LOVESICK

ALSO BY ÁNGELES MASTRETTA

Tear This Heart Out

Translated from the Spanish by

MARGARET SAYERS PEDEN

ÁNGELES MASTRETTA

LOVESICK

RIVERHEAD BOOKS
NEW YORK
1997

Riverhead Books
a division of G. P. Putnam's Sons
Publishers Since 1838
200 Madison Avenue
New York, NY 10016

Library of Congress Cataloging-in-Publication Data

Mastretta, Ángeles, date.
[Mal de amores. English]
Lovesick / by Ángeles Mastretta : translated
from the Spanish by Margaret Sayers Peden.
p. cm.
ISBN 1-57322-062-0 (alk. paper)
I. Peden, Margaret Sayers. II. Title.
PQ7298.23.A795M3813 1997 97-2077 CIP
863–dc21

Printed in the United States of America
3 5 7 9 10 8 6 4

This book is printed on acid-free paper. ♾

BOOK DESIGN BY LAURIE JEWELL

FOR HÉCTOR AGUILAR CAMÍN,

FOR THE IMPLACABLE ORDER

OF YOUR MIND AND THE GENEROUS DISORDER

OF YOUR HEART

LOVESICK

CHAPTER

1

DIEGO SAURI was a native of a small island that still floats in the water of the Mexican Caribbean. An audacious and solitary island where the air is a challenge of profound and auspicious aromas. In the mid-nineteenth century all the land in those environs—firma or floating—belonged to the state of Yucatán. The islands had been abandoned out of fear of the repeated attacks of pirates who sailed the peace of that sea and its twenty shades of blue. Not until after 1847 did men return to them.

The last rebellion of the Mayas against the whites of that area was a war as long and bloody as few Mexico has known. The Mayas, divided among themselves but united in their opposition to the strange and mysterious cult of a cross that talked, threw themselves with machetes and English rifles against the people who had settled in the jungles and coasts once ruled by their ancestors. Fleeing from the horror of what came to be called the *guerras de casta,* the caste wars, a number of families set sail for the white coast and green heart of Mujeres Island.

As soon as they disembarked, these people, Spanish and mestizo, who had descended from shipwrecked voyagers and who now had nothing to defend other than their lives, agreed that each of them would take as their own all the land they were able to clear. And so by weeding out undergrowth and thorny plants, the parents of Diego Sauri came into possession of a stretch of transparent beach and a long strip of adjoining land, and it was there they built the palm hut where their children would be born.

The first color that struck Diego Sauri's eyes was blue, because everything around the house was as blue and clear as the heavens themselves. Diego grew up racing through the jungle and rolling on the invincible sand, caressed by the calm waves, another fish among the schools of yellow and violet. As a youth, he was brilliant, polished, bathed by sun, and heir to inexplicable desires. His parents had found peace on that island, but somewhere in him burned a war yet to be fought. His grandmother used to say that his ancestors had come to the peninsula in their own brigantine, and more than once he heard his father respond—half proud, half joking—"Because they were pirates."

Who knows from what past he may have come, but the boy who grew up to be Diego Sauri longed with all his heart for a horizon that was not framed by water. What soon became his passion was the art of healing. His father had discovered Diego's gift when he saw the boy surreptitiously revive a gasping fish intended for the dinner table. When Diego was thirteen, he had assisted during the pandemonium of his mother's most difficult delivery, and from that moment had demonstrated such manual dexterity and such a cool head that other women in the same uncertain condition began to call on him to help them. In lieu of formal training he relied on instinct; he had the adroitness and aplomb of a Mayan priest and was as quick to call on the goddess Ixchel as the Virgen del Carmen.

By the time he was seventeen, Diego Sauri knew everything there was to learn on the island about herbs and potions, had read every last book to find its way there, and was the fervent enemy of a man who frequently appeared on the island carrying large sums of money that smelled of blood and nightmares. Fermín Mundaca y Muchaga was an arms trafficker who had benefitted greatly from the interminable *guerra de castas* and whose respite from his trade consisted of fishing and swaggering around among the peaceful island dwellers. That alone would have been enough to make him Diego's enemy, but in his role as a young *curandero,* Diego knew a different story about him.

One night Diego had opened his door to the ravaged face of a woman who had been seen with Mundaca. She had bruises on every part of her body, and could not summon the strength even to moan. Diego healed her. He kept her in his parents' home until she was able to walk again without fear and look at her face without remembering. Then he put her on the first sailing ship to leave the island. Before she boarded the small vessel, she wrote the words *Ah Xoc* in the fine-grained, shimmering sand. In Maya, *Ah Xoc* means shark, which was what the Mayas called Fermín Mundaca, the man who sold the government ships that would transport troops to fight against the Mayas as he sold the Mayas their arms. At that moment, the pale, timid woman opened her lips and spoke for the first and last time to say, "Thank you."

That same night five men surprised Diego Sauri as he was making his daily round of the houses of his patients. They beat him until he was nothing but a pile of rags. They tied his feet and hands and split his lips, but not before he cursed them. His eyes closed on an image he would hold forever: an enormous moon that looked like the yellow, mocking grin of a god.

When he was able once again to question what was happening to him, he felt water moving beneath the cell in which he was imprisoned. He was on a boat, going God knows where, but instead of being flooded with fear, he trembled with curiosity. However unfortunate the cause, he was on his way toward the world.

He never knew how many days he spent locked up. A darkness, then another, then many more, passed above him, until he lost all sense of time. The ship had docked more than five times before the man who brought him scraps of food each day opened the door.

"Well, here we are," the giant redhead said in English, looking at him with all the compassion he was capable of summoning.

"Here" was an icy port in the north of Europe.

SEVERAL YEARS and many apprenticeships later, Diego returned to Mexico as someone returns to, and fails to recognize, his own being.

He could speak four languages, had lived in ten countries, worked as an assistant to doctors, scientists, and pharmacists, walked through streets and museums until he had memorized the twisting alleys of Rome and the piazzas of Venice. He was a cosmopolite and an eccentric, but more than any mortal man before him, one who hoped that his most recent fortunes had led him by the hand to the same bowl of soup beneath the same roof for all the days left for him to live.

He was just twenty-seven years old the evening he disembarked in the balmy ardor of air he knew as well as his own soul. The port of Veracruz was related to his islands, and he blessed it, even though its soil was dark and its waters murky. As long as he didn't look down, he thought, he would feel he was back home.

Walking with the haste of the curious, he plunged into the sweltering uproar of the port city. He headed for the plaza, where he went into a noisy inn. It smelt of newly roasted coffee and fresh-baked bread, of tobacco and anise. At the back of the room, through shimmering waves of sound, among animated conversations and waiters coming and going as if blown by an unremitting wind, he met, once and for all time, the eyes of Josefa Veytia.

Diego had spent too much time in pursuit of his destiny not to know it when he saw it. He had wandered all those years, all over the world, only to have life turn around and hand him his future at the same meridian where the past had taken it from him, and as he approached the woman's table he never broke stride.

Josefa Veytia had traveled to Veracruz from Puebla with her mother and her sister Milagros to await a ship from Spain carrying her uncle, Miguel Veytia, her father's younger brother, in whose hands her father had been inspired to entrust his family before betraying them by dying when Josefa was only twelve, Milagros sixteen, and their mother that ambiguous and unvarying age into which women settle when they wish to ignore the question.

Their uncle, Miguel, lived half the year in Barcelona and the other half in Puebla. In each of the two places he devoted a good part of his time to discussing the business and complications he had in the other. His life was as peaceful and pleasant as an endless Sunday. Monday lay forever on the far side of the ocean.

As the Veytias learned that afternoon, the Republic had been proclaimed in Spain two weeks before, and his uncle's liberal emotions had forced him to stay until the celebration deteriorated into tedium.

"Who knows what's going to happen in Spain," Diego said to the women, installed among them as if he were an old acquaintance. And with no further invitation he began to expound upon the republican fervor of some Spaniards and the monarchist leanings of others.

"I wouldn't be surprised if in a year's time they will want a king again," he prophesied in the impassioned tone politics always evoked in him, in the meantime combating a passion more tangible than his prophecies.

In December 1874, the Spanish proclaimed Alfonso XII king and Diego Sauri wed Josefa Veytia in the church of Santo Domingo, which still dozes two blocks from the main plaza in the most noble city of Puebla.

CHAPTER

2

CAPTIVES IN THE FERMENT of life, the Sauris enjoyed ten years of unhurried and harmonious matrimony without either by chance or good fortune producing a child. At first they were too preoccupied with themselves to be perturbed that their euphoric daily encounters had no consequence beyond the peace of their bodies. They began to wonder about a baby only when they knew each other so well that with eyes shut he could picture the shape and precise size of the dainty and immaculate toenails on each of his wife's feet, and she could in her memory reconstruct the exact distance between her husband's mouth and the tip of his nose as her finger traced the curve of his profile in the air. Josefa knew that each of the white teeth revealed in Diego Sauri's smile, however identical they seemed, varied slightly in color. And Diego knew that in addition to being a kind of goddess ruled by the laws of intense harmony, his wife had a highly arched palate and invisible tonsils.

There may have been some inconsequential part of their bodies that remained unexplored, but no more of the other's than their own. So they set about trying to have a child who would tell them what not even they imagined of the twists and turns of their desires and their breeding. Certain they had done everything one does to engender a human being, without achieving it, they decided to try things they had not thought necessary: from drinking infusions of an herb that Josefa Veytia called *damiana* and Diego Sauri's botanical expertise had taught him was *Tornera diffusa* to counting the quarters of the moon to learn the days Josefa was fertile and during that time escalating the bodily passions that with such commitment became even more spirited and impetuous than usual.

All these steps were taken in consultation with, and following the counsel of, Dr. Octavio Cuenca, a doctor whose acquaintance Diego had made on the crimson-streaked evening he arrived in that city, and whom with the passage of time and sharing of discoveries he had come to love like a revered brother.

From the time Josefa's menstrual period had burst upon her precocious adolescence one fierce and favorable May until the time of their endeavors, she had received the visit of the red caller when the moon was in its fourth quarter, so that every month, thirteen days from that date, Diego Sauri closed the pharmacy and for the following three days did not so much as read the newspaper. They rested from their intense creative labors only long enough for Josefa to drink long drafts of water in which they had boiled for two hours the bulb of lilylike flowers the old woman herbalist in the market called *oceoloxóchitl* and Josefa's husband knew as *Tigridia pavonia.* Diego had come across the flower's scientific name and the description of its curative effects in a book written by a sixteenth-century Spaniard who had wandered over New Spain making an inventory of plants used by the ancient Mexicans. His heart had beat a little faster when he read: " 'Tis said that if women imbibe the brew they will thereafter conceive." Diego had placed his hopes in this Indian lore because he was beginning to lose faith in the science of medical doctors as well as in the extracts and tinctures he prepared in his own pharmacy. He had taken, and had Josefa take, every pill found on earth, and was rapidly losing patience, his hopes turning to ice, congealing even the tranquility of the days that were the city's gift to them.

Diego and Josefa lived several years frustrated because their bodies, so skilled in coupling, were so inept when it came to tripling, until one Day Thirteen Josefa dressed in the very early morning, and when her husband opened his eyes to the duty of making a baby found vacant the place on the left side of the bed that was ordinarily warmed by her body.

"I'm not playing anymore," she said when he walked into the kitchen, looking for her with amazement still written on his face. "Open the shop."

Diego was one of those rare men who unquestioningly respect the designs of the divine authority incarnate in their wives. Reaching his status as an agnostic had cost him many years of study. He had even convinced Josefa that God existed because man desired a god, yet he had faith in the Holy Spirit he sensed on the brow of his wife. Which is why he dressed and went downstairs to forget his sorrow among the flasks, scales, and fragrances of the pharmacy he operated on the first floor of their home. He did not ask anything of Josefa until several days later. Then one early morning when the light had begun to sink into the darkness of their bedroom, he dared ask if she wanted to do it just because. She agreed, her peace restored, and thereafter did not speak of a child. Little by little, they even came to believe it was better that way.

IN 1892, Josefa Veytia was a woman of thirty-some years who had acquired a way of walking that recalled the proud carriage of a Flamenco dancer, who always awakened with a new plan in her head and always went to sleep having carried it out, who reciprocated her husband's affections at the hour of desire and had never refused him the pleasure of knowing he was accompanied in the game so many men play alone. There was always a question in her round eyes, and on her lips the contagious peace of one who does not press for answers. She wore her hair combed up above the proud neck Diego liked to kiss in the late afternoon as a kind of foretaste of the light her naked body would shed upon his night hours. For if it was little, Josefa had the gift that balances the need for words against the urgency of silence. Conversations between them never died. Sometimes they talked till midnight, as if they had only just met, and other nights the dawn waked them with the compelling need to tell each other their latest dreams.

THE NIGHT Josefa discovered that the moon had waxed to double the size it normally was when the first red spot on her snow white underdrawers would announce the torment of menorrhagia, she opened their dialogue by saying that she felt afraid. She knew of nothing more punctual than her agonizing menstrual period. The first time in her life she had felt something trickling down her legs it was ten-fifteen on a Saturday morning, the fifth of May, a day when the entire city of Puebla trembled from the smell of gunpowder and pride, shortly before the start of the mock battle that celebrated their triumph over an invading French army several years before. When the great bell of the cathedral rang hoarsely to announce that the hour of combat had arrived, Josefa and her sister Milagros were on their balcony waving their handkerchiefs at the groups of uniformed troops and armed citizens who were hurrying through the streets to take their places in the trenches and on the high vantage of the churches. The world then had the habit of war, and celebrated grave danger as habitual vertigo. As part of that world, when Josefa felt the blood running down her thighs, instead of feeling afraid she whirled in a circle shouting, "I am wounded, but I shall not surrender!"

That night the moon had been in its fourth quarter. Ever since, invariably, for 215 months, blood had accompanied that moon. And that was why Josefa had said "I'm afraid" when she saw the full moon and realized that not a single drop of blood had appeared to nullify her procreative hopes.

Looking up, Diego Sauri's eyes softened as he contemplated his wife, surrendering to her scolding that leapt without transition from the moon to his regard for the lies printed in newspapers. Because it was the fault of the newspapers alone, he heard her say, to which he dedicated a good part of his life, that he had gone for three whole days without listening to a word she said, his head swimming with news about the march against the reelection of the president of the Republic. That dictator had been in power for seven years when Diego began saying that he could not last much longer, and another nine had gone by without Josefa's having any further indication of his fall than the hopes her husband concentrated on seeing it happen.

Fearing that the reproaches would never end if he did not react to the matter of the moon, Diego got up and went out the dining room door into the warm June night. An enormous moon ruled the brilliant sky.

"It's no wonder the ancients worshiped it," he said as he felt his wife's warm, placid body pressing against him.

"You want me to do it?" he asked.

"I think you already did." Josefa's words were spoken with such melancholy that her husband dropped his arms and stepped back to search her face and ask what the devil it was he had done.

"Made a baby," Josefa said, and the words seemed uttered with her last breath.

GUIDED BY the absolute curve of his wife's growing belly, Diego Sauri insisted that what was inside was the answer to his dreams of a baby girl. Josefa asked him not to try to predict what he couldn't know, but he replied that he had been certain from the fifth month, and that she was wasting her time knitting with blue yarn because the baby would be a girl and they would name her Emilia in honor of Rousseau, and to insure that she was an intelligent woman.

"But why would she be stupid if we named her Deifilia?" asked Josefa, caressing the syllables of her grandmother's name.

"Because she would begin life with the mistaken idea that, as her name says, she was the daughter of God, not us. And this baby is *our* daughter."

"Not until she sees the light of day," argued Josefa, who had spent a large part of her pregnancy in fear that the miracle might escape her.

Like any good Caribbean man, Diego Sauri was not given to questioning miracles, and he always laughed when his wife expressed her fears, doubting her ability at the prescribed moment to form the folds of an ear or to match perfectly the color of both eyes, because how could he know what was happening if his contribution had been limited to that of a decanter?

"A love-crazed decanter, if you please," said Diego Sauri, getting up to give her a kiss.

Diego was of average height, about the same as the father Josefa guarded in her memory. He had strong shoulders and light eyes that relieved the darkness of premature circles beneath his eyes, palms marked with a riddle, and clever, accomplished fingertips. He still moved like the swimmer he had been, and he awaited a wink from his wife with desire eternal on his lips.

"Don't start that," Josefa scolded. "All this time you've been going in and out of where the baby's going to come out, with no respect at all. We might hurt her."

"Don't repeat those old wives' tales, Josefa. You sound like a *poblana,*" he said, kissing her again.

"I am a *poblana,* I'm proud of being from Puebla. The fact that you come from a land of savages isn't my fault."

"Savages? The Mayas?" asked Diego. "Long before a human foot trod this land, Tulum was an empire with earthly gods."

"The Mayas disappeared centuries ago. Now there's nothing but jungle and ruins," she said, playing on her husband's pride.

"It's still a paradise. You'll see," Diego answered, pulling her up from the wicker chair where she was knitting and guiding her toward the bed as he unbuttoned her nightgown.

An hour later, Josefa opened her eyes and said, "You're right, it is a paradise."

"You see," her husband said, patting her round and palpitating belly. Then, coming back down to earth as men do, he asked, "Is there anything to eat?"

AS HE LAY WAITING, remembering the words of his good friend Dr. Octavio Cuenca regarding the precise ratio between the moment a pregnant woman feels the first weak contraction and the imminence of birth, he heard Josefa dash like lightning from the kitchen.

"My water's burst," she cried.

Diego jumped out of bed as if he thought she was falling, but in that instant Josefa acquired a calm worthy of a woman who has given birth to a dozen children. She took complete control of the situation, refusing to let Diego call a doctor to help.

"You swore to me you would do it yourself," Josefa reminded Diego.

"When was that?" he asked.

"The night of our wedding day," Josefa replied, and ended the discussion in order to devote herself fully to the furor taking over her body.

For a long time she had believed that pain would be a kind of luxury. During the hours that followed, she never doubted that for a minute, but every last inch of her body learned that some luxuries cost what they are worth, and that the intimate orgy of giving birth is, more than pain, a fierce and desolate battle that fortunately is forgotten with the end of hostilities.

Nine hours later, Diego placed the warm, satiny body of their baby in her arms.

"You see, I was right," he said, licking away the large tears running down his face before he smiled.

"And she's perfect," Josefa sighed, checking the baby girl as if the little body contained the sun, the moon, and the stars.

"You are braver than Ixchel," Diego avowed, handing Josefa a piece of cotton soaked with alcohol and a solution of marijuana. Then he kissed the tip of her nose and carried away the still naked baby. The cold sun of Mexican winter was just beginning to rise. It was seven o'clock on the morning of February 12. Josefa closed her eyes and slept with the peace of mind that had deserted her nine months earlier.

Near noon, she awakened from the first unfinished dream of her lifetime.

"Diego, who is Ixchel?" she asked, still clinging to the images of her chimera.

Radiant as a girlish grandmother, Josefa's sister, Milagros, hurried to tell her that Diego was sleeping and that Ixchel was the Maya goddess of the moon, water, and *curanderos,* and therefore charged with protecting women in childbirth and pregnancies.

"Have you seen her?" Josefa asked.

"She's angel embroidery," Milagros answered with the confident tone that had benefitted Josefa since they were children. Older by four years, Milagros had given Josefa the poise their mother lacked, and had loved her for all the brothers and sisters she didn't have. She was a little taller and quite a bit more stubborn; like Josefa, she had prominent cheekbones and thick dark hair, and could smile like an angel or loose a blinding fury worthy of all the devils of hell. Josefa was proud to be related to her. Although people found them so different it was difficult to imagine how they got along, there was between the two an old pact that allowed them to understand one another with their eyes. Milagros had the same deep-set, curious eyes as Josefa, except that she was never at peace without answers; she needed to know them all, be informed about the world down to its last hidden valley, and shred her doubts as soon as her throat tightened voicing them. These were the reasons she had never married any of the many men who wanted her. They did not know the answers, so why hand her destiny over to them? Milagros's freedom was her primary passion, and daring her best vice. She could cut short an argument with the ominous, scornful flash of her eyes; she read more than most women and was more erudite than any. She enjoyed challenging men with her store of scientific knowledge and for pleasure memorized poems and sought out challenges. She despised embroidery but was a wizard when it came to designing dresses or changing the look of a room merely by moving a few paintings. She was drastic in her judgments and demanding of those around her, guarded with her affection, generous with her belongings, captivating with her tales. She felt a partiality for her sister, Josefa, that she had never tried to hide, and with her was able to set aside any or all of her weapons. Simply because Diego Sauri had fallen in love with Josefa at first sight, Milagros loved him like a brother and would have given her life for him as freely as for her sister. In addition, she shared her brother-in-law's political beliefs and fantasies, and helped him withstand the criticism and pleas for sanity that Josefa fired at him from time to time, relying for effect on her sharp and pertinent tongue. Unlike Josefa, whose conciliatory spirit helped her wend her way unscathed through the precepts and prejudices that ruled the world they lived in, Milagros raged every time someone's opinion seemed disrespectful or insufficiently universal. She never missed an opportunity for an ideological battle over God, religion, faith, the absolute, and other perilous subjects.

From her bed, Josefa watched as Milagros went to the cradle where the infant was sleeping.

"According to the hour and day of her birth, your baby is an Aquarius with ascendant Virgo," said Milagros. "A juncture of passion and sweetness that will provide as much happiness as sorrow."

"All I want is for her to be happy," was Josefa's wish.

"And she often will be," said Milagros. "Her life will be lighted by the fourth quarter moon still visible in the sky when she was born. That month is ruled by Ursa Major, the Hair of Berenice, Procyon, Canopus, Sirius, Aldebaran, the Austral Fish of Eridanus, the Boreal Triangle, Andromeda, Perseus, Algol, and Cassiopeia."

"Will the light of so many stars make her a woman in command of herself, with an intelligent mind and a heart devoted to life?" asked Josefa.

"That and more," said Milagros, her head beneath the netting over the cradle.

Josefa asked her sister if she would recite the charm the women of their family always chanted when a child was born. Milagros agreed to yield to family tradition so that nothing would stand in the way of the rite that would make her a godmother. She placed her hand on her niece's head and recited:

"Child, may you sleep beneath God's gaze. My wish for you is that you never stray from it, that you travel through life with patience as your best ally, that you know the joy of generosity and the peace of those who expect nothing, that you understand your sorrows and know how to comfort those who sorrow. May you have clear eyes, a prudent mouth, an understanding nose, ears deaf to intrigue, precise and calming tears. And may you have faith in eternal life and the tranquility that faith bestows."

"Amen," said Josefa from her bed as the tears began to flow.

"And now may I say mine?"

Milagros was more than a beautiful woman who sometimes dressed like a drawing from *Le Moniteur de la Mode* and wore the finest chapeaux Madame Berthe Manceu designed; she also had in her clothes-press a collection of the finest *huipiles* ever embroidered. She often wore them on solemn occasions, and had been known to walk down the street with her hair in braids across her head, Indian garments rippling like a bright banner down her body. She was wearing a *huipil* that morning. Josefa looked at her admiringly, and asked her to proceed.

"Child," said Milagros, with the solemnity of a priestess, "for you I wish madness, valor, yearning, impatience. May you have the good fortune of love and the delirium of solitude. A taste for comets, water, and men. Intelligence and wit. Curious eyes, a nose that remembers, a mouth that smiles and curses with godly precision, legs that never grow old, tears that restore wholeness. For you I wish the sense of time of the stars, the temperament of the ants, and the doubt of temples. And may you have faith in auguries, the voices of the dead, the lips of the adventurous, the peace of men who forget their destinies, the strength of your memories and of the future as a promise that holds all you have yet to experience. Amen."

"Amen," echoed Josefa, blessing her sister's faith and imagination.

SHELTERED IN her godmother's wishes, Emilia ate and slept with sensual placidity the first months of her life. The horror stories her father read in the newspapers did not reach her ears, although every morning she heard him read aloud what had happened in the world, offer opinions on things that disturbed or saddened him, and describe the surprises of the day with the absolute certainty that they moved her as much as they did him.

Josefa assured her husband that the baby was too young to be interested in the rise of the Labour Party in England, the annexation of Hawaii by the United States, the failed crops and cattle deaths across their nation. She scolded him for making the baby sad by talking about the ban on bullfights, the disaster of the reelection of the governors, or the waste of one hundred thousand pesos a month on the impossible project of draining the Valley of Mexico. Diego's reply was that she was worse, talking about the England of Charlotte Brontë and reading *Shirley* aloud to the baby.

"I do that to put her to sleep," her mother said.

"What interest can she possibly have in the avatars of Julien Sorel or the suffering of Ana de Ozores?" asked Diego. "At least I tell her about reality."

"Yes, but every detail of reality. Does the poor child have to hear about the tobacco tax? And when they closed *El Demócrata,* you recited the names of the jailed editors for a week."

"I used the excuse of telling her so you would hear," said Diego Sauri. And then, turning to the baby: "Finally I impressed on your mother at least one example of governmental arbitrariness."

"I know them all. But I don't encourage your anger because I don't want you locked up, too."

"Me? Why?"

"You want me to tell you?"

"No." Diego fingered the reddish mustache he had grown to celebrate his daughter's birth.

ALTHOUGH THEY SELDOM SPOKE OF IT, they both knew that Josefa was right. For more than three years, people had been meeting in the pharmacy who, whether for legitimate cause, old longings for democracy, or pure conspiratorial bent, had something against the government. First, chance brought them together, then like minds, finally necessity. And toward that moment, every day or so, some customer came into the pharmacy prepared to insult the governor in front of anyone who chanced by. That being the case, it did not take Diego long to pass from opposing reelection to being daringly outspoken, and then, as is the way of the world, from outspoken to fanatic—and from fanatic to prisoner was just a matter of time.

"We're going to move the political group to Dr. Cuenca's house," said Diego.

"Thank God," said Josefa, calmed by that news.

"Which god?" asked Diego.

"Whichever one inspired you to do it," his wife replied.

CHAPTER 3

IN 1893 Dr. Cuenca had in his favor, in addition to fifty-four years of living, a well-warranted and firmly established professional reputation. He had clung to that unwaveringly since the death of the woman with whom he had engendered two children and whose presence he missed as he awoke each morning, as if that day were the first he greeted without her.

He had lived with her—and continued to live with her memory and their children—in a house near the maize fields encircling the city, seven blocks from the *zócalo* and the cathedral. It was a house ruled by two hubs, the indelible and mythic company of its garden and the large sala devoted to the Sunday meetings. Dr. Cuenca played a sweet and ambiguous flute that contradicted the military rigidity with which he marched through life during the week. Some of his closest friends were musicians or writers, and they visited on Sunday to pass on the latest news or play as a group. In contrast, during the week his behavior was marked by a professional rigor that commanded the respect of even his enemies, a sense of duty and order his children feared even after they were grown, and a verbal austerity that in her lifetime had made his wife one of the most skillful decipherers of silence in the long history of that avocation among women, and that after her death had caused her to return from time to time to brush his forehead with her eyelashes and listen to his silence telling her all the things that weighed upon him.

Dr. Cuenca had been born in warm country, in the always humid town of Atzalan. His father's name was Juan Cuenca and his mother had been known from childhood as Manuelita Gómez, the daughter of the priest. According to her descendants, Manuelita's father had donned the cassock to fulfill a vow made to the Virgen del Socorro during the War of Independence, when, one evening at twilight, pursued by Spanish troops as one of the *criollo* leaders rebelling against the Crown near Veracruz, he had been found hiding in the ironing room of a house whose ladies, fortunately, had the habit of wearing layers of white starched petticoats. They hid him behind racks of clothes to be ironed, among baskets filled with crinolines and full skirts of taffeta and lace, sheets, towels, pillow slips, and bedspreads.

He heard the soldiers rush in cursing his name and shrank back as swords pierced through clothing in search of his body, trembling for the first time. He was a still youthful widower, and wanted to live to a ripe old age. So on that unforgettable Tuesday evening, he promised the Virgin he would wear the cloth if she saved him from that predicament. When the men gave up their search and his soul returned to his body, he trembled again, this time recalling his rash promise: he would have to become a clergyman, making his daughter Manuela the daughter of a priest.

Perhaps as vaccination against her father's vow, Manuela married Juan Cuenca, a liberal landowner with dark skin and gleaming eyes, whose laugh shone with teeth so large they were evident even when his lips were closed. Juan Cuenca owned fertile land, rivers, and cattle in such quantities that he could look after himself without God's help. Thus he allowed himself the luxury of being a confessed non-believer and a trustworthy man despite his prominent teeth and long silences. With him, Manuelita enjoyed a calm, uncritical marriage that produced ten children. Octavio was the third, and wanted to be a doctor. He could not, however, escape the war that consumed the life of his country during most of the nineteenth century, and he studied medicine at the University of Jalapa only to end up a doctor in Juárez's army.

Jacobo Esparza, his classmate, was also his companion in arms. The first time Octavio Cuenca went home with him, he discovered the shining lips and uncompromising tongue of Jacobo's younger sister. María Esparza was two and was engaged in one of the many homely liberties she indulged in throughout her lifetime: she was in the middle of the corridor among the ferns and geraniums, sucking a red lollipop and sitting on her potty. Nearly two decades later, after years of study and several wars, believing he knew all there was to know about love and its upheavals, Octavio ran into María among the plants of her immutable house.

"Marry me now, Doctor, you're getting old," she proposed.

"I have a son by another woman, and I'm twenty years older than you," Dr. Cuenca answered.

"I know," she said. "That's why I'm hurrying you."

DR. CUENCA'S HOUSE had a large carved-wood door adorned with an iron knocker that resounded through the garden and corridor till it reached the kitchen, where someone interrupted her chores to run and open it to the person who was knocking. It was a house that kept its door closed because in Puebla doors were always closed, as if from constant fear of invasion from the outside world. But in hospitality, the door of that house was open, like the doors of houses in the warm country. Everyone who knocked was entitled to come in and take a seat under the trees in the garden, a chair in the sala beside the piano, or at the dining room table before a bowl of rice soup.

It was a house where children could race around noisily and where adults held their weekly meeting without being overly concerned with the quarrels and uproarious good times of the young ones. It was, then, an ideal house for parents who had children at the age of breaking things, and for souls at the age of intelligent conversation. For that, and for reasons of simple affinity, the Sauris spent many of the brightest Sundays of their lives in that house.

* * *

THE FIRST TIME they took their daughter Emilia to visit, she was three months old and had few charms other than smiling and kicking her legs when possessed by what her father thought to be an inordinate gusto for life. Josefa Sauri came to the meeting that Sunday with the face of someone hiding something exceptional in her arms. Her husband came behind her carrying a basket lined with organdy, which he kept knocking against people's legs as he said hello. They were preceded by Salvador, the older of the two Cuenca Esparza sons, a lad of eight, talkative and lively, who compensated for his mother's absence by loving his father doubly well. Following them, intent on finding out what Josefa was carrying so carefully, came Daniel, the younger son, a boy whose eyes, somewhere between brown and green, and mocking gaze reminded Cuenca of his María Esparza. He had named him Daniel, as his wife had had time to request, and had placed responsibility for his upbringing into the hands of Milagros Veytia, as she had begged him to do. María Esparza loved Milagros the way you love friends with whom you share basic tastes and deepest secrets. When she saw death approaching, her one obsession filled her mouth: *Give the boy to Milagros.*

Dr. Cuenca swore to her he would and, as long as his son was still a baby, allowed Milagros to keep him with her. However, as soon as he knew that the child no longer needed her to change his diapers or be fed, the doctor wanted him back so he could train him to be a man by following the course of discipline he had used with Salvador.

Milagros wept secretly for months, mouthed a daily curse, and delayed the return with as many pretexts as she could invent, but from having shared so much with her friend, she knew Dr. Cuenca inside out, and realized from the beginning it would do her no good to show anger. Neither, as she respected the peace of the dead, did she appeal to María, knowing that might cause a posthumous dispute between her and her husband. Milagros returned the boy to his father after his third birthday, refusing to accept in exchange the speech of thanks he attempted to deliver.

"May I still act as his aunt?" she asked as she let go the boy's hand.

"It would be an honor for us," Cuenca told her, with those words reinstating her right to intervene in his destiny.

Because she was still the child's comfort, Milagros exercised that right, spoiling him more and correcting him less. That afternoon, foreseeing the risks that could result from the child's probing mind, she cautioned him to be careful because there was a baby girl in the basket. As answer, Daniel tugged at an end of the bundle Josefa was carrying and gave Milagros the most seductive smile any man could ever offer.

Pausing in the threshold of the sala, Josefa scanned the guests until she located her husband in the midst of the gathering, basket on his arm and political speech on his lips. She called from across the room. Rooted in place, Diego Sauri motioned for Josefa to come on in, but she stood in the doorway, debating whether she should brave the smoky hubbub of the salon. Meanwhile, the Cuenca boy again tugged at the coverlet that enveloped the baby, uncovering her to the world whether the befuddled mother intended it or not.

The poet Rivadeneira, a man with a disenchanted expression and the features of a finely bred animal, a prisoner of his love for Milagros Veytia, started toward Josefa to see for himself the treasure of the Sauris, and was surprised to see how much she resembled her aunt. He had come to understand the reasons Milagros gave for not marrying him, or any other man, but even if he hadn't, he would have accepted them as part of a fate it did not behoove him to rebel against and from which he could never escape. He found no reason, therefore, to look for love elsewhere.

Milagros took the child from her sister's protective arms and paraded her around the salon, holding her high in the air. Everything in the sala smelled of the world of men. The few women scattered among them were there because they had been motivated to resemble men in their method of reasoning and of reaching wrong conclusions. Not because that may have been the best of all methods for them, but because it was clear that a man's world could be breached only by behaving like them. Anything else bred suspicion.

Josefa Sauri herself, who spoke so well and at such length when she was alone with her husband, felt like an outsider in the masculine kingdom of those gatherings. It did not really concern her because she knew she was well represented by the enterprise of her sister, who was impossible to pin down and who preferred to reject matrimony rather than give up what she considered to be the privilege of living like a man.

It's my good fortune she's my sister, Josefa thought that Sunday as she watched Milagros show off her daughter as if she were playing with a doll.

Milagros wound in and out among the men, the baby shedding layers of coverlets and the noise level growing louder, until suddenly the entire sala, down to its broken chandelier, was rocked by a piercing scream. Tugging at Milagros's skirt, hair unruly, enraged, Daniel Cuenca had yelled at the top of his lungs to demand a view of the baby; in the same second the adults fell silent and the Sauris' treasure let out a deafening cry of distress.

Embarrassed, Dr. Cuenca went to collect his son Daniel and, favoring him with an eloquent glance of reproach, told him to say he was sorry, speaking in a tone that implied his own guilt for having such a son.

"He's only four years old, Doctor," Milagros Veytia declared, nullifying the reprimand with the anise of her breath. Then with her free hand she took the boy's hand and fled through the unexpected but perfect corridor opened by men laden with books, cigars, French snuff, and scientific prejudices.

"Look at Milagros, will you, with a child in each arm," said the poet Rivadeneira. And remembering a game that consisted of appropriating other poets' verses to express one's own sentiments, he asked as she passed by: " 'What, Lucero, do you think/ of the force of my misfortune?' "

" 'As you have not my courage, I think you must feel envy,' " she replied, and went on her way.

In three steps she reached the doorway, where Josefa was waiting, shaking her head. As soon as she was close enough, without letting go of Daniel, she handed her sister the screaming child. Then she led the way to a bedroom where there was comparative quiet. Josefa sat down in a large chair and held Emilia at a level with the eyes of the boy who, as soon as he was able to see her, leaned forward, forehead nearly touching hers, and told her he was sorry he had frightened her.

"That's all we need, a four-year-old Don Juan," said Milagros.

When he heard her laugh, Daniel straightened up, the contentment of satisfied curiosity vanishing from his face, and ran from the room.

Josefa unbuttoned to the waist the front of her high-necked blouse and sent her sister back to the meeting, giving her breast to the baby sighing against her body.

THERE WAS a newly learned pleasure in that ceremony. Josefa was immersed in it when she felt a hand lightly touch her naked breast. She opened her eyes and saw Daniel Cuenca with his face pressed to that of the baby affixed to her breast. As soon as he knew he'd been seen, he backed to the door and vanished. Shortly after, Josefa saw him reappear at the garden window. By then she had buttoned her blouse, so she got up from the chair, pretending she hadn't seen him.

"Men are like that from the day they're born," she told her daughter Emilia as she lay her in the basket. "They want everything, but they don't know how to ask."

The baby allowed her mother to bundle her in the covers as if seeking sleep to unravel an enigma. But not in this or any other slumber was she rid of the bewitchment of the meetings in that house. That evening she experienced the uneasiness of its inhabitants, and from that moment was disturbed by the agitation that ruled its Sundays.

CHAPTER 4

THE SAURIS' HOUSE was part of a very old colonial mansion that had heroically survived not only the eleven sieges suffered by the city of Puebla during the first sixty years of the nineteenth century but also the division of its three patios into the respective centers of distinct houses. It was Josefa Veytia's sole inheritance, but more than enough to make her the most satisfied of any female heir of her time. The house had a long history, but Josefa inherited it knowing only the most recent. Don Miguel Veytia, her father's brother, a fan of bull- and cockfights whose dearest possession was a bookshop above the Iturbide arcades, had been so bold one dazzling April afternoon as to wager his shop on the courage of a speckled fighting cock. Veytia's friend in drinking and dominos, a Spaniard with no coat of arms who in 1881 was the city's most successful businessman, insisted in challenging the bravery of that cock.

"That creature looks pure Indian to me," he had said, chewing on his cigar.

"And all the braver for it," Veytia replied. He shot dice every night with the businessman, and they had an ongoing polemic about which was the more valiant blood, Indian or Spanish.

"Would you bet your store, books and all, on him?" the Spaniard asked.

"What are you betting?" was Josefa's uncle's reply.

"My part of the Casa de la Estrella," he answered, pulling from his pocket the ancient deed of the partitioned house.

Miguel Veytia accepted the bet, shaking hands with his friend and apologizing because he wasn't in the habit of carrying the deed for his bookshop with him. Fate decreed that the speckled Indian cock bit the dust four seconds after the red one. By then Veytia's Spanish friend was as full of alcohol as a wineskin, but no one was ever more rigorous in paying off a bet. No matter how much Don Miguel protested, the title of the Casa de la Estrella was repeatedly and stubbornly slipped into his pocket. Finally Veytia accepted, thinking that the next day he would return the deed, without objections, to the prudent and sensible businessman from Asturias his friend became in sane moments. Unfortunately, there was no next day for that loyal bettor. Before dawn, he got into a knife fight with someone drunker and better armed.

"Tell Veytia to keep the house," were his last words.

Through the days of weeping the loss of his rowdy, fair-going companion, Miguel Veytia kept the title in a drawer, and eventually forgot it. But when his niece Josefa fell in love with the newly arrived Diego Sauri, the honorable expert in rare books could think of no better owners for the Casa de la Estrella than those two young people possessed of a fire the likes of which his gray head retained only the memory of a few ashes. Because of his gift, the conjugal pair formed by Josefa Veytia and the unmonied pharmacist Diego Sauri began the unknowable journey of matrimony without major economic pitfalls. They did not actually have a notion as to how they would live, but at least they knew where.

The Veytias descended from a Señor Veytia who emigrated from Spain in 1531 to help found the city. And since that first Veytia had dared cross the ocean the way it was crossed in those years, all those who inherited his surname, with the recent exception of Josefa's Uncle Miguel, inherited with it the certainty that Puebla was the best place to live and die that any human could choose. As a result, no Veytia had ever included among his ambitions that of travel, and in 352 years none had the least desire to go on a honeymoon that involved the risk of losing sight of the volcanoes. Knowing that, Josefa kept Diego Sauri's travel plans for them a secret, saying nothing until the Holy Mother church had imposed upon her the obligation to obey her husband above all others. Since, however, they could not think of anywhere near Puebla they could spend their wedding night, Josefa spent her first week of love with Diego in the nearly empty, sunny Casa de la Estrella.

The whole city knew that for a week the Sauri Veytias did not leave their bed, and that Josefa did not go to the door even for her mother when on the fourth day that woman, who thought herself a model of prudence, was bold enough to call on them to make sure they were still alive. The new bride had come out on the balcony with her hair flying, covered only by the white shirt her husband had worn at the wedding, and in a voice that reached the clouds said that she could not come down.

After that scene, it seemed inconsequential that the bridal pair was undertaking a wedding trip without a set destination, one dedicated to traveling the country for several months gathering herbs and potions. Instead, the family was rather relieved that the bizarre couple was allowing them to draw a free breath while they worked up the spirit to accept them as they were.

When Diego and Josefa returned with a collection of chests handled as if they contained the treasure of the British crown, having wandered through every possible mountain or valley within a radius of five hundred kilometers, the family welcomed them as the most beloved and truly missed prodigals since the one whose story is told in the Bible.

In the peace of that welcome, Josefa and Diego settled into the Casa de la Estrella and devoted all the time and money they could invest through the years to making it the silver goblet it once had been.

ON THE LOWER FLOORS of the house, Diego Sauri set up a pharmacy that smelled of wood and shone like porcelain. The shelves that held his jars, the counter, even the worktable in the laboratory behind the shop, were all of cedar, and there was no remedy he could not provide. Diego found an answer for every ill among his white flasks and hundreds of numbered, aromatic little boxes. In a very short time his shop had become something more refined and complete than the ordinary pharmacy. He had everything from Anhalt water for the weaknesses of the elderly to cocaine powders.

During the time he lived in Europe, he had collected small samples of the principal remedies of each region. He learned the formulas for many of them and knew what the powder in each of the boxes was for, although anyone else would have confused them with bath talcum.

TOWARD THE END of the century, the mirrored corridor on the second floor of La Casa de la Estrella was crowded with flowers and plants and lit by an almost brutal sun. Emilia discovered the delights of that brilliant tunnel as soon as she was able to crawl, and for several months her knees and hands would become dirty from the dust on the mosaic tile that, until then, had been invisible.

The first time Emilia stood alone clutching the edge of a flowerpot, her head lifted like a ballerina's, Josefa discovered her from a distance and blessed the day she had planted the row of potted ferns that made a jungle for her daughter's daring. Emilia met her mother's eyes, heard her call in a low voice vibrating with the apprehension of someone watching an artist on a high wire, and let go one pot, risking two steps to the next, as Josefa drowned in the salt of two enormous tears.

Unaware of the great feat taking place overhead, Diego Sauri was in the laboratory behind his shop preparing batches of General Quiroga's famous dental powders—a mixture of red coral, cream of tartar, dried boar horn, Venetian talc, cochineal, and essence of clove—which had become fashionable that year but which Diego always sold with the unprofitable admonition that the best dentrifice was much simpler: a mixture of two parts burned bread crust and one part cinchona bark, all finely pulverized.

As he stood preparing his mixtures, Diego Sauri liked to sing fragments from famous arias. His wife's joyful entrance into his laboratory surprised him in the middle of *Se quel guerrier io fossi*.

"She's walking!" Josefa announced, bending down to set Emilia on the ground. She held her by the waist and told her husband to kneel down and tell the baby to come to him, but he refused, horrified at such an experiment.

Mocking his fears, Josefa let Emilia go, and Diego had no choice but to kneel down to her level. He saw his daughter standing in the middle of his laboratory, dressed in pale blue, her hands clutching air, her doll feet unsteady in new boots. Her eyes were far below the level of the table, but she recognized this room as the haven of the man who when he was wearing a long white apron was in a place that seemed the best of all possible worlds. Many afternoons he had brought her downstairs with him and sat her in a high chair to watch while he mixed his ingredients and sang, but this was the first time her feet had touched the floor.

The pharmacist opened his arms to his daughter, a flask containing a different tincture in each hand. Emilia's eyes fastened on the deep purple, and she started toward her father.

Shouting bravos, Diego relinquished the flask with the essence of Florentine iris to the hesitant grasp of the daughter whose steps he saw as a miracle, then bestowed on his wife predictions of their daughter's glowing future.

This blissful speech ended when Josefa, practicing the female duty of divided attention, saw an Emilia stained with lilac from her bangs to the tips of the white boots the cobbler had delivered only that morning.

NIGHT FOUND THEM ALL in the bathroom, Emilia's purple only partially faded, and they lamenting the first squabble of their long married life. Amid a dozen basins and the dizzying scent of the soap the Droguería Sauri ordered from an importer of English products, Josefa called Diego irresponsible and Diego defended himself, calling his wife petulant in return. By nine Emilia had been put to bed, still half-stained with lilac splotches, and Josefa sat down to weep on the bathroom floor, where she had returned to pick up Emilia's boots. The Sauris' bath was out of the ordinary. In addition to the tub with lion feet and the three porcelain pitchers with matching washbasins, Diego had installed a shower that provided the exceptional pleasure of clean water flowing over their heads, while freeing their hands from having to hold a pitcher.

"Why should plants have a better bath than we do?" Diego had asked Josefa when he saw her watering the pots in the corridor.

Three days later he had convinced a blacksmith to fritter away some time in trying to build a large-scale watering can. The man acceded when Sauri smoothly assured him that if their contrivance worked out well he would sell dozens in his pharmacy, recommending it as the most advanced means of preventive medicine.

The apparatus did not have the success he expected with his clientele, but that did not dampen his spirits. The fact was that in his shower, beneath leaded windows admitting the same blue light of his childhood, he was the happy king of his bathroom. The novelty also pleased Josefa, who sang waltzes beneath it every morning, observing the shine of the body that intoxicated her husband.

WHEN DIEGO CAME to apologize, admitting that it had been a mistake to give the flask to his daughter, the floor on which Josefa had sunk down to cry was still wet from the chaos of bathing the baby.

"There's nothing to forgive," she said, with the beginning of a smile that Diego stooped down to kiss. From there they went off to bed.

Josefa clung to her husband as a natural right, with the peace of one who is reclaiming her soul as she caresses the rare treasure of a man able to say he is sorry.

IT WAS their good fortune not to have another falling-out until the night years later Emilia came into their bedroom sobbing as she hadn't done since the nightmares of her second year.

Only shortly before, they had wakened, touched by the same desire, and had sought in the darkness to exorcize it with the balm of their united bodies, pulling one another from the edge of the same precipice.

Josefa kissed her husband's shoulder, grateful that his haste had not given her time to remove her nightgown completely, and refastened it with an agility that, had it not been for the child, she would have invested in consummating their holy war. She asked her daughter what she had dreamed, and let her climb into bed to cuddle and be calmed. Emilia answered she didn't remember.

"Try to remember," Diego said in harsh tones befitting an enemy.

Emilia's answer was renewed weeping, and Josefa tried to answer for her by saying the child was afraid about having to sing and dance at the Cuencas' the following Sunday. Furious at having been brought back to earth so abruptly, Diego told his wife not to interpret their daughter's emotions, and demanded the child tell them what her dream had been and then go right back to bed. Emilia's hesitant answer was that she had dreamed about the Devil, and although her father had explained a thousand times that the Devil did not exist, she had seen him wearing the mocking face of Daniel Cuenca in her dream saying, "Yes, I exist!" When he heard that, Diego berated Josefa for allowing the girl to associate with people who talked about the Devil, and Josefa defended herself by saying it was the Cuenca boy's face, and not the Devil, that had frightened their daughter. Diego called Josefa a jackass, and she told him he was the one doing all the braying.

Day dawned with the Sauris in separate beds for the first time in their many years of married life. Josefa had unknowingly fallen asleep beside Emilia. The last thing she remembered was that for a while she had rubbed her back and laughed at the Devil *and* Daniel Cuenca. What she dreamed wasn't clear, but she awakened with a weight like a flatiron in her heart. She slipped out of bed without making a sound and went to her sewing room on the opposite side of the house. There she had a high-backed chair in which she sat to read or embroider; a blond oak round table, where there was always a flurry of papers, some of which had recently served to teach Emilia her ABCs; a small bookshelf; and a desk with small drawers and cubbyholes, where she kept assorted papers, from the deed that made her mistress of her house to bills from the notion shop and the grocer's. She searched through a felt-lined drawer, took out a piece of light-colored paper, and wrote: *Beloved. You are right. The Devil does not exist, and the child is not bashful. Truce! Josefa.*

When she returned from the market there was a bouquet of pastel flowers on the dining table and a brief note Diego had written on the paper he used for his prescriptions. It said: *Yes, the child is bashful. Her father hopes to surrender his arms to you on a better occasion. Diego.*

Before dinner, the pact was sealed on the same ground where shots had been fired the night before. Diego had been whistling when he came upstairs from the pharmacy and headed straight for the bedroom. Josefa recognized his footsteps and hurried after him, trying to hear whether he was in his stocking feet. If he took off his shoes during the day, that was the signal for a holy war; if not, she knew that he was going to their room only for a catnap he took with his shoes on, as was the custom in the Yucatán. At least that is what Josefa believed, since her only connection with the peninsula was her husband. She attributed anything Diego did differently from her fellow *poblanos* to his place of birth. Calling her "my little lettuce" in his most rapturous moments was an unequivocal example of Yucatán behavior. Which is what he called her that afternoon before he surrendered his arms. The next day Emilia went to her first rehearsal at the Cuencas'.

CHAPTER 5

THAT WAS a memorable Sunday.

Growing up, Josefa Veytia had been taught that Sunday clothes must be elegant, and that everyone from the youngest to the most elderly were obliged to show off their best outfits on that day. Only among that group of bizarre friends her husband and Dr. Cuenca had been cultivating would anyone show his face on Sunday in more slovenly garb than that worn during the week.

"That's how it's going to be in the future," Diego told her, pulling his most ancient coat from their wardrobe. "And we are the ones who must lead the way to that freedom."

"That's your responsibility, too?" Josefa was incredulous. "Diego, please stop taking on so many burdens. One group of thirty madmen cannot change everything."

"Well, not everything. I can't see any reason at all for changing the little frown some women get when they're arguing that there's no reason for change," said Diego, slipping into the jacket that had a hole in one elbow and a rip in the lining.

"I don't believe that in a hundred years any woman is

going to want to go outside in the getup you're talking about," said Josefa, ignoring the personal reference.

"What a shame I'm not going to be here to show you."

"We agree on that point. People like you should live forever, but for now, Emilia is going to do what other little girls do."

"Why are you crying?" her father asked when he saw Emilia decked out in ruffles, with a pink sash around her waist. "Your mother has you done up like a china doll."

"That's *why!*" Emilia replied, running to hide her face in the drapes in the sala, so no one would see her cry.

By the time they were ready to leave, she had recovered, and came and stood beside her father with a smile while her mother admired her as she would a masterpiece. Only then did they set out for the Cuencas'.

MILAGROS VEYTIA was waiting at the door, watching the Sauris stroll toward her as if they had all the time in the world. At her side was Daniel Cuenca, at ten wearing his first pair of long pants and a blue linen shirt inherited from his brother.

"They dressed their little girl up like a china doll," said Daniel. "That's why they're late."

"Don't you dare pester her," Milagros ordered when the Sauris were twenty paces from the door. Silently, she watched how Emilia was scarcely able to walk for all her ruffles. I wonder why Josefa insists on dressing her like that, Milagros thought, feeling a certain compassion for her godchild. Nevertheless, as she came closer, she could only surrender to the force of those dark, almond-shaped eyes. She had been right the morning that little girl was born. The eyes were a crystal-clear sign that her goddaughter would never know the delights of innocence.

"Don't hurry," she said sarcastically when the Sauris could hear. "Don't feel you've kept everyone waiting for two hours."

As Diego said hello and kissed her, she greeted him with a request. Would he take charge of hanging the stage curtain they needed to make the sala look like a theater? Then she asked Josefa if she remembered the accompaniment for the song the children were going to sing, and if Emilia had learned the words.

Emilia felt Daniel's mocking eyes on her and said she'd forgotten them, but Milagros, as if she hadn't heard, told her to go teach Daniel because he didn't know a single word. Then she took Josefa's arm and led her away.

"Don Porfirio himself couldn't be as bossy as you when you're in charge of a theatrical production," Josefa chided.

"Don't call him 'Don' Porfirio. He's an arbitrary, petty, dried-up, evil old dictator."

"Surely he's not that bad."

"Ask your husband."

"I don't have to. He says things like that all day long."

"And you turn a deaf ear?"

"Of course. I don't want him killed for talking out of turn."

"Even deaf mutes are going to die, Josefa. It doesn't help to hold your tongue."

"Don't say those things," Josefa pleaded.

"As if you didn't know them already," was Milagros's answer.

THE CHILDREN had stayed behind, near the fountain. Daniel had a stick in one hand and was scratching in the dirt as he examined Emilia with a critical eye.

"Don't look at me like that," she said.

"I'm not looking at you," Daniel replied, laughing, his eyes very different from the ones that had terrified her in her nightmare.

"I know I look awful."

"You're not awful, but you can't run," said Daniel.

"I can beat you," she answered.

"Try," he challenged, darting off at top speed.

Emilia ran after him as if she were not hindered by stiff crinoline petticoats; she followed him to the back of the garden and watched as he scrambled up a split-branch ladder to the middle of an enormous ash tree. She knew that in her ruffled dress she would never get past the second rung. She slipped out of it. Then came a starched petticoat she also discarded. Thus liberated, she climbed the ladder.

Daniel did not say a word but never took his eyes off her as, still panting, she straddled a large limb and leaned back against the tree trunk. He took in her flushed, shining face, her dangling legs, her white knee socks, the bow-trimmed shoes swinging back and forth like the clapper of a bell.

"How does the song go?" he asked.

The lemon tree has to be green
before the purple's revealed,
and so if love's to endure,
first it must be concealed.

As Emilia sang, her feet moved as if she were dancing on air.

Daniel listened, following the swinging legs, letting an enchantment steal over him that matched the way he felt when he watched his kite knife through the air. He would let out a lot of string, and when it was high above, but tied to him by the string that made him its master, he would shout with as much pride as if he himself were soaring in the heavens.

Emilia discerned something of this flight, and stopped singing to give him one of her most self-satisfied smiles. At that, Daniel jumped to the ladder and scooted down like a cat chased by a broom.

"And that's where you'll stay," he said, looking up once he was on the ground, swooping up the dress his feet had landed in.

Shortly before his wife's death, Dr. Cuenca had built a pond at the very end of the orchard, which she had stocked with trout. It was toward that pond Daniel ran with Emilia's dress. Salvador, his older brother, was already there with a friend, smoking a cigarette he had filched from a visitor and watching his brother running toward them like the pest he always was.

Daniel, on the other hand, did not see them. He paused for a moment on the bank before throwing the mass of ruffles into the water. He knew this would not be the best way to avoid being shipped off to boarding school, but he could not deny himself the pleasure of seeing the dress float in the pool like a ship under full sail, so he threw it into the air and watched it flutter until the ruffles, and the reverence with which Josefa had sewn them, lighted upon the water. The dress pirouetted in the gentle breeze with no sign of sinking, as if in fact it had been intended to float like a ship.

"Dumb asshole kid! Whose is that?" asked Salvador, communicating a certain admiration.

"Mine!" yelled Emilia, pushing Daniel from behind to join the dress in the pond.

Neither Salvador nor his friend had seen her coming. But nothing could have amused them more than the screaming little girl who had suddenly appeared in camisole and underdrawers, looking like a half-skinned rabbit, to extract her revenge. Despite the fact that Daniel was treading water and saying it felt great, Salvador knew all too well how to recognize his brother's injured pride.

He and his friend laughed so long and hard that, as they puffed on the cigarette, Emilia stopped celebrating long enough to remember she wasn't wearing a dress. She felt the older boys were branding her with their laughter and could think of no better escape than to jump into the pond and hide her confusion in the water.

And that was how that day's rehearsal ended.

Soon after, Dr. Cuenca concluded that Daniel must be torn from the indulgent skirts of Milagros Veytia and conform to the standards his father thought appropriate once and for all.

Milagros, cleverly playing on the argument that her legitimacy as Daniel's tutor originated in the very last words María Esparza had spoken, was able to obtain Dr. Cuenca's concession to postpone the boy's departure and allow her to keep him with her at least to the end of the century. It is difficult to know what chord she touched with that plea, but the upshot was that Daniel stayed in Puebla one more year, under the care of the honorary aunt who was indispensable to him if he was to escape unpunished from the constant trouble he created.

Not until 1901 was the rebellious mind and enigmatic laughter of Daniel Cuenca packed off to the school for young men run by Don Camilo Aberamen, a strict Italian who specialized in forming the character of difficult boys.

By then Emilia and Daniel had exchanged combat for complicity. They spent Sunday afternoons climbing trees, trading stones they had collected during the week, and paddling their feet in the pond while they took turns scratching each other's back. This last activity in fulfillment of a contract Emilia had established to avoid an argument with her friend.

One afternoon as they dabbled their feet in the water with the feeling they would never be free of the cough they shared, Daniel asked her to scratch his neck.

"How long?"

"Until I say."

"No," said Emilia. "I'll scratch your whole back, but I'll count to sixty and then it's your turn."

The idea had seemed fair to Daniel, and from that agreement had come their accord.

The last Sunday of that February, each of their games took on the weight of ritual. The stone trading took less time than usual, because that day Emilia did not have to show each of the additions to her collection to see whether Daniel would trade one of them for the smooth, black stone, shiny as silk, that he called his amulet and carried with him everywhere. He put it beneath his pillow before he fell asleep, and it was the first thing he touched when he woke. They had come upon it together, one dry winter morning when Milagros took them for a walk beside the Atoyac River. Emilia had seen it gleaming among the other stones but had wasted time pointing to it. Daniel followed her finger with his eyes, stooped down, and grabbed it.

"It's mine," they had shouted at the same time, but it was in Daniel's hand and there it stayed for several months of trading, during which time Emilia tried everything from condescension to blackmail, without success.

"Open your hand," Daniel said as they began their session that Sunday.

Emilia held out her hand and felt the stone drop into her palm. Daniel's amulet shone a second beneath the pale sunlight.

"Are you sure?" Emilia asked, as if it were a diamond she was holding.

"Race you to the pond," said Daniel, who ever since he was a little boy had found it difficult to show his generosity.

They dipped their toes into the icy water of late afternoon. The circles they made with their feet frightened the fish along the shore.

"Shall I scratch your back?" asked Emilia.

"Up to sixty."

Emilia's slim fingers began to move up and down Daniel's back as she counted more slowly than she had ever done. She was to twenty when Daniel's arm crossed hers and he returned the favor. He did not count at all, and at twenty-three Emilia stopped counting. They sat silently for a while, feet stirring the water, until Emilia dropped her hand and dared say:

"I don't want you to go."

"What good does that do?"

"I promise I'll look after your stone."

"It's yours."

"Will you look for another one there?"

"No. There aren't any stones there," Daniel said, pulling his feet from the water.

"And girls?"

"No girls, either."

They walked back to the house carrying their shoes, their throats filled with February's cough. Milagros Veytia had come out to meet them, pretending to be annoyed.

"What a pair of crazy kids. What were you doing getting your feet wet?"

"Saying good-bye," answered Emilia, who had learned from her mother to state the heart's tribulations openly.

Milagros took them to a bedroom, rubbed their feet with alcohol, brewed cups of aromatic herbs, and told them one of her adventurous and heroic tales. When Josefa came to claim her daughter, she found Milagros wearing a strange smile, sitting on the edge of a bed where two exhausted children lay sleeping.

"I'll help you carry her," Milagros told Josefa as her sister moved to wake Emilia.

"She can walk when she wakes up."

"Not today," said Milagros, as if there were no question that she was the ultimate authority. And Josefa obeyed as if in fact she was.

Diego Sauri saw them as they came out into the corridor together, carrying the slack body of his daughter, and once again confirmed his belief that those were the two best women in the world.

MONDAY MORNING, Dr. Cuenca and his younger son began their journey to the boarding school in Chalchicomula. Only in that way, Dr. Cuenca told himself, only by having Daniel live near his brother in a world organized to train boys to be men, would Daniel recover from the babying he had experienced in the care of his wife's overindulgent friend.

Milagros Veytia was confined to bed for a week, using the pretext of the worst case of flu in her life. Josefa came by on Tuesday to make her soup and give her the youthwort pills and Tolú balsam tree syrup her husband had sent.

"It's absurd," Milagros told her. "It was the children who got wet but I'm the one who's sick." Then she coughed twice and sobbed out her abandonment on her sister's knees.

CHAPTER

6

EMILIA BEGAN with a cold as monstrous as Milagros's and ended with chicken pox. For two weeks all Josefa could do was bathe her with black nightshade soap several times a day and bear the criticism nearly everyone had to make of this treatment, which was Diego's innovation.

"Are we doing the right thing?" Josefa asked him one morning as the pharmacist was reading *Regeneración* with the same patient concentration he accorded the newest medical prescription.

"No. I don't think it will work."

"Do you think it will leave scars?"

"He's already scarred by his infamy."

"Diego, I'm talking about Emilia. At this moment I am not concerned about the fate of the governor of Sonora."

"He's the governor of Nuevo León."

"You're not listening. I'm going to have to be hired by a newspaper before you listen. I'll offer my services to the *Imparcial* this very day."

"Don't even mention the name of that rag."

"Emilia looks terrible, and you don't care," Josefa reproached him. Just looking at her daughter made her want to cry. Her body was a mass of sores. Her throat hurt, her back itched like fire, her fine little features were marred by hundreds of waxy pimples.

"Don't worry," her husband said. "In less than two weeks her skin will be absolutely normal."

Josefa was skeptical.

"Other people don't bathe their children," she said.

"Because the rationale is imperfect." Diego Sauri never lowered his newspaper. "Everyone believes he's right until someone else improves a treatment. And medical treatment changes very little. There are still eminent physicians practicing bloodletting."

"But now we're the ones who look like barbarians."

"Doesn't matter," Diego proclaimed. "People who search do more for medicine than those who accept."

"Do you have doubts when you tell me how to treat Emilia?" Josefa asked.

"Anyone who doesn't errs twice."

"Just so she doesn't end up with scars."

"She won't have scars with either treatment. It's just that with mine she'll be cleaner."

In assenting, Josefa's voice expressed the irony she felt when her husband claimed something was irrefutable that she found questionable.

One week later, Emilia lost her last scab in the tub in the blue bathroom and was able to return to the school her parents had chosen after much discussion and many doubts.

"Anything's better than sending her to the nuns," Sauri had said when it was time to think about his daughter's education. "The only thing they'll teach her there is prayers, and what we want to do is try to form a creature who can understand the contradictions of the modern world."

"At seven?" Josefa asked, and they became entangled in a discussion that ended with Emilia's being enrolled in a school run by a severe and meticulous spinster who carried with her a history of forbidden loves.

The catechism was taught in her school, but the Sauris countered that information by telling Emilia that it was a theory like any other, just as important, although perhaps less authentic, than Milagros's theory of multiple gods. So Emilia grew up hearing that the mother of Jesus was a virgin who proliferated into many virgins with many names, and that Eve was the first woman, formed from Adam's rib and guilty for all the ills afflicting mankind; at the same time she learned about the patient goddess Ixchel, the ferocious Cuatlicue, the beautiful Venus, the fierce Diana, and Lilith, the other first woman, rebellious and unpunished.

In the afternoons, Josefa taught Emilia piano and a passion for novels, while Diego talked ungovernably about politics, travel, and medicine. When she was eleven, Dr. Cuenca began teaching her to play the cello. He was a demanding teacher with few words, but Emilia learned to love him because he loved her like the daughter he'd never had.

WHEN EDISON'S KINETOSCOPE came to Puebla it cost thirty centavos for a thirty-second performance. It was there Emilia was first touched by the dream of knowing the world, a dream her father nourished constantly. North Africa, St. Petersburg, Pompeii, Naples, Venice were some of the first places her eyes saw from afar as she listened to the voice of Diego Sauri, youthful and enthusiastic in the midst of silence, saying:

"You must go there someday."

One night when she returned from the wooden shed they called a movie theater, Josefa admonished her husband.

"You are going to turn Emilia into a perpetual malcontent. If you keep filling her head with impossible ideas she'll grow up like a potted jungle plant confined to a patio. I don't want you to tell her again that travel is a form of fate."

"Do I say that?"

"You stir her up too much. I'm forty years old and I've never been outside Mexico. How can she ever get to a third of the places you tell her she will?"

"She is going to live her entire life in a new century," Diego replied, his voice sweet on the air that reigned in his home.

While Emilia was growing up sheltered by the freedoms of that air,

Daniel Cuenca was learning about the world under the harsh tutelage of Don Camilo Aberamen, a man of anarchist leanings who placed the force of his convictions behind educating the group of boys he selected from the applicants to his remote school, precisely for the fiery temperament that was the cause of their being sent to him. He was convinced that intelligence thrives in youths with indomitable spirit. And it was both his pleasure and his pride that he taught them to be rational and to control their emotions without losing their courage. Studying with him, they learned as much music as Latin, and spent as much time on mathematics as climbing mountains and leaping over obstacles intended to train their bodies for the battle of life.

In December and January Aberamen's students were allowed to leave the school, which was buried in a dusty village in the foothills of the volcano Citlalpetl. During that period Daniel returned to his father's home and to his games with Emilia.

One of those times they went together to see the ocean.

Diego Sauri, Manuel Rivadeneira, the Veytia sisters, and Emilia left by train from the Puebla station. Milagros, who for the first time in her life displayed in public the fact that occasionally she ceded a bit of her freedom to the poet Rivadeneira, had, after long discussions with Josefa, invited him to go with them on the train.

"If I invite him, you're going to want me to marry him. And I'm not willing to run that risk," she said. Nevertheless, the morning the train left, she appeared at the Sauris' accompanied by Rivadeneira and his inexhaustible erudition.

Manuel Rivadeneira was a wealthy man with simple pleasures. He enjoyed what life offered and never asked for more than was given. With that resignation he had accepted Milagros's refusal to marry him, and with that wisdom he had managed to stay close to her without further explanations.

He lived alone, but had moments of sunlight no married man could dream of. He saw Milagros whenever she wished to see him. As a result, he never saw a cross face or the darkness of boredom in the smile of the woman who filled his life. He read without a schedule and lived without haste. His house was as silent as a church.

As the train pulled away from the station, Emilia was flushed with excitement. She was beginning the first of the thousand journeys her father wished for her every day.

Three stations and almost two hours later, they reached San Andrés Chalchicomula. When the car they were traveling in slowed before the station platform, Emilia could see her tall, strong-headed friend through the train window. A long curly lock of coppery hair fell over his forehead, and at his feet was the leather suitcase he carried back and forth to school at year's end. As soon as he saw them, Daniel pulled a small flute from his pocket and began playing a melody of his own composition.

"You can see that boy's free spirit the minute he's on his own," said Milagros, watching from the window with all the smugness of the mother she wasn't.

"What you can see is that you adore him," said Rivadeneira.

As soon as the door opened, Daniel burst into the car, making more racket than the midway of a carnival. Emilia screamed her welcome. They hugged one another, laughing and rolling on the floor, and only when the train began jolting down the track was Josefa able to tempt them with playing cards and crackers into adjoining seats.

They played card games and argued until they reached the hills of Maltrata. The train was laboring up a steep mountain and they were surrounded by clouds. A fine drizzle was falling over the mountains that burst through the fog, and the valley they had traveled through for so long had become a cliff punctuated with occasional small houses and rushing streams. Everything around them was green and watery.

They traveled several hours through that landscape, until they fell asleep against one another. They were beginning to feel cold when a long whistle blast announced they had reached Boca del Monte. The doors of the car opened wide and the train stopped in front of a building where a table was set and a great colorful fire was roaring. Ever after when she felt cold, Emilia longed for the night they spent beside the fire in that inn.

The next morning when they reached Veracruz and checked into the Hotel de Mexico, which was located on the pier overlooking Emilia's first view of the ocean, she was introduced to the heat of the tropics and to the café where her parents had fallen immediately and everlastingly in love.

OTHER VACATIONS, Milagros took them all over the state of Puebla. She showed them the valley that by her lights had been governed by the designs of the god Xólotl, and talked to them for hours about the knowledge of the heavens that was an integral part of venerating a god whose name means Celestial Traveler. She also took them to Cholula, the most important religious center in the valley of Anáhuac, to climb the pyramid built in honor of Quetzalcoatl, god of the air.

"He was an intelligent god, an exemplary god. He taught men the art of working metals, and the even more difficult art of governing," Milagros Veytia told them as they approached his temple in a mule-drawn trolley. "When anyone spoke to him of war, he covered his ears."

The children jumped out and ran up the hill toward the flat top of the pyramid, to the church the Spanish built in the sixteenth century atop the great temple, with no respect for the god the first inhabitants of Mexico had confused with those men who came from the sea.

"The Spaniards were high-handed," said Daniel, contemplating the landscape that spread before the atrium of the church constructed for the Virgen de los Remedios.

"It was their religion and their time that was high-handed. Furthermore, a child should never criticize his ancestors," Milagros told him.

"My ancestors were Aztecs, not Spaniards," Daniel insisted.

"And that's why you have a matador's buttocks? You aren't what you choose to be, you are what you are," his aunt said.

"And the Aztecs were high-handed, too," Emilia chimed in. Her cheeks were blazing and her moist bangs clung to her forehead.

"When do you go back to school?" she asked.

"Tuesday," said Daniel, and slipped his arm around her shoulder as they walked toward a woman selling oranges.

That Sunday, for the first time, Emilia was driven to ask something of two different gods. Neither Quetzalcoatl nor the Señora de los Remedios, however, came to her aid in preventing Dr. Cuenca from taking his son back to Chalchicomula.

"Now I know why you don't pray to any god," she told her parents after some time had passed.

"You do?" Josefa asked, looking up from the napkin she had been embroidering.

"They don't answer your prayers anyway."

"The only answer to anything is life," Diego interposed from behind the pages of his fourth newspaper of the day. "And life is generous. Often it gives you what you haven't even asked. But it's never enough."

"It's been enough for me," Josefa confessed.

"That's because you were born with the full moon," Diego told her.

"And me, what was I born with?" asked Emilia.

"You were born with electric light," her father answered. "Who knows what you will want from life."

EMILIA MISSED DANIEL most on Sundays. The Cuencas' garden had become as immense as time was long.

Her girlfriend Sol García's parents seldom let their daughter go with Emilia to what they called anarchist meetings. So while the adults were envisioning democracy, Emilia paced through the house like a bored cat or sat quietly in a wicker chair listening to discussions about music and poetry. She entertained herself by watching them from a distance as they plotted and argued about the future as if it depended solely on their designs. As she spoke, Milagros moved her hands in a way Emilia found eloquent in itself. Watching her was to witness an unforgettable dance that belonged to Emilia alone, one she kept forever in that deep cavern where we store our best memories.

SOMETIMES THE SAURIS were late to the meetings at Dr. Cuenca's home because as passionate as Diego was about republican politics, he was equally intense about the bulls, something he intended to pass on to his daughter. This was perhaps one of the few disagreements between Milagros and her brother-in-law. What he touted as an art form she considered butchery.

All during the nineteenth century, the matter of bullfights was the source of arguments not only among married couples and family members but in Congress as well. In 1867, President Juárez outlawed what he thought to be "a barbarous, savage, and stupid entertainment that only a despotic government could tolerate."

On this point, Diego was at odds with the president he referred to as "the implacable and upstanding Señor Juárez." So when bullfights were again approved in the Chamber, he was among the first to celebrate.

The Sauris had met many unforgettable people during the long journey in search of medicinal herbs they referred to as their honeymoon. Their friendship with Ponciano Díaz, the premier Mexican matador of the period, dated from that time and began on a difficult trip between Querétaro and Guadalajara. When Díaz was invited to fight his first bull as a full-fledged toreador in the Puebla Plaza de Toros, he stayed with the Sauris, drinking his way through his days with them. He quickly became famous.

Emilia first saw that simple man one afternoon when her father took her to the bullfights dressed in a *china poblana* costume and carrying a bouquet of carnations bigger than herself.

Halfway through the afternoon, Diego took his daughter down to the ring, where she handed the flowers to a sweaty and exhausted man in the traditional Andalucian suit of lights; the officials had just decorated him with a green, white, and red sash identical to the one worn by presidents of the Republic.

Emilia gave Díaz the carnations with a shy smile, and he, seeing his friend Diego Sauri standing behind the child, was inspired to pick her up in his arms and dance her around in circles.

Díaz had been crowned with laurel, his dark suit was stained, and he smelled of blood as if he himself were a wounded bull.

I don't love Mazzantini
or even Cuatro Dedos,
the one I love is Ponciano
Who's king of all toreros

the crowd sang, in time with the dance of their favorite matador.

When Ponciano set Emilia back down, after kissing her and congratulating Diego Sauri for his "beautiful little heifer," Emilia looked at her sequin-embroidered skirt, soiled now with blood and dirt, looked at the tiers of seats where people were still cheering in patriotic delirium for the best matador in Mexico, and bit her lip to keep from crying. From that moment on, the bullfight evoked a mixture of horror and enthusiasm she found difficult to hide.

Thirteen months and two days later, the famous Mexican bullfighter died of what was reported as liver failure. Diego knew exactly how many drinks had caused it.

Throngs of grieving fans filed before Díaz's coffin. Emilia came into the dining room one early morning as her father was reading an account of the burial in one of the five newspapers spread before him on the table.

"We'd be better off if it was the other Díaz who'd died," she heard him say as a large tear rolled into his coffee cup.

Porfirio Díaz had been in power for twenty years. Twenty years during which he progressed without qualm from republican hero to dictator. Which was when Diego Sauri had become his personal enemy.

It was just growing light. Emilia was cold. She was barefoot and half-naked.

"I pricked my finger," she said, holding it out so Diego could see the blood on the tip of her index finger.

Her father examined the tiny wound, sucked it, and then gave her a kiss.

"Why did you lick it?"

"Saliva disinfects. You stuck yourself somehow."

"What with? I was asleep."

"Mama will know," Diego said as his wife came into the dining room. After she kissed them both, she agreed that Emilia had stuck herself.

"What with?" Emilia repeated, still shaken by the suddenness of her awakening.

"Some kind of wire," her mother said, leading her off to get dressed.

"It wasn't your friend Ponciano, was it?" Emilia asked Diego. "They say the dead come back."

"They come back, but not that way," said Diego Sauri, plunging back into the newspapers with heart and soul.

AT MID-MORNING, Josefa showed up at school to take Emilia home. The puncture wound in her finger had been caused by the tooth of a large gray rat they'd found beneath her bed.

Back home, gathered around the rodent Diego had somehow caged, were Dr. Cuenca, Milagros Veytia, and even the poet Rivadeneira. Everyone was staring at the rodent with the horror of those who see in it the threat of rabies and the bubonic plague, but as Emilia came in they hid their panic while she said hello, kissing them one by one and showing them her bite.

Dr. Cuenca's opinion was that there was nothing to be learned at the moment, and the Sauris decided to keep the rat and observe it for a week. Diego set the cage in the back patio and waited for time to pass. When after ten days the rat was still alive and healthy, it was clear Emilia had been spared any harm. By then Diego and his daughter felt a certain affection for the rat, and every afternoon they delayed its execution till the following day. After a month, they no longer spoke of killing it, and the rat became a habitual guest to whom Diego brought carrots every morning and Emilia visited when she came home from school.

"That little creature has charm," said Diego at dinner one Thursday. "I actually think I see something of Ponciano in him."

"People aren't reincarnated in animals. You die and that's it," Josefa declared.

"What does it mean, 'that's it'?" Emilia asked.

"Who knows, daughter," Josefa answered, and with such sadness that it made her daughter shiver.

"My Aunt Milagros says you become a tree. Sol García says you go to heaven. Señorita Lagos says you go to hell. In Dr. Cuenca's house they believe that spirits linger in the air, and you two say 'who knows?'"

"That's what we say," Josefa agreed. "So I can assure you that the rat isn't Ponciano. Poor man, all that effort just to have someone see him as a filthy rodent. It's time for it to go, Diego, give it something."

"I'm going to take him down a glass of port," said Diego, pouring himself a brandy. "You want some, Emilia?"

"My friends are right," said Josefa. "We're raising a very strange child."

"She'd be a poor thing indeed if we let her be like the others," said Diego.

"I am like the others," said Emilia. "You're the ones who're strange, and not like other parents," she commented before getting up with the rat's port in her hand. "If he drinks it, he was the matador; if not, we'll poison him," she said on her way out of the dining room.

THE RAT DIDN'T LIKE the port, but Diego had become so fond of it that fifteen months went by before he agreed to get it out of the house, and then only to set it free.

Early one morning, driving one of the first motorcars in the city, the Sauris left Puebla far behind. The liberation ceremony had taken on such importance that Milagros Veytia and Sol García accompanied them as guests. The automobile had been lent to Diego by his friend, the poet Rivadeneira, who besides his passion for Milagros Veytia could count among his blessings a fortune much more accessible than an ungrateful, brilliant woman.

At an appropriate spot they stopped and formed a somber procession headed by the forceful presence of Josefa Veytia y Rugarcía, as Diego called his wife when she assumed the duty of acting as the one member of the family with her head screwed on right.

They walked through the purple flowers that dotted the fields in October. Diego carried the cage in one hand and with the other led Emilia, who was humming a little tune her father insisted on whistling in the early mornings: "I would love to be water where you go to bathe. . . ." They looked for the center of the level field.

"Here's fine," Josefa decided after a few minutes.

Diego Sauri stopped and set the cage on the ground.

"I'll open it," said Emilia, stooping down to lift the latch that opened the little door. In one second the rat had flashed away to explore the field where it would disappear.

"Farewell, Ponciano," said Diego, as he watched the rat scamper into some brambles.

"Ponciano had better manners than that," said Milagros Veytia, taking up her brother-in-law's game. "This fellow didn't even say thank you."

"You're right," Diego agreed with melancholy. "You Veytia women are always right."

"Until we believe someone from the Yucatán," rejoined Josefa, who had taken a tablecloth from her basket and was snapping it in the wind, intent on spreading it on the grass without a wrinkle. Five times she let it settle and five times she lifted it again because she didn't like how it lay. The sixth time she gave up and left it as it was, to avoid her sister's teasing about being such a perfectionist.

Milagros sat on the ground, watching her sister set out plates, glasses, wine, cheese, salad, bread, butter—even a flower vase she filled with flowers gathered by Emilia and Sol. Milagros detested the kinds of chores tradition had relegated to women; she saw them as busywork in which thousands of major talents had wasted energies that should have been devoted to more useful endeavors.

Every time she got on that subject, her most fervent partner in the conversation was Diego himself. So both spent that afternoon mapping out a bright future for Emilia, and for other women on the planet, while Josefa laughed and the girls ran off until they were two dots on the horizon, then raced back to play Chinese checkers or have the fun of interrupting the adults' conversation.

"That's how the work is divided. He spends all day in the pharmacy and he doesn't complain," Emilia heard her mother say as she put cheese on a hard roll.

"That's fine, Sister. What isn't fine is for Emilia to see your attitude as something natural and inevitable. Because she may be your daughter, but she's my goddaughter, and she may have a different future in store."

"I'm going to work in the pharmacy," Emilia threw in as she went by.

Diego nodded. "She will be living in a different century."

"We're already living in a different century." Milagros had found an opening for another of her speeches.

"Bless you, Sister-in-law . . . someone realizes that." Diego took a long swallow of red wine.

"We've realized it for five years now. And what good has it done?" Josefa asked.

"Among other things," Milagros replied, "the governor has been reelected for a third time, right under our noses."

"And what kind of change is that?" Josefa wanted to know.

"The kind you don't see till you see it," Diego answered.

"Your husband's waxing philosophical," Milagros laughed.

"You started it," Josefa accused. "With all that talk about the Flores Magóns having to leave the country, and about going to visit them in Canada."

"There won't be enough time. They'll be back before that."

"They'll be locked up the minute they get back," Josefa surmised.

"They'll announce their arrival with bullets, not speeches," said Diego.

"Don't frighten Josefa," Milagros warned.

"Don't try to protect me, Sister. That talk about rebellion is ridiculous. It will fail. I don't know why you two can't see that." Josefa turned once again to the argument she never tired of repeating. To have an anti-Reelection club was fine and good, but to turn it into a group that professes justice at the end of a gun is crazy.

IT WAS GROWING DARK. The girls returned from their latest expedition, and everyone helped put the utensils back into the basket.

"Did you fall?" Diego asked Emilia.

"No."

"You have blood on your skirt. Now what bit you?"

"Nothing. Where do I have blood?"

"Where else?" said Milagros. "Something else the years do to you."

"Don't tell me, don't tell me," said Josefa, marking the sign of time on her daughter's skirt, in the pallor of her youthful face, the surprise in her eyes, the haste with which she thrust her hand between her legs.

"What do I have?" asked Emilia, who saw an answer in the expressions of the others.

"Woman's curse," replied her friend Sol, who was a year older and for some months had adapted to using that dark phrase and clean white rags to resolve the monthly question.

Diego Sauri realized he was out of that conversation. He started walking back toward that other mystery, his friend's automobile, and left the women talking among themselves under a sky where three stars were just beginning to shine.

After a while, the women declared their conclave over. It was beginning to rain. They sang on the way home, led by Milagros:

Santa Barbara, dear lady, you who once were a star
protect us from thunder and lightning afar.

Josefa was struck dumb, unable to find words.

Several times during the night she awoke to cry over the first change of her personal twentieth century.

"Don't you like the changes the century's brought?" her husband asked.

"No," she answered, her head hidden in her arms.

"And I don't like this one," said Diego, softly stroking her back.

CHAPTER 7

THE CENTURY was changing many things, not only in places Emilia believed existed in her father's imagination alone—like Panama, where a treaty had been signed with the United States to build a canal that would cut right through the middle of the Americas, or England, where a queen who had lived an eternity had died, or Japan and Russia, where a war had been raging for four years—but in Mexico, too. This was the news that disturbed the breakfast hour in their home, and in Puebla, the city she had learned to love, following in her mother's footsteps and listening to her aunt's sharp tongue.

Sheltered by the habit of peace, more novelties had come to the country than Diego Sauri could ever have imagined. Twenty thousand kilometers of railroad tracks cut past mines and through fields sown with henequen, produce, and grain for export. Beds of gold, silver, copper, and zinc ore created towns overnight. English and North American companies competed for the bedeviled bounty of the oil fields. Textile plants and foundries multiplied, along with paper, jute, glycerine, dynamite, beer, cement, and soap factories. All of it at an ungovernable speed that invited catastrophe.

In 1904, the meetings in Dr. Cuenca's house began to yield time formerly devoted to innocent musical and literary diversions to endless discussions of the problems brought on by the bonanza of modernization and the regime that encouraged it: wages bought less and less, the country was helplessly tied to the ups and downs of the U.S. economy, the railway was making the wealthy wealthier, and mine operators were rejecting traditional Mexican manual labor; the course of the Republic was moving toward disorder, and the rules of politics were governed by improvisation and caprice.

On Sunday nights the poet Rivadeneira returned home to the privacy of his diaries, where, aided by total recall, he wrote down each commentary he had heard. He more than anyone knew which of the guests was most lucid, who was most skillful, who had the most bluster, and who was truly brave.

Midway through 1907, he recorded the outpouring of rage and despair provoked by news of the slaughter of workers in Cananea, a copper mine in the north of the country. That information, brought to the meeting by a man named Aquiles Serdán, slim, half-bald, with burning eyes and a firm voice, the son of an impoverished family of shoe manufacturers, drew everything from shouts of fury to stony silence.

Once back home, Rivadeneira summarized what had happened while he was waiting for Milagros Veytia to climb into the bed they shared on nights they chose to hoard happiness against the remainder of their destiny. That afternoon, Dr. Octavio Cuenca had made the best analysis of any that could be made.

Saddened, he had said, "This society, which for fifty years has dreamed of being republican, democratic, egalitarian, rational, is surrendering to the governance of a minority that is authoritarian, sluggish, closed to outside influences, and knit together by the worst colonial traditions."

Later that same year, an obsequious committee of Puebla's city fathers were motivated to present a gift to Governor Mucio Martínez, the man who for many years had been imposing his will upon the people and land of that state.

In their attempt to think of a gift for someone who seemed to have everything, these gentlemen had come up with the idea of a large album in which they would collect the appreciation and signatures of the most important men of the city.

There was no shortage of people willing to seek out such men. Nor was there any scarcity of important men agreeable to signing. What person who owned anything, if nothing more than prestige, would not lay it at the feet of someone who protected his right to have it?

Everyone signed. Large landholders who in a day's time could not travel the length of their property by train, factory owners whose employees worked eighteen-hour days, merchants, luminaries . . . Every possible endorsement, and even several that should not have been considered.

When the sponsors brought the album to Dr. Cuenca, it was already filled with good wishes and notable names. No one could question the inclusion of a man who was so austere and so generous, a man so precise in his medical practice, a man so refined that he was embarrassed to collect his fees, a man whose only peculiarity consisted of treating the poor without charge.

Diego Sauri came to visit, with Emilia in tow, on the afternoon Dr. Cuenca was smilingly reviewing the verbal genuflections of his fellow citizens.

"What do you think of this, my friend?" he asked Diego.

"Pure groveling," said Diego, taking a look. "What will you do?"

"I've already done it," the doctor replied, dispassionately.

Diego picked up the book and paged through it until he came to his friend's entry. *I leave but one bequest to my children: paralysis of the spine before the tyrant.*

Diego smiled and passed his hand over his face.

"With your permission, I'm going to cut out this page. Surely you don't want to take on a fight of this size. I doubt if I have to remind you who the governor is."

"No," said Dr. Cuenca. "But let's leave the message. Some pleasures in life should not be denied. Isn't that right, my child?" he asked Emilia.

THREE DAYS LATER came the order for his arrest: a week in jail for public drunkenness at three in the morning.

"You've never been drunk in your life." Diego Sauri was incensed.

"But it isn't a bad charge," said Dr. Cuenca. "The complaint is signed by three of my neighbors. Don't worry, nothing will happen to me. You've seen how many times José Olmos y Contreras has been in and out."

Olmos was director of *La Voz de la Verdad,* and in fact Diego Sauri had seen the newspaperman going in and out of jail like someone on his way to church: imperturbable.

Which was how Dr. Cuenca left a week later. At the door of the jail, close to midnight, his Sunday-afternoon friends awaited, headed by the pharmacist Sauri and the Veytia sisters, who were dying for sleep.

FROM THEN ON, the doctor and his friends were listed as dangerous. Suddenly, two or three friends of friends of friends wanted to attend their meetings, and as there was no way to deny entry to anyone who affected a great interest in art, medicine, and intellectual exchange with people so well known, the Sunday meetings abruptly lost all political content and focused on theater, music, and other arts. Dissimulation was the watchword.

There was very little reference to social problems or criticism of the government; all the talk was of songs and poems, but everyone who was supposed to know something knew it, and any secret communicated in that world of conspirators was guarded as carefully as a state treasure.

After receiving his college degree, Daniel Cuenca had decided to study law, like his brother Salvador, at a university in the United States. He was not yet twenty when he began traveling through the states of Chihuahua and Sonora to get to know the groups of liberals primed to rebel against Porfirio Díaz. Nothing of that, however, was spoken aloud on Sundays; questions were resolved by asking the doctor about his sons' health, and how they were getting along with their studies.

During the week, from mouth to mouth and letter to letter, the drums muffled on Sunday thundered for war.

EMILIA SOMETIMES HEARD those drums from afar, sometimes throbbing at the very center of her brainy and beautiful adolescent head. Her fifteenth birthday party, a kind of coming-out, became the occasion for holding the first meeting of an anti-Reelection club in the Sauris' home. Such groups not only were not forbidden, but abounded as a relatively harmless demonstration of the government's disposition toward democracy. Emilia's birthday ended with shouts of *"Long live Mexico!"* and *"Death to authoritarianism!"*

"Is that dumb Daniel going to come home someday?" Emilia asked Milagros at about three in the morning, half-tipsy from the port her father had served as a seasoning for democratizing festivities.

THE NEXT SUNDAY Emilia arrived at the Cuencas' with her parents and the cello she had agreed to play in public for the first time.

Over the years, Milagros Veytia had taken charge of directing plays and organizing programs. That evening she did not let her niece go into the sala with everyone else, but made her go through the garden and crawl in a window behind the stage curtain.

"That way no one will see you ahead of time."

"But they've seen me hundreds of times," Emilia protested.

"Not as you are today," her aunt said.

Milagros had always thought Emilia was an exceptional child. But that afternoon she found her to be as if newly gifted with a strange and mysterious grace. She was growing up well. She still had her mother's perfect nose, although the chicken pox had left a tiny mark of its passing. Milagros argued that the hint of imperfection made the nose even more eloquent.

"It's so perfect—it suggests an ambiguity," she told Josefa when she worried over the scar.

The eyes Emilia's father had brought her from the coast were as dark and large as an enigma. Milagros had forever praised her good facial bones. Because, as she told her sister Josefa, it pleased her to see herself in them. Like Milagros, Emilia had prominent cheekbones, a broad brow, and arched, perfectly drawn eyebrows.

When she was a little girl, no one had thought Emilia would be very tall. Milagros had had an irrefutable response to those predictions.

"Perfumes have never been bottled in carafes, and diamonds don't come in the size of bricks."

As if she had to invalidate such expectations, between her eleventh and fifteenth birthdays Emilia had grown to be slightly taller than her aunt.

"Stop growing now," Milagros told her the afternoon of the concert. "You're like a tropical plant."

"Oh, Aunt Milagros," Emilia answered, shrugging her shoulders.

"'Oh, Aunt Milagros.' What kind of answer is that? Don't answer like that. If you don't know what to say, it's better to say nothing."

Emilia picked up her bow and drew it across the strings, this time answering Milagros—who had gone to stand beside the curtain, signaling Emilia to go to her chair in the center of the stage—with a brusque, surly sound.

"Now that's a better answer," Milagros whispered before she turned out the light and left Emilia groping for the chair in the dark.

EMILIA WAS WEARING her first long skirt that afternoon. Her mother had made her a light silk dress identical to the one shown on the next-to-last cover of *La Moda Elegante.*

"She still walks like a little girl," Milagros Veytia said to herself, pulling the cords that operated her curtain and turning on lights to start the show.

Emilia did not look at the people applauding, welcoming her as if she were on the stage of a grand opera house. She closed her eyes and began to play the difficult Bach piece she had studied with Dr. Cuenca two afternoons a week for the last three years.

Her audience was a group of eccentrics banded together in the heart of a city that recognized only the art of money, that in war had forgotten the desire for harmony that had given birth to it, that gossiped in the streets and prayed behind closed doors to an uncompassionate and illiterate god.

On Sunday afternoons, her audience was shaping an audacious chimera: angels had *not* come down from heaven to lay out the streets of their city. That legend was false, as legends usually are. Angels were born in these very streets; it was merely a matter of recognizing them and educating them to their winged, mysterious profession.

Within that dream beat the irrepressible liberalism of the nineteenth century, but also the conviction of every good *poblano,* no matter how illuminated or agnostic he or she might claim to be, that it was not possible to denigrate the city's acceptance of those who had led it prior to the blazing May 5, 1862, when Ignacio Zaragoza had defeated the perfect French army in the battle of Loreto and Guadalupe.

Puebla was the Puebla de los Angeles. If no angels flew through its skies, it was because they were to be found on earth. At least, that Sunday, that's what the men and women believed who applauded the angelic Emilia Sauri.

EMILIA WAS USED to the warmth of that group, but she did not know how to accept their applause without a touch of embarrassment. The moment she stopped playing, she bowed and ran to hide behind the black cloth Milagros had rigged as a stage curtain.

In the small space between the cloth and the door to the garden stood, applauding noiselessly, the performers of the numbers to follow Emilia: the poet Rivadeneira, in his role as master of ceremonies; a songwriter with his guitar and three women dressed as Tehuanas who would dance to his new composition; an opera singer who was looking for employment in the city and in exchange for three Italian arias had deigned to accept their invitation to dine on *mole* with sesame seeds; a couple costumed to dance the "Umbrella Duet"; and an eight-year-old girl who sang in Nahuatl.

Among them, blocking her path, Emilia saw the conspiratorial expression of a boy who had grown so much that he was no longer the Daniel of her memory. He had the same smile, the same mischief in his eyes, but when he pulled her to him with a hug and a few words in her ear, the new Daniel instilled in Emilia Sauri the fear she would feel for an intruder. She had never felt her heart beating so low in her body.

"Emilia, say hello later," Milagros Veytia whispered with a grimace. "Go out now to say your thank-yous."

Emilia again took the stage and acknowledged her applause with long bows and a quiet smile.

"Your eyes are like a celebration," Daniel told her when she was close again.

"When did you get here?" she asked.

"I never left," Daniel answered, stroking her forehead and hair with the fingers of one hand.

THEY HAD NOT SEEN each other for three years, and each had changed; at the same time, something unaccountable and timeless wove a strand between them.

"Emilia, go back out there," her Aunt Milagros prompted.

"I don't want to," Emilia answered, squatting down, grinning, and waving her hands before her as if she couldn't hear.

"Devilish girl," said Milagros in a low voice, closing the curtain before turning her attention to guiding the singer to his place onstage.

Pure sounds of a sad melody issued from the guitar played so quickly that at times it sounded like a harp. Emilia and Daniel stood with their heads together and talked quietly below the sorrowful voice slicing through the air of the sala.

Neither of them would recall what was said, because more than hearing, they absorbed the words. Daniel examined Emilia with the surprise of someone who discovers a toy has metamorphosed into a goddess. She had the lively eyes of the little girl he had known, but now she had the knowing gaze of a woman, and her mouth had become a miracle he coveted for himself. Emilia could not believe that the defiant, untamed eyes of the Daniel she had known in childhood had taken on the satisfaction that now lighted them. His hands were large, with long fingers, and she could see the veins pulsing beneath the skin. He was slimmer; he looked almost malnourished, and his tanned skin gave him a look of the outdoors. Just from feeling him close, Emilia let two tears typical of her Sauri blood fall that her Veytia blood hated with all her heart.

"Tears of celestial blue," Daniel sang, repeating the words of the song in the background.

"Idiot," Emilia answered as she jumped to her feet.

"Teary, and irritating, too," Daniel said, following right behind.

Emilia jumped out the window into the garden. Again he followed.

"You're not afraid of ghosts any longer?" he asked when he caught up in the darkness.

"Not as much as I'm afraid of you," Emilia replied, turning her back but still pressed close against him.

"Afraid of me?" He circled her shoulders with his arms.

"Yes," she said, peering into the darkness, not turning to look at him, but frozen as if by something very familiar in the arms holding her.

"Turn around, let me look at you," Daniel said slowly.

Emilia kept her back turned. She did not want to look at him, but neither did she want to resist the hands clasping her shoulders or want to run away from his words. She stood quietly, listening as if to a soothing waterfall.

What he said was not important; we never remember the individual words whose sum convinces us. Word by word, we would never have believed them.

Emilia opened one of his hands and placed the palm to her lips. She tasted it a moment, and then bit down on it, with that act swallowing everything she was unable to say to this eloquent friend who had been away so long.

"Have I forgotten everything I was taught?" she asked, letting herself be embraced.

MILAGROS RUSHED into the darkness of the garden the minute the curtain opened on the next-to-last number of her show, a tiger on the trail of her niece and nephew.

She always liked the shadows and dampness of the garden, but not even that calmed her. Daniel was the last person on the program, and how was she going to explain that he was lost?

She saw them from a distance, sitting with their backs against a tree, and the thought crossed her mind that if she weren't so furious she would have to confess that she envied them.

"Can you two explain why you've run out on your responsibilities?" she called out to them so they would hear her coming. "You, Daniel, how quickly you forget your revolution. Yesterday you were ready to burn down the country, but that fire seems to have fizzled out pretty fast. And you, Emilia, how are you going to explain to your mother where you got that mud on your dress? Come on, snap out of it, we barely have time to get this devil on for his number," she said, slapping Daniel on the back.

"What's he going to do?" asked Emilia, who couldn't imagine that her friend had become a singer or a poet in the time he'd been away from her.

"He's going to say a few words," her aunt said.

"More words?" Emilia said quietly to herself.

DANIEL AND HIS BROTHER, Salvador, were in Puebla to attend a clandestine meeting of several anti-Reelection clubs. They'd come back from the north filled with information and fired anew with rage. Two weeks earlier, they'd been with Ricardo Flores Magón and other Mexicans jailed in California. They'd come back together on the train. Every so often, they stopped to talk with other dissidents. One year ago, an attempted armed revolt against the government had failed, but prison and dead comrades would not deter a second. This information could not be spoken before a heterogeneous group like the one gathered at the Cuencas', but in an effort to throw the informants off track, and to convince the indecisive in an address about democracy and its imperatives, it was thought that a few words from Daniel were in order.

Emilia found a place on the floor beside Milagros. She sat down more to look at Daniel than to hear what he was saying. She was fascinated by his long legs, his slim back, and tense shoulders. She liked his voice and the enchantment in his eyes.

SLOWLY AND CEREMONIOUSLY, Daniel began with the need for change in their society that would make it possible to replace the honorable vestiges of the past with new blood. But the bewitching eyes and smiling mouth that had mesmerized Emilia began to paint a picture of a country wounded by the infamous actions of the doddering old men governing it. Daniel had grown to manhood under the influence of anarcho-syndicalism and of social currents that held sway in a few classrooms and many unions in the United States. He was filled with faith and fervor. He spoke with the passion of a soldier sounding a call for war. Listening to him, Emilia felt out of her depth, and in truth was as afraid as she'd said she was.

It was only a few years before that they'd traveled to Veracruz by train with her parents and her aunt, who had scolded them every time they stuck their heads out the window to smell the brilliant green of the fields. It was such a short time since they'd run along the beach of the first ocean they had ever seen, so recent that Emilia thought she still knew the bony-kneed Daniel who'd pushed her into the water. But in fact, an eternity had passed.

Why did men grow up to become strangers? Why were they seized by that passion for politics that frightened her as much as it did her mother? Why was she listening to Daniel recount one tragedy after another, and why instead of stopping her ears and running to hide, was she sitting as quietly and calmly as if she were beside him at the pond, listening to his week's adventures?

Because he had come back, and that seemed to be the thing that tipped the scales, leaving the taste of prophecy in her mouth and fueling the euphoria that made Daniel predict a fair and just future, a country that would suddenly, and with no turning back, experience the vertigo of democracy.

He hadn't said anything that wasn't in the newspapers, nothing Emilia hadn't heard from her father, but everyone was shouting *Bravo!, Viva!, Death to tyrants!,* and there was only silence when Aquiles Serdán, the most radical of the anti-Reelection leaders, took the podium to recognize the two Cuenca boys as militants indispensable to the cause of liberty.

Emilia was the only one displeased by his praise.

"Surely the cause is based somewhere else," she commented to Milagros Veytia.

All around her the air was electric. Men and women who came every Sunday were even more ecstatic than usual. Many came over to hug her and thank her for her music, to congratulate her parents on the little girl who had grown up so suddenly, to tell them how pretty she was and how much everyone admired her.

The cello and its enchantments were forgotten; Emilia wasn't interested in anything but how long that lying Daniel was going to be in Puebla.

"He said he'd come back to see me," she told her aunt and mother.

"Didn't that make you happy?" Josefa asked.

"I thought he'd come back to stay."

"Impossible, child. Don't hold that against him, there will be time for him to stay after things change," Milagros added.

"And when are things going to change?"

"Don't ask me to predict that. Guessing is your father's specialty," said Milagros.

"When is he leaving?"

"It will have to be soon, but I don't know. You ask him."

"I don't want to see him. Let's go," she begged Josefa, in a voice that clashed with the general jubilation.

From a group near the three women, from the midst of a conversation that was rolling to a boil, came the voice of Diego Sauri, who could always listen to two things at once, asking Emilia where it was she wanted to go. He received no answer. His daughter's lips were pressed together and there was anger in the eyes that met his.

Diego was standing in a cloud of cigar smoke; before leaving his attentive audience, he completed his criticism of the aged president of the Republic:

"Another man would hide his atrocities, this one parades them. 'Reestablishing order,' he calls the crimes of his rural guards. And, as if it were nothing at all, he sets out with four trains filled with riffraff to inaugurate more railroad track. And you, Emilia, don't be talking about going off somewhere, come and let me hug you. I'm proud of you. Women like you will change this nation."

"What are you talking about, Papa?" asked Emilia, who was in no mood for speeches.

"About you," he said, coming to give her a kiss. "What's the matter? Aren't you happy? You played very well, your friend Daniel is here. So why do you look like you have a toothache?"

"Daniel came just to go away again."

"So that's it?" Diego asked, and abandoned his fellow guests to devote himself completely to explaining to his daughter how important Daniel's work at the northern frontier was. "Don't you want a friend who does his duty?"

"I want a friend who doesn't go away."

Diego heard thunder rolling from his daughter's lips. He had never wanted to accept that she was growing up, yet at that moment, in the face of that voice and those flashing eyes, he had to acknowledge that she was as different and distant as someone he didn't know. An unimaginable sorrow knifed through his heart. Things were not the same. To hold on to her as she had been, if only a brief while longer, he put his arm around her shoulders and they walked together toward the pond. That was the only place at the Cuencas' where Emilia could have long conversations.

Diego and his daughter had never had a disagreement in all their lives. She had always loved her father so much that she never felt a need to defy him. She always believed that the soundest reasons and the best ideas came from him, and that if she ever thought him mistaken, their difference was so insignificant that she didn't feel she had to contradict him. It was the same with Diego. To him, Emilia was as perfect as the future he predicted.

As soon as they were near the pond, Emilia emptied her heart of a flood of complaints against those friends of his who were molding a future that would bring about unrest and changes she saw no need for. Her voice ripped through the garden in protest. Diego had sat down on a tree trunk near the pond and was listening with his head in his hands.

"You and all those other people want to get us into a war," said Emilia. "Why do you think it's so great for Daniel to go off to see if he can get himself killed? To have someone else to mourn over? Someone else to provide an excuse to say bad things about the government? I hate all of it. You've even made that idiot Daniel think he's important. Why are you sending him to the United States? So he can be locked up like Flores Magón? I hate all of it. I hate all of you."

Josefa, who had been searching the garden for them, heard her daughter's voice in the distance. She ran through the trees, and as soon as she saw them could not restrain herself.

"Emilia, what's got into you?" she said, appearing out of the darkness like a ghost, filled with a fury she did not recognize. "Where did all that nonsense come from?"

"From her heart," said Diego in a defeated voice. "Don't you hear what she's saying?"

"That's very bad, Emilia," Josefa scolded. "It seems everything your father has told you all these years has fallen on deaf ears. You have to think about the people who are suffering in this country."

"And who's thinking of me? Even you don't care what happens to me."

"That's very foolish," Josefa objected. "It must be the strain. You'll think differently tomorrow, but for now, ask your father to forgive you if you're to deserve a place to sleep tonight."

"Don't fuss at her, Josefa. She's sad and there may be something to what she says. God knows I wish I could put Daniel in a closet and keep him safe for her." Diego got up from his tree trunk, waving his hands before his face to ward off his dejection, and walked toward his newly adult daughter.

"Don't hate your father, silly girl. You don't yet realize that I'm the only man in the world who will always adore you without asking for anything in return." He pulled from the pocket of his ancient jacket the handkerchief on which Emilia had embroidered his name in her first sewing class in fifth grade.

Emilia thanked him, adding a faint smile to the torment in her eyes. She hugged her father, who began to sing the pirate song his grandmother had sung to him. He didn't have to apologize. As he sang, Emilia was putting back together the bits and pieces of judgment that had earned her a reputation for having good sense, and soon her heart and head were accepting what she had known since Dr. Cuenca had been jailed—that her parents' friends were a group of apostates the government considered its enemies, and that they had no alternative but to play a part in the conspiracy that would bring it down.

Emilia heard Daniel's voice from the house, calling: "Where are you? I'm leaving."

"At the pond," Emilia answered, calm as the ocean after a storm. "Come on out."

"Not to the pond, you'll push me in," Daniel said as he came into view.

He was wearing his overcoat, something Diego noted nervously.

"So you have to leave immediately?"

"By morning someone will have reported we were here and where I said we've been. I talked too much."

"Be careful," Diego warned.

Before Josefa followed her husband, she asked Daniel to give her a kiss.

Daniel's heavy overcoat was like the ones worn by the soldiers of Porfirio Díaz's army.

"Aunt Milagros got it for me," he told Emilia as he stroked her dark hair.

"Don't save anyone who doesn't deserve it," Emilia asked, burying her head in Daniel's lapel.

"Did you lose my stone?"

"It's under my pillow," she replied as her fingers combed back the lock of hair that always fell over his forehead.

CHAPTER 8

"REMEMBER ME once a day. The rest of the time, put me out of your mind," Daniel told Emilia, tracing her profile with his finger as if he would carry her portrait with him. Then he dropped his hands, turned, and ran away.

As he rushed into the house he ran into Milagros Veytia. He stopped to give her a hug.

"You're tearing me in two, and I'm not fifteen," Milagros protested.

"Convince Emilia," he said, winking. Then he went to find his brother.

Salvador Cuenca was four years older than Daniel. He had been studying law for three years at the University of Chicago before his brother enrolled. From then on they had shared their fervor for the dream that some imagined as a great revolution and others as a magical entrée to a new regime that would grant them the right to elect their leaders like any other modern country.

They were a lot alike. Salvador, too, was distant, but restless, not talkative but emphatic when he did speak, elusive and smiling, with an imaginative mind and strict code of behavior.

That night, while Daniel was communing with Emilia

and their memories, in search of something to hold on to, even though it would make him vulnerable at the same time, Salvador had discovered Sol García. He had glimpsed her among the shadows when she rose to shout her applause after the concert. Then, as the stage lights rose again, he looked at her for a few seconds in the half light and felt that in his entire life he had never seen anyone so luminous.

After Daniel's address, the chandelier in the sala revealed her in detail, and he was drawn to her side as if it were the most natural thing in the world.

"My name is Salvador Cuenca," he said, holding out his hand. "And yours?"

"Soledad García y García," said Sol, with a radiant smile. "Are you Daniel's brother?"

"He's mine," said Salvador.

"And I'm like a sister to Emilia," Sol explained.

"How did that happen?"

"Because we want it that way."

"I can't think of a more legitimate reason," Salvador replied. "Where do you live? In heaven?"

"Here in Puebla," said Sol.

"Why haven't I ever seen you?"

"I live in another Puebla."

"Which one is that?" Salvador gestured toward a nearby chair and invited her to take a seat.

Attracted by the magnet that always summoned her to a difficult situation, Milagros Veytia joined them to tell Sol she should be asking the questions.

"Where do *you* live?" Sol asked, happy she had not had to explain the world she lived in.

"In Chicago. Daniel, who can never keep a secret, already made that public," Salvador said, and began describing the difficulties they had encountered in returning home, how little time they had left, how he saw things in the country, how much they needed an organization that would unify the dissidents who opposed the dictatorship, and everything he had on his mind from one day to the next.

Sol listened so intently that Salvador was moved to tell her everything about himself. He told her how he was tongue-tied with most people, about his thoughts and his ambitions for the future, for a time when the dictatorship was gone, and people like himself could live with a clear conscience and a less uncertain future.

When Dr. Cuenca came to advise him that it was time to go to the meeting at the Serdáns', Salvador did not want to leave his listener. Sadly, he held out a strong hand and in exchange was favored with Sol's smooth hand and wide eyes, but not her words. She was always shy, but she had never felt so incapable of speaking.

"They call me Sol," she said finally. "Sol, with only one García."

"Thank you, Madame Sol. I hope you don't end up with two more Garcías," Salvador joked as he said good-bye with the crooked smile of the Cuencas.

WHEN SOL WAS BORN, her parents argued so long, and with so many people, about what to name her that at the moment of the baptism they still had not come to an agreement. To avoid problems, oversights, and family resentment, they gave the parish priest a list of names that, along with the holy water, he dribbled over her head as someone in the habit of perpetrating horrors anytime he was called on to perform that sacrament.

So the innocent babe was suddenly saddled with the name María de la Soledad Casilda de la Virgen de Guadalupe de los Sagrados Corazones de Jesús y María.

That litany pleased her father, who thought Soledad was a ringing and impressive name worthy of accompanying his daughter through life; her maternal grandmother, who had insisted on the child's carrying her own solid name; the baby's mother, who like every Mexican woman with dangers in the present and fears of the future took all her concerns to the sweet, mute figure of the Virgen de Guadalupe; and the paternal grandfather, who did not have much truck with saints because he thought it stupid to ask something of someone who despite many good qualities could not hold a candle to the authority of the blessed hearts of Mary and Jesus, who, as anyone should know, were essential figures in the power structure. Not for nothing was Jesus one-third of the Holy Trinity and Mary his mother.

In short, from all this confusion, it happened that the little girl grew up with two names—the one her father had chosen and the one her mother gave her out of the desire to please everyone, including the two into which her mind was always dividing the world in order not to have to make too many choices: María José was what she called the baby from the time she held her in her arms on the way back from the christening until the child was seven years old and saw her baptismal certificate as they took her to enroll in school. That was when she learned that her first name was Soledad and that she had a name that *meant* "solitude" and that she must live alone with her *soledad* and with the severity of the nuns who called her by that name.

By then, Evelia García de García, Sol's mother, a woman whom the patient Josefa had kept as a friend more out of loyalty to their shared childhood, when they loved each other, than for any other interest or affinity, had begun bringing Sol to visit the Sauris. Emilia was the first to call her Sol.

Soledad would never forget that day. She was sitting beside her mother in one of the overstuffed chairs Josefa Sauri kept in her sala against all laws of traditional elegance but to the benefit and comfort of those who used the room, when in from the garden, all rosy-cheeked and sparkling, came a little girl a year younger than she, who from that first day took charge of her as if she were the older one.

"Why don't you ask Soledad to go and play with you?" Josefa suggested when she saw her daughter in the doorway.

"Come on, Sol. I'll show you my treasures," said Emilia with no further ado.

They became friends that afternoon, and grew up in each other's company, knowing intuitively that one had what the other lacked and that there was no better way to feel whole than to do things together. Over time, each learned so much from the other that at first view their differences were not readily apparent. Only they knew that in extreme moments each was the other in some vague and intense way.

Which is why, when Salvador left her confused about their conversation, and after seeing Daniel run past her, Sol looked for her friend, knowing, without ever having been there, that she would find her in the garden.

Emilia was still sitting beside the pond. A fine rain was beginning to fall.

"Are you crying?" Sol asked, bending down to look in her face.

"I'm about to finish," Emilia answered, taking an imported linen handkerchief from her pocket. Then she put her arms around her friend. Sol held her without saying anything, and they sat there until they began to rock gently back and forth.

Emilia started whistling a little song to which she and Sol, arms about each other, moved in time like two dancing bears.

"I met Salvador," said Sol.

"Did you like him?" Emilia asked, interrupting her tune.

"Yes."

"Poor Sol," Emilia said, and began to whistle where she had left off.

AND WHEN JOSEFA SAURI went to look for them that was how she found them, whistling and hugging each other. Josefa had helped her sister clean up so they wouldn't leave the Cuencas' house a mess.

"You're soaking wet," she told them.

"The outside of us, Aunt Josefa, is the least of our problems," replied Sol, who knew all about the disagreement between mother and daughter, and wanted to smooth things over.

"Poor girls. Come on, let's see if any of us can sleep."

"No one can sleep when they're carrying around the dream of revolution," Milagros Veytia said, overhearing her.

"Did Sol tell you she bowled Salvador over?" Milagros asked Emilia.

"She couldn't do that."

"But I saw it."

"Couldn't *tell* it," Emilia clarified.

"And what did you think of him?" Josefa wanted to know. "Your mother will think he's a very poor choice."

"What do you think I thought of him?"

"That he's your ideal," said Emilia.

"Almost. Luckily, it will be so long before he comes back that I'll be married by then."

"Who to?" Emilia wanted to know.

"Someone," Sol replied in the tone she used to communicate her mother's incomprehensible designs.

"That is, if you want to," was Milagros Veytia's comment.

"Oh, I'll want to," replied Sol, as if she could see the future.

"Right now, we're going home, or you'll never be able to come with us again," said Josefa, glancing at the large grandfather clock in the Cuencas' sala.

THE NICE but not terribly clever Evelia García, as Milagros called her, and Evelia's irreproachable but short-tempered husband, as Evelia herself called him, were standing waiting for their daughter in the doorway of their house facing the Plazuela del Carmen.

It was ten-fifteen when the four women drove up in the automobile Rivadeneira had lent them.

As soon as they came into view, even before the car had come to a stop, Señor García began yelling. Ignoring all the amenities, he declared the Veytia sisters and all the people they met with on Sundays immoral, and reproached his daughter for what he considered an act of debauchery that stained the good honor of his name and placed her good reputation in jeopardy.

"But no one looks after his treasure better than we do," growled Milagros when she had parked.

"Better not say anything, Milagros," Josefa said when she saw the Garcías' expressions. And she leapt from the car with unusual agility to apologize for being late.

"I have no forgiveness to waste on you two, we know all about you," fumed Señor García, whose wife was paralyzed with fear. "And when do you plan to get out of there, Soledad?" he asked.

"When you lower your voice," answered Milagros Veytia.

"I will speak in whatever voice I want, señora," said García. "Soledad is my daughter and she does what I say. It is my extreme good fortune that it did not befall me to be your father."

"We agree on that. Life spared us that particular misfortune," said Milagros.

"Let my daughter out immediately, if you do not want me to inform the authorities what your meetings are all about."

Sol was sitting behind Milagros, and in a low voice asked her please to let her out.

"As you see, the child wants to get out," Milagros told Señor García. "It was the same at the meeting we've just come from. She wanted to leave much earlier, but we wouldn't allow her. We thought it necessary that you realize she is safe at any hour if she is in our care."

"So, you agree there is the possibility of danger?"

"Oh, yes," said Milagros. "Including from the police. Any danger you can imagine."

"I never imagine, señora."

"Oh, I'm so sorry. I should have known that a man like you would not suffer that vice," said Milagros, opening the door and stepping out of the car to let Sol out.

For the evening's gathering, Milagros had worn one of her most exquisite *huipiles,* and she looked so imposing that as soon as she stepped from the car the entire atmosphere changed. Her richly embroidered elegance seemed to calm even Señor García.

"After all, nothing happened," he said, checking his daughter as he tried to imagine, perhaps for the first time, what the devil Milagros Veytia was made of. He spoke in a moderate tone.

"Somewhere, some man must be worried about you ladies. What news do you have of your husband, Josefa?" he asked, trying to atone for his rudeness.

"Josefa's husband is a man of great judgment," said Milagros, getting back into the car and pulling away with all the uproar of a full-scale battle.

Anselmo García had spent the morning at his ranch, watching his cattle being branded with the large G of his surname. For him, it was late, and anger had drained the little energy he had left. Fortunately for the women of his family, he was exhausted and sleepy, and he went back inside without another word.

"YOUR POOR FRIEND," said Milagros Veytia on the way to her sister's house. "It must wear her out living with a man like that. And she calls him 'my angel.' If he's her idea of heaven, can you imagine what her idea of hell must be? She has good cause to be so frightened of damnation."

"She's afraid of everything. I've told you that again and again," Josefa replied. "And fear clouds your reason. I think fear kills more people than bravery."

"But you feel it, so what can you do?" asked Emilia.

"Don't let it win. Anyone who never feels afraid is suicidal, but so is the person who feels nothing *but* fear."

"Well, right now that's the only feeling I have."

"You're just tired. Tomorrow you'll feel brave," her mother promised. "You'll spend the night with us, won't you, Milagros?"

"If I'm needed."

"You're always needed," her sister assured her. Diego would not yet be home from the secret meeting, and Josefa would have to remind herself of her theory on fear in order to get to sleep.

Two hours later, she heard Diego coming up the stairs. A great crash announced his arrival, because as he came into the room he tripped over the long sand-filled cloth cylinder she placed against the door to keep out the cold air.

"I'm at the age that I feel drafts," she had said when she put it there three months earlier. The same three months Diego had spent protesting what he called a ridiculous artifact typical of the high plateau.

When she heard him fall, Josefa ran to him without putting on her robe or thinking of the dangers of a draft.

"Are you all right?" she asked when she saw him on the floor, biting back a string of insults, hands clasped over his head.

"What's the matter?" called Milagros, running out into the corridor to find her sister kneeling over Diego's body and speaking into his ear.

She shuddered. In an instant, her mind was filled with dire questions. Was someone chasing him? Had he been shot? Was he dead? Damn the blessed Revolution, anyway! Why had they gotten themselves into something no one had asked them to?

"He fell over that thing I use to keep out the night air," Josefa explained, answering the question her sister had voiced, as well as the ones left unsaid.

This, Milagros told herself, is going to lead to a husband-and-wife quarrel that I want no part of, so she turned away after waving to her sister to signal her support.

"What are they arguing about?" a sleepy Emilia asked when Milagros returned to the bedroom they sometimes shared.

"Nothing serious, your father fell." But she could not shake off the sense of catastrophe triggered by her imagination.

"He what?"

"He fell as he came in, but he's fine," said Milagros. "You know, Emilia, I'm afraid of a revolution myself."

Emilia was used to Milagros's talking in her sleep, but not to her muttering misgivings as she paced around the bedroom in the long white robe that made her look like a ghost. So as soon as she felt completely awake, Emilia got up and went out into the corridor to see what was happening.

By then, Diego Sauri was sitting up and Josefa was apologizing profusely.

"Oh, what happened?" said Emilia, rushing to her father. "My dearest papa, my sweetheart, my hero, my treasure."

"I was thinking about you, and I forgot abut the trap your mother had set for me," Diego answered, letting himself be fussed over by his daughter.

"Are you sure you weren't worried about that late meeting?" asked Josefa, who suddenly stopped feeling she was the culprit and decided to throw the blame for everything on the meeting at the Serdáns'. "Why did you have to get together at midnight? They lead everyone around by the nose. Since the meeting is in their house, they don't risk being out at all hours, walking through the city as if it were completely normal."

"In Madrid at this hour, people wander around the alleys singing! The fact is that this city is as backward and boring as a church," said Diego Sauri as he got to his feet.

"Don't start that, Diego, you live here because you want to. Where you come from, you'd have been eaten up by now, by pirates or the Mayas or the Federales." Josefa took any attack against her city as an insult to her family.

"The Federales are going to eat us no matter what," said Milagros, coming back to join them.

"Why?" asked Emilia.

"Don't pay any attention to your aunt, you know how she exaggerates," Josefa said.

"Why deceive her?" Milagros pressed. "If we're going to be involved in this, let the girl know what's going on. She's not a baby anymore."

"What do you mean by 'this,' Milagros?" Josefa asked.

"Being against the dictatorship, having friends who are working to overthrow it, knowing where political exiles are hidden and how many weapons their followers have."

Emilia's eyes grew wide as she listened. Daniel had already told her a few things. She had sensed danger in the fact that he'd had to leave, but it hadn't occurred to her that the peace of her own house could be threatened.

"You're right, Milagros," Diego agreed. "How sleepy are you, Emilia? You look bright-eyed as a squirrel. Come on. Let's go talk somewhere away from this draft that may kill your mother."

"Well, at least you see there is a draft," her mother said, taking Diego's arm and walking with him to the sitting room in the center of the house.

She went to the kitchen to prepare orange blossom tea to settle everyone's stomach, and then came back to sit beside him as an adjunct to the conversation.

It was after two when Emilia went back to bed.

"We'll have to try not to be afraid," she told Milagros, who was still up, pacing around the room.

"Nothing is going to happen to your Daniel," Milagros assured her, coming to sit beside her on the bed.

"I hope Ixchel can hear you."

"She's already listening," Milagros answered as at last she slipped into bed.

THE NEXT MORNING Josefa overslept; it was she who traditionally bore the responsibility of serving as an alarm clock. It was nearly eight when she was awakened by the noise of the birds in the corridor, who, used to her punctuality, were protesting that she had not removed the covers from their cages. Like the birds, Emilia and Diego awakened protesting how late she had let them sleep.

Emilia went off to school with her braid half-brushed and a crease mark from the sheet still fresh on one of her cheeks. Diego opened the pharmacy without having prepared the rhubarb syrup and peptone wine that had been on order since the preceding Saturday. Milagros, however, had disappeared with the morning light. Because that's how she was. She could smell the dawn, and spontaneously her eyes and the path of her obsessions would open before her.

Despite the confusion with which the day had begun, Josefa thought as she aired her sheets, everything was brighter following their midnight conversation, and aside from the unexpected there was nothing to fear.

"Of course," Milagros told her when she met her coming back from the market. "In such cases, the unexpected is precisely what one should have foreseen."

"That's why I love you, Sister," Josefa smiled. "That delicate way you have of upsetting my life."

"I want you to be realistic, Josefa, but you're never going to leave the world of your novels. It's no use trying, you like to see everything through rose-colored glasses."

"But novels are filled with catastrophes," Josefa demurred.

"Then don't complain about reality."

CHAPTER 9

OVER THE YEARS, Josefa Veytia became as avid a newspaper reader as her husband. Every day the accounts of what was happening to her country kept her as enthralled as the serial novels that caused her to wake at midnight, trying to imagine what would come next.

Her passion for writers and their inventions diminished in the face of the stories reality offered every morning. She read as many newspapers as Diego, and devoted even more time to them than he. She knew who wanted this and who predicted that, who was seeking and who opposing the eighth reelection of the dictator who in her memory was the hero of many important battles, and, in her judgment, the man who as long as she could remember had provided years of tranquility, something appreciated by her and her parents, born in the war-torn nation of the nineteenth century.

Nevertheless, after reading in the newspapers every day the praise that those who favored his regime heaped upon the old dictator, and then comparing that with the dozens of clandestine pamphlets that reported the arbitrary acts being sanctioned throughout the country—and, in the case of

Puebla, the perverseness of its governor, whom the dictator had backed for years—Josefa had stopped calling the aged tyrant *Don* Porfirio and become another militant in the anti-Reelection cause.

Diego began to realize the advantages of lulls in his conversations with Josefa only when they were lost to him, when Josefa had begun to think like another of his comrades in the struggle. All his wife wanted to talk about was Madero's chances for election, the anti-Reelection club, and what Diego thought of the steady flow of pamphlets and books coming out on those subjects.

I don't know which is worse, Diego Sauri mused one Wednesday during dinner, Josefa's previous silence or this endless discussion. Ever since the old man declared that he's ready for democracy, every word of gossip turns into a pamphlet and every spell of delirium becomes a book.

"Who can understand you, Diego? Weren't you forever complaining about the alarming silence in this country?" Josefa asked him.

"Yes, but naïveté can be boring. Who can possibly believe that Madero's candidacy and his spiritualist dreams can accomplish anything?"

"I do. I who don't want a war but am as fed up as you with this peace."

"You used to like peace."

"I still do. That's why I support Madero, because he has the face and actions of a peaceful man."

"Well, neither one of you is going to get anywhere."

"Now you're being a pessimist, Papa," chimed in Emilia, who lately never missed a word.

"Daughter, I see things. Looking has always been my favorite occupation."

"You're going to hurt my feelings if you say that again," Josefa said archly, glancing up from the newspapers she read in the evening.

"Egotist," Diego answered, biting off the end of a long cigar.

"You're the egotist, you who walk the righteous path of truth and cynicism."

"Josefa, I have always recognized your talent for predicting the outcome of a novel, but this is different. The logic of literature, in which you are expert, doesn't apply. Madero is going to lose."

"Milagros doesn't think so."

"Milagros, like me, believes that if that moth-eaten old man did not tolerate the pitiful game of General Reyes and his followers, he most assuredly will not consent to an election between him and Maderos, one Maderos might win."

"What happened with General Reyes?" Emilia wanted to know.

"General Reyes was governor of Nuevo León. He became the candidate of some naive state politicians who believed the talk about a transfer of power, imagine. And all because Díaz wanted to impress some gringo newspaperman, telling him things like he would take it as a sign from heaven if an opposition party sprang up in this country. Wonderful, just wonderful. Let us heed El Señor Presidente, let us look for someone to replace the doddering old fool."

"And?" Emilia interrupted the chortles that choked off her father's story.

"Their fun didn't last very long," said Diego. "Díaz called Reyes, Reyes recanted, leaving the Masonic lodges, the minor bureaucrats, and the army out on a limb. He withdrew his candidacy and threw his support behind Díaz's reelection. As a reward, he was removed as governor of Nuevo León and sent to Europe to study new techniques of war. He's a sly fox, our famous Díaz," said Diego. "And your mama believes he can be undone by a rancher from Coahuila turned overnight into a visionary, an orator whose assets are courage and fire and having written a book filled with historical disquisitions that don't really lead anywhere at all."

"Oh," said Emilia, trying to organize all this information in her head. "Daniel told me in a letter that he's a good man."

"He is a good man, Diego, accept it," urged Josefa, for whom goodness was a virtue greater than any other.

"All we needed was disorder to add to the disorder we already have," said Diego.

"What disorder?" Josefa asked.

"You haven't noticed? Only the state of Puebla has ninety anti-Reelection clubs."

"I know that. What's bad about that?"

"Everyone is fighting everyone else. Having ninety is like having none."

"That isn't true, my love."

"Josefa, don't tell me that what I see with my own eyes every day isn't true. I talk with people, you read about it."

"You read about it, too," put in Emilia.

"Only to see how they never do what they say," Diego explained, his playful tone changing to one of regret. He didn't like to see his house turned into a verbal battleground. More than war, he feared losing the quiet, Edenic sanctuary of his harmonious married life.

"Diego," Josefa continued. "Aquiles Serdán was in jail two months for practicing exactly what he preached."

"He was in jail for being foolhardy. Who would have dreamed he would march with his anti-Reelection group in the annual Independence Day parade? And then afterward give himself the luxury of writing a letter to the president to complain about how badly he'd been treated by the governor. Do you believe it? 'Your words are well known: *We must have faith in justice.* But the truth, Señor Díaz,' " Diego imitated a petulant child, " 'is that if justice does not prevail in this instance, neither my colleagues nor I will ever see it.' It sounds daring, Josefa, but it's pure foolishness. As if Díaz were the kind of authority one could complain to. And in that regard, Serdán is like Madero. They're fighting the government—and such a government!—but they want that same government to treat them well."

"And they're right," said Josefa.

"But here everything is ruled by illogic. The workers in the factories in Orizaba are right, too, and the mine workers in Sonora, and we've seen the response their logic got."

"So what do you suggest, Diego? That we go on as we are?"

"Don't be insulting, Josefa, you're a newcomer to all this. For twenty-five years I've been talking to you about something that's just now become fashionable."

"You're absolutely right," Josefa conceded, getting up from her rocking chair and dropping the newspaper she had held throughout their argument. "That's why I love you, because you're so stubborn."

"What a sensible woman," said Diego, relaxing his shoulders and shaking himself like a goose. "Time for dinner?" he asked, consciously calming himself.

"Yes, now while there's still something to eat," added Milagros Veytia. She had been standing in the doorway listening to them.

"What a thing to say, Milagros. You're more pessimistic than Diego."

"I'm less optimistic," she said as she kissed her niece, then asked her about her friend Sol, changing the subject to lessen the tension during the dinner hour.

As Sol García had correctly predicted several years before, her mother, an obsessive and efficient matchmaker, had succeeded in placing her daughter's shining virtues in the direct path of one of the heirs of the wealthiest family in the country. It had not taken long for that same scion to lose even his appetite—until then his one passion—over Sol and to seek a way to win her. Owner, with his family, of various haciendas, sugar mills, tobacco lands, houses, and money inside and outside Mexico, the boy had conquered Sol more quickly than Emilia could ever have imagined. And when needed—because from time to time a firefly of doubt flickered in the girl's heart—her mother pulled out the old but efficient chestnut about how her daughter was a jewel and, being a jewel, must be safeguarded in a luxurious coffer. So matters moved along, and preparations were being made for a wedding that would be remembered down through history.

"Is the princess's trousseau complete?" Milagros asked as they were sipping their soup.

"Not yet," Emilia informed them. "They ordered everything, even her lingerie, from Paris, and there are trunkloads still to arrive. Some got as far as Veracruz but others haven't been shipped yet. At the rate they're going, she'll have to be married in the lace petticoats that arrived from Brussels yesterday."

"This girl inherited your sharp tongue," Josefa said to her sister.

"Lucky for her," Milagros replied. "And tell your matchmaker friend that if her daughter doesn't get married fast, she's going to be marrying a man in financial ruin."

"But they own half the state of Puebla and part of Veracruz. Why do you think Evelia is marrying her daughter to him?"

"Because she has never had a gift for looking ahead, and because she's infected with her husband's materialism."

"Well," said Emilia, "let's hope she's good and infected. Sol already is. Yesterday she talked for an hour about all the things she's going to have. The house on Reforma, the English furniture, the Bavarian china, the Swedish crystal. She's really hard to take—sometimes she makes me want to abandon her to her fate. You know, she's convinced she's going to be madly happy."

"You wouldn't wish anything different for her," Josefa said sympathetically.

"Josefa, there's no understanding you," said Diego. "You have to be *for* one side and *against* the other, you can't be for everyone at the same time."

"Why do you say that?" Josefa asked as she sniffed at the fish. "I think I got carried away with the chili."

"What Diego means," said Milagros, "is that you can't hope to change things and yet have everything stay the same for the people on top. And yes, you were a little heavy on the chili, but it's delicious."

"No, it isn't," Josefa brooded.

Diego insisted. "It's better than ever. Don't you like it, Emilia? Why aren't you eating?"

"Sol's ring covers half her finger. When she walks, she looks like she's tilting to one side."

"And that's why you're not eating?" Josefa asked.

"I'm not very hungry."

"Eat anyway," said Milagros. "Store something in your hollow leg for when there isn't enough to go around."

"Why are you always harping on that?" her sister asked.

"Because I've read a lot of books about war."

"Don't tell us about them," Diego pleaded. "And you, Emilia. Just in case, don't waste your food. Do you want a ring like Sol's?"

"Why would she want that?" asked Josefa. "Emilia is a sensible girl."

"To be foolish," said Milagros. "It's only logical that a sixteen-year-old girl doesn't want to be sensible."

"I don't want a ring like Sol's," said Emilia, tasting her fish.

"But you do want to be foolish. Shall we go to the circus on Friday, or do you think you're too old for that?"

"Oh, let's go, Aunt Milagros," said Emilia, once again abandoning her fish. "When is it?"

"There's one performance tomorrow and another on Sunday."

"What circus are you talking about?" Josefa asked.

It was the Circo Metropolitano, Milagros told them. The owner was planning to donate half his profits while in Puebla to Madero's campaign.

"If he makes that known, he'll lose a third of his public," commented Diego.

"But he won't. I know only because I spent last evening convincing him."

"How did you do that?" Josefa asked.

"Conventional methods, Sister. Don't worry, I didn't sully our good name."

"If there's anything left of it," said Diego.

"If you want to know the truth, we still haven't recovered from Josefa's wedding. Marrying a nobody who just arrived from the Caribbean coast."

"I came from the coast, but I wasn't a nobody. If no one here knew who I was, it was because they were ignorant. You *poblanos* think that if you don't know it, it doesn't exist. But I was famous in my part of the world," said Diego, nuzzling his wife's ear.

"Come along, Emilia, these two have important business to attend to. You want to come with me to visit your father-in-law?" Milagros asked, referring to Dr. Cuenca.

"Yes," said Emilia, leaping up from her chair.

"Don't encourage her, Milagros," Josefa warned. "One fine day Daniel is going to show up here with a gringa wife, and then how will you cure her of her broken heart?"

"No one recovers from a broken heart, but what we can do is nourish hope. We'll just run to see whether a letter came, and be right back," said Milagros, who of the two seemed the adolescent. "Come on, Emilia, give your mother a kiss so she won't wither away while you're gone half an hour. We'll see you in a while, Diego. See whether you can calm down our new radical."

"Don't make fun, Milagros," said Josefa.

"I say it with enthusiasm, Sister," Milagros replied as she said goodbye, tugging at Emilia, who had gone back to the table to dip her finger into the flan.

One hour later, they were back in the Sauris' warm sala. There was no sound but the lights were still on.

"Your parents burn electricity as if it were free," said Milagros. "Just look, they left all the lights on. What does Daniel have to say?"

"You know, lies," Emilia answered, and folded her letter into a small square she slipped inside her blouse.

Milagros dropped into a chair as if she had been dancing and was out of breath. Emilia sat opposite her in a wicker rocker, folding her legs beneath her like a yogi.

"In that position, you look like a snake."

"I'm a Maya goddess."

"Goddesses don't sit like that."

"My papa has one that does," said Emilia, unfolding herself to go look for a figure Diego Sauri kept in a desk drawer and that she had always thought of as one of the most valuable objects of her potential inheritance.

She returned with the sculpture and handed it to Milagros, who turned it over in her hands.

"Sit like her again," she asked Emilia, setting the small figure on the table so she, too, could try to imitate it.

"Is there some advantage to this posture?" she asked.

"Peace. At least that's what Papa says, but you know he has an overactive imagination."

AFTER LISTENING to her daughter and sister for a while, Josefa came from her dark bedroom to join their conversation. Emilia began telling them things, and an hour later their tongues had warmed the air to such a fever that they woke Diego.

"Aren't you girls ever going to bed?" he called from the bedroom. "It's midnight."

Settled comfortably in her chair, Josefa asked him to come join them.

"We're setting the world right, and your advice would be valuable."

"My 'valuable' advice always helps you do just the opposite," said Diego without lifting his head from the pillow.

"But it's a point of reference, my love," Josefa assured him. "Come out here with us," she again invited when she saw him in the corridor, a promise that the conversation would continue for at least two more hours.

"They are taking political prisoners to Quintana Roo," Milagros informed him as soon as he sat down. "People are terrified, and now they don't want to come welcome Madero."

"Tomorrow I'll visit the clubs and report that. People are afraid of snakes and heat, too, but you survive it."

"It's beautiful there, isn't it, Papa?" asked Emilia, who from the time she was a child had heard about the fragrance of pineapple and flowers that blew across the lonely islands of the Caribbean. There was no light like that in all the world, or comparable perfume, or birds or lobsters like the ones there.

"Let's go there so you can see for yourself. You'll see I'm telling you the truth," Diego began, with a look of faraway memory in his eyes. He did not often speak of his homeland, but once he began it was a matter of listening for hours, without interruption, without doubting, believing as only daughters believe their father's stories.

"And you truly believe that the only way is with weapons?" Josefa asked, interrupting the play of his imagination.

"I'm losing all my beliefs. Now I only suppose," answered Diego, whose head was still whirling with visions of his green island. "Everyone has ideas, all of them different. We'll see how it goes with Madero's visit. For the moment, he doesn't even have a place to stay."

"He can stay here," Josefa offered.

"So that three days after he leaves they take you off to jail?" questioned Milagros.

"Would it be that bad?" asked Emilia.

"Why," her father replied, "do you think there's no place for him?"

Milagros reported that someone had told her that perhaps José Bracheti, the Italian who ran the Hotel del Jardin, would house him.

"I hope so," said Diego. "Even so, we don't have permission to use any public plaza or hold meetings in the theaters. We may have to hold the rallies in an empty lot in the barrio of Santiago. And see who dares come."

"Don't worry about it anymore." Josefa hated to see Diego so dejected. At such moments, she consoled him as if he were her child.

"Maybe what you need to do is fix us some camomile tea," Milagros suggested, familiar with her sister's habit of brewing herbal teas anytime that external forces seemed out of control.

"I'll make some from linden flowers," said Josefa, who hadn't heard the irony in Milagros's voice.

"You'll do no such thing," Diego directed. "Come to bed. And you, Milagros, don't go back home now, it's too late. I'm going to bring a coverlet," he said, patting Emilia, who was spread out asleep in a large chair, her hair spilling over her face.

"I don't know whether your husband is better when he's sad or when he's bossy."

"Bossy." Josefa had no hesitation. "When he's sad, I don't know how to deal with him. When he's bossy, I just don't pay much attention."

"I won't pay *any.* I have to go," said Milagros, throwing a rebozo over her shoulders.

"Be careful," Josefa pleaded. "I'd die if anything happened to you."

"What's going to happen?" said Milagros from the door before starting down the dark stairs. A minute later, the large door to the street closed behind her.

"Who's that?" Emilia asked, waking.

"No one, my love. Your aunt left, come to bed now." Josefa helped her daughter to her feet. As Emilia leaned against her mother, she felt her tremble.

"Why did you let her go?" Diego asked, returning with a quilt.

"Because I can't do anything with her."

"My aunt left?" Emilia was suddenly wide awake. "I wanted to go with my aunt."

"Don't even consider it." Josefa poured herself a cup of cold tea. "Come to bed," she said, and combed Emilia's hair with her fingers, as if she were still the child she had been such a short while ago. "Come on, I'll sing to you and rub your back." She led Emilia toward her bedroom, her voice a hypnotic drug, a lingering perfume of childhood that Emilia could not resist.

THE NEXT DAY, when Josefa went out to walk through the city, as she did every morning, she found the walls covered with large yellow posters telling of the arrival of the candidate Madero and inviting people to welcome him at the train station.

To go to Milagros's house, Josefa walked straight down the street for seven blocks and then two to the left. Now she flew along them. She always carried the large key to Milagros's door in her purse. It was like an amulet against some catastrophe. She went into the house and through the patio that was at that moment flooded with golden light. She ran up the stairs two by two, and hurried into the warm sala. The piano was open, as it always was, because Milagros claimed that closing it would bring bad luck. Everything else there also had its reason for being and its destiny. Everything was ruled by a silent but deliberate harmony.

Josefa did not pause, as she always did, to see what new antiquity her sister had acquired; she went directly to the bedroom and pushed open the door, making a terrible racket. The shutters that blocked out the sun and the noise of the street were all closed along the long balcony that overlooked the Plazuela de las Pajaritas. Josefa closed her eyes, trying to adjust to the darkness, but when she opened them she could still see nothing but a blackness that sent chills up her spine. She groped her way toward the balcony, looking for the latch on the shutters.

A slash of light poured noiselessly into the room and fell on the sleeping body of Milagros, as immutable as the volcano Iztaccihuatl, dressed in the clothes she'd been wearing the day before. She had not even removed her shoes. On the floor, beneath an arm that hung in the air as if she had barely the strength to release them, were some of the thousand posters that had papered the city bright yellow.

"Sister?" Josefa whispered as she unlaced Milagros's shoes.

"What?" Milagros's voice was muffled as she burrowed into her pillow.

"I love you very much."

"I know."

"Are you dead?" Josefa prodded, sure that she had never seen her sister so exhausted.

"Yes," and Milagros sank deeper beneath the covers to escape the light that was washing out her fantasies.

"Thank God," sighed Josefa, closing the shutter.

"Which god?" came Milagros's lethargic voice.

"The god of war."

CHAPTER 10

GOING BACK to the Casa de la Estrella, she had walked slowly, whistling as she went. It was getting late, and she imagined her husband in the pharmacy with Emilia, who in recent months had been going down early with him and spending the entire day among the bottles and scents of the laboratory. She had learned many of the compounds from her father and some of his skills; while he sang the sad arias that brightened his afternoons, she had read a third of the medical texts scattered about the tables and worked on straightening the shelves she had dusted since she was a child.

Once she had everything arranged, Diego objected. He was sure he would be lost in all that order.

"You have everything all turned around," he said, holding his head in his hands as he went to sit on a tall stool from which he could demand justification. "That's why I never let your mother fool around in here. How will I ever know where to find things?"

"They're all in alphabetical order. I've spent my life watching you paw through the clutter looking for something. It would take years to understand how you manage on intuition and memory. Do you ever listen to yourself? At least twenty times a day you say, 'Now, where did I put that?' It will be easy now."

Diego listened to her pontificate, thinking how he still wasn't ready to acknowledge she was grown up.

"You're so proud of yourself," he said, "let's see if you can find the preserved Indian laburnum."

Emilia wheeled in her tracks and went straight to the third shelf.

"Which do you want, flowers or powders?"

"Flowers," Diego murmured.

Emilia took down an amber glass bottle, half filled with a syrup in which small white flowers floated. She pulled the cork and sniffed it before handing it to Diego, who did not have to look any closer to know that it was the correct bottle.

"What is this for?" he challenged.

"I don't know," said Emilia, taking her place on the light-colored wooden stool that had always been hers.

"It's used as a purge for people with delicate constitutions."

"Why do they put it in honey?"

"Because as Nicolás Monardes said in 1565, the year he published his *Herbolaria de Indias,* 'with knowledge and sugar you remove tartness and septicity.' "

"Ask me another."

"Sassafras bark."

"You'll find that under *s* because there's both bark and roots. And I don't know what it's for, either. I only know that Mama takes it when she's feeling muddled," said Emilia, handing her father a huge tin filled with bark and twigs that looked like cinnamon sticks.

"It has a thousand uses," Diego explained. "They say it works as a love potion, too."

"We'll need to give some to Sol. I don't think there's ever been a bride less in love and closer to marriage than she is."

"This very afternoon we'll fix her a syrup," said Diego. "Where are the bezoar stones?" he asked, to continue the game.

"Fifth shelf, very handy. And they are a very powerful antidote to poison."

"How do you know that?"

"Isn't that what it says in the Spanish soldier's letter you keep in the drawer with your Maya goddess?"

"Yes, exactly. Did I ever read you that letter?"

"Never," replied Emilia, thinking that now she was of an age to grant her father the pleasure of telling once again a story she'd heard twenty times.

When Diego saw his daughter biting her cheeks to keep from smiling, he remembered that reading it had been his thirteenth-birthday present to her, but Emilia insisted she knew nothing about it and urged him to tell her the whole story about the bezoars described in the letter of Don Pedro de Osma y Xara y Zejo. She was aware how highly her father regarded the sixteenth-century Spanish soldier who had abandoned the battles of the Conquest to devote himself to locating and learning the virtues and benefits of the plants of the Indies. It warmed his heart to hear of a man who when he had to choose between war and science had chosen science. Her father told the story with such passion that she vowed aloud she would never forget it.

As he heard his daughter promise like someone taking a solemn oath, Diego wanted to shower her with compliments, but fathers of that day thought praise did not build character, so instead, restraining himself, he asked Emilia to bring him the herb called Juan Infante.

"It cures cuts and arrow wounds. That's what your book says. It's in the first volume of Infante."

"Look at this carefully," said Diego. "It has tiny, fuzzy leaves. It's easy to find in the countryside, but you have to know how to tell it from one that doesn't do anything. This one heals the gravest wounds. And carbolic acid?" he continued.

"Right here, maestro," said Emilia with a bow.

Entranced with their game, Diego then asked for arsenic powders, belladonna, and any name that came to mind. Emilia responded, without a truce, until a client came to interrupt their dialogue.

THAT CONVERSATION acted as the seal on a pact whose foundations had been lain so long before that it was impossible to pinpoint the date. Father and daughter became a dedicated and happy pair that even on Sunday spent the mornings amid the mingled odors that curled through the laboratory. Which is why it was there Josefa went to look for her Emilia.

"You want to know where your daughter is?" Diego asked, signaling for Josefa to approach quietly.

He turned to the shelves behind the counter and looked along the second shelf to the left for the apothecary jar marked *Cannabis indica*. Josefa knew the secret. When that vessel was removed, you could look into the laboratory through a glass pane set right at eye level. Diego had installed it when he opened the pharmacy so he could work in the back but keep an eye out for customers.

Silent as a thief, Diego took down the jar, handed it to his wife, made sure Emilia was still on the other side, and stepped back for Josefa to have a look. She peered through the opening between the jars, stared for three seconds, and fell back into the arms of her husband, who, as soon as he had deposited her gently on the floor, ran to get a wad of ammonia-soaked cotton.

"Don't put that awful stuff anywhere near me!" Josefa commanded, getting to her feet in less time than it had taken her to faint. She ran her hands over her face. Was that her daughter she had seen?

In the laboratory, on tiptoe, swaying as if ruled by internal music, Emilia was kissing another woman on the lips, stroking her face, weeping and laughing at the same time. Josefa could not see, but beneath the rebozo that covered the "woman's" face and hair, it was Daniel's hands that enfolded the waist of the happiest Emilia who had ever set foot in the pharmacy.

Dressed sometimes as he was, sometimes as a wealthy young playboy, sometimes as a campesino, Daniel had crossed the border and arrived in Puebla after such a long absence that to him Emilia's lips were the first draft of cool water after an endless desert.

"They're kissing," said Josefa, undone.

"Only logical," said Diego.

"And is this something else that will be normal in the twentieth century? I'm going to have to die, I don't belong in this century."

Still kissing, but wanting to see Daniel's face, Emilia loosened the rebozo and pulled off the wig. Then Daniel himself took off the long-sleeved blouse buttoned up to his chin and pressed his naked chest against the light dress covering Emilia's tingling nipples.

"Where were you?" she asked, running her fingers up and down his back.

"Here," said Daniel, placing a finger between her teeth, a seal of fire against her tongue, and she closed her eyes so that nothing would distract her from that discovery.

Diego had replaced the jar of marijuana and, more overcome by jealousy than by worry about twentieth-century sexual mores, diverted himself by focusing on Josefa's anguish. He called her a Puritan, put his arms around her, dried her tears, and led her upstairs to have breakfast.

A woman came into the pharmacy. Finding it deserted, she banged three times on the counter, something Diego had asked his regular customers to do when they wanted him. The sound brought Emilia back from the vast seas upon which she had been sailing. With a start, she jumped away from Daniel and called, "Coming," as her father always did and, after smoothing her hair, went into the shop wearing a smile as white and perfect as the porcelain of the jars at her back.

The woman had come for the pasqueflower drops that allowed her to exist without constant dizziness. When she saw Emilia as glowing as a ray of sunlight cutting through the rainy morning, she felt the world was a better place, thanks to the blessed intervention of the herbalist Sauri.

The minute he saw the woman leave, Daniel came out to join Emilia, only now in a cashmere suit and silk necktie. He had dampened his hair, and for the time being it was combed back from his face. He could easily pass for the son of an honored statesman, but even in this disguise, his courageous air and fiery eyes shouted defiance.

For the first time in his life, the pharmacist closed his doors at midmorning. Emilia and Daniel went upstairs to have breakfast with the Sauris, who were still lost in deep discussion of the advantages and disasters of the new century. Diego had calmed Josefa by telling her that the source of her fright was in fact Daniel in disguise. Even so, when she saw him come into the dining room with his arm about her daughter's waist, she nearly fainted a second time.

"You look very handsome," she said with the boldness women use only to praise men who could be their sons. Daniel hugged her without letting go of Emilia. He had eaten poorly and lived with danger for months; he desperately needed shelter and affection, a taste of childhood and of bread baked in the kitchen of people who loved him.

As they ate breakfast, Daniel told them about the state of Madero's campaign in other cities around the country, and brought them up to date about the complex division among anti-Reelectionists in Puebla.

"Madero isn't the best thing that can happen to us. He's the only thing," he said as they were drinking their coffee.

Diego recognized that it pleased him to hear someone with good sense, and both men criticized Madero for wanting everything to happen at once when, as they knew, in politics wanting everything at once meant failing in nearly all of it. Then they went back to the subject of Puebla. There were ninety small groups in a state of greatest confusion. The principal anti-Reelectionist clubs were divided between moderates and radicals, and they had no agreements or coherent projects; nothing, in fact, but confusion.

"Madero is a good man," Josefa said quickly.

"What does that mean?" Daniel replied.

"It should mean something."

"Politics is for bad men," said Emilia, with all the assurance of youth.

Daniel turned to contradict Emilia, and Diego to contradict Josefa. All of them debated whether there should be so many anti-Reelectionist clubs, whether the moderates or the radicals were right, whether Madero should back one or the other, whether there was a risk of war, and whether war always burdened the ingenuous, the dreamers, the young, and the poor. Until the conversation finally wound down, with only Josefa left to answer her husband.

Daniel and Emilia had opened the doors to the balcony overlooking the street and were leaning against the railing gazing toward the west. The dark blue of the volcanoes pierced the sky; nothing seemed to change them.

"Do you miss them?" Emilia asked Daniel.

"When I can."

With no touch of resentment, Emilia wanted to know what he was doing with his life She knew too well that Daniel could live without her and without the volcanoes, as easily as he had learned to live without his home, his surroundings, and his games when he was a young boy. For a long while, she listened to him talk about the elections. They were his immediate obsession, and Emilia had learned early that with Daniel, as with any man, you had to listen to a long list of immediate obsessions if you wanted to get down to the essential questions. She heard him explain why he was sure the elections would be a disaster and that it would be better to save themselves the effort of waiting until July to find that out. He said that in this regard the radicals were right, but that he would be with Madero until his prudence betrayed him, and that he loved Emilia more than he loved democracy . . . although he was living his life in the reverse order. Then, putting his arm across her shoulders, as he had when they were children, he asked her if she wanted to go with him to the barrio of Santiago. They ran downstairs, counting the steps in time to an old childhood game.

"They make more racket than a revolution," declared Josefa, who was watering the plants in the patio. As they went by, Daniel gave her a kiss and told her they would see each other at dinnertime. Josefa nodded. And, turning to her daughter, asked where she thought she was going, because that neighborhood was dangerous and Daniel was in no position to protect anyone, not in his wildest dreams.

Emilia was about to start groaning and protesting but was spared the effort. As always when she was needed, Milagros appeared to help her. She was feeling quite smug after admiring her work of the previous night, and she disputed Josefa's opinion, saying that Santiago wasn't all that dangerous, that Diego had relieved Emilia of her duties in the pharmacy, and that they would be back in the blink of an eye. As she talked, she pushed the young people toward the door. Behind her, she heard the voice of her sister, who had not had time to get a word in edgewise.

"Milagros! I've already blinked twice!"

THE CITY, and particularly the barrio of Santiago, where Madero was to speak two days later, was besieged with police from all over the state. Although they had orders not to attract attention until Madero had left with his entourage and the flocks of journalists who followed him everywhere, they had nonetheless continued to focus their suspicions on anything that seemed a little out of the ordinary. As, for example, Emilia, Milagros, and Daniel, who were too well dressed for Santiago, a place crammed with the earth and adobe huts, despair, and mud of the poor.

The threesome was even more obvious as they entered the small plaza bordering the church because a clutch of children ran to meet them. Milagros was a frequent visitor there. So frequent that the children all ganged around her, calling her "Auntie," to the great surprise of Daniel and Emilia. Clinging to her petticoats, one little boy asked what she'd brought. She replied by pointing to her niece and nephew. One little girl dressed in rags, filthy from head to toe, wanted to know what else she had.

Emilia was carrying a gunnysack of small bread loaves, and Daniel's heavy sack disgorged all kinds of things. Milagros stooped down to the level of her questioners and began handing out caramels and oranges, even medicines and advice. Her goddaughter watched with a mixture of admiration and horror. She did not think she could ever muster her aunt's casualness in dealing with people so destitute. She nearly screamed when a boy covered with running sores touched her; she had to make an effort not to run away, cringing from a sorrow and fear she had never felt before. It wasn't that she hadn't seen poor people in the city, begging on street corners and in the entryways of the churches, or even that like everyone else in her world she hadn't learned to accept the idea of their existence, but this was the first time she had seen poor people in their own domain, away from the buildings and streets in which they were treated as intruders. Emilia felt ashamed and guilty. Two sentiments she had not yet had the misfortune to experience.

She wanted to run back home to the bright and cheerful heart of the city, she wanted to close her eyes and hold her nose, she wanted to be out of that dirty barrio with its squat hovels, away from the voices, pleas, and offensive stench of those children, but Daniel and her aunt did not even notice her discomfort; they had begun handing out treats and chatting as if they were sitting beside the fireplace in their own salas.

Somehow Emilia had been left holding the bread sack, the bottom of which was filled with quantities of the fliers Milagros had pasted up in the center of town.

"Share now, share," Daniel called to the children running off with small armfuls of bread.

Up to that point, the police watching from the doorway of the *pulquería* El Gato Negro had limited themselves to observing. But when all the bread was gone and the posters heralding the Monday meeting began to fly from the gunnysack like doves, the police dropped the indulgent air with which they had watched this seeming display of charity and came out from where they were hiding.

"Drop everything and run," Daniel told Emilia, who finally had relaxed and was talking with a little boy who stroked the perfumed luxury of her hair.

He must have been about ten. When he heard Daniel, he leapt away with the alacrity of a squirrel and told Emilia to follow him. All three ran behind him to one of the houses that to Emilia all looked the same. She had already been thinking that if she got lost she would never find her way out of that labyrinth. And that was before; now they were running from one house to another through windows and false walls of straw matting.

They followed the boy through a series of warrens with small cooking fires and odd sticks of furniture. The floors were always dirt, and cradles or rope sometimes hung from the ceiling. They tripped over children and turkeys, unflinching old people and women at their chores, but, led by the boy, they never slowed until Emilia saw Milagros disappear behind a pile of firewood and felt Daniel tug at her sleeve, directing her to the mouth of a *temazcal.*

They crawled through the narrow opening that served as an entrance, and the boy covered it with a straw mat, closing them in a round room where neither could stand. Emilia had never been inside that kind of bathhouse, although her father had described to her how before the Conquest priests and warriors closed themselves in that warm darkness to think and rest. Just in front of the entrance was a fire. On top of the fire were heated stones on which water and fragrant herbs were thrown to create a vapor that filled the round-walled room.

"Take off your clothes," Daniel said, unbuttoning his shirt and muttering that if they looked inside and found them wearing clothes, he was as good as dead.

The panic produced by those words dissipated any hesitation Emilia might have had. She quickly stepped out of the skirts and petticoats a woman of that time wore. When she was down to her camisole and lace-trimmed underdrawers, Daniel told her to hurry, and picked up a jug of water to wet down the red hot stones. A warm vapor misted the air. Emilia was about to say something, but Daniel placed his finger on her lips to counsel silence. Outside, she heard the footsteps of the police, their voices asking questions, the boy replying with vague answers.

Emilia loosened the braid she had wound around her head, and her curly hair fell down her back.

"Look in there," one man ordered.

"My sister's bathing in there," said the boy. But a policeman again ordered another to look inside.

Emilia signaled Daniel to hug the wall. Then with her fingers she combed her hair over her face and crept to the matting that covered the opening of the entrance. She pushed it aside with one hand and then thrust half her body outside.

The police saw a naked-to-the-waist Emilia amid the steam pouring from the hole, damp hair spread like a net over her breasts.

Several mangy dogs, lips curled, began nipping at the heels of the police, sending them on their way. The boy again covered the glowing entrance with the mat, and Emilia crept back into the round refuge, where a dazzled Daniel awaited her. A hundred words fell like water on her ears as he lay beside her. Emilia pressed against Daniel's strong, sweating body, feverishly exploring it, trembling but unafraid, sure that she had no reason to envy even the highest goddess.

Milagros had come out of her hiding converted into an indigent wearing the smoked glasses of a blind woman. As the light began to fade, and while her niece and nephew returned to reality, she looked for a comfortable place on the ground and fell asleep. Two hours later, she interrupted the warm silence of the *temazcal.*

The three of them emerged from among the warren of houses as it was growing dark. It had rained the way it rains in May, a downpour that sent people scurrying into their huts and the police into the cantina, where they entertained themselves with the dice of the one-legged ice cream vendor the children called Satuno Posale.

They trudged through the mud to the edge of the barrio. When they came to a field of young maize, they ran through the rows yelling and feeling freer than they ever had in their lives. A road that ran alongside the train tracks led them to the outskirts of the city. Emilia might just as easily have been at a ball in Paris.

"Do you have to wear quite such a happy face?" her aunt asked when they were in the mule cart carrying them back home.

IT WAS ABOUT SEVEN when they reached the Casa de la Estrella, laughing at the police and at life. Josefa heard their story without forgiving them for the fright they had caused her by being so late. She accused them of being irresponsible and arrogant, she wept with anger, and threatened to lock up all three until the fever of the elections had passed.

"You're not interested in elections any longer?" Diego asked, anticipating the sweetness of the days when only novels interested his wife.

"I detest them. I'm going back to Zola and to poetry."

"Zola?"

"Because then if there's danger, it's just in a book."

"And love?" asked Daniel, looking at Emilia with the delight of complicity.

"That, too," Josefa replied.

CHAPTER

11

DANIEL SAID GOOD-BYE and left with Milagros, but returned to the Casa de la Estrella after midnight. He opened the front entrance with a key his aunt had lent him. Noiselessly he climbed the stairs, crossed through the sala, and slowly pushed open the door of the room where Emilia was sleeping.

"Marry me," he said, taking off his clothes to slip into her bed.

"How often?" Emilia answered, pulling her nightgown over her head.

"Many times," Daniel entreated as she pulled him toward her in the darkness.

THEY DID NOT SLEEP. Nor did they talk much. For hours they played, each a prisoner of the other, adventurous and curious.

"You have a star on your forehead," Daniel said, exhausted on her breast.

Emilia stroked his head, then he buried his head in her lap and wept as if he had to rid himself of some deep anguish.

With the dawn, they fell asleep. They did not disentangle their lethargic legs until the sun was high and the smell of coffee seeped into the room to stir the air and the memory of their shared dream.

Emilia heard Josefa singing in the kitchen and opened her eyes. She saw Daniel breathing beside her. From the toes of his feet to the curls of his unruly hair, he seemed the finest sight she had ever seen. She thought that not only her memory but the very air would always be marked by his presence.

"What are you dreaming?" she asked as she saw him waking.

"Lies," he answered in a drowsy voice and with the angelic face that visits those blessed in love. Once again he took refuge in her, as he told her that in all the world there was no other hiding place for him.

They did not eat breakfast. Just before ten they ran downstairs and slipped quietly through the patio. Emilia opened the door and Daniel kissed her before he ducked out. She went into the pharmacy with a blissful expression on her face, but Diego asked nothing and she offered no explanation. They had many things to do before their midday meal.

At two they went back to the house without having spoken Daniel's name, only playing guessing games. There, over soup, they had to face Josefa, whose love for clear words equaled what Diego felt for his medicinal plants.

"Did Daniel sleep here?" she asked.

"Yes," said Emilia.

"God help us," prayed Josefa. "And don't ask me which god."

WHEN THEY HAD EATEN, Milagros came to pick up her niece to take her to the circus.

"I don't feel too secure about your taking Emilia with no protection but your blindness to danger," Josefa said when she saw her sister.

"When has anything ever happened to Emilia when she's with me?"

"Nothing, till it happens. But what can I do, loving you has always had its risks."

"You'd think I was a mountain climber. Let's go, Emilia, I can hear music on the air," said Milagros, looking at the clock.

The circus tent seemed to Emilia the best place she could find to lose herself. There were so many people crowded inside that when she squinted her eyes the bright clothing looked like a handful of confetti thrown in her face. They had good seats, and arrived in time to watch the parade of monkeys and elephants, tightrope walkers, animal trainers, lions, and trapeze artists. Emilia was so happy she could even laugh at the clowns that had frightened her as a small child.

"Why is it that circuses make you sad?" she asked Milagros.

"With what we get from this performance, we can buy some prisoners out of jail," her aunt answered without answering, because she hated not to know answers, and because the circus made her sad, too.

Staring upward, not at her aunt, Emilia said:

"She's going to fall."

And with her eyes fixed on the woman who had just leapt from one trapeze toward her partner swinging on another, she asked:

"How many are there in jail?"

"Many," Milagros answered. "She didn't fall."

"Not this time."

"You sound as if you were the one up there." Milagros's voice was ironic.

"And you don't? Who decides which ones get out?"

"This time I do."

"And who are you going to free?" Emilia applauded the trapeze artist who had lifted her arms to celebrate her triumph.

"Tonight, Daniel."

Emilia held her breath, missing a beat of her applause, but did not yield to fear.

She knew Milagros had no patience for swooning and did not tolerate women who turned pale and silly.

"When this is over?" she asked.

"We'd better. If we want him alive."

"What are they doing to him?" asked Emilia, abandoning all pretense.

"Better not to think."

Emilia gazed sightlessly at a living doll who was standing on a horse cantering around the ring. It seemed as if she were gambling, and with every stride of the horse winning from life her right to live. She stood as erect and smiling as if she were on solid ground, as if what she was doing were completely logical. She maintained the same expression and same apparent calm when six additional horses circled the ring shoulder to shoulder so she could leap from one to another in time with the music played by the band.

With her teeth gritted in a blatantly false smile, Emilia felt the ground moving beneath her own feet, as if she, too, were leaping from horse to horse. When the tiny woman dressed in white and gold threw down her dancing whip, straddled the horse, and stroked the mane of its arching neck as she talked into its ear, Milagros Veytia put her arm around her niece's shoulder and said:

"We'll get him back in one piece."

"What does Daniel do to make them chase him this way?"

"Nothing, child, he's alive and wants to be free," said Milagros, ramrod straight in the white *huipil* graced by three silver-and-coral necklaces.

"I want freedom, too, but no one's after me."

"It won't be long now," Milagros told her.

THE POET RIVADENEIRA was waiting near the gate in his small 1904 Oldsmobile, a dark green automobile that in place of a steering wheel had a mechanism Rivadeneira correctly called "tiller steering" and a front that curved up from the ground and turned back like the runners of a sled. Around 1910 those automobiles were no longer the last word—there were more expensive, more modern vehicles—yet that small curved dash thrilled Milagros Veytia, who grew increasingly more expert in driving it at speeds as reckless as thirty miles per hour.

Rivadeneira knew just how deeply Milagros was involved in the intrigue against the government. He had begun by helping her and ended by getting deeply involved himself, except that because of being a wealthy landowner and having the reputation of being a levelheaded gentleman, he carried on his activities in the background. That night was an exception, however. Milagros thought it would be helpful if he went with them to the jail. A man with his prestige and his automobile would have an effect on the guards they would have to bribe on the night shift.

Milagros had received information that no one had yet connected

Daniel with the energetic young man who was the right arm and leg of a prominent Madero collaborator. When they arrested him for handing out propaganda, he had spoken to the policemen in English, claimed he did not understand Spanish, and pretended he was not only a gringo but stupid to boot. That was what he had planned with Milagros and the members of her anti-Reelectionist club. If it came to looking for him in jail, they would ask for Joe Aldredge; he would cling to that identity even if they cracked his skull or drowned him.

THE JAIL OCCUPIED a huge area surrounded by very high walls and even higher towers at every corner. It loomed out of the night like a monster, sending a shudder down Emilia's spine.

"They have him here?" she asked.

"That's what I hope," said Milagros.

"He should be here," Rivadeneira confirmed in his quiet voice. "Did you notify his father?"

"Of course not," said Milagros. "Poor man, he has enough trouble. If he hears that Daniel's a prisoner, he'll come rushing to look for him and end up in the cell with his son."

"And how are we going to get Daniel out?"

Milagros explained that some of the guards accepted bribes in exchange for playing dumb and letting an unidentified prisoner go free.

"They're hungry for money. I know through a boy who works as a doctor inside. There are four that will help us. One is the *jefe* of the night shift. He's the one who's going to turn the 'gringo' over to us. What time is it, Rivadeneira?"

"Eleven-thirty. It's time." The poet Rivadeneira always dressed like an elegant Frenchman in suits cut in Mexico City by a very exacting tailor on Alcalcería. His shirts were from Lévy and Martín, and they all bore a small, intricately initialed monogram over the heart.

Milagros made fun of his clothes every time life placed her in the position of allowing something more than a few caresses from that man who never in all his life experienced a more intense and desolate emotion than his love for her. That night he was wearing a new derby he had just bought in a shop in Portal de Mercaderes, famous since 1860. Emilia thought that in all that finery he deserved their compassion, crowded as he was between her and Milagros, who never entertained the least thought of letting anyone else drive. When the poet got out of the car, nonetheless, his clothing was somehow wrinkle free and aristocratic. Milagros looked him over with a smile, and not without reason told herself that his dandified appearance would greatly help them in the challenge ahead.

Fortunately, Emilia, too, was dressed like a doll from a fashion magazine, because Milagros's white *huipil* was of questionable impact, even though it made her look like a beam of light rarifying the night.

The entrance to the jail was a small door cut in the wall. They filed through one by one and asked for the guard whom they knew to be in charge of that shift. The young doctor had already spoken with him and he was alerted to what they wanted—in fact, he had already set a price for his services—but he made them wait a while in order to give himself the importance he thought he deserved.

When he appeared, he greeted them effusively and accepted the envelope Rivadeneira handed him with such embarrassment and so little practice that he blushed the color of a chili pepper. He chose Emilia to come past the barred door and follow him to the large holding tank where all the day's prisoners were collected.

They had not taken the time to list the men's names. They had simply thrown them in the cell to wait until the next morning. Or week. Some spent months there before their names appeared on the list of new prisoners. They disappeared, and that was that. It did no good for their wives to come day after day asking the guard at the gate for news of their husbands. They were not on the rolls. They might never be.

Milagros watched Emilia disappear behind the bars and looked for a bench on which to deposit her body and her fears. If her sister knew what she had done she would never love her again. But the girl's soul was split into two precise halves, and Milagros believed that if one half could save the other, she would not be the one to prevent it. Rivadeneira sat down beside Milagros and consoled her by patting her hand. Only she could know what that meant, coming from him.

FOR SEVERAL MINUTES Emilia and the jailer walked through a dimly lit corridor. Finally they came to another set of bars, this one blocking passage to a large, darkened room. Emilia pressed her face to the bars, searching for Daniel.

"That's him," she said, pointing. His chestnut hair set him apart from the twenty dark-eyed, dark-skinned men jammed together in that room.

"Where did they get this guy?" the *jefe* asked the guards.

"Dunno," one of them answered. "He was here when we came."

"Poor gringo," said Emilia, calling upon all the histrionic talents she had learned in their Sunday theatricals. "That's what he gets for touring the cantinas. I shouldn't have come to look for him, but he has better ways to spend his time. And if you knew how important he is in his country, you wouldn't keep him another minute. By tomorrow morning the American consul will be here complaining."

"Bring 'im here," the *jefe* ordered the jailers.

It wasn't necessary. Daniel had seen Emilia, and was pushing his way toward the door to the cell. From several feet away Emilia could see his expression of fury. He was biting his lips, and fire she had seldom seen flashed in his eyes.

"I'm very sorry, you should not be here," he said in English, when he was close enough to see Emilia's blessed eyes.

"I'm just fine," she replied in the same language, feeling tears rising from the pit of her stomach. The strain of the farce was beginning to tell.

"So here's your gringo for you," said the jailer in charge of the holding tank, an ugly man, as jailers should be, as crude and brutal as everyone imagined them. Emilia nodded because words forsook her. Then she gathered herself together, looked up, and in the sweetest tone she had ever uttered asked if it would be possible to let him out.

"Get the lead out, fuckup," the *jefe* ordered the man at the door. "Let the gringo through."

Accustomed to commands peppered with curses, the guard turned the key with the same unvarying slowness of everything he did. In silence, her eyes staring into the shadows of that pigsty, Emilia waited without blinking an eye.

"Are you cold, honey?" the jailer asked, putting an arm around her waist and pulling her against his hard potbelly.

"A little."

She struggled not to lose her poise. Again she was struck speechless as he put his hand on her breasts and squeezed them one by one as if choosing fruit in the market.

"Take him now, beautiful," he told her, "because who knows what tomorrow will bring."

"Oh, thank you," Emilia replied, without pulling back or trembling, without losing the smile of gratitude pasted on her lips.

Then, as smooth as silk, with regal delicacy, she moved out of his embrace. Once free, she took the hand Daniel held to her as he came through the barred gate.

"Don't touch him or they'll kill us," she said, employing the English her father had made her learn when she was sure she would never have use for it. She held the smile all the way back. Not even when she saw Milagros's face, anguished for the first time she could remember, did she drop her frozen, beatific expression.

"EMILIA IS BLESSED," said Daniel as he tried to fit himself into the poet Rivadeneira's small Oldsmobile. He sat her on his lap, kissed her, and laughed at her composure and her theatrical talents. "Without her, Aunt Milagros, they would never have let me go."

"We'd already paid him," Emilia said, pressing against him and ignoring the pigpen stench that clung to his body.

"If she hadn't stopped me, I would have killed that brute, even if they killed me for it. But do you know what she did, Aunt?"

"Don't tell her," Emilia pleaded.

"I can imagine," said Milagros.

Saving some of the story for them, Daniel insisted on telling part of it, reporting, through his daze:

"She controlled me with her eyes. In a sweet-as-sugar voice, as if she were a diplomat greeting an ambassador, she spoke in English to tell me not to do anything, but in the clearest Spanish on earth, she telegraphed a military command with her eyes. She's amazing, Aunt. I'm going to be afraid of her, you don't know how cool she is in a crisis. The *jefe* was actually convinced that the farce he'd agreed to was true."

"I can imagine," Milagros repeated, drying a tear with the tip of the handkerchief Rivadeneira offered her.

"No, *tía,* you can't imagine. She's a monster," said Daniel, hugging Emilia tight.

"I can imagine, but I don't want to. You hear me, Daniel? I don't want to, and I mean what I'm saying."

"It wasn't all that bad, Aunt Milagros. That's how we always test oranges, and no one gets upset," said Emilia.

"You are not an orange, Emilia. If your papa hears, he will die!"

"Right. But he isn't going to hear. So don't worry. Where are we going now?"

"You are going home," said Milagros. "And this troublemaker is coming with me. He's foolhardy, and from now until Tuesday I'm going to stick to him like his shadow."

"So am I," said Emilia. "Because we don't want to be throwing any more money around."

"But who's going to do my job?"

"No one is indispensable," said Milagros. "We'll find someone, someone less well known."

"I can do it," Rivadeneira offered.

"Oh, Rivadeneira, Rivadeneira. You are such a good man, but always so misguided," Milagros told him. "This boy runs like a hare and yet they caught him."

"All right," said Rivadeneira with his habitual restraint. "But it's not all about running."

"He can take my place in some things. Others, he can go with me," said Daniel.

"You see, Milagros. You never think I can do anything."

"I don't? I've always said you're an excellent poet and that no one knows as much about Sor Juana as you do, not even Amado Nervo, who thinks he discovered her."

"Justice, bestow your laurels," said Rivadeneira. "Thanks for glorifying me that way. Until now, you've always thought you knew more than I do."

"Everything, in the end, is sacrificed upon your divine altars!" said Mila-

gros, in turn quoting the venerable Sor Juana out of context. *"Doubly foolish is he who, besides being foolish, wishes to display it!"*

"How should I take that?" asked Rivadeneira.

"As an act of humility, something I have little of. So enjoy it."

"My love, if you be prudent, then give shelter to my own," said Rivadeneira, unable to disguise his pleasure.

WITH NO PRUDENCE at all, and forgotten by the two who were exchanging lines from centuries-old poems, Emilia and Daniel rained kisses and caresses on each other in the warm May night.

When Milagros stopped the automobile in front of the Casa de la Estrella, the two young people leapt out and waved good-bye, without making a sound.

"Don't try to exercise your authority now, because it's too late," Rivadeneira told Milagros, fearing she would try to take Daniel with her.

"You're right," she replied, resting her head against him, exhausted from the strain of never allowing herself to give in. After all, her niece and nephew shared a halo and she was not going to interfere. "Love me," she said to Rivadeneira, who could count on the fingers of his right hand the number of times he had heard such a plea.

Emilia threw a kiss to her aunt. Daniel winked and formed the words "I love you" with his lips. Then Emilia took the large key to the front entrance from her purse and handed it to Daniel, who like an expert opened the cranky lock of the Sauris' house.

DIEGO AND JOSEFA, half-asleep, were waiting in a large chair in the sala, and heard the sounds of love from the bottom of the stairs.

"Hasn't Daniel left?" Josefa asked.

"He was in jail," said Diego, sinking deeper into the chair. "But I see that Milagros was able to get him out."

"How long have you known that?" Josefa asked reproachfully.

"Oh, a while."

"Who told you, and when?" Josefa was flushed and unhappy. "Why on earth didn't you tell me?"

"I didn't want to worry you for nothing. You see, he's here now. He's lucky."

"Worry me, but don't keep me out of the picture."

"I won't from now on." Diego rose to greet the young couple, as well as to escape the wrath he felt building in his wife.

"How could you sit there and beat me in chess knowing something so horrible?" Josefa wanted to know, as if glued to the chair.

"Because I'm a good strategist, and I try not to worry about things beyond my control," said Diego, opening the door to the stairway and the enthralled pair.

Emilia came in with a loosened tongue and an unsteady heart. She did not stop talking for more than an hour, mixing together, in the confusion of her elation, the jailer with the trapeze artist, her aunt with the need for a revolution, Rivadeneira with the lion tamer, and Sor Juana with the young horseback rider. Nevertheless, she was careful not to tell what had happened when she went beyond the gate, following the jailer to look for Daniel. She skipped over that part as if it had all been needlepoint and singing.

At times Daniel interrupted to heap praises on her. He was sitting on the floor rolling a cigarette with the paper and tobacco that Diego offered as soon as he saw him sink down onto the rug with a weariness that reminded him of his days of confinement in the hold of Fermín Mundaca's ship more than thirty years before.

He couldn't help it, he liked the man Daniel had become, and did not view as dramatically as his wife the fact that Emilia was so in love with him. Possibly it was better than some other delirium. After all, he and Josefa were themselves tied up in the intrigue against Porfirio Díaz. And maybe none of it was as dangerous or as unusual as it seemed. He hoped Josefa was right, and that as easily as breathing Madero would establish a democracy. After he handed Daniel the tobacco, he returned to sit beside his wife.

"WE KNOW THAT you slept here last night," Josefa fired directly at Daniel as soon as Diego was back beside her.

"I know that you know," he replied, asking himself how it was possible that he hadn't feared the interrogation he faced in the jail but was so apprehensive about the one Josefa was threatening.

"I invited him, Mama," said Emilia, snuggling closer to Daniel's filthy shirt.

"For how long? He just got here and he'll be leaving Tuesday afternoon with the Hero of Liberty," said Josefa, who did not want to hear Madero's name ever again.

"Josefa," Diego said. "Times have changed. What more can we ask for our daughter? She's fallen in love, what does it matter if that love doesn't fit the normal rules and ceremonies?"

"It matters. Why wouldn't I want for her what we have had ourselves?"

"Because you know that history doesn't repeat itself."

"Don't make one of your speeches, Diego. This is already too complicated to be further muddied by your speechifying."

Diego agreed. For a while he sat in silence, puffing his tobacco. Then he moved closer to his wife, his need to touch her that of someone swimming toward solid ground.

As she felt him near, Josefa said grudgingly, "I wish I could agree with you about something. Because lately I haven't found a single thing we agree on."

THEIR ARGUMENT continued for some time without spectators. Emilia and Daniel did not want to waste their time that way. They had closed themselves in the blue bathroom, and when Diego and Josefa, going round and round, had worked their way back to the point of disagreement and were close to screaming at each other as they had never done in their entire lives, they were stopped short by mingled sounds of laughter and the running water of the shower.

"What more do you want, Josefa?" Diego asked, hearing the music just beneath the sound of the water. "Think how there are hundreds, thousands, millions of human beings who will never catch a glimpse of the miracle Emilia is living."

"She's barely sixteen," Josefa reminded him.

"All the better. More time to enjoy it."

"In bits and pieces," Josefa lamented.

"Because the only unalterable emotion is boredom. That lasts forever. But love," said Diego, twirling his eyeglasses by one stem, "comes in fits and starts. You know that."

"Yes, I know that," Josefa replied, her head hanging. "Today, for example, I haven't loved you at all."

"Don't pretend you don't understand what I'm saying."

"I understand, you're all too obvious, but tradition is tradition. Grant me the right to be sad."

"As long as you're not jealous," Diego said, getting to the heart of what was bothering her.

"Are you planning to leave me for an adolescent love?"

"Not right now."

"Then right now I'm not jealous."

Diego smiled.

"Don't get the big head. I have enough with your being a liberal, I don't need you to find something else to be vain about."

"What's vain about being liberal?"

"The vanity of those who think they know everything."

"The ones to blame for that are those who say they know everything God's thinking."

"Oh, no you don't, Diego. That's all I need, to end up talking about God. You'll do anything to change the subject. The child is going to suffer terribly and we'll be to blame."

"It isn't our fault that she wants something specific from life and goes out to look for it."

"She doesn't know what she wants."

"Don't underestimate her good judgment. She knows she loves Daniel."

"Well, she's making the mistake Chinese women make," Josefa stated flatly.

"And what mistake do Chinese women make?"

"This kind," Josefa answered with a sigh. "The same mistake Emilia's making. But it's all my fault because I let you take her to that rehearsal at the Cuencas'."

"What rehearsal?"

"The one she didn't want to go to because she'd had a bad dream the night before."

"Josefa, I thought we'd settled that years ago."

"It was never settled. This is the same discussion we were having eleven years ago, and I'll tell you one more time, that Cuenca boy is dangerous."

"Which Cuenca boy?" asked Daniel, who had emerged from the bath with shining eyes and the devilish smile he'd had all his life. His hair was wet and uncombed, falling over his forehead.

"You," said Josefa, pointing.

"Aunt Josefa," said Daniel, patting her cheek, "I know I'm not the best thing that could happen to Emilia, but I'm not the worst, either. Here, let's count. I'm not a drunk, I don't gamble, I don't chase women, I'm against Porfirio Díaz, and I don't have gonorrhea. I know how to play the piano, the flute, the violin, and the *chirimía.* I've studied history, I can speak English, I'm a good reader, I do not believe in the alleged natural inferiority of women, and I worship this one."

"God himself would tell you he's good, Mama," said Emilia, who had appeared rosy pink and happy and with a brush in her hand and a towel wrapped around her head.

"Don't ask her which god," Diego counseled, laughing aloud.

"You two think this is some kind of game. That you're going to be in each other's arms forever. But are you ready to have children?" Josefa asked Daniel, who still held the hand where he had ticked off his virtues on her fingers.

"I don't think they would turn out too badly," Daniel answered, kissing the implacable warrior he had for a mother-in-law.

"Where did you learn to play the *chirimía?* I can't believe that gives you the right to spray children around." Josefa's reprimand sounded in her voice.

"Mama, it took you twelve years to have me," Emilia interrupted, now face-to-face with her mother.

"And what if you're like my mother?"

"That would be trouble," she said, sitting down beside her father. "But I might be like Aunt Milagros and never ever get pregnant."

"Stop talking such nonsense." Even as she scolded Emilia, Josefa could not help but feel a certain pride. The love potion her daughter had drunk had lighted in her eyes a confidence that had not been there the week before. "I'm going to fix us some cinnamon tea. God help us all," she said, walking past them with the ballet dancer's erect shoulders and slender waist that Daniel realized she had bequeathed to Emilia.

Diego watched Josefa, acknowledging there was truth in her arguments but being careful not to show it when she turned to look at him as she headed for the kitchen, warning him with her finger:

"And you, don't dare ask me which god."

"I'd have to be crazy to do that," Diego answered, getting up from the chair and following her.

WITHOUT FURTHER DISCUSSION, Daniel settled into the Sauris' house and for the next few days turned everything upside down. Emilia did not return to work in the laboratory; Josefa stopped reading and began trying out recipes with the fervor of a newlywed; Flaubert the parrot went mad trying to get used to the silence of the mornings and noise of the night; Cassiopeia, the cat who kept Josefa company when she was reading, was banished from the room where Daniel and Emilia lazed until long after breakfast; and Futuro, the black dog that accompanied Emilia on her afternoon walks, had to put up with being left behind and locked up by his mistress.

The house was suspended in a state of constant tumult. Nighttime conversations went on without rigor or agreement until early morning, dinner was never earlier than five o'clock, and there were usually four different breakfast hours.

The many clubs that fought over leadership of the anti-Reelection movement in the city had in common, in addition to their interest in Madero, another tie: their respect for the independent and tenacious posture of the group of friends who for twenty years had been meeting in the home of Dr. Cuenca. Perhaps for that reason, perhaps for his audacity and his skills at reconciliation, Madero chose Daniel to prepare the way for his visit to Puebla.

Since it was risky for Daniel to move about in the streets, Diego Sauri offered his house for the meetings and pacts among the representatives of the various clubs backing Madero. So for several days, from seven in the evening until daylight caught them drowsing at the dining room table, the house was besieged with visitors, enlightened with all manner of plans, and blessed with the luxury of sheltering unreserved passion.

"Emilia, do you have to run your hands over Daniel in front of Aquiles Serdán?" Milagros asked her niece one afternoon, leading her to a corner in order not to distract those who were discussing whether they had enough supporters to make a crowd at the railroad station.

"Absolutely necessary," Emilia replied.

"Why?"

"Because Daniel spreads some rare disease. Something like a sadness. When I want to get over mine, I need to touch Daniel."

"And how often do you need to 'get over it'?"

"Almost all the time, Aunt," Emilia asserted with a fleeting, downturned smile.

CHAPTER

12

THE FOLLOWING TUESDAY AFTERNOON, Madero arrived. A crowd was waiting at the train station shouting *"Viva!"* and working up a democratic fervor, the largest show of anti-Reelectionist strength ever seen in the city.

In the whirlwind of such dizzying activity, Emilia lost Daniel. She did not try to hold him back. She kissed him in the middle of the street, a long, slow kiss, until she was left with the savor of his tongue on hers. Then, without a word of reproach, she let him follow Madero. She watched the crowd close behind him and turned to seek comfort in the eyes and arms of Diego Sauri.

"Want some coffee?" Diego asked, putting his arm around her waist and feeling more useless than ever.

"Let's go to the meeting," said Emilia, countering his offer with a smile.

As they had suspected from the beginning, the authorities had not granted permission for a public demonstration. The persecution that had resulted from their efforts in the barrio of Santiago a few days before had been worthwhile, since it turned out they were able to hold the clandestine meeting there; so many people came that soon after it began anyone would have thought that "clandestine" meant a boisterous celebration.

There were various speeches, high spirits, complaints, and curses galore. As soon as Madero spoke his last word, Emilia and her father returned home, walking slowly and speaking very little. Diego did not want to muddy his daughter's sadness with his political laments, and Emilia thought her father did not deserve the spectacle of her grief put into words. Only after they had stepped across the threshold of the sala where Diego met the eyes of Josefa, clearly awaiting answers, did he allow himself to voice his complaints.

"Terrible," he said, throwing himself into a chair. "This man is going to get us into a mess that even he can't get out of. He has no idea what he wants. Everything is good intentions and fuzzy plans, if sound ideas. While they're locking people up just for speaking his name with some enthusiasm, the man goes around wanting to stay in good with the church, the poor, the rich, the whores, and the ladies of San Vicente. What a miserable speech! I wanted to crawl under a rock."

"You're exaggerating." Josefa had chosen to stay home rather than claw Daniel's eyes out when he left. "What did you think, Emilia?"

"The same," she replied, languid and dreamy.

"But she says that because she's jealous. I say it with total objectivity."

"Jealous? Not at all. As far as I'm concerned, Daniel can follow that chubby little man to every committee, club, or sect he wants to," said Emilia, who joined her father in his chair.

"Sol came to see you," Josefa reported, hoping to distract her. "She's radiant."

"She's getting away from that mother," Diego explained.

"And her father," Emilia added, pretending to nip her own father's cheek.

"Aren't you going to go see her?" asked Josefa. "She's getting married next week and you haven't spent any time with her."

"I got married last week and she didn't spend time with me. When it comes to marrying, Mama, two are involved."

"Not always, Emilia."

"Would you have wanted me to get married like Sol?" To better confront her mother, Emilia jumped up from where she was sitting near her father.

"I don't know," said Josefa, trying to bite off her embroidery thread with her teeth.

"Yes, you would have liked that. Why don't you use the scissors?" Emilia handed Josefa the small pair in her lap she seemed not to have noticed.

"Because I'm an idiot."

"Madero's the idiot," said Diego. "Off in the clouds somewhere while all the time he's laying kindling for an inferno."

"Is that all you can talk about? I don't want to have to start over again in defense of Madero's moderation. I'm going to bed." And Josefa began putting away her thread.

"What do you want us to talk about?" Diego asked. "The other subject is weddings. Do you want me to say you're right, that we shouldn't have allowed Emilia to love Daniel without some ceremony because the boy had to leave at any moment? I'm not going to say that, my beloved Josefa. This country is about to go up in flames, and a girl's virginity is not going to concern anyone, least of all our Señora de Guadalupe."

"I'm going to bed before you get to the part in your speech about how democracy has a civilizing effect."

Josefa got up from her easy chair and started out of the room, pensive and annoyed. Diego watched her, unable to avoid the old enchantment his wife aroused in him at the least expected moments.

"Don't be angry," he pleaded. "What do you want to talk about? What are your dreams? What star fell on you?"

"Don't be a pest, Diego," said Señora Sauri, backing away from the arms her husband opened to her.

Emilia smiled at their game, and a kind of consolation washed over that peculiar pain called adolescent love, suddenly gone from her life, its absence as overwhelming as its arrival.

"Tomorrow I'll go see Sol and help any way I can. I promise," she said, hugging her mother as if she were the daughter.

Standing in the middle of the sala, each supporting the other, they seemed to Diego the center of the world.

They're as wrung out as two Amazons after a battle, he thought, gazing at the two of them. Beautiful and strong. Identical and different. What was a war compared to them?

THE NEXT DAY mother and daughter left early for Sol's house. From the vestibule they could hear the commotion on the second floor. Emilia and Josefa stepped into a bedroom piled with all the lingerie one woman could wear in a lifetime, along with enough towels, sheets, and blankets to last twenty years. There the young bride of the house was standing on a chair, trying on the dress that besides having just barely arrived from Paris was unfortunately two sizes larger than the wearer.

Josefa thought how much better it would have been had they called on the best seamstress in Puebla instead of having to battle this disaster at the last minute, but she held her tongue, guided by her dislike of irrelevant comments. Not content with that forbearance, she offered to make the dress cling to Sol like a second skin. She asked for pins and began adjusting the darts with a dressmaker's skill. In half an hour the dress fitted Sol's body perfectly. Only then did Sol get down from the chair, where Emilia helped her undo the row of tiny buttons that ran down her back like a shiver.

"You're going to be beautiful," Emilia assured her friend, and kissed her to excuse her absence for so many days.

Sol stood half-dressed in her whale-boned camisole and linen petticoats.

"What happened to you?" she asked Emilia in a low voice, almost whispering in her ear.

"I got hit by a train," said Emilia, savoring her memories.

They cleared a space amid the underthings scattered across the bed, and sat down to chatter while Josefa and Sol's mother went to entertain themselves in the room with the gifts.

Shelves had been installed along every wall of the huge room but there was not an inch that wasn't filled.

"Where did you put mine?" Milagros Veytia asked as greeting, sweeping into the room ready to examine everything with an appraiser's eye. She walked past silver, china, and cut crystal with a stride that threatened the collapse of all the shelves. "There's enough here for an army."

"They're going to have two haciendas, a house in Mexico City, an atelier in Paris, and pied-à-terres here and there. They will need it all, don't worry," said Sol's mother, affecting a modicum of modesty when actually she was beside herself with pride. She followed Milagros farther down the rows of gifts. As if transported, she stopped before a clock with inlaid wood. A jewel of marquetry that bore the card of Milagros Veytia. As she read it, she dissolved in praises and thanks.

As response to such effusiveness, Milagros limited herself to ask, not without condescension, how she could be helpful. Josefa had sent a message asking her to come and now explained that the cause for the urgency lay in the hundred tucks to be taken out and redone in Sol's dress.

Milagros was exhausted from Madero's visit, but instead of trumping up some excuse and escaping the chore, she told herself that a little time for reflection and sitting in a chair doing something with her hands would do her good. In recent days she had walked miles from one end of the city to the other, so the idea of sitting in the sewing room and talking with her sister seemed very pleasant.

"That woman could drown in a puddle," she said as soon as Sol's mother hustled off to resolve another of the twenty thousand mock problems weighing on her.

"And as for you, you're shameless. I saw you switch that card," Josefa accused, interrupting her sewing to peer into Milagros's innocent eyes.

"But you won't tell on me, will you?" Milagros reassured herself. "It seems insane to spend money on a gift for a girl who has presents from the wealthiest families in Mexico. I can get twenty men out of jail for what that clock would have cost me," justifying her action with the illuminated smile of a saint.

THE WORLD KEPT SPINNING during the days that followed, until life seemed nearly normal. In the mornings, the Veytia sisters chatted over Sol's dress. Anyone who saw them from a distance, seemingly without a care, stitching away on the dress of the girl who would marry the younger son of one of the wealthiest families in the state or the nation, could not have imagined the tenor of their conversations. Josefa knew through Milagros that in the days following Madero's visit, dozens of his most enthusiastic supporters had disappeared. To add to their woes, Milagros told her that one night a train had left carrying a hundred prisoners whose punishment was to be sent to Quintana Roo, that imaginary land of marvels her husband felt such nostalgia for.

The more she thought about it, the more difficult it was for Josefa to believe that such a paradise could be considered a punishment.

"They take them there to do forced labor in murderous heat," her sister said. "They're not going there to fish and doze beside the sea that stirs your husband's memories. They're going to an impenetrable jungle to sleep among snakes and mosquitoes, to attack the mountain and build roads, to eat what they can get their hands on . . . to die."

"All because they want fair elections?"

"All because of that." For the first time, Josefa could sense her sister's dejection.

"Come live with us," Josefa urged as she saw that at this moment in their lives her sister felt unprotected.

"It's not that bad. Solitude has its pleasures."

"Marry Rivadeneira," Josefa suggested as she cut a thread.

"And ruin his life?"

"You're already doing that."

"How's Emilia getting along?" Milagros asked, sensing danger in that conversation.

"Getting along," Josefa replied, knowing her sister to be much more disconsolate than she would ever show.

SEPARATED FROM DANIEL and his embrace, Emilia tried to bury herself among the bottles and scents of the pharmacy. Her father welcomed her back with *Ritorna vincitore* but did not again bring up the theme of missing someone.

Diego was sure that nothing he had to say could help his daughter as much as engaging her mind, so he challenged her with one of humanity's most consuming problems: how to discover the causes of illnesses in order to prevent them.

With the ease of someone who has never had anything else on her mind, Emilia returned to her father's medical books.

"Look what I have for you," said Diego one afternoon, flourishing a huge book with loose and yellowed pages.

Historia medicinal de las cosas que se traen de nuestras Indias occidentales was a study written in 1574 by Nicolás Monardes, a Sevillian doctor, recounting discoveries made in the New World.

"Your hero," said Emilia.

"One of them," Diego replied, laying the reference book on the main table of the laboratory.

Emilia pulled up a tall bench and began looking through it.

"It says here they knew the uses of the oil of the sweet gum tree," she said, looking up and turning to find her father. "Why did you tell me it was an original preparation of the Sauri pharmacy?"

"It was original with us because its applications had been lost. Time is the best friend of originality."

"Monardes says it warms, comforts, resolves, and mitigates pain. Maybe I'd better rub a little on myself."

"Everything is good for lovesickness, sweetheart," Diego told her. "As long as the afflicted person is intelligent, any oil will cure her, and you are a very intelligent sufferer. So much so that sometimes you fool us. I could almost believe you've forgotten your illness."

"I'd be crazy to pull a sad face before Josefa Sauri. If she thinks you make too many speeches about the elections, imagine what she'd do if she saw me looking dreary. She'd never forgive Daniel as long as she lived."

"Your mother has a soft spot for Daniel," Diego invented, terrified by the mere idea of a break between his wife and his daughter.

"You have a good imagination, Papa," said Emilia, winking. "Like Monardes. Have you seen all the things he says tobacco is good for? He says it heals wounds and relieves headaches, rheumatism, chest pain, stomachache, bloating, worms, swelling, flatulence, toothache, carbuncles, and sores. I guess there's nothing my Aunt Milagros can't cure by lighting up a cigarette."

They spent the afternoon reading and transcribing everything about tobacco and its uses. When they closed the pharmacy to go up to dinner, they took the book with them and wore Josefa out with strange anecdotes about opium and the ghosts and fantasies it produces.

"Do you know what Monardes wrote?" Emilia asked her mother, quoting: "Five grains of opium kills us Spaniards, although the Indians take sixty grains for good health and relaxation."

"By chance does it say how many it takes to 'derange' mestizos like me? Because there are times I would love to 'lose my reason and see things and visions that provide contentment,'" said Josefa, parodying the descriptions in the book.

"The Spaniard's five grains would be enough to kill you," her husband told her.

"And I suppose you're going to tell me you're Indian and can tolerate fifty?" asked Josefa, ironic and amused.

"I'll show you."

"Don't think of wasting it," said Emilia. "With that much we could cure five dying patients, and it could kill you."

"Kill me? You don't know what I'm made of," boasted Diego, smug in the peace of his favorite chair.

THE POET RIVADENEIRA erupted into that peace, looking as burned out and pale as a candle stub.

"They've arrested Milagros," he reported. And sounded as if those might be the last words he spoke.

"We'll go get her," responded Emilia, believing that all they had to do was repeat the tricks of a few days before.

"It won't be that easy this time," said Rivadeneira. "They know her too well in the jails, we can't pretend she's a foreigner. Worse, the governor has detested her ever since the night she asked his wife how she could stomach living with a murderer. She was arrested on his orders, not the police's. Of course, I can't find any record of her arrest in any of the jails." Rivadeneira had never felt better informed or less useful.

Diego Sauri went to sit beside Josefa, who, mute from the time of Rivadeneira's entrance, was quietly but uninterruptedly weeping. In her head resounded the thousand times she had reminded her sister of the obvious benefits of a calm life. And she trembled remembering how Milagros always replied with an uncompromising edict: "If you want to see me quiet, you'll have to bury me."

FOR A FEW MINUTES, Rivadeneira paced in silence, back and forth across the sala, watching Josefa vainly attempt to stop crying, Diego bury his fingers in his unruly hair as if to pull it out by the roots, Emilia biting her left thumbnail, her lips moving as if repeating a curse she could not say aloud. Then out came a chaotic spate of words; he babbled as one does in dreams, as if in hearing himself he might find an answer. The Sauris did not understand a word of his monologue; they listened as if to a madman combing through his thoughts, but they listened with that patience that comes only with anguish.

None of the three dared interrupt the incoherent stream, incoherent, though no more than any words they could muster. They were frozen in a time that seemed both brief and eternal. A time ruled by the shared wish to see Milagros walk into the room to solve everything with her charmed presence. Silence moved among them as slowly as a legion of idle angels.

Only then did Rivadeneira stop his ranting; he put on his jacket, walked to the mirror of the tall umbrella stand, smoothed his hair, and took down his hat.

"What I must do is get her out of wherever she is and once and for all take her to a world that is less deafening for her," he said, donning the hat. "I'm not going to ask. I'm sick and tired of giving in, tired of her treating me as if I don't exist, of her picking me up and dropping me as if I were the wife of some general off at war," he said as again he strode back and forth in the Sauris' sala, silencing them with a belligerence they had never seen.

Josefa stared at him; for the first time she could glimpse the nature of the nearly secret relationship between her sister and the only man who had taken the measure of her desire for freedom.

"Do that. It seems like a marvelous idea." Josefa jumped up and rubbed her face with her hands as if that might erase the panorama of her feelings. "How are you going to get her out?"

"By asking the scoundrel who's holding her," the poet answered, displaying a determination he doubtless had always possessed but was not accustomed to showing. "I hope I will not be long. Thank you for clarifying things."

"What did we clarify?"

"Everything," said Rivadeneira. Diego Sauri followed him to the door, intending to stick with Rivadeneira wherever it occurred to him to go.

It was ten o'clock at night when they presented themselves at the home of the governor, accompanied by a jittery notary public, a friend of Rivadeneira's. Two guards stopped them at the gate and one blew a whistle. At his call, in less than a minute's time, came thirty men armed as if to repel an assault. Rivadeneira straightened his jacket, assumed his most elegant tone, and asked to see the governor.

The guards looked him over from tip to toe, as if he were a madman. They said the governor was not in and that this was no time to come looking for him. As if he hadn't heard, Rivadeneira took out a card with his name and handed it to the man who seemed to be in charge. At the same time, in the most pleasant tone Diego had heard in all his dealings with this noble man, he said the matter was urgent and that they would wait as long as necessary.

Five minutes later, a man wearing a dark suit with a vest appeared and introduced himself as the private secretary of His Honor the governor and, after ceremoniously consulting the exact hour on his pocket watch, asked whether they had been well treated and informed Rivadeneira that it would be an honor for his employer to receive him. Escorted by Diego Sauri and the notary, a short man who blinked nervously the whole time, as if a pair of hummingbirds were fluttering in his eyes, Rivadeneira climbed the stairs of the palace where the dispenser of favors and disasters in the state of Puebla lived.

First they walked down long, bright, deserted corridors. They went into a large room and from there to a reception room; from the reception room they passed to a smaller room and finally to the smallest of all. In this last room, the secretary asked them to wait a moment and disappeared through a glass door.

"What are we going to say to this devil?" asked Diego Sauri.

"I know what I must say." Rivadeneira acted as if he had been planning this meeting for a very long time.

The secretary returned wearing a fixed smile that might have been pasted on his lips on the day of his birth, and with a gesture invited them through the door. They saw before them a large room presided over by the portrait of Benito Juárez. At the rear, behind a desk large enough to seat twelve for dinner, was the governor.

"My esteemed Señor Rivadeneira," he said, rising as he saw them enter, "I am at your service."

"Let my sister-in-law go," said Diego Sauri, without preamble.

"I do not imprison anyone, señor, uh . . . ?" said the governor, examining Diego Sauri as if trying to determine what rock he had tripped over.

"Diego Sauri," said the pharmacist, with no further explanation and without offering to shake the hand of his powerful host.

"My friend Diego Sauri," said Rivadeneira, "is married to the sister of Milagros Veytia. And Milagros Veytia should be married to me."

"And you came here to tell me that?"

"To ask you to set her free, and to guarantee that I shall be responsible for her from the moment you hand her over to me. I am prepared to sign a statement to that effect before a notary public," said Rivadeneira, solemn as an emperor.

"I would have to break the law. Milagros Veytia is a prisoner because she is a dangerous woman."

"You don't have to tell me. I've always known it. But she is also a luxury, and luxuries, as you and I know, are expensive."

"How expensive?"

"As much as all the land belonging to the Hacienda de San Miguel. Three thousand hectares with their own river."

"That know-it-all is worth that much?" asked the governor, arrogant and scornful.

"I will not tolerate insult," said Rivadeneira. "These are the titles to the property. I shall sign them as soon as you deliver Señora Veytia to me."

Without a word, the governor reviewed the papers, page by page, with the gluttonous look of someone seeing three thousand well-irrigated hectares pass before his eyes, one by one. Then he laughed uproariously as he rang a bell. The secretary appeared in the instant, bowing.

"Have they brought Señora Veytia?" the governor asked. "Our friend Rivadeneira has given me very wise and judicious reasons to believe in her total innocence."

"She's here. Shall I bring her in?" the secretary asked.

"Wait," said Rivadeneira, "I'll sign first," subjecting his desire to see Milagros to his wish to conceal the source of her freedom. Diego Sauri watched him, wondering what god he should thank for the good fortune of having this man as a friend. No one had ever signed a name with such certainty that it would open the gates to a paradise.

"You must be crazy," said the governor, taking the papers and with his eyes signaling his secretary to bring in Milagros Veytia.

"Believe me, it has been a pleasure," said Rivadeneira.

"I think it would be better if we met her outside," counseled Diego Sauri, but by then Milagros was through the door and facing them, as unchanged and haughty as if she had not just been spirited from a secret prison.

"What did this thief ask you for?" she demanded of Rivadeneira.

"A list of your good qualities," he replied, taking her arm and hustling her toward the door, fearing the governor might regret his bargain. Give up Milagros? Would *he?* Not if they deeded him the whole country with its surrounding seas.

ONE WEEK LATER, during the religious ceremony of Sol's wedding, Milagros Veytia, who always attended such rituals to enjoy talking all the way through them, promised the poet Rivadeneira that after the elections she would go with him on a trip devoted solely to loving him.

"And then you'll have to tell me what you did to get me out," she whispered as they knelt during the blessing.

"And then . . . ," Rivadeneira whispered as if he were praying.

The poet smiled, clutching his secret to his heart while a children's chorus sang Handel's *Hallelujah* and Sol took her husband's arm to begin the march back up the aisle to the door of the church.

Emilia, standing between her Aunt Milagros and her mother, saw her friend turned into an exquisite, quivering doll, and tried to concentrate on the music.

"What a disaster we're allowing!" Milagros said in her ear.

"What could we do? Rescue her from her happiness? How do you convince the sky that it isn't blue but transparent?"

"Emilia, you're getting too wise too quickly," said Milagros, kissing her.

"Did you know that the red carpet starts at her house, crosses the park to the church, and then continues all along the sidewalk to the garden where they're having the dinner?" asked Emilia. Then, as if one thing followed from the other, as Sol walked past them, a yearning vision in white, Emilia said, in an almost normal tone, "I think Daniel is wasting his time in this thing about the struggle for equality and democracy."

"You may be right," Milagros answered after smiling patronizingly at the bride and groom.

"Of course I'm right. Don't you see? If all this comes from exploiting the poor, why would anyone want to help them?"

"Because they won't have any other choice."

"Why won't they, Aunt Milagros? They own everything."

"I know, my darling. Until they *stop* owning everything."

"Papa never tires of saying that in order for that to happen, there will have to be a war."

"I hope not," said Milagros. "In any case, we're not going to settle that today. What do you say we walk down that red carpet to find the bride and groom and the party?"

"Don't coddle me as if I were some silly girl. You won't make me any less sad. You're the only one who hasn't worn herself out trying to distract me," said Emilia, speaking loud enough to be heard over the music, but just as the music ceased.

Like everyone else, Diego and Josefa had followed the bride and groom out. All that was left in the church were Emilia, Milagros, Rivadeneira, the cloying perfume of the tuberoses, and, just behind Emilia, a man in an impeccable frock coat who when he heard her last words turned lithely and said in the rotund voice of discovery: "I am Antonio Zavalza and I would be enchanted if I could continue to listen to your conversation."

CHAPTER 13

Who this Antonio Zavalza was—besides a diligent eavesdropper—was something the family learned in detail in less than an hour, because the man's tongue knew no inhibitions, and he was lonely. He had been in the city barely four nights, he said, but for several years had dreamed about it. He wanted to live there, walk through it at night, learn the twists and turns of its streets. He wanted to be well liked, to be everything but a stranger.

He left the church determined to convince Emilia that he was not a spy but a captive of her voice. And by the time they reached the party that followed Sol's religious ceremony, anyone would have sworn they had been friends since childhood. Antonio Zavalza was a nephew of the bishop, although they had little in common beyond the family name and inheritance. Zavalza had spent five years in Paris studying medicine, and had come to Puebla with the desire to make it the site of his first consulting room.

As soon as Sol's mother saw him waltzing with Emilia as if they had practiced for two months, she came hurrying to the Sauris' table to fill in all the details about the new arrival. In addition to being handsome, Antonio Zavalza was one of the most important great-grandsons of the Marquesa de Selva Nevada. His father had died the previous year and left him a small fortune, which the young man had chosen to dedicate to creating a foundation to benefit the elderly. For self-esteem, he wanted to earn his own living. He was a doctor; he had graduated in Paris with honors; he was not a fan of Don Porfirio; he said to anyone who would listen that the church was an antiquated institution; and he had broken an engagement the bishop had arranged on his behalf with one of the De Hitas' daughters.

"In your eyes, he must be quite a black sheep," Diego commented. "Why did you invite him?"

"Because his uncle asked me to, he wants him to meet the best people."

"Well, he picked a poor place to start," said Milagros.

"You dearly love to denigrate your family. Can't you see the boy is enchanted with Emilia?"

"They've just met," Josefa demurred. "Don't start plotting anything."

"You see that my plotting bears fruit. Sol is happy," her mother said.

"She's naive," Milagros contradicted. "Did you do her the favor of telling her about things, or is she due the surprise of her life?"

"I have explained, of course, how she should act with her in-laws. She conducts herself like a queen, she's elegant and discreet, and she doesn't speak out of turn or ask anything she shouldn't."

"And it doesn't matter to you whether she's happy in bed," said Milagros, causing her sister to pale.

"That, dear, is not your concern, but God's," said Sol's mother. "The less time she spends thinking about that, the better."

"Poor child," ventured Milagros, whipping open her fan as if with it she could lighten the heavy atmosphere.

Emilia and Antonio Zavalza arrived at just that moment.

"Sol wants to talk to you before she goes. Instead of throwing her bouquet, she wants to hand it to you."

EMILIA LEFT HER FATHER talking with the recently arrived doctor and went to look for Sol, who once again was nearly buried among petticoats and dresses and standing in the middle of her bedroom struggling with the laces of a corset that nipped in her waist and gave her the poker-straight body of a mannequin.

"Your Aunt Milagros is right. These are horrible contrivances," she said, smiling as she saw Emilia. "My mother says that matrimony is not unpleasant, but that there are moments when it is best to close your eyes and pray an Ave María. Do you know about that?" Her eyes were filling with tears.

"Oh, pretty, pretty, Sol," murmured Emilia, hugging her. Then, holding her close and patting her back with fondness, Emilia offered her friend a quiet lecture.

Downstairs, the music of one of the orchestras was playing a waltz by Juventino Rosas, and the heavy scent of tuberose on the air announced the coming of dusk.

Emilia took a small handkerchief from her bosom and offered it to her friend. She looked through her purse for a small bottle of beet juice to mask the pallor her descriptions had occasioned. Then, as if she were dressing a doll, she helped Sol into the complicated traveling suit created by the famous Madame Ginon on the Calle Pensador Mexicano. When she had fastened the last hat pin, she stood back and examined Sol from head to foot, as if she were a work of art.

"You haven't changed your shoes," she said, going to the armoire where Sol had kept her high-button shoes, viewing the desolation of that emptied closet.

"I feel as wooden as that armoire," said Sol.

"In the worst of cases, you can help things along with your imagination," Emilia told her, kneeling with the buttonhook.

"Don't do that," Sol asked, tugging at one of her curls.

"Do you hear what I'm saying about imagination?" asked Emilia, still concentrating on the shoe buttons.

"Yes," Sol replied.

"The bird that will help you fly away is right here under your hat," said Emilia, standing up and touching her friend's temples.

AN HOUR LATER, at the moment of leaving for the first night of her honeymoon, already in the seat of the Panhard Lavassor to which her husband was devoting more attention than to her, Sol sought her friend's eyes among the crowd and, when she met them, tapped her temples and winked.

"What is she telling you?" Antonio Zavalza asked.

"That she will try to be happy," Emilia replied, waving good-bye to the bride.

THE NEXT DAY, because she had forgotten to close the wood shutters, the early-morning sun came pouring into Emilia Sauri's windows, denying a repeat of the happiness she had allowed herself the day before. She cursed without opening her eyes. Silently, she groped for the source of her overwhelming need to cry. Aloud, she asked herself that same question, and with moist eyes once again counted the beams of the ceiling. Then she pulled the pillow over her head and for two days wept disconsolately, without stopping and without opening her door.

Her parents, who from the time Emilia was a child had seen her lock herself in her room to cry, spent the first morning without being unduly concerned. But when the clock struck eight that evening without a sign of Emilia, even at mealtimes, Josefa could no longer contain the "I told you so" she had been choking back all day. Her loosened tongue was as sharp as a sword, wounding her husband's ears until sleep overcame her about three in the morning.

The morning light was very pale when she resumed combat. By noon of that Tuesday, when Diego came up from the pharmacy for the fourth time to ask if things were any better and he might therefore hope for a bowl of warm soup, his wife's fury had turned to melancholy. She had been knocking at her daughter's door for an hour and a half, without so much as a sob in response.

"Daniel is an imbecile!" cried Diego, to his wife's surprise. "I agree with you completely that Daniel is an imbecilic young man!"

"I never said he's an imbecile," Josefa clarified. "I have always said that he is extremely intelligent, but he's selfish. As are all these people bent on saving everyone who can think of nothing but attracting notice to themselves. They sent the poor boy off to boarding school, so he never had enough affection, and now that he's out on his own he's looking for recognition."

"That's why! He's an imbecile!" shouted Diego, punctuating his wife's comments. But nothing happened. Emilia did not budge from her retreat despite the uproar her parents were making. She might as well have been dead. At least that's what the Sauris believed.

After several more hours of that unresponsive silence, Diego himself began to sob with such anguish that Josefa shifted from berating to comforting him. She was patting him and whispering to him when Milagros Veytia came into the room and stopped dead before them. All she had to do was look at her sister's face to see that things were not going well with Emilia.

"Is she locked in her room?" she asked, assuming it as fact.

"And I can't find the spare keys," explained Josefa, as if it were a novelty to lose keys in her household.

"One kick and that door opens," said Milagros.

"Stop crying, Diego," said Josefa, knowing how close thought was to deed where her sister was concerned.

Five kicks from Milagros and the stout German lock charged with guarding her niece's door died fulfilling its duty.

Emilia's bedroom was revealed in brilliant and harmonious light. The last rays of the setting sun fell across her iron bed and white cotton spread. But there was no Emilia lying there with face pressed to tearstained pillow. In fact, Emilia seemed not to be there at all. Shattering the silence that paralyzed her sister and brother-in-law, Milagros Veytia asked loudly whether the girl might have sneaked out by the balcony, and started toward the sunny rectangle of sheer curtains. Diego was offended by the question, wounded by the mere idea that someone could think his baby had something to hide from him.

Josefa Sauri started to step in front of her sister but stopped short as if the floor had dropped away. At her feet, huddled in the pink nightgown of her last childhood years, deaf to her parents' cries and Milagros's battering at the door, lay Emilia, as if under a spell. There was no way to know how long she might have been asleep. She looked absolutely exhausted.

Exhausted from growing up, thought Josefa.

Diego Sauri ran to kiss her forehead, to check whether she had a fever. Then he looked up at his wife. This was how Emilia had slept as a child, with the same total abandonment of consciousness. Except, of course, she had not had an irresponsible father and aunt then. Maybe Josefa had been right when she bewailed the freedom Milagros and Diego were burdening her daughter with.

Josefa seemed to read his expression.

"There are some basic things people with new ideas can't seem to understand," she said to him.

"What basic things?" Milagros asked, raising her voice.

"Men have passions, we women have men," Josefa replied. "Emilia is not a man. You cannot treat her as if she had feelings as poorly adjusted as a man's."

Diego countered with favorable arguments for his point of view, climbing onto the bed as he was, shoes and all, to be closer to his wife. But not even when her nostrils were filled with the wood-and-tobacco scent that bound her so tightly to her husband did Josefa cease her recriminations.

"What a fool I was, standing by while you two made Emilia and Daniel's bed. As if it were some kind of game to let him rob Emilia of her peace."

"Peace is for the ancient and the bored," said Milagros. "Emilia wants happiness, which is more difficult, and shorter-lived, but better."

"Speech me no speeches, Sister," Josefa entreated her sister as she was leaving the room. "I have passed the point where I can tolerate speeches."

"It terrifies me when Josefa gets angry with you," Diego told Milagros.

"Don't worry. She knows we're right. It's just that it's very difficult for her to accept it."

"I'm not so sure at this moment that we did the right thing; maybe we should have insisted that Emilia get married like any other girl. New ways can be torturous."

"Old ways even more so. And if you want to bring up that subject, Díaz's old ways are the most torturous of all. I don't know what we're going to do. If he continues to be so stubborn about staying in power, this is going to turn into an infernal mess. The electoral campaign is a farce. The only election the man wants is his own. And the more people are hounded, the more radical they become. Some are wanting to take up arms now."

"Save us from the fate of crusaders," said Diego.

"Tomorrow morning some of Madero's representatives are coming from Mexico City to try to talk Serdán into abandoning his idea of armed rebellion and agreeing to use the law as his weapon."

"I don't think they will get anywhere. Who can reason with that bundle of passions? He wants to be a hero. And that is very dangerous. Heroes always end up somehow as dictators. You just have to look at how that great hero of the Republic, General Díaz, turned out. Would you believe me if I tell you I'm frightened? It's one thing to want to live in a society worthy of being called that, and to seek justice for others as a way of assuring it for yourself; it's something else to start a war."

"They swear it would be a short one," said Milagros.

"There's no such thing as a short war. Declaring war is like making a little rip in a feather pillow," said Josefa, coming in with a pot of tea. "That's why I like Madero, because he's a man of peace."

"And blindly naive," said Diego.

"He's a good man. Like you."

"With the difference that it would never occur to me to lead anyone."

"I'm going to leave you two as much in agreement on that subject as ever. I'm off to see what happened at the meeting because I'm already late."

"Don't go, Milagros. If you miss one day it won't matter," Josefa pleaded.

"I've already missed it. I'm just going to see how it ended."

"I want to go with you," said Emilia, getting up from the floor, alert as a rooster at dawn.

"Well, where did you come from?" asked Josefa with a smile.

Diego had picked up a pillow from the bed and had removed the pillowcase to feel the feathers. They were so soft, so pliant to the touch. If only that could happen with his wife.

Milagros told them good-bye and ran downstairs. Ten seconds later they heard the street door slam.

"She closes doors as if she wanted them never to open again," said her sister.

"More like she wanted to knock them off their hinges."

Emilia asked if she could have some soup with bread and cheese. Josefa served her bean soup. She had never tasted anything so good. As she ate, her face slowly changed. By the time she finished her second helping, she was a new girl.

"When are you going to learn not to confuse hunger with sadness?" Diego asked. "You've been crying for two days—one and a half were from hunger."

"Don't try to get yourself off the hook, Diego."

"I am off the hook. Is it my fault, Emilia, that you adore Daniel?"

"Who thinks that?"

"Your mama."

"What an idea, Mama. Papa is only one-fourth guilty. Another fourth is my Aunt Milagros's fault for introducing me to Daniel as soon as I was born. And of the remaining half, part of the blame is yours, because I liked it that you didn't like it, and I'm guilty for what's left, for being stupid."

"I like that distribution," said Diego. "I'm prepared to bear the blame for my quarter."

"At least," murmured Josefa, pouring her husband more coffee.

That evening, the linden flower brew Josefa had prepared was dark as India tea. Emilia poured in a little milk and sipped hers. An angel flew over the table, and in the silence of its passing they heard knocking at the downstairs door. Diego speculated that it could only be Milagros, and followed his wife, who went to peer over the balcony to see who it was. A cluster of heads were pressed close to the entry. The Sauris had no idea what was happening, but without a second thought Emilia ran downstairs and threw open the door. Two wounded men scarcely able to stand spilled inside, along with a third young man carrying one more over his shoulders, with her Aunt Milagros shepherding her ill-fated flock.

Government troops had closed in on the meeting as it was about to end. People had fled in whatever direction their instincts led them. These four had come to the Sauris', bringing with them the stench of gunpowder and panic, guided by Milagros's certainty that there was no safer shelter in the world than that afforded by her family.

As if she had been forewarned, without a flicker of surprise, Emilia led them to the book-filled room next to Diego Sauri's ground-floor laboratory. She turned first to the most seriously injured youth, while Milagros buried her face in her hands, the first time her niece had seen her totally undone.

The young man was clutching his belly. Emilia loosened his grip to look beneath his clothing. Sure that he would require morphine, Emilia asked her father, who had just appeared, to bring it to her. Diego did not entirely approve of what he was hearing, but the mature confidence with which she asked him a second time to prepare a syringe caused him to turn and obey.

Emilia was taking the boy's pulse when her father returned with syringe, morphine, and the conviction that his daughter would not know how to administer it. But Emilia, who had ripped off the bottom of her petticoat to make a tourniquet for the lad's arm, held out her hand without a glance for his hesitation. She found the proper vein and injected the morphine as smoothly as a professional would have done. Then she stayed beside the stranger a moment, stroking his forehead and talking quietly to him.

Josefa came in with the rags and hot water and reported that Milagros had gone for Dr. Cuenca and listened to her daughter comment that she doubted very much anything could be done for the boy.

The young men who had carried him in did not have the least idea who he was. They said they had seen him running, and then he fell. They didn't even know how they had managed to carry him. They heard his cries above the shots raining all around them and the voice of Milagros calling for help. They had picked up that one because he was yelling, but there were many left behind on the ground.

Diego asked if any were dead, but they told him it wasn't a good time to hang around investigating the fate of others. Then they retreated into silence, pale from the emotions of the night.

Milagros returned with Dr. Cuenca. Recent years had hastened the decline of age, but his hands were still skillful. He immediately began to probe for the bullet in the boy's body.

"He's going to die anyway," whispered Emilia. "Why torture him?"

"That's something you never say," Dr. Cuenca reproved her. "Help me."

Emilia obeyed. She knew how obsessively Cuenca bore the medical standard, battling death to the very last moment. But she had seen the damage from the bullet and could not imagine it was possible to save the boy.

Both the Veytia sisters were sickened by the sight of blood, so they left Dr. Cuenca to his work, aided by Diego and Emilia. They did what they could to treat the less serious wounds of the other three youths, and to talk with them and calm their fears.

Two hours later, when it was clear that Dr. Cuenca had been right, Emilia stroked the sleeping boy's eyelids and kissed his face as if he were holy.

Watching Emilia, Diego Sauri did not detect a single tear, not one gesture of repulsion, during all that time. At moments he saw her blinking rapidly, as if that might erase the sight of the disembowelment that lay before her. And occasionally he saw her bite her lip till it bled. But she never trembled, never showed fear. She might have been an old woman inured to pain and its infamy. Only the circles under her eyes grew darker until they were two purple stains.

The wounded boy would have to stay under the Sauris' roof because he could not be moved. Emilia knew that, and she also knew that Daniel's father was counting on her to act as his patient's nurse. So she asked if she could be excused for a moment, and when she obtained his permission ran from the room as if chased by devils.

She went up the stairs two at a time, ran through the living room without a word to her mother and aunt, and rushed into the bathroom without stopping to close the door. Bile was rising from her stomach, and she could no longer hold it back. For long minutes that to her mother seemed eternal, the two women heard her vomiting interspersed with loud curses and distorted prayers.

DR. CUENCA HAD come upstairs behind her, as valiant and noble as a fine wine. He was not a man to call attention to himself or act the hero, but that evening he had won another battle, and its success was cause for allowing himself a loquacity and jubilation that in him were nearly scandalous.

"Is the girl vomiting?" he asked with a smile, stopping in the doorway.

Josefa Veytia nodded, and two large tears trickled down her face. Dr. Cuenca stepped into the room and lit a large cigar that had been rolled in Havana.

"There's a lot of vomiting before you become a doctor," he said, "but the girl has the talent and the passion. Feed her well and she'll make it."

Then he asked Josefa if he could have some of that tea she made to cure just about anything.

Diego Sauri seized the opportunity to look for brandy for himself and for his boneweary sister-in-law, who had just returned from checking on how things were with Emilia in the bathroom.

"Now all of a sudden she wants to be a doctor," he told Milagros as she accepted her brandy.

What followed was a bedlam of reproaches and questions. Steady as a rock, Dr. Cuenca explained that Emilia had traded her cello lessons for classes in medicine. They had mutually agreed to keep them secret for the pleasure of being free of observation and expectations, and Emilia had become a good student. Adding what she knew about pharmacology to what she had learned from Cuenca, she already knew at least a third of what she could be taught at a school of medicine.

"I feel like a deceived husband," said Diego, complaining about the secrecy. "You're going to have your dream of having a daughter who's a doctor."

"I hope so, I only wish she were my daughter. But I didn't have the blood to produce girls," said Cuenca, and changed the subject from Emilia to his constant preoccupation in recent times: war as augury and prudence as the last duty of an old man whose life had been lived in the most war-torn and painful century of Mexican life.

He feared things could not be reversed, but struggled to moderate the haste of those who practically guaranteed that a rebellion in Puebla would bring all the country along with it. He did not trust those who believed it would be easy to take the barracks, storm the stores, and instigate strikes, those who would let themselves be consumed by haste and excess over moderation and ideas. He held politics, the political enterprise, as the most generous of all undertakings, and patience above wrath. Like Diego, he distrusted men who were prepared to kill and to die and in the process destroy the habit of peace that to him was so precious. He did not believe like others that for the last thirty years things in Mexico had been fair. He believed that the dream had been betrayed, because life always betrays dreams. The republic his generation had dreamed of should have been democratic, egalitarian, rational, productive, open to new ideas and to progress. But he had grown old watching it turn into a kingdom for the extremely wealthy, still a land of inequality and authoritarianism. It was as it had been when he was born, the way it had been when his grandfather had fought to free the nations from Spanish colonialism—a society ruled by the most stubborn Catholicism and led by the favored, the privileged, and the politically powerful.

Even so, many things had changed. The world was a different one from that of thirty years before. Many things had not changed, but others changed so quickly that there was scarcely time to register it. There was poverty and stagnation everywhere, and, interwoven with that, wealth and change. And to top it off, the old insisted on governing a country that was by now a land of the young for whom the only world, the only passion, was the future.

They talked a long time that night of anguish and anxiety. Josefa had triple-locked the large front door, ensuring that if anyone among the beings for whom she lived and breathed wanted to remake the world within the next few hours, they would have to do so from her house using the peaceful arms of imagination and words.

Dr. Cuenca tried once, at about eleven, to leave, but as Señora Sauri refused to unlock the door until the light of dawn spilled freely through the streets of the city, he returned his hat to the hall stand and accepted his first brandy.

There was no reason to carry his sorrows elsewhere. Those who suffered for their country in the house that night were, in addition to his sons, his entire world, and for some time his sons had been roving the world looking for the politics and freedom they could not find at home.

CHAPTER

14

Emilia Sauri was not a participant in that council. She had left the bathroom and passed through the sala trailing a scent of flowers and aromatic herbs.

"I'm going to look after my patient," she said, and disappeared.

Her patient was sleeping. She checked his pulse, his temperature, and pulled up a chair to sit beside him and watch over him. She sat quietly in a spooky silence until she, too, fell asleep.

She had no idea how much time had passed when she was awakened by the sound of the lock on the front door slowly turning. She shuddered as she pictured the onslaught of the police whose force and barbarity she had heard so much about, but after her first thrill of fear, she remembered she had to protect the wounded man in her care, and went to the door. She watched as a chink of light appeared; she saw how the darkness of the street shrank the pale light of the lamp on their patio, and stood erect, waiting for a uniformed figure to order her to perform who knows what horror. The door opened wider and there stood Daniel, a shadowy figure draped in a peasant woman's rebozo, a disguise he had used before. She began to tremble as she had promised herself she would not do before the police.

They did not speak. Each lived hearing the echo of the other's voice, and voices now would be no release for the impetuous love they were occasionally allowed. Emilia's favorite fantasy was imagining herself taking Daniel's clothing off, piece by piece, and when she did that in the darkness that flooded over them, there was in her fingers an ancient skill and on the air that burned her lips a flame she knew was always waiting.

BEFORE DAWN, Dr. Cuenca slipped down to the study. As he walked into the still dark room, he was met by the ghostly figure and voice of his son Daniel. Just surfacing from their lovemaking, his son and Emilia were breathless and beautiful. Emilia could feel her cheeks blazing, and Daniel's heart was racing under the shirt he began to button.

"Making love like that can be harmful to the health," Dr. Cuenca said, with one of the few smiles he bestowed upon the world throughout his frugal existence.

TWO DAYS BEFORE, by government order, Madero had been arrested after delivering a speech they called "an incitement to rebellion and insult to authority." He was being held prisoner in San Luis Potosí, and there were orders to jail any and all of his dangerous friends throughout the exploding Republic, especially those older men who had been General Díaz's friends in the times of his republican youth. For them—for disagreeing, for being worse than the rebellious youths, for being traitors to Díaz—things would get worse, and quickly. Among them was Dr. Cuenca, something his sons realized better than anyone. They had met in San Antonio even before they'd imagined that Madero could be arrested and had decided to take their father somewhere safe, because to leave him in the hands of the group that met every Sunday did not seem the wisest course to follow. So Daniel had come to Puebla to take his father to the United States. Once in Puebla, he had thought it best to take Milagros Veytia as well, and, along with her, all three Sauris.

To his misfortune, his wishes were not orders, and he would find that none of the ones for whom he had made the trip wanted to go anywhere with him. None except Emilia, who in two hours' time had forgotten her nursing duties and was ready to follow Daniel wherever his whim might lead him.

"When it's light, we'll discuss it," Cuenca told them finally, to free himself from the reasons his son was offering.

He turned his attention to the wounded boy and called on Emilia to help him dress the wound. Daniel turned on the electric light Diego had installed in his office. Then watched as his father and Emilia gave themselves to their shared passion. He passed from feeling that he was the center of Emilia's life, the Emilia he had made love to that night, to being a mere bystander in a universe of cues and terms that was not only unknown to him but responsible for the first stirrings of a feeling he had never known: jealousy raged in him as his father and Emilia wove between them the most complicitous and perfect web he could have imagined. His father and his wife knew things about each other he didn't know, they shared a language he could not decipher. And watching them move in concert, sharing something that was entirely foreign to him, perturbed him so deeply that he did not know which of the two he loved more or which he hated less.

Emilia read the mind of that laconic man who had been like a father, and that father talked to her with a gentleness he had never shown his sons. Together they seemed to be dancing a pas de deux around the stranger to whom they were ministering as Daniel could not believe they would minister to him. Emilia loved another Cuenca besides him, and his father loved Emilia in a way he had never demonstrated to him.

Only when they finished did Emilia turn to Daniel a face lighted by the first rays of morning seeping through the window. Her hair was pulled back into a hasty braid and an aureole of new hair had escaped to frame her face. She gazed at him as one gazes at infinity, closed her eyes, and then quickly opened them in a wink with which she asked forgiveness for the hour of happy infidelity he had witnessed.

And Daniel forgave her. And loved her again with the same heart-twisting urgency he had felt as he turned the key that opened the lock to her house.

* * *

After breakfast, Dr. Cuenca agreed to leave the country with his son. He was too old to be running risks that did nothing but put others at risk. He did so because of his absolute certainty that Milagros, Rivadeneira, and the Sauris not only moved in his circle but were so closely linked with his name that they, too, were in danger.

Once again his house was being watched; it was not going to be easy to see his sons during the next months, perhaps years; and since his classes with Emilia had been discovered, he no longer had to worry too much about her education. Emilia was prepared now to seek the instruction she needed, and perhaps if he went ahead, the Sauris would soon allow their daughter to enroll in a university in the United States. Then, if luck was with them, and if the sun warmed the dictator's rusted heart, maybe Madero might be allowed to win the elections and he, Cuenca, could return to await the birth of a grandson who had the eyes of his student, Emilia Sauri.

Emilia would have preferred not to part from her mentor. She had enough with all the times she had to tell Daniel good-bye, so many that now even when he was near she could not allow herself the peace of knowing he was hers. She felt that almost as soon as he arrived, and they embraced, it was also their farewell. Because she looked for Daniel everywhere, she had fixed on his father as the nearest thing to him. To lose that comfort as well seemed a double punishment. She did not want to cry or complain in front of her mentor, though. She owed him so much. She had learned too well from his silences and his words that a good doctor never lets herself be crushed by pain; only as she hugged him could she shed the last tear of her childhood.

They had revealed their greatest secret, and yet after two years of knowing medicine to be one of the two essential passions for the girl who was half daughter, half accomplice of his self-centered old age, Dr. Cuenca took comfort in knowing they were bound by shared rituals.

He had taught her to be attentive to her patients' breathing, to listen keenly to the sound of their blood beneath the skin, to look into their eyes to discover the source of the illness afflicting them, to examine carefully the underside of their tongue, the top of their tongue, what that tongue told or kept silent. He had taught her that no one heals without the intense and single-minded desire to be a healer, that no doctor can allow himself to exist divorced from that desire. He had taught her that the lives of others, the pain of others, the relief of others, must rule the breathing, the early dawns, the courage and peace of every doctor. He had told her that a person's gut knows more than his heart, and that a person's head breathes the air the heart sees fit to send it. He had convinced her that no one survives a wish to die, and that there is no illness that can kill someone who is determined to live.

In addition, he had gifted her with the one asset an unremunerative profession could offer, the more than a hundred personal discoveries from his long commitment to medicine and its enigmas. Emilia knew where every screw went that held the body together. She knew the color of the internal organs, how the blood flowed and through which arteries and veins, which murmurings explained which pains. She knew how to extract babies from the blue cave in which their mothers guarded them for nine months, she knew how to stitch wounds, reduce inflammation, stop diarrhea. She already knew that the paths of human suffering lack a set course and sometimes have no end. But she also knew that suffering could be eased, that from the beginnings of time humanity had found ways to relieve pain, that there was no absolute medical truth, and that there was always something new to be learned from others' research.

"We doctors know nothing except what we continue to learn," said Cuenca, turning to leave without saying good-bye.

Daniel took his father's arm, and once again gazed helplessly at Emilia.

"You know what I have to say," he told her.

"You're going off to war?"

"There won't be any war," said Daniel. Emilia wanted to believe every word.

THE NEXT WEEKS were difficult for everyone. After the elections, Milagros Veytia was so drained and so despondent that for several days she could not even pull a comb through her hair. She moved all her things into her sister's house because the solitude she had adored rang in her head like the clanging of a frying pan. Before she moved, the poet Rivadeneira had been so tormented by Milagros's refusal to go on the promised trip that he decided to go anyway, in yet another of his daily attempts to find a way to live without her.

Well before the election, it was clear there would be fraud. Neither Diego's nor Josefa's nor Milagros's name appeared on the lists the law required be published one week before the voting. And, like them, many others never received cards authorizing them to vote.

The "friendly" guards had disappeared from the jails. Since her arrest, Milagros had not been able to go out alone without running the risk of being arrested a second time. All three Sauris replaced her in the work of buying freedom for Madero supporters. But even Emilia, calling on the tricks she had used to save Daniel, was able to set only one prisoner free.

Then one day they arrested the only son of the woman who every week came to the Casa de la Estrella to pick up Diego's shirts and every week returned them starched and ironed white as sugar. Her tears fell like summer showers the day she told them her son had been taken to the train station and that it could only mean they were shipping him off to die.

Since her parents were busy listening to one of Milagros's speeches, Emilia went with her to the train station to look for someone, anyone at all. It was growing dark as they walked onto the platform. The magnificent engine shuddered into life, throwing heavy steam into the air. Emilia breathed it in, let it circulate through her lungs, and thought she felt the echo of a secret voyage. Her feet, her tongue, her throat were light as that air as she flew in search of the man in charge of the carload of prisoners. She climbed the steps and banged on the door, insulting her mouth with the arrogant screech of a demanding *patrona*. She added the name of Sol's husband to her own and unhesitatingly wielded the influence of the family that owned more than half the state. She said that the boy who was Doña Silvina the washerwoman's son was a servant in her house and that she could not imagine any reason for his being held prisoner. When they told her it was because he had been leading a strike, she reacted with a show of surprise. She stared at the guard with the superior gaze that horrified her in Sol's inlaws and declared that was impossible, she had seen him around the house for the last five months, day and night. Having convinced the military man in charge of the train station of her family's position, she took the boy with her, after signing her borrowed name to the papers that made her responsible for his life and loyalty to his country.

Doña Silvina was so grateful that the next morning she presented herself in Emilia's house with one of her nine daughters. As payment for the return of her sole male child, she thought it only fair to hand over one of her girls. The child was a waif of thirteen, undernourished and pale, who smiled with a mixture of timidity and self-importance as her mother explained to Emilia the reasons for her offering. Emilia did not know what to say. She knew that it was a great insult not to accept a gift from someone poor. But from that to accepting the woman's daughter as if she were a plucked hen was a gargantuan leap.

For a moment the verbal facility that had stood her in such good stead the previous day deserted her. She stared at Doña Silvina as if trying to determine what she was made of. She looked at the daughter, trying to summon the words for an answer, and dug her fingernails into the palm of her closed fist until the child interrupted the meandering path of Emilia's pain with her hoarse doubts.

"Don't you love me?" she heard the child ask.

Emilia answered that it wasn't that, and saw the girl's nervous smile turn to satisfaction as she told her mother to go on home. The woman uttered her thanks once again and was nearly out the door before Emilia tugged at her apron and said she couldn't do this. Emilia spun a verbal skein of lace to explain why she could not take the daughter. Doña Silvina did not understand, but in the end accepted her reasons, convinced more by Emilia's tears than by the flow of honeyed words.

When finally they left, Emilia ran to look for Milagros, who was editing a manifesto calling for a meeting to protest electoral chicanery. Writing was now her sole consolation, and she wrote manifestos every day and at all hours—whether or not they were published, whether or not they ever left her disorderly desk.

"You would have done her a favor to keep her," said Milagros. "She must be half-starved."

Emilia remembered the child, her half-pleading, half-complacent expression, and thought that maybe Milagros was right. But she also was convinced she was more at peace for having refused.

"Peace is what we don't have," said Milagros, waving away the brush Emilia had picked up to use on her aunt's hair.

First she braided the thick hair in which more and more white was showing, and then twisted it into a nearly perfect chignon. Time had chipped away at Milagros's beauty, but her features were as striking, arrogant, and noble as in her wild younger days.

Josefa had always said that intelligence was the canvas on which life painted her sister's face. And looking into her eyes that morning, Emilia recognized that truth above any other spoken of her aunt.

Disheartened intelligence is dangerous, however, and Emilia was sad to hear Milagros predicting catastrophes. The Apocalypse, and an abysmal despair Emilia was not prepared to accept as her future, resounded in her aunt's voice. So she set herself the task of contradicting the predictions Milagros saw so clearly in her personal crystal ball.

Emilia devoted the rest of the morning to listening to Milagros as no one had listened in a long, long time, and bet the twenty-two inches of her flyaway black mane that Madero would be the next president of Mexico, even though neither Milagros nor her father—nor, apparently, God the Father or Coatlicue—believed it possible.

"And I will bet you the light of my left eye it *doesn't* happen," Milagros said, amused by her niece's offer. Then she went to the desk that had belonged to her father and rifled through one of the drawers.

"Here," she said, holding out an unopened envelope addressed to Emilia in Daniel's writing. "Someone can still protect you from this life."

THE DISCUSSION Milagros and Emilia's parents had been having when she left them the night before had to do with that envelope. The three of them knew what must be in it, because with it Milagros had received a letter from Dr. Cuenca commenting on the one in her hand. As soon as they deduced what the letter contained, the Sauris had wanted to hide it from Emilia as long as possible. In that conversation, Milagros had tried to convince them that it is not possible to block out the sun with a finger, much less an unsteady finger, but Josefa had won out in the end, convincing Milagros that it was better to wait.

The one concession Milagros had won from her sister was that she would be the one to keep the letter. Along with the right to decide when she could wait no longer.

In the letter, with the same straightforward manner he had in past months written about the climate in Chicago, the latest film by Chaplin, or the plots of the novels he had been reading, with the same quick irony with which one day he had recounted the story of the founder of the Boy Scout movement and another described the size of the Manhattan Bridge, which would be completed later that year, Daniel's irregular and cheerful handwriting communicated to Emilia that for a while she would not be receiving any further news from him. Madero had broken loose from the confines of house arrest in San Luis Potosí and arrived in Texas. From there, he and others opposed to the reelection of Díaz had sent out a document declaring the elections invalid and calling for an insurrection to begin precisely at six o'clock P.M. on November 20. Daniel was going to cross the border to Chihuahua and join a group of muleteers and miners who would form one force in the uprising destined to awaken the country from its lethargy.

After that announcement, Daniel recommended that Emilia read the third symphony of an Austrian Jew capable of commanding twenty horns and sixteen trombones in an orchestra. "If he weren't from Vienna he would be from Guamúchil." Then he went on to say goodbye with a kiss for her visible lips and another for the smile below.

Emilia read the letter slowly, folded it with a circumspection that surprised her aunt, then surprised her again. "Rivadeneira will be here at three for dinner," she said, and smiled the smile of a well-behaved child. Then she went to her bedroom, took out the cello she had set aside, and embraced it, caressing it with her bow and drawing from it a beautiful, lugubrious sound that sang the burning pain she was determined not to express in words.

It was the end of October, and Sol had not returned from her honeymoon. Rivadeneira had run into her in New York, pleasant, bored, and exquisitely turned out. He did not want to say it, but it was the vision of that couple that had sent him bounding home like a deer to the unpredictable Milagros Veytia. He wanted to be with her forever, and with great ceremony, a toast, and a speech at the end of the meal, he asked whether he might grow old by her side.

"Rivadeneira, my love. I am sorry to say that we have already grown old together," Milagros replied.

A week later she moved into the large house on Reforma that smelled of old manuscripts and a solitary man.

CHAPTER

15

THE REVOLUTION DID not begin at six P.M. on November 20, but it began. Many different times on many days following the morning of the eighteenth in Puebla. That morning, the government ordered a raid on the houses of certain anti-Reelectionists who had long been under suspicion. Alerted, Aquiles, Máximo, and Carmen Serdán, known to be the most radical of the rebel leaders in Puebla, awaited the arrival of the military, prepared to start the rebellion two days early.

It was eight in the morning when the knocking came at the door. As if happy to receive a visitor, the Serdáns opened without a moment's hesitation. A man with eyes like a crow, known to everyone as the chief of police, walked into the patio of the house on Calle Santa Clara with a pistol in his hand. He stopped short when he found himself facing Aquiles, carbine in hand, and without a word fired a shot. The bullet missed completely, and Serdán did not wait for a second. He squeezed his trigger and shot the police chief dead. Some of the chief's subordinates ran toward the interior of the house and others fled. One of those who ran inside started up the stairway toward Aquiles. Then Aquiles's sister, Carmen, dressed in white and with her hair tied back at her neck, stepped into his path, her gun pointed at his chest. The man asked her not to fire.

"Then give me your pistol," Carmen replied, her aim never wavering.

Obedient, the soldier retreated down the few steps he had climbed and dropped his weapon. His chief lay dead in the patio, like a specter, arms flung wide and eyes protruding.

Everyone in the house realized that in very short order there would be a ferocious attack. Sixteen of the Serdáns' friends barricaded themselves along with the family on the roof of the home, behind large clay water jars or behind the rim of the flat roofs. Soon afterward an overwhelming number of police opened fire on the house.

Milagros Veytia was drinking coffee in Josefa's kitchen when the distant shots broke a tense silence. The gunfire was coming from the church of Santa Clara, across from the Serdáns' home. There could be no mistake. As soon as she heard it, the first thing that occurred to Milagros was to run outside and try to reach her friends' house. The police, however, had closed off the neighborhood and were stationed on the roofs of the churches, preventing the arrival of any form of help. As the airwaves communicated the progress of the unequal, intense battle, Milagros cursed the poet Rivadeneira for having refused to visit the Serdáns the night before, and sank into inconsolable grief.

Diego Sauri closed his pharmacy and went upstairs to tear his hair out in the company of his family. No need to say what had not been said; no need to hope to avert what was inescapably predictable and dark. The Serdáns, along with everyone in the house, could not defend themselves for long.

A few of the rural guard loyal to the government climbed onto the roof of the church of San Cristóbal on the side of the Serdáns' house that was crackling with furious gunfire. After a half hour of shooting, they succeeded in inflicting damage. At almost the same time, an army squadron attacked from atop a hotel on the other side of the house, and a second scaled the walls of the orphanage behind the flat roofs from which the rebels were shooting.

Milagros listened to the skirmish slumped on the floor, biting her fingernails and loathing the world. Emilia sat beside her, stroking her head in a vain hope she could calm her.

"We should be there. Dying with them," Milagros said at one point in her disjointed conversation with her brother-in-law. The pharmacist Sauri refused to feel guilty that he neither had a weapon nor wanted one.

"An absolute prohibition against killing a fellow human being should be the basic principle of any coherent ethical code. No one has the right to kill anyone," he said, as he always did when he needed an argument to oppose war.

"You talk as if there were some other way," Milagros responded.

"There must be another way. I don't want to be a hero. Heroism is worship of murder."

For more than two hours the sound of the bloody battle tormented their ears. Then gradually the shots began to thin out, and silence like a prophecy fell over the city.

Máximo Serdán and nearly all the rooftop defenders were dead. Carmen advised her brother Aquiles. His mouth twisted in a grimace his sister would carry in her memory for the rest of her life, and he stopped firing. A number of the rural guard moved toward the front entrance. Beside herself over her brother Máximo's death, Carmen said to Aquiles, "Look, let's finish them off."

He merely stared at her, disconsolate.

"Their leaders are not with them. If I knew that the death of these men meant we would win, I would kill them all, but the jig is up for us, no matter what," he said, taking off his overcoat. "I'm going to look for somewhere to ride this out."

While Aquiles looked for a hiding place, Carmen continued to fire from the window until Filomena, Aquiles's pregnant wife, tugged at her skirt and forced her to stop. Speaking quietly, she led her to the room where she and the Serdán brothers' mother had taken refuge throughout the battle.

About then the Federales broke down the door and rushed into the house. Searching for Aquiles, one of the officers came to the room where the women were gathered and took them prisoner.

Hiding in a cold basement and sweating from the combat, Aquiles caught a chill that within a few hours turned into pneumonia. By midnight, he could no longer keep from coughing. The men standing guard in the dining room, where the trapdoor to the cellar was covered by a rug, heard him. An officer lifted the door to the cellar, located him, and fired at point-blank range. The result of the rebellion: twenty dead, four wounded, seven prisoners, and defeat.

In the following days, two hundred soldiers arrived from Mexico City. More than three hundred militiamen descended upon the city, mustered from various towns in the mountains; the chief of the military zone bought up all existing weapons from local dealers to prevent them from falling into the hands of his enemies; and the pay of the Zaragoza battalion rose to thirty-seven centavos per day for common soldiers. The government ordered local political leaders to hand in two reports daily detailing any unusual activity in their districts.

As if further intimidation were needed, the authorities put the body of Aquiles Serdán on display. Milagros insisted on going to see it. Rivadeneira went with her, clinging like a shadow. They came home staring at the stones of the sidewalk, leaning on each other.

"He chose the best way," said Milagros as they crossed the threshold of the world that would be their shelter.

THE REBELLION IN PUEBLA was a failure, but it spread through the country like wildfire. By the time of Emilia's birthday in February 1911, the rebels in Chihuahua had driven the federal army from their land and extended their movement to the mining region in eastern Sonora state. There were uprisings everywhere. Many failed, but then others picked up the cause, and many more celebrated in private the success of their victories.

The first letter from Daniel after the conflict arrived by regular mail, dirty and well traveled, at the end of April. He had mailed it in a post office in a village in northern Zacatecas. It was signed with a "ME" in large letters and was a list of "I love yous" and "I miss yous" with no further details and no target but the heart of "Doctor Sauri."

"Me, a doctor? All I needed was *that* lie to top off his list," said

Emilia. For months she had been cursing the uncertain times that kept her from attending the university to study to become a real doctor. Her father kept telling her that doctors are not made with diplomas, and that if she knew how to cure sick people she would be a doctor, whether authorities at the university wanted it or not. In fact, he could testify that there was more than one owner of a diploma who couldn't cure a simple scratch.

To escape the rigors of life in the Republic, and of arguing with her father, Emilia had again started working mornings in the pharmacy. In the afternoons, she ran like water to her new teacher. That newcomer, Dr. Zavalza, placed at her small feet his person and his knowledge, and invited her to observe during his consultations.

In contrast to Daniel, who shone brilliantly but in bursts—and who had been absent now since the previous year—Zavalza's less extreme but more generous nature grew on Emilia; she saw him as an intelligent and good man, one of those who, as Josefa said, are few and far between.

Besides, Emilia could not have found a better teacher. Zavalza had an endless store of knowledge and shared it without making a show of it. He liked what Dr. Cuenca had taught Emilia and enjoyed listening to the ethical arguments she had learned by heart from the aged maestro. Between patients, Emilia sprinkled the consulting room with Cuenca's maxims and aphorisms, and Zavalza listened the way one listens to a sonata by Bach. Her voice had enchanted him the first time he heard it, so much so that at night, when his silent bachelor's chamber would not allow him peaceful sleep, he closed his eyes and heard her voice like the echo of desire. Her voice rang of crystal and ruin, and she sang the final syllable of her words as those do who have lived every hour of their lives among bells. And if that weren't enough, she was fascinated by the same driving curiosity about medicine that had caused Zavalza to forget about the money and commerce, travel and estates, power and inheritance meant for him. His father had yielded to his whim to be a doctor, but he had always believed that when his son completed the degree he would choose the comfort of administering an inheritance over the purgatory of the putrescence and discouragement that can fill a doctor's life. The father's blessing was to die before having to do battle with his son's determination to follow his profession. He left that fight to his brother, the bishop of Puebla, a cleric for whom Zavalza had no respect and would never have obeyed. He much preferred to devote his talent and his time to disagreeing with the bishop and to learning everything yet to be learned about medicine. Besides, in recent months, he could enjoy listening to Emilia tell him things he already knew with the fervor of someone discovering them as precious new information.

Watching Zavalza, Emilia verified the things she had learned from Cuenca. Every afternoon she rediscovered that no two human beings are alike, and surprised her friend by suggesting remedies to cure what his science could not cure. She was intuitive and decisive, simple and alert. She talked about Maimonides, the physician of ancient times whose books her father venerated, as if he were an old acquaintance, and about medicinal herbs doña Nastasia sold in the market; with the same enthusiasm she listened to Zavalza tell of recent discoveries by Austrian and North American doctors.

All medicine, she agreed with Zavalza, even that which bases its doctrine on abstractions and its reasoning on inferences, has something to teach. From metaphysics to observation, all methods seemed good to them. Emilia learned not to disdain anything. Least of all the language of facts, which finds something unique in every change, even if that knowledge derives from general doctrines. To heal, she believed, you use anything from the doctor's hand on the patient's head to her papa's Tolú pills and headache plasters. To heal: from a long conversation to opium capsules. To heal: from soap and water to tartaric acid. To heal: from powdered marshmallow root to the discoveries of Dr. Liceaga, a friend with whom Zavalza corresponded every week, whether from Mexico City or Saint-Nazaire, where he had traveled for the purpose of studying everything known at the time about the rabies virus. To heal: from the navelwort tea recommended by Doña Casilda, the Indian midwife who spoke Spanish only to insult, to the indispensable pasqueflower of the homeopaths. From the *xtabetún* Diego Sauri had sent from his islands when a patient came to him with kidney stones to small doses of arsenic or Chinese massage on a patient's toes.

In early May 1911, Diego Sauri received a letter from Dr. Cuenca. As he read it, he felt the walls of his pharmacy and all its apothecary jars whirling around him. In his ornate and trembling hand, Cuenca communicated his fear that Daniel was either a prisoner or dead. Diego ran to tell the news to Josefa and they agreed that Emilia should not be told one word. They spent several sleepless nights, until the evening that Milagros and the poet Rivadeneira returned from an extremely difficult trip to San Antonio, bringing with them Cuenca's apologies for having alarmed them for nothing. Daniel was safe and the rebels were taking city after city.

That night the Sauris slept for nine hours in a row, but Diego awoke as exhausted as if he himself had attacked Ciudad Juárez, for when Milagros had told him about its capture, she had filled his ears with descriptions that made blood run as copiously through his dreams as must be flowing throughout the country—with no way to avoid it and no way to stop it.

"If you defend yourself, it's still murder," he told Josefa at dawn. The monster loves masks.

Josefa turned over and slowly kissed Diego's moist brow and dry lips. She, too, was terrified by the war, the ripped feather pillow of their democratic dreams.

Milagros and Rivadeneira returned from San Antonio with a confidence they had lost during the repressions of November. They spent days busily putting out a clandestine newspaper. Josefa suspected that they also were working as go-betweens for the revolutionary cells and the men daring enough to sell them weapons and mounts.

They heard rumors of uprisings in textile factories, of strikes in cotton mills, of haciendas and villages that were the scenes of skirmishes and deaths. Emiliano Zapata, leader of the revolutionaries in Morelos, found devoted followers in Puebla, who in bands of several hundred each fought to take over towns and the Ferrocarril Interoceánico rail lines. Every day the government tried to belittle these incidents, saying they were the work of common murderers and thieves, not rebels.

The Church came down squarely on the side of the government, and sermons against the revolt were preached from every pulpit. Zavalza and his uncle the bishop had a falling-out, which the Sauris celebrated by inviting the doctor to dinner. They drank their last glass of port at four in the morning, with Diego recycling his pacifist speeches, Josefa humming a popular song about Madero, and Emilia dancing with Zavalza, free of memories, and happy.

One afternoon at the end of May, Milagros came in with news burning her tongue. Porfirio Díaz had resigned. She could not say it enough, as if repeating it would make it believable at last.

The next day, the aged dictator sailed for Europe from the port of Veracruz.

"They have unleashed a tiger," he proclaimed before boarding the ship that would carry him into exile.

"That's all I need, to end up agreeing with him," Diego Sauri muttered as he busied himself among his bottles and eyedroppers in the room behind his shop.

SOME WEEKS LATER, Emilia found her father clutching the breakfast newspapers with greater than usual fervor. A truce had been declared. The Revolution had triumphed, and peace accords were to be signed that would lay the groundwork for a provisional government.

Emilia passed her hand over his head and sat beside him to drink her coffee and listen to his predictions. Nothing could compare to her father at that hour of the morning, there was nothing like the scent of his freshly soaped neck, the light in his seer's eyes.

"You will have to decide," Diego told her, concluding a long dissertation on the possibilities of the government that would be headed by Madero. He did not have to say more.

They were enjoying their last swallows of coffee when Josefa burst in with the news that Madero would enter Mexico City on June 7. Milagros and Rivadeneira were going to witness the spectacle of the welcome and wanted permission to take Emilia.

"The girl makes her own decisions now," Diego replied, knowing that his daughter would go even if they made the error of saying no.

On the fifth, the three of them left on a train plagued with surprises. When not stopped by mounted men trying to climb aboard, horses and all, they were stopped by hacienda owners trying to climb aboard, hacienda and all.

"Don't ever forget a minute of this, because you'll never see anything like it again," Milagros told Emilia.

The poet Rivadeneira had a brand-new apparatus for taking photographs, and Milagros's admonitions were in his view the perfect accompaniment to the images he was recording through the eye of his camera.

In Mexico City, they stayed in the Colonia Roma in a small house belonging to an English friend of Rivadeneira's. He had left for Europe the previous November, once he saw what was awaiting the regime with which he had enjoyed such good business relations. As he told Rivadeneira and Milagros good-bye, the Englishman promised he would return as soon as everything calmed down, and left the next day, as if going on vacation.

He told them to think of the house as their own, and they cared for it exactly as if it were, ocasionally living there for brief periods. It was a beautiful small house in the French style, like most of the houses in that zone. To add to the decorative excesses, Milagros had scattered pre-Hispanic idols and pots around the sala.

Their first night there, they were wakened by an earthquake that shook the city at 4:26 A.M.

Emilia was sleeping alone in a bedroom where the rose crystals of the chandelier began to reverberate like a tiny maddened campanile. Milagros ran in to tell her not to be afraid, and found her still in bed, captive to the strange thrill of watching everything sway as her iron bed rocked like a cradle. She had been seduced by tremors ever since she was a little girl, and was not afraid of them. She had inherited that detachment from Milagros, who during the three minutes the quake lasted walked around the house, experiencing the sensation and laughing at the rage with which Rivadeneira berated her for not immediately running outside.

"Don't you understand that this city is built over water? It's an aberration. Everything can collapse and kill us," he repeated over and over after the earth and he had stopped trembling. They did not go back to sleep. Madero was scheduled to enter the city at ten, but they left the house by seven. They bought newspapers and settled in to read them in a Chinese café near Reforma. With their large cups of milk and a basket of breakfast breads, they read and talked for more than two hours. Then they tried to go to the station, but men on horseback, a mix of recent rebels and perpetual peons, refused to let them pass. So they went to the Alameda Central and walked around until, about eleven, the news filtered through to the bench where they were resting that Señor Madero's train was nearing the platform. By twelve-thirty they had managed to squeeze into the crowd standing along Reforma near the statue of Columbus.

People had clambered up on the monuments and it was impossible to see exactly which hero was concealed beneath the bodies clustered on shoulders and knees, hanging from arms, and treading on toes. Cheers for Madero rippled through the crowd, and everything was one unceasing, chaotic roar. After standing two hours in the boiling sun, Rivadeneira had the brilliant idea that they should go back home. Instead of listening to him, Emilia climbed up on the statue of Columbus. The catlike hand of a young man lifted her off the ground, and she scaled the statue with her skirt clamped between her teeth, revealing her legs to loud whistles.

Once ensconced, she waved at Milagros Veytia, who was leaning with strange formality on Rivadeneira's arm. Then she concentrated on the stream of sombreros and horses passing before her eyes. Dust-covered and dark, the men gave the impression of wearing uniforms, even though no two were dressed alike. Wide-brimmed sombreros with pointed crowns were interspersed with military caps and tangled hair wet with sweat. Suddenly, between a rotund man with cartridge belts crisscrossing his chest and a tall man dressed as if by Señor Madero's own tailor, Emilia saw the only person who interested her among that throng. He sat his horse gracefully, with an almost juvenile air of elegance.

"Daniel!" she screamed, deafening the others clinging to the statue with her. And that one heretical yell amid the general uproar was enough to make the mercurial youth grinning beneath a huge straw sombrero so like the many others turn in the direction of her voice and see someone waving and leaning toward him as if she could reach him from where she was.

With an exclamation of surprise, Daniel checked his horse, whipped off his sombrero, and searched the crowd for the owner of the voice calling his name. Emilia once again secured her skirt in her teeth and hopped down from the statue like a bird. Shoving and pushing, feeling she was drowning one minute and flying the next, she reached the edge of the crowd lining the street and held out her hand toward Daniel, who on the other side of the wall of shoulders and heads offered his hand to help her slip through. They threw their arms around each other and kissed right there in the middle of all the shouting, the finest moment of the spectacle that had spilled into the streets of the city. Emilia's tongue pushed into Daniel's mouth.

To get as close as he could to the perfume of her body, Daniel placed one hand behind a neck regal as a scepter. He smelled of days of hard riding, and Emilia tasted dust in the ear she was slowly kissing. The column of men and horses parted around them as they hugged and whirled around in a circle. Emilia stroked Daniel's back as if she owned time. Then her hand explored his chest muscles, and from there slipped inside the trousers hanging loosely from his gaunt body. She caressed the skin of his firm buttocks. But only for a breath. Summoned by yells from his disappearing companions, Daniel removed his hand from her neck, his lips from hers, and pulled away from the hand searching beneath his clothing.

"I have to go," he murmured.

"Always," said Emilia, turning her back to him.

Before he remounted his horse, Daniel promised to look for her that night.

"I hate you," she said.

"Liar," he replied.

Motionless in the middle of the path of horses and men captive to a different passion, Emilia watched Daniel fade back into the parade. As he rode away, his face showed a mixture of relief and pride.

From a distance, Milagros had watched the whole scene as she struggled to make her way to the edge of the sidewalk. Hearing Milagros call her name, as if cheering her, Emilia was shaken back to reality. She fought back toward Milagros's arms, mouthing the insults Daniel had left too quickly to hear, and cursing the rest of the parade.

Because it was always the same: always a glimpse and then abandonment, always a surprise and then departure, always the waiting as the one constant in her destiny.

"But destiny is what is yet to happen to you," said Milagros, putting her arms around her. "It's never the same."

A few minutes later, Madero passed by. Afterward, even Rivadeneira and his camera were enveloped in the euphoria of thousands of people celebrating hope. Nothing was certain yet, nothing except the future. From that time forward, all that lay ahead was unbounded dreams, and at that moment few could imagine that nothing is as bounded as a dream fulfilled.

They got back home after five. Exhausted, as if they had fought the war fought by the men they had watched file by. Emilia had time to give Daniel the address where she was staying, but when dark began to creep through the windows and they had to turn on the lights, she said she didn't want to see him anymore. Not that night, not any night. She remembered the affront of the urgency that had torn him from her that morning. She had sensed in his body a fire that more than ever she recognized as a rival, something that was totally separate from her.

She was discouraged to be jealous of something so amorphous and yet so implacable. One part of Daniel, the man she had thought she knew inside and out, was escaping her, was always going to escape her, because she did not understand it, because that part of Daniel had grown from the lives and battles of others, but it was so intense that it had spread through his body, filling places she had once filled.

During the early hours of the night, Milagros and Rivadeneira waited with Emilia while she talked about her conflicting emotions and about her unequivocal anger, listing her feelings and describing them with a nearly scientific precision. They listened to her elaborate her feelings, unable to believe, considering their niece's vehemence, how it was possible she had gained those insights during an embrace that lasted two minutes, and were little convinced that their words could calm her before they drifted into a remote dream.

Emilia waited all night for Daniel. From time to time, Milagros or

Rivadeneira waked and said something to break their niece's vigil, until she took mercy on them and, as if they were a pair of children, led them to bed. She turned out the light and returned to the sala. She wasn't sleepy. Desire is an enemy of sleep, and Daniel wasn't coming, never came.

Alone, beneath the funereal gaze of a saint painted during the time of the colonies, Emilia longed for the peace of her bottles and books, for the quiet diligence of Antonio Zavalza, for his mouth, a balm that would soothe her longing for Daniel.

When they awoke with the sun the next morning, Milagros and Rivadeneira found Emilia still dressed, bleary eyed, and skeptical. To cheer her up, they decided to tour the city, spoil her, buy her things she had never dreamed of wanting. That was their plan, and a successful one, for dredging a wounded heart from the swamp of despair. So it was not until night that Emilia finally wept out all her rage.

Three days later, without having seen a hair of Daniel's head, they took the train back to Puebla. Emilia was wearing new clothes from her skin out and an extravagant, arrogant smile only disappointment can engender—disappointment, that is, mixed with shopping in the City of Palaces. When Josefa saw her daughter coming toward her down the platform, she told her bedazzled husband:

"God save Zavalza from that smile."

CHAPTER

16

NOTHING WAS as changeable in those days as routine. The world outside the pharmacy and its unvarying aromas was coming unraveled, and everything that had been anticipated there among its bottles was coursing through the country, disturbing even the atmosphere.

An interim government was preparing for new elections to be held in October 1911. Every morning, the newspapers, newly awakened to their freedoms, insulted whoever seemed the best target. And every evening, some group that disputed the results of their first war again took up arms against the fearsome determination that had animated the rebel troops but not gained anything for them.

In the Sauris' house, the future of the country was discussed as matter-of-factly as the day's chores in other homes, and the pharmacy resembled a rowdy cantina where the customers dissolved their loyalties and ambitions before going upstairs to continue the discussion over the bean pot Josefa kept going for anyone who passed through her dining room.

Everyone had their own account of offenses and their own assessments of misfortunes; of what they were witnessing, everyone believed what looked best, and, of what they didn't know, what they wanted to imagine. But everyone, everyone, agreed that Madero and the officials who had been installed to prepare new elections were totally ineffectual in trying to guard themselves from the claws of a tiger unwilling to be placated if it was not being fed.

The city, and perhaps—who knew?—the entire country, was in the grip of the same people who had fought for power in the past, with the added vexation that now you didn't know who was who, what was behind the words of a millionaire Díaz supporter who'd converted to a passion for Madero, or what was behind the rage of a disillusioned Madero loyalist who kept a good pistol as he turned in, as proof of his confidence in the government, a bad rifle.

Taking advantage of such chaos, conservatives returned to the political fray, hoping to use the new circumstances to obtain a governor close to their interests. And to oppose them, the revolutionaries could think of nothing but to destroy each other. Instead of choosing a single candidate, each group put up a different one, until Madero succeeded in imposing his own choice.

Diego Sauri was distraught, maddened. During the day he listened to all the news and tirelessly discussed it with anyone who came into view. At night he slept mulling over that news, as if he thought that by thinking about it so much he could dilute the strength of his fear.

Josefa, who was cooking for an unpredictable number of daily visitors, left to Milagros the responsibility of reading the newspapers, gathering the bad news, and keeping her up to date about any horror that happened. To her misfortune, Milagros performed her duty fully. She felt she was obliged to do so because, among other things, she and Rivadeneira ate there every day. Milagros never learned to contend with the kitchen, and it seemed ridiculous at her age to pretend to be interested in something she considered so ethereal. She would arrive at an early hour with a pile of newspapers and a pencil, and spend an hour before breakfast and two afterward reading even the advertisements. As soon as she finished, she presented Josefa with a résumé of the worst occurrences, a list of the most horrible headlines, and a description of the bloodiest caricatures. By that time she had fewer political duties and more doubts than ever. She did not know what group to join, and although she did not agree with the way Madero was operating, she did not want to oppose him, hoping that his good intentions would outweigh the perverse innocence he displayed after coming to power.

"Some of Rivadeneira's idiotic sanity must be infecting me," she told Josefa a few days before July 13, the date Madero was scheduled to visit Puebla again.

Her help had been essential in organizing the new visit, but she had not put half her characteristic energy into it. Of course, many recent Madero converts would gather at the train station, along with a few passionate supporters, most of them complaining, people who wanted to recount problems they were still suffering from. Milagros and the Sauris did not plan to show themselves at all. Despite the supposed peace, there were still sounds of war in the air, and they were too disillusioned to go out and cheer for anyone.

Josefa limited herself to counting the number of shots she sometimes heard in the distance. She knew with absolute precision when they were coming from the north and when from the south, when from the factories near Tlaxcala, when from the fields on the way to Cholula and when, as in the long night of July 12, from a place as nearby as the Plaza de Toros.

Very early on the morning of July 13, while the chords of Emilia's cello reverberated on the air and Josefa was assiduously stirring a stew, Milagros came in with news of the day's dead. It seemed unbelievable, but federal troops, troops of Madero's provisional government, had killed more than a hundred Maderistas.

The rest of that day went by without a word from anyone. As silence thickened into tension, Madero himself came to town.

Everyone waited for the man to publicly condemn the federal army for murdering his followers. But no such thing happened.

"You can't be neutral when people are killed in your name," Diego said that night with a deep frown between his eyes.

That frown wasn't there before, Josefa thought when she saw it, now ineradicable, the next morning.

DURING THOSE MONTHS, Emilia heard the most extreme opinions about the most extraordinary events of her life. When she was in the dining room, she kept busy writing them all down, and when someone changed his mind without anyone's seeming to notice, she took out her notebook and recorded the new thesis without taking time to criticize the inconsistency. Her father had friends who ten times within a four-week period changed from loyalty to Madero to anti-Madero fury, and back again.

She had given herself that task as consolation for her own doubts. If people changed their political orientation so often, why couldn't she detest Daniel's memory one morning and long the next night to be pressed to his sex?

For weeks the same questions had been circling through her mind, although she dared not repeat them to anyone. Everyone was too preoccupied by larger questions. Who cared whether Daniel came back or what he might have become?

One morning in mid-August, she went downstairs to the pharmacy, groggy with doubts, alone, because her mother claimed that she saw the weariness of the last months in the circles under Diego's eyes and had made him stay in bed to rest awhile. Emilia left them eating a late breakfast and told her father she would take his place behind the counter that morning.

She opened the front door, filled some prescriptions, and propped the sliding ladder against the shelves. The ladder was oak and always shone as if it had just been varnished. They used it to dust the porcelain jars that dazzled against the white walls. Standing on the top step, she began to run a clean cloth over them, one by one. What would become of her if Daniel never came back?

His memory was engraved on her fingertips. Some mornings she actually believed she was running her hands down his back. Even so, she sometimes had fantasies about losing him. When reason denied her peace, she fantasized about his death. Then, amid a calm distantly shadowed by guilt, scenes flowed before her like a river: What if someone suddenly advises me he's dead? What if someone knocks at the door and hands me a telegram? What if the next letter I open brings a sympathy note from a friend explaining the details of the skirmish that killed him, telling me about the last hours of his life, how with his last words he seemed to speak my name?

She pictured him dead and at the same time closer than ever, unable to leave her, bound to her every time her mouth called him, her body shivering with the certainty that his ghostly arms would enfold her anytime she wished.

She was swimming in that fantasy when a small boy with dark eyes and alarmed eyebrows came screaming into the pharmacy. His mother's face, he said, was purple, and instead of pushing hard to produce another brother for him, all she was doing was quietly asking for air and not moving.

Emilia, jolted back to reality, asked him whether he had looked for Doña Casilda, who was midwife to half the poor of Puebla. The other half was so poor that their women gave birth alone, as alone as when they had been born, and as alone as they were when a man left his keepsake implanted between their legs. They knew how to give birth to babies as well as she did to ghosts, with no help but their blood; they called the midwife only when something went wrong.

The boy told Emilia that Casilda was in her pueblo, as if begging her not to make him go back over the same ground. Then she suggested he go find Dr. Zavalza. But he had just come from doing that, and hadn't found him. Emilia finally came down from the clouds and the apothecary jars where she had been hovering half the morning and, with a half thought for where Zavalza might have gone without telling her, dropped everything and ran after the boy.

His name was Ernesto, and he was the oldest of the five children his twenty-year-old mother had given birth to, him when she was just thirteen. Emilia knew her because twice she had filled Dr. Cuenca's prescriptions without charge when the mother had come to her with a baby on the verge of death.

A few months later, Emilia had seen her walking past the pharmacy, her belly growing large once again. She had called to the woman and asked her to come in, and they had talked for a while.

The girl had told Emilia things she tried to forget during many sleepless nights. Fifty times she awakened, feeling guilty for having a bed, for having breakfast and lunch and dinner, for knowing how to read and having professional ambitions, for having a father and mother and aunt, for having Zavalza, and for having glimpses of heaven in her passion for Daniel. This woman was only two years older than she, and had never known anything but abandonment and hunger, misfortune and abuse.

Perhaps what most disturbed Emilia was remembering her as she told the story of her life. Having had five babies by the time she was twenty, three of them now dead, having different men in her life and no house except the one-room hovel she was jammed into with this man's relatives in the barrio of Xonaca seemed not to sadden her as much as having lost her teeth, being the size of an eleven-year-old boy and carrying through the world the sixth get of a man who had never one night stirred her emotions. In love? What was that?

Leaning against the counter as she drank the orange juice Emilia had given her, she spoke rapidly, laughing from time to time to mock the questions the pharmacy lady was asking her. What did her three children die of? Well, what did Emilia think? God didn't want them to make it, she said, without emotion.

THE OLDER of her two living children led Emilia down the other side of the San Francisco River, the other side of the gentle and sweet-smelling world in which the passions and verities Emilia thought essential had been formed. They went past a group of children playing on a garbage dump; past a woman who was bringing water from the river, her back bent double; past a cantina that stank of vomit and a drunk sleeping off his sorrows on the filthy shreds of an old petticoat; past two men who were throwing a third out of a store and kicking him so hard he was blubbering and farting and begging for mercy.

Emilia clung to the boy's hand and let herself be led blindly to blot out the horror around her. At the end of the farthest street, they ducked into a room where the only light came from a rag-shrouded window and there was no bedding except the straw mat the laboring woman was lying on. Around her, offering contradictory advice and opinions, were five women of undetermined age. They were all in agreement that the girl wasn't trying hard enough. More than helping her, they were scolding her, but constantly wiping her forehead, legs, neck, and belly with wet rags.

The only man in the house started beating the boy for having taken so long. Emilia tried to stop him and explain the reasons for the boy's delay. The man didn't want to hear but stopped, intimidated by this stranger. Questions replaced blows. And as the boy explained how he hadn't been able to find anyone else, Emilia joined the circle of advisers harassing the prostrate woman.

Emilia's own heart sank once she was close enough to listen to the woman's weakened heart. It would have done no good to try to get the women to leave her alone with the ailing girl, so she merely asked them to make room by her legs and then placed her hand between them and sought the source of the bleeding. Who knew how long her life had been draining away? Who knew what had been torn apart inside her, or how?

The aspiring physician's entire arm was bathed in blood. She felt she would die with the girl, from fear and compassion, but she was able to cloak her sorrow with a flurry of useless actions. She looked for the sedative drops she had put in her bag when she still believed they were all that was needed for a delivery, and emptied the whole vial between the girl's caked lips. Kneeling beside her on the ground, she checked the color of her eyelids, just to be doing something, with a devastating sense of helplessness. Almost nothing seemed to be left whole in the girl's body, she must be feeling as if her entrails were ripped apart, yet she did not complain.

"How did this happen to you?" she asked.

"I did it to myself," the girl replied.

Emilia kissed her, sympathizing from the bottom of her adolescent heart, and again felt the weight of guilt fall like a blow. She could not hold back any longer. She wept a long while there beside the dying girl, who gazed toward her as if toward a far horizon. She wept for the friendship they never had, for the distance between their worlds, for the exterminating angel on the girl's lips. She stayed with her until she was lost in her pallor. Then Emilia Sauri rose to confess there was nothing she could do.

The man railed at the boy, who was crying soundlessly, and stormed from the room, cursing. He left without a backward glance, as they say men do when they know they cannot return.

The woman who owned the hovel then told them she had heard

the girl moaning when the sky was still black, but had thought the sounds meant the man was on top of her. She said she had taken her in because she was with her husband's brother, an irresponsible drunk who did not have anywhere to sleep and always asked them to take him in when he had a woman.

As she told the story, she identified as the culprit the only man Emilia had seen there. He was, all the women agreed, a no-good bastard who did not deserve any help. They had accepted his woman because she laughed as if she had reason to, and because her boy was very helpful, but if the girl died, that drunken bum—they swore—would never set foot around there again.

A priest with light in his face came into the room like a drop of water. His cassock was threadbare and the yokelike neck was unbuttoned. Emilia knew him. He was the only priest her father considered a friend. The only priest who didn't pray out of duty or speak of God when it wasn't timely. This Padre Castillo was from the Yucatán, like Diego, small, prudent, inexhaustible, and a good conversationalist. He came by the pharmacy every two or three days to have a cup of coffee. It was from him Josefa had heard that war was like a ripped feather pillow.

As he came in, Emilia felt the warmth of his eyes and was nearly able to smile. She felt so lost, so incompetent. She went to him to tell him what was going on. He patted her shoulder and fished for something in the pockets of the trousers beneath his hiked-up cassock. After some difficulty he found his stained stole and asked them to leave him alone with the girl. The women left to follow the shade of the one tree in the vicinity.

Emilia was talking with them, immersed in a world that frightened her, when the priest returned. The girl had died.

"She's at rest now," said the owner of the hovel. They all hurried inside to look at the dead girl, as if she had not been there before. They put flowers around her and stuck candle stubs in the tamped-down earth that formed the floor. They asked the priest to pray for her and bless her.

Castillo did so with the docility of one who fulfills his duty without protest or presumption. Emilia noticed that his lips were locked as tightly as she had decided to lock hers. She had never seen anyone die, but neither had she seen more of that woman's life than her laugh. The boy Ernesto stood beside her, his tears dried.

"Where did she go?" he asked Emilia, as if she were biting her tongue. She wanted to answer "nowhere," but the word refused to come out, though reason asserted its truth.

"Where the dead live," she answered instead.

The next day, after going with the boy to bury his mother in the city cemetery, Emilia held out her hand to tell him good-bye and be rid, finally, of the nightmare. She had planned to walk back to the pharmacy with Castillo, meet Diego, and go upstairs and try to eat something in the safe shelter of Josefa's always snow white table. But as soon as the boy had her hand in his, he clung to its comforting softness and asked her to take him with her. His younger sister had been given to some señora, he said, and he didn't know where to look for her. Nor did he know who his father was, and that night he wouldn't have a place to sleep if she left him behind.

"Where does this end?" Emilia Sauri whispered into Padre Castillo's ear.

"In nothingness," said the priest, taking the child's free hand.

ANTONIO ZAVALZA and Diego Sauri were chatting behind the counter of the pharmacy when the strange trio arrived. Zavalza was wearing his eyeglasses because he had been examining one of the old books Diego read to satisfy his yen for traveling. Having traveled around half the world only to spend the greater part of his life in the same spot, tied to the same eyes and same rapture, occasionally made him a little restless. Then, sure that to attempt any other course would be ridiculous, for several nights Diego Sauri would bury his nose in the pictures in his books and travel through India and Morocco, Pakistan and China. After several days lost in this battle with his desires, he would return to his living room and shop counter, renewed and again himself, one hundred percent sure he had chosen well in not venturing outside the invisible wall that surrounded the city of Josefa Veytia.

He had never told anyone about those escapades until he met Zavalza. They shared a knowledge of other worlds and a passion for

Veytia women. Each, one by the mother, the other by the daughter, had been driven mad by these simple but sinuous, quiet and topsy-turvy, reckless and smiling, trembling and powerful females.

Zavalza had come to the Casa de la Estrella that evening with his desire like a knot in his throat, wild to spill into Emilia's bosom the last drop of his uncertainties. During the three hours Emilia was at the cemetery, he had time to get away from everything and even to accompany Diego through Turkey and the Persian Gulf.

With his head, the pharmacist thought there could be no better man in all the world for his daughter than this physician, but he also knew that things are not as one might choose but as they are, and that Emilia was irrevocably committed to a different magnetism. He had, however, learned from Josefa to put as soft an edge as possible on half-truths when it was best not to tell the whole truth. So he did not discourage Zavalza, but left the responsibility for dispensing disillusion to whomever it might befall. Emilia is a twentieth-century woman, he told himself proudly, and she will know what to do.

ZAVALZA HAD not removed his eyeglasses when he saw the young woman to whom he owed his torment and for a second thought that it must be a flaw in the lenses that made it look as if she were rushing toward him, nearly dragging the boy and the priest who held his hand.

Emilia winked a greeting to her father, dropped Ernesto's hand, confident the priest would unfold that tale, and headed straight for Zavalza. She offered him her hand, confessing how painful her inability to help had been and how much she had needed him there with her. All this in a murmur that sent the doctor into a near ecstasy. Still holding one hand, Zavalza stroked Emilia Sauri's cheek.

"Doctors who don't feel pain are terrible doctors," he told her and, as if praising her sadness, told her everything promising and beautiful that lay in the depths of his heart.

Emilia did not have to ask him to take the boy into his house. He himself proposed it as soon as he had recovered from the hug with which Emilia rewarded his words and his comfort. She had held him a long while, like someone discovering a treasure. She had never known such a feeling of peace, and wanted nothing more in life than to feel it always.

"Will you stay with me?" she asked Zavalza.

"Do you think I have any other choice?" he replied.

ONE MONTH LATER, the bishop sent to the Sauris' home a letter with his personal seal, announcing his intention to call upon them and requesting them please to notify him if such a visit would be propitious. Diego replied immediately that it would be a pleasure to receive him any and all times he chose to visit them in his role as the uncle of Dr. Antonio Zavalza, but never under any condition as bishop. He did not refrain from stating that in his family church dignitaries were not respected merely for being who they were.

The bishop deemed that reply to be one more insult among the many already received from the pharmacist, not least among them, having procreated the girl who had his nephew head over heels. As a result, the official conversations intended to convey the matrimonial proposal of Antonio Zavalza ended before they began. The unofficial ones, in contrast, were moving along at a smooth clip. After Emilia's consent, Zavalza spoke with Josefa, visited Milagros—who was as amicable as her fierce partisanship for Daniel allowed—beat Diego in a game of chess, and began to spend Sundays in the company of the family. To the Sauris' surprise, and Milagros Veytia's panic, Emilia had agreed to marry Dr. Zavalza with the same ease and firmness she had displayed in picking out new clothes when they went shopping in Mexico City. Without showing a moment's hesitation, without a quiver in her voice or a single teardrop, she erased Daniel from her conversations, and apparently from her expectations.

It was not even as if they had killed him, because one speaks of the dead with more passion and lingering endearments than of the living. No, it was as if he had never been alive. A thousand times they tried to ask about Daniel, and those same thousand times Emilia avoided the questions as if she hadn't heard them. All the things that had made his name resplendent Emilia made sure to obscure with silences and evasions.

She had decided to marry Zavalza, despite the fact that it seemed hasty to her family, that for the first time in her life, Milagros had wept for all one afternoon and night, begging her to be more prudent, that Josefa drowned her in teas and hugs, and that her father handled the matter by pretending it did not disturb him. She would marry Zavalza because she felt calm in his eyes and confidence in his hands, because he loved her above all else, and because he had relieved her of the constant pain of loving Daniel.

ALL OF THESE THINGS, whose mere enumeration wearied even the clearheaded Josefa, who after the least effort at trying to absorb them felt as if all the birds in her upstairs corridor were fluttering inside her head, had happened in only five months. It was the end of September when Josefa found a letter from Daniel in the mailbox. When she saw it, her stomach turned over as it had when she was a girl and something unpleasant happened, and her shock was doubled because for such a long time she had forgotten that lurch in the solar plexus that feels like a rabbit scrambling out of its hole.

"Now we'll see whether she's as set in her mind as she thinks she is," she told Diego, holding the letter the way she might have held a dagger.

Diego shrugged his shoulders and ran to take refuge among his bottles of distilled water, pretending to look for something he urgently needed. He did not want even Josefa to see how upset he was over his daughter's falling in and out of love. Once hidden behind the amber bottles, he bet his wife that nothing would change, and watched her disappear up the stairs calling for their daughter.

CHAPTER

17

EMILIA SAURI took her time opening the letter. For once she didn't rip open the envelope, nor did her hands tremble as she held the six pages of Daniel's account of his exploits of the last months. It was a long missive, written as kind of a diary, sounding at times as if it were to be delivered by hand and intended only as a guide for Daniel himself to expand upon each of the stories. At the beginning it had the playful tone of their good times, but as it went along the prose turned to a feverish, sad voice Emilia did not recognize.

It began with an apology, listing the reasons he had been unable to see her in Mexico City. All reasons having to do with politics and the Revolution that wounded the self-esteem Emilia had sworn to maintain in order not to be hurt again by the banal but inevitable feeling of always playing second fiddle to the country. She read hurriedly, the way we read lessons that don't engage our minds. Daniel told her in minute detail every last pursuit and scrape of his life as a rebel soldier. One whole paragraph was devoted to describing in brotherly detail the looks and behavior of a textile worker named Fortino Ayaquica. Another was about the sexual habits of Francisco Mendoza, a man from the country around Chietla, and there was a third, still more extensive, describing the poetic sensitivity he had discovered in the heart of Chui Morales, who owned a cantina in Ayutla. Morales, Mendoza, and Ayaquica were the leaders of Zapata's forces in Puebla. Each of them had brought with them three hundred rebels in bands that fought furiously, though as if in some inexplicable chess match, for control of towns and villages. Daniel had been sent to live with them and act as Madero's delegate. In a short time he had learned to drink and talk like one of them, to see the world and decipher it through the eyes of those men whom he soon considered exemplary fighters and exceptional human beings. Daniel explained that he had ridden with them to Mexico City the day Madero arrived, and that it was his responsibility to stay with them, which was why he had not been able to get away.

Daniel wrote that his father was not entirely happy that his son had ended up where the fighting was heaviest and where there was little need for lawyers and educated men, but he thought, and wanted to tell Emilia, that every minute he had lived with those men had taught him things he could never have learned at a distance.

Then he theorized about the dangers that same distance had generated in cultivated liberals, and in Madero himself. It was a distance that led them to attempt such things as to want people to agree to stop fighting and go home without having achieved anything more than a simple change of names in the governing body. He ended the letter by saying he regretted that the deaths on July 12 had kept him from coming to Puebla when Madero visited. Things being as they were, he had to stay with the men who needed him and not with those who were deceiving the downtrodden who had won for them the privilege of choice and power they didn't deserve.

Here and there, among the political commentaries Emilia read with the same objectivity she devoted to dinner-table conversations in her house, were paragraphs in which Daniel complained about how hard it was to be so far from her beautiful breasts, or an incoherent string of words that flooded her ears as, lost, he spilled into her the blessing that obtains all pardons and eases all afflictions.

Only while reading one of those sentences, which were always preceded by "You want to hear?" did Emilia Sauri allow herself for an instant to glimpse the turmoil in her heart. In his closing she learned who it was who had died on the twelfth, how anger had churned through the south that afternoon when not only men, but boys and women were returned to their towns slung over the backs of mules that had taken them to Puebla alive, excited, and gullible as they would never be again.

The description of that return was so dark and oppressive that as Emilia read it she longed to erase it from her memory. That page ended with Daniel's asking whether she knew if there were any Maderistas left in Puebla. He wasn't one any longer. Then, as if he didn't want to hear himself any longer, he said good-bye, sending a kiss with all the pain his heart could hold.

Emilia folded the letter, tears pressing like stones against her eyelids, but without shedding a single drop she turned toward her mother's expectant gaze and told her that Daniel sounded about the same as always, that he loved them and missed them very much. Then she tore the already folded pages into tiny pieces and handed them to her mother, saying she could throw them in the cook stove.

Josefa longed to reach out and caress the face that had turned as cold as the March sun, but she did not dare upset Emilia further by showing a compassion she knew Emilia could not bear. In that and a thousand other ways, her daughter was just like Milagros. No one better than Josefa knew the strength of the walls those two built around their emotions.

"They put up walls of water," she had once told Diego, "and you have to swim through them."

The moment she left her daughter, she abandoned the cool and collected pace with which she had made her way to the door and ran as fast as she could to a table in her bedroom. She locked the door and piece by piece fit together the jigsaw puzzle Emilia had handed her. To add to her labors, Daniel's letter had been written on both sides of the pages, and it took the morning to read it. She had to put each page together twice in order to read first one and then the other side, but Josefa was so skillful that by the end of three hours she not only had succeeded in reading the complete letter but had the process down well enough to repeat the trick first for Diego, and then later in Milagros's house, for her and Rivadeneira, who as he watched her put it together and take it apart marveled at the unrecognized art that lay in that skill, one as demanding as poetry and, were it possible, even less valued. By nightfall, once they had all learned the letter's contents, Josefa took the pieces to her daughter's bedroom and left them on the dressing table beside the brush Emilia pulled three hundred times every night through her mane of dark curls.

Since one inherits more than vices, Emilia was able to put the letter together with the same proficiency her mother had shown. She read it over and over until dawn. Then she put the pieces in a cigar box Diego had given her after he had smoked the four hundred Cuban *puros* it contained. It was a memorable box because Rivadeneira had brought it back from a trip to Cuba, and Diego had never found cigars anywhere in Mexico with the same savor. Emilia was ten when the box became hers, and with it, though she hadn't realized it, had begun her long love affair with boxes.

Once locked away within those aromatic walls, Daniel's message ceased to interfere with Emilia's future. The same was true of her family's curiosity; no one asked about Daniel, not even when Dr. Cuenca's name came up, always favorably, during the course of conversation. Daniel's name disappeared from their lips, seemingly from memory, anytime they were with Emilia. That was what the four of them had agreed to do after reading the letter. If Emilia could live in that silence, they told one another, they were not the ones to thwart her will.

ONE WEEK BEFORE the October elections, the Casa de la Estrella formally accepted the addition of the wisdom and patience that characterized Dr. Antonio Zavalza. The dinner Josefa prepared was unforgettable, not only for the occasion it marked, but also for the ambrosial bouquet of peaches that clung to the chicken she served. Like any bachelor, Zavalza was devoted to home-cooked chicken, something that could not be said about the tastes of Diego Sauri, who like every respectable husband looked upon chicken with the coolness of those who have forgotten the deprivation of not having it. So Josefa invented the dish with the peaches to satisfy in one plate the longing her probable son-in-law felt for domesticity and the ambition for adventure that Diego sought to appease at mealtimes.

Politics was always one of the most important herbs for dishes served at the Sauris'. Josefa had known it to be her ally for a long time, and to assure that she could always have it on hand, it had occurred to her to put something on the table beside the salt and pepper to represent it, a small container filled with gravel-sized stones that rattled when it was shaken. With that talisman before her, Josefa felt sure of success anytime she was worried about a gathering. At first the stone-filled saltshaker had been the cause for hilarity among family and friends, but over the years it had become so familiar that no one gave it a thought. It still sat in the center of the table on the tray that held the oil and vinegar, freshly chopped chilies, salt, and spices.

That night each of them seemed to have decided to pass over the subject of politics. With their consommé, they talked about traveling. Zavalza thought it paramount that Emilia know Europe, and Diego agreed with him that a person was different, better, after having walked around Paris until he knew it as well as Puebla. Making a virtue of prudence, Josefa did not remind them that she was who she was without having once crossed the Atlantic, and from across the table signaled her sister with her eyes please not to mention that. So the chicken was served without interrupting the peace of conversational trivialities. Maybe everything would have gone as smoothly as it had been going, had Zavalza, reaching for the pepper, not confused it with the pebble-filled talisman; when he shook it over the chicken it made a sound like stones rolling in a river. Everyone laughed and a few moments were spent in teasing Josefa about her faith in her talisman's powers to stir up something political. But only moments later, they heard in the street the sound of a flute that vibrated in Emilia's ear before anyone else heard it and caused her to jump up from the table without saying a word but with a smile that glowed like a jewel. Her face paled one second and burst into flame the next. No one but Daniel played a flute like that. Emilia opened the balcony door and leaned over the railing. When he saw her, Daniel sang at the top of his lungs the last two lines of a plaintive melody that knifed through the air like a stiletto:

And the comfort I have left,
Is that you will remember me. . . .

Zavalza had never heard that flute, but merely by looking at Emilia he understood as well as her family that she would follow it. He did not try to hold her back. No one did. Everyone looked toward Zavalza as if they owed him an apology, and in return they saw in his eyes the mark of breeding that occurs very rarely in any century. It was his voice that broke the ice congealing the atmosphere, as with words of utter tranquility, Dr. Zavalza calmed them, confessing that he had known all too well that something like this was bound to happen sooner or later. He said he did not want to mislead them by boasting that he truly understood or have them believe he thought things were better this way. He had hoped it would happen later rather than sooner; he even joked about what a fiasco his carefully planned trip to Europe was turning out to be. Then, with a gentility a prince could envy, he resumed his meal, comparing Josefa's chicken *à la pêche* to the delights of a stay in Paris, making sure that dinner was the pleasant occasion they had planned. He entertained his hosts as if he were the one who owed them an apology. In Diego's honor, he described the itinerary of his trip to Morocco and for more than an hour had them all captive to the perfume of mint that fills its streets, the mystery and waistlines of its women, the wondrous language sung by its men, and an enumeration of the Arab secrets that permeate the Spanish culture. After that he talked about medicine and poetry. When it was time for Josefa's teas, he listed the curative properties of each of her herbs and then indulged himself by asking her to play the piano so he could sing with her a song about star-crossed love from the repertoire of the last operetta company to come through town. When the light of dawn seeped into the dining room, Zavalza said his good-byes, feeling that at least the two Veytia sisters and the men who lived with them had allowed him into their family, the family he had always longed for. He did not want to think about Emilia that morning; his body still felt her tearing herself from him despite the enormous effort of will she had put into loving him. The rational Emilia had loved him more than anything. But love is not everything, and because he knew that, he did not feel her abandonment as an offense.

THE FLUTE DANIEL had played to summon her was thrown on the floor beside his shoes. Emilia Sauri opened her eyes to the ten o'clock sun flooding the bedroom, and then focused on the reed flute she had run after the night before. She smiled. She needed to laugh to forgive herself. What was to be done about her? She was hopeless. She had not stopped to invent an apology, she had not tried to say a word. But why? What could she have said that everyone there didn't already know? What was new about her bonds? Antonio Zavalza knew about that better than anyone. No one deceived him. Even when she had fooled a wary Josefa into believing she had forgotten Daniel, she had not washed from Zavalza's eyes the last dark line of doubt that made his black eyes even blacker. He knew the source of her spells of silence, and of her talkativeness in others. And she? What could she say about herself? She was happy. So happy she could not torture herself for her lack of character and good sense any longer than the three minutes she contemplated the reed flute. She would follow it again, any time she heard it.

They had slept in the house Milagros had not given up when she went to live with Rivadeneira. Daniel had the key with him and had never been parted from it even in those moments in battle when you give up anything to save your life. He wore it around his neck and it was his assurance that he had a home, that someone was always waiting for him, that no matter how much danger and death he survived, life was waiting around the corner and he had only to run and find it. Emilia was there for him. He never had a moment's doubt about that. He knew all the hidden places of that body, he traveled with her memory and her mind as much a part of him as his own body. In his mind, Emilia was fighting alongside him in the war, awaiting the peace to get on with the unsigned agreement of their lifetimes together.

When Emilia asked why he had come back, Daniel told her he missed the moles on her left shoulder. They did not speak of Zavalza. Daniel knew that if he gave his tongue permission to speak on that subject, he would end up screaming insults. He would rather touch Emilia again, probe to see whether she was keeping secrets from him, while he explored the last withheld fold and wrinkle of her body, come to know it and sow in the very heart of all her desires the enervating pleasure he knew once again was only his to give.

Emilia Sauri closed her eyes and saw the sea, saw an enormous moon low against the sky, saw Daniel when he was twelve, waiting for her at the train station of his boarding school, saw the tree in the garden, saw the pond where they dangled their feet, saw the black stone in his hand, the faint darkness of the *temazcal*. She imagined her inner self: wet, belligerent, triumphant. And for the first time she blessed the fate that called to her, for the first time she did not try to hold inside the sound of the mountains erupting from her body. The others were not there. The ones who protected her, the ones who gathered around her, understanding her, the ones who had made her doubt her fire because at times she also seemed a part of them. Her war and her armistice with Daniel were theirs alone, only with him did instants seem like years, and the confirmation of her plaint shattered the air in shards that screamed through the plaza.

That morning, Milagros came to her sister's house early. She sat down to drink *café con leche* and try to begin a conversation.

"We women never seem to tire of losing perfect men," she said.

Josefa shrugged her shoulders, unable to think of anything to say, upset, but sure that things were better this way, and that her sister had something to do with the latest turn of events.

"You mean, the women of our family," she said, pausing to hear whether the teakettle was whistling at the very moment all the birds in the corridor burst into a concert rare when the sun was so high.

CHAPTER 18

IZÚCAR WAS A HOT, rough town. No one could have thought of it as a good place for a honeymoon, but the moon was pure honey above the heads of Emilia Sauri and Daniel Cuenca the night they lay in the grass in the dark, warm solitude beside the cane fields. There was no room for doubt or sorrow beneath the canopy of those heavens. They slept as few have slept upon earth.

The next morning, they went into the town of dirt streets dominated by the smell of fermenting sugarcane. Squat houses lined the streets where already people were moving about, men in white cotton pants and straw sombreros and barefoot, malaria-ridden women with children hanging from their arms like fruit. In the doorway of a building slightly taller than the surrounding houses, two men were holding cups of pulque aloft like fencing swords. In his left hand, one of them held a large, gleaming clay jug from which he had filled his own and his friend's cup. They were looking at each other with great seriousness, as if with that drink they were sealing their fate.

Near them were a dozen men in deep conversation; in the center of their group were three little girls with grimy dresses and mud-splattered faces that hadn't been washed for several days. The eyes of the smallest shone like stones from between the legs of the men raising their cups above her head. In her hands was a rag doll, and she was staring straight ahead, as serious as if she, too, were there to get a glimpse of her life.

"What are those three little girls doing in that crowd of drunks?" Emilia asked Daniel.

"Testifying," he said, putting his arm around her shoulder to guide her across the blistering street.

As they approached the group, a dog playing at the knees of an old man rushed toward them, his bark loud as a police siren. To Emilia's amazement, Daniel called the dog by name and quieted him by patting his back. The person with the pulque jug came toward Daniel, mysterious and warm. He was Chui Morales, cantina keeper and leader of the local revolutionaries. Daniel introduced Emilia as his wife, and Emilia felt a hand squeeze her heart. Morales took her hand and with a few courteous words announced himself at her service and then informed her that almost everyone there had known her for a long time.

The little girl with the doll came to tell Emilia that the dog belonged to her. Stooping down until she was at the child's level, Emilia asked what she and the other girls were called.

One man who had just arrived from Morelos shifted his eyes from the bottom of his pulque cup to say that women weren't allowed, that if Morales let this one come in there wouldn't be any meeting, or peace accord, or shit.

"No women, only little girls?" Emilia asked.

"These dirty ones here," said the man, indicating the girls with a nod of his head.

"She's one of them," said Daniel. "She's cleaned up because we went to see her godmother, but she'll be dirty soon enough."

"Get rid of her," said another of the men.

"No one tells me when to come and no one 'gets rid' of me," Emilia cut in, standing up in front of the girl.

"I'm not talking to you," said the man, touching his sombrero.

"Oh, but I'm talking to *you*."

"You don't want to go in, Emilia," Daniel told her. "Cantinas are no place for women. These men are right."

"Of course I'm going in," said Emilia, walking to the door of the *pulquería* and stepping inside before anyone had time to stop her.

After the brilliant sun outdoors, the darkness of that stinking room was a violation. Two men were dozing on the sawdust-covered floor. Emilia did not have a chance to get close enough to see if they were alive because another man came stumbling out from behind stacked barrels and fell upon her as if she were a ghost. He kept calling her *Virgincita,* and asking a thousand pardons for being drunk, telling her as he clung to her how devoted he was to her and how he had never thought that he would touch, or feel the protection of, the Mother of God.

It took Emilia a couple of seconds to recover from her fright, but when she did, she pushed the man with all the strength of her anger, and struggled with him until she escaped his stench and the beard scratching her cheek. The man was strong, but he was so drunk that, helped by her push, he fell to the sawdust, out cold. Emilia turned on her heel and went back to the sun outside.

"When that bastard comes to, he'll be knocked over again when he remembers what a woman did to him," said Chui Morales, who had never loosened his grip on the jug. He looked for a cup for Emilia, to celebrate her backbone, and, laughing, convinced the men to let her have a drink with them.

"As far as you're concerned, they can eat me alive, can't they, stupid?" Emilia shouted at Daniel, who was unmoved as she pounded her fists on his chest.

Stepping into the fight with a naturalness that defused Emilia's anger, the eldest of the little girls handed Emilia a cup, and Chui Morales came to fill it from the clay jug that seemed to hold a river of pulque. Then he took Daniel's cup and filled it with the viscous liquid Emilia had always thought the most revolting drink ever invented by her compatriots. Everyone, including the little girls, held out their cups. Morales went around filling them all, nearly dancing, jug held high, as if performing an ancestral ritual. Finally he poured his own and proposed a toast to the newcomer.

All that time, Emilia had been contemplating the contents of her cup with revulsion. She told them she appreciated their welcome but that she wasn't very thirsty.

"You don't drink pulque because you're thirsty," said a short man with a captivating face, whom Daniel introduced as Fortino Ayaquica. Emilia offered her hand and Fortino raised his glass to toast her, at the same time reciting a litany of the virtues of the pulque that flowed from the jug Morales flourished.

"This isn't the same as that stuff inside," Chui Morales told her, emptying his cup and still holding the jug.

The pulque indoors, they explained, stank because it was *tlachique;* they let it go bad and never washed the kegs before they filled them. What Chui Morales had in the jug came from maguey cactuses on a hacienda they'd captured during the rebellion. It was clean as a mountain spring.

"White as the butts of the young ladies in the Casa Grande," said Fortino, laughing aloud.

"Go on, drink up," said Chui with a guffaw that made his curling mustache dance up and down.

Emilia placed the cup to her lips. She cursed the day she had chosen to follow Daniel and took the first swallow, wondering how many things she already had to curse him for, how many lay ahead because of her obsession, which inch of his lips she would die for, really die, not die of disgust. Before she realized, she had drunk the entire cup.

"Some woman!" said Chui, clapping Daniel on the back as he hawked up cottony phlegm.

Daniel thanked him for the compliment, while Emilia, who had squatted down to talk with the girls, had her cup filled again and drank it much more rapidly than she had the first.

"We'd better go," said Daniel, using the pretext that it was getting late and he had to take her to a friend's home so the men could get the meeting under way.

"That's all I need now," Emilia pouted. "For you to say when we go." She sat down on the ground and asked for more pulque. At that moment Francisco Mendoza arrived, the third of the rebel leaders Daniel had to talk to. With him was a strong woman with a tender mouth, frank eyes, and a black mane of loose curls, who acted as if she knew Emilia and without further ado plumped down beside her.

From above their heads, Chui Morales poured the woman's first glass with masterful precision and again filled Emilia's cup, who, head reeling, was beginning to feel like dancing and yelling. The woman who had just arrived put her arm around her and began jabbering away. Her name was Dolores Cienfuegos, she said, and she lived up to the fires of her name.

"You, are you going to get drunk?" asked the little girl with the doll, watching Emilia pet the dog who had stretched out beside them.

"I already *am* getting drunk," said Emilia, her eyes fixed on the varied shades of green stretching toward the mountain across the sweet-smelling, bristling fields that lay around the village.

THE GIRLS at the cantina were the daughters of Chui Morales and Carmela Milpa, a paralyzed woman who in exchange for the use of her legs had the silky voice of an angel. She sang the most desolate love songs and the most timeless lullabies. She, with her daughters, and Dolores Cienfuegos, with her fire, lived in a house with a floor of warm bricks on which they scattered a vine with a pale flower that in the evening smelled like jasmine and in the morning carnation. Francisco Mendoza and Chui Morales left them there when they went off to fight. And there they found them when they returned, whipped or triumphant.

There among the adobe walls and dark-skinned, doe-eyed women, Emilia learned that the men's leaving and returning was not a pain reserved solely for her. She learned that women weave life from memories and she grew stronger every time the men rode away. She learned to get along on her own, to stifle what was irrelevant, to hum to herself, to mock the war, and to grapple with fate as a plant grapples with weather. She learned the value of a bean, a jug of water, a top, a nut and bolt, a nail, a shoe, a piece of rope, a rabbit, an egg, a button, the shade of a tree, the light of a candle. And in return she taught them how to bring down fevers, boil water, soothe headaches, stitch a wound, hem a skirt, paint butterflies, sail paper boats, clean teeth with burnt tortilla, brew *pirú* leaves and *tabachín* flowers to kill the worms that gnawed in the children's bellies, to know which days each month a woman is fertile, to blend *epazote* and *yerba dulce* with coconut butter to rub in the vagina and prevent pregnancy, to distinguish poisonous plants from medicinal ones—all knowledge learned from doña Casilda and the herbalist in the market. After two weeks she had adjusted Dolores's menstrual problems, cleared the jaundiced skin of two of the girls and the smallest one's fever blisters. Best of all, she had relieved Carmela's insomnia. In a mortar she ground a paste of white sapote leaves and tincture of marijuana; when that was applied to Carmela's legs at night, she enjoyed a restful sleep she had not known for the last three years. Half the village seized the opportunity to talk to Emilia about their ills. Every morning she worked in an improvised consulting room at the door of the cantina and examined anyone who wanted to come see her, children with a cough or diarrhea, sores, injuries, swollen bellies, back pains, infections, terminal diseases. In the afternoons she went around the village visiting those too sick to come to her, and all day long she despaired of her ignorance about an infinity of things, as well as the lack of any drugs or medicines except those she could obtain from local plants. Fortunately, the earth was lush and fertile in that region, so early mornings she went out with Dolores to search the mountainside for leaves she recognized. But there were many ills and she did not know how to help a child in convulsions or treat gonorrhea or syphilis. There were times she didn't even know what the illness was she was seeing. Despite her success in curing sicknesses caused by poverty and poor hygiene, such as stomach parasites and minor infections, she was too often aware of her limitations, and at those moments she thought of Zavalza and drew strength from the consolation he would have offered. There were a hundred things he would have known to do when she could only hold her head and curse.

While the men were away, the women worked from sunup to sunset. There was no rest from their labors or respite from their tongues. Emilia learned that she could go on long after she felt tired, that after four hours of work, if she took a deep breath, she could begin another four. She discovered her true worth, leapt several times across the chasm of her fears, and learned that affection is never spent even though it is fully given.

She spent less time with Daniel than she did bathing at the river with Dolores, and she romped more often with the Morales girls than she was allowed to touch the heavens and count the comets. But she was content with what she had. When after five weeks Daniel said they had to leave, she wept as if her world were breaking in two.

THE ELECTIONS had given Madero an undisputed triumph. But his presence in the government had not in any way improved life for the campesinos. After the persecution that wiped out their villages and harvests, Daniel's friends had decided to take the land and rebel against this government that had not delivered what it had promised in exchange for their support. They did not want a peace of lies; they could not go back to their people, after so much death and tumult, to say that the peons were still peons and the haciendas still belonged to their old owners. There was no word, no message, no command, that would convince the campesinos to resign themselves and accept a return to the old ways. Disgusted and ashamed to represent Madero's lackluster performance, Daniel decided to join the new uprising. To do that, the first thing he had to do was get Emilia out of Izúcar, where her very face and way of walking would put her in danger when war broke out.

Emilia did not want to go. After several nights of arguing about the difficulty of life in that world, Emilia refused a thousand times to go home. She swore she would rather die there than lose Daniel again. She screamed until the trees trembled under the crystal sky. She wept, she stopped eating, she cursed Madero, the Revolution, injustice, the feverish night she had rediscovered Daniel's love, and the way her lips trembled when he was near. Daniel listened to all her arguments, but rejected any that did not mean taking her back home to the Sauris.

"It will take more than all your army of rebels to get me out of here," said Emilia. "You are not going to decide my life for me."

"But I am going to see that you don't die," he replied.

He knew how many people depended on the light in Emilia's eyes and did not feel he had the right to risk that. He loved Milagros and the Sauris as much as he did his own father, as much as his cause. Not he, not his cause, not anyone, was worth putting Emilia at risk. If he had to tie her up, he would tie her up, but he was not going to leave her as near the center of danger as that place would very soon be.

"This is not your war, Emilia," he said, holding her close the last night they slept beneath the Moraleses' roof.

"What is?" Emilia asked.

"The Casa de la Estrella, medicine, the pharmacy, my heart . . ."

"So be careful I don't cut it out and preserve it in alcohol," Emilia said, curt and furious because of the truth she had to face. "I'm in your way, but if you stay, then it's my war, too. I'm not going anywhere you won't be."

Tired of arguing to no purpose, Daniel got up and walked out into the darkness.

"Men," said Dolores Cienfuegos, coming to comfort Emilia. "A wonder we don't kill them, or they don't kill us."

They walked down to the river and sat on the bank beneath a weeping willow, the sound of water running over stones the only other presence. Dolores was nearly thirty and was not a shy woman, or particularly discreet, but she found it hard to begin the conversation. She had grown fond of Emilia and admired her educated voice, the ringing precision of her words, her ability to use them. She felt more than ever incapable of expressing things with the clarity and emotion of her thoughts. Not because she lacked intelligence but because poverty had denied her the chance to develop it. She had not realized that until Emilia arrived and she had measured her emotions against Emilia's and heard her say the things Dolores felt, with an ease and skill she had always envied but never found on her tongue.

"Things don't work out the way you want; it's more like, what can you do?" she said to begin, looking at Emilia without pity, but also without envy.

Then all the things she had dammed up in her head began to pour out. If Emilia stayed in the village, she said, she would end up being a burden; they would have to protect her, feed her, spend too much time taking care of her. On the other hand, if she went back to Puebla and helped them from there, she could be more useful than in a camp of armed men. She knew how to heal people, speak English, make sense of the language the government people spoke, prepare medicines. She understood laws, deals, books, things that no one there understood. Being far away, she would be close; her being secure would give them confidence; understanding that world, she could better defend theirs. She was needed, and much beloved, but her work was elsewhere. And no one knew that better than she did, no matter that for five days she had been refusing to accept it. Why cloud the hours she and Daniel had left by thinking about the future? This was not a time of luxuries, and time was a luxury she shouldn't waste in grumbling. She must understand, follow her destiny as the men obeyed theirs.

Emilia listened to everything Dolores wanted to say without lifting her head from the lap Dolores had offered when they stopped beneath the willow. Dolores's voice blended with the sound of the water rippling over the stones. Emilia had to agree with what Dolores was saying, and as she listened saw her in all her aspects: quick, stealthy, daring, beating clothes on one of the flat rocks in a calm bend of the river, tasting the beans in the palm of her hand for salt, cleaning a rifle with the lace handkerchief Emilia had given her, shaping tortillas with the skill of a sculptor, blowing on the charcoal under the brazier, playing hide-and-seek with the little girls, shouting her passion for Francisco Mendoza high on a hill where no one could hear them, then two hours later dressing him down like a fellow guerrilla.

"Look, don't bother me with that shit!" Emilia heard her say the first morning they shared the poverty of their room with Emilia and Daniel. All her life she would remember her delight.

From the first words, Emilia had realized that Dolores was right; the rest of the time she listened, thinking how she already missed her. The morning she left, the two of them went to the cantina for pulque.

"Health and heaven," Dolores said, squinting her eyes to gulp down the drink.

EMILIA AND DANIEL reached Puebla in the early-morning hours. They had planned to sleep for a while in Milagros's hideaway before going to the Casa de la Estrella, but on the way to the former they passed the latter, and the roads of the heart become clear only as we are walking them. It was before daylight but a street lamp shone palely on the balconies of the house. Emilia Sauri imagined her parents asleep behind the shutters. In each other's arms, as she had seen them sleep since she was a child, as they continued to sleep, even though they woke with aches and pains. She imagined the smoothness of the eiderdown on her bed, the gleaming wood floors, the peace of curling up in one of the armchairs in the living room, the smell of the morning coffee, the early riot of the birds, the slow hours spent among the bottles in the pharmacy listening to her father's dreams of travel, the calm at bedtime when she dipped some of her mother's bread in her milk. She ran to the door. She didn't care about the reasons not to, or the caution Daniel thought necessary. She grabbed the knocker and banged it as only her Aunt Milagros could.

Josefa leapt out of bed at the first sound that reached her ever-alert ears; she heard Diego grumbling about Milagros's habits and hours, as in the dark she fumbled for the sleeves of her bathrobe. She crossed the corridor damp from the dawn darkness and went running down the stairs.

"Emilia?" she asked before she opened the door. Because who but Emilia could have made her heart plummet to her boots?

CHAPTER

19

DURING THE TURBULENT, deeply troubled months that followed the night Emilia crossed the Sauri threshold, lifted over it by a copper-skinned, tangle-haired Daniel, Josefa kept repeating a saying about time doing to emotions what wind does to fire: "If it is low, like a candle flame, it snuffs it out. If it flares like a bonfire, it feeds it."

Emilia let Daniel leave without a single reproach and without wanting to know where he was going. Zavalza received Emilia without asking where she had been and without a single reproach. Time began to flow over everyone's heroics and hurts.

Days became months, and life, with its havoc and dangers, an intense struggle. Zavalza and Emilia were working together again. Always talking about the ill, about putridity and suffering, about possible cures or inevitable deaths; they were a pair unable to rest. They learned to be close one day and the next like gears of the same clock. Every day more and more people came to Zavalza's consulting room looking for a cure, and found it in the stubborn pair willing to joust with fate over the most unforeseen physical misfortunes.

One noontime in September 1911, Zavalza came to the

pharmacy to tell Emilia and Diego that he had somewhere he wanted to take them. Diego had an idea of what Zavalza had in mind, and thought he deserved the pleasure of showing it to Emilia in private, so he excused himself, saying he could not leave the pharmacy unattended, and watched Emilia, innocent and eager, follow an impatient Antonio.

At the beginning of that year, the owners of an estate on the outskirts of the city had put it up for sale at a price far below its value because they were fleeing the country as if the plague. Zavalza heard about it from Josefa, and hurried to snap up the bargain. For several months, he kept secret what he intended to do with it. Emilia frequently saw him go off at mid-morning or come a little late to his five o'clock office hours, but said nothing.

"He has a sweetheart and wants to keep it a secret," Emilia told her mother.

"Impossible," Josefa said with conviction. "Those are the first secrets everyone learns."

With the money he would have spent going to Europe and getting married, Zavalza had converted the house into a small hospital. Finally it was ready to show Emilia.

"It's almost everything I have, and much more than I could have hoped for," he said as they came to the door.

Emilia Sauri's enthusiasm surpassed what she would have felt for any of the marvels of Europe. She ran from one room to the next, imagining how to arrange the furniture, she opened and closed windows, approved the exact green of the grass in the garden, and just when she thought she had seen everything, a beaming Zavalza led her to a small operating room where all the instruments and equipment were as up-to-date as those in a movie.

Zavalza had obtained the equipment through the good offices of Puebla's North American consul, a ruddy-faced, smiling old man whom Zavalza had cured of a dyspepsia he thought was chronic and who was, therefore, at least as devoted to Zavalza as to his country. The U.S. ambassador in Mexico City had a personal commitment to destroying Madero's regime, and in his desire to do so reported to his government all kinds of tales about dangers to North American lives and property. To back up his accounts, he made up story after story about some recent appropriation or other, some group of persecuted or bankrupt compatriots, some major misadventure. He had ordered the equipment gleaming in Zavalza's operating room to substantiate a costly anecdote about an unhappy—and nonexistent—doctor who, after shipping very expensive machines to Mexico City had abandoned everything because, as a foreigner in the midst of the Madero regime, he was intimidated by the persecution and horror around him. Once the ambassador had proved his story, he put the evidence up for sale, and through the smiling consul in Puebla, Zavalza had bought it for a fifth its price.

As Emilia listened to her friend tell that story of a political intrigue that had played out to his benefit, she walked from one side of the room to the other, touching and feeling everything. Finally she stopped before Zavalza and hugged him.

"I thought you had a sweetheart," she said.

"Have you lost your senses?" asked Zavalza, burying his nose in the balm of her curls.

"I don't have the right," said Emilia, sheltered in Zavalza's arms and good nature. He smelled of tobacco and cologne. In that embrace, peace washed over her and she found the feeling so new that she began to sing a love song and sway to its rhythm.

During the year of his absence, Daniel's letters arrived from the most unexpected places. Sometimes they were playful and written with haste. At times slowly, and sad. Emilia's humor changed with the letters, the ups and downs of the rebellion Daniel had espoused when he did not find in Madero the just leader he had expected.

Daniel had returned to the state of Morelos and the southern part of Puebla; he had been assigned to work as courier and contact between the campesinos of the south and the anti-Madero rebels in the north; he had traveled, written proclamations, helped draft plans, and been hungrier than ever before. For a while the rebels in the north made the country tremble; they took Chihuahua and part of Sonora before the government could realize what was happening. Daniel accompanied them as a journalist, writing dispatches for one newspaper in Chicago and another in Texas. He also was with them when they began to be pushed back by a strong military force organized by a general inherited from the days of Porfirio Díaz. The man's name was Victoriano Huerta, and Madero had put him in charge of the campaign in the north. Daniel had had only intellectual and legal duties until the rebels had to face the new army in Rellano. That day even boys fired against the federal troops. After that, it was all losing and running, until there was no choice but to flee to Texas.

When he opened the door of his house in San Antonio, Dr. Cuenca, as erect and haughty as in his best days but nearly blind and with all the ills a failing heart can inflict, could not believe that all his efforts to educate his son had led to the ruinous state he now saw him in.

"What mistake did you step out of?" he asked.

A castaway would have looked better than the bag of bones Daniel had become. He reeked of a mixture of gunpowder and hell, he had scabs on his face, the right shoulder of his shirt was ripped open, his too-large pants were riddled with holes, the soles were hanging loose from his shoes, and there was pain on his face as he tried to smile.

After he had eaten and bathed, he slept for three days and nights. He awoke one Tuesday at about six in the evening to meet the vigilant gaze of Dr. Cuenca. The aged man's features conserved the serenity that had ruled his life. Daniel rubbed his eyes with his hands, as if to imprint there an image of unequivocal harmony.

"Too bad I didn't take after you," he told his father.

For the next week they talked night and day, ate strange food at strange hours, slept long stretches at erratic times, and reached an agreement. Daniel had been losing his strength and his usefulness in an attempt to lessen the power of a man who had no power. He had fought beside that man's weakest enemies, against those who fought in his name but would turn against him sooner than one could imagine. Then the freedom of the press, speech, and ordinary talk that no one had valued sufficiently would again be buried beneath the corpses of innocent men. The others, those who had nothing to lose, would kill each other off chasing inevitable and impossible causes and names, and the Revolution would race through the country, without check or objective, until God knew when.

It was not easy for Daniel to accept his father's arguments, but after he had worn out his tongue repeating them and Daniel had rearranged them so often in his feverish brain, he had no recourse but to see with the lucidity of a disenchanted old man things the febrile intelligence of a twenty-four-year-old had failed to comprehend. His brother, Salvador, an indefatigable compañero in the early struggles, was wasting his time in less dangerous but equally pointless pursuits. He had returned to the political world of Mexico City to work with the Maderistas. Dr. Cuenca would have given everything he owned not to have sown in his sons the passion for politics that now consumed them. It was too late to try to eradicate it, so he would spend his last breath looking for ways to keep them out of danger.

Despite having convinced Daniel of the need to abandon a war that had no future, one he would understand less every day because no one can understand anything in an atmosphere of unleashed hatred, Dr. Cuenca had little luck in coming up with either an acceptable mission or a destiny for his son. He had a number of friends in San Antonio, and in the law offices of one of them found a place for Daniel. Daniel, however, did not want to practice in English or arrange inheritances and divorces for unhappy people with no greater cause than themselves. He did not want to live his life as a lawyer, even less in a country that was not his own, but just then he could not think of anything more agreeable than the tranquility surrounding his father. He knew Cuenca was weaker than he appeared and sicker than he admitted. To leave him alone at that time would have been the worst of follies. For the moment, Daniel had no war to wage, no higher duty than that of keeping his father company. He worked in the mornings and in the afternoons kept an eye on the doctor. San Antonio was a placid city with a slow pace that mitigated its brassiness and lulled Daniel into a calm that was at times comparable to happiness. Dr. Cuenca knew, however, that his son's peace was artificial, and that if he did not soon point him toward some new passion he would find one on his own, which surely would be a return to politics.

"Write about your country, don't fight it," he said one day, hopeful that writing might be Daniel's salvation.

He knew his son had the ability to write in two languages; he remembered the eloquent Spanish of his letters and the success of his English-language dispatches to the newspaper in San Antonio. He suggested that Daniel become a full-time journalist, that he travel the world, look for assignments as a correspondent for several North American newspapers, and that he cull from his notebooks and manuscripts everything he could preserve about the Mexico that was vanishing and the one in the process of being born.

Daniel mulled over that idea for some time. He could not believe it was possible to earn a living doing something so pleasant, but it seemed a good way to continue practicing his ambition to perform the impossible. The very next day he went to the offices of the newspaper where for a year he had been sending dispatches from Chihuahua and Sonora. He was greeted by Howard Gardner, a slightly unfocused young man whose nervous conversation was a happy mixture of conviction and skepticism. He was the copy editor, and in practice the managing editor, because the nominal editor was the owner, who came by less and less frequently with more and more directives. He would issue ten instructions, four would be observed, and then life would flow on like the calm, transparent waters of the river that could be seen from the office windows. It turned out that Howard was an ardent fan of Daniel's articles. He told him, laughing, how he had come to count on the arrival of one of his stories to break the boredom consuming his afternoon; he asked several times how things were going "down there," lamented the war, embraced the correspondent as if he had missed him personally, and had money still owed him sent over from accounting.

"I always knew you weren't dead," said the editor, with a warmth in his eyes that made Daniel blush.

He had not expected someone like Howard, he had envisioned an indifferent gringo and once again had to recognize the truth of one of Milagros's sayings: *The purpose of life is to keep us on our toes.* He unhesitatingly accepted this friendship that was being offered when he most needed it, and left the office chatting with Gardner as if he had known him for years. At the end of four hours, and more than four beers, each knew the other's life history. As they left the dark, noisy bar that had witnessed their confessions, they were sharing a last secret, arms around each other's shoulders, each sure he had found a kindred spirit, a conviction visible in the drunken and meditative cadence of their footsteps. A million stars pierced the night sky.

"What a night for kissing your girl," said Howard, pointing to the heavens as he said good-bye.

Daniel was whistling as he entered his father's house, and he took a chair near his to report the glory and omens he had discovered. Dr. Cuenca listened, remembering, with the delight fathers feel when they discover in their sons the light that once fired them.

"It seems you met your Diego Sauri," he said, referring to the friendship that bound him to the pharmacist. And as if that allusion had unraveled a knot tangled in his chest since he first set eyes on his son, he finally dared ask about Emilia.

"Emilia is a treasure," Daniel replied, emphasizing each word. Then he sank into a sea of drunken, overwrought tears, unrestrained grief he had never allowed himself to express.

When he decided to stay in San Antonio, he had written Emilia, giving her an exact account of his situation. In the envelope, along with the letter, he enclosed a lock of his hair and a photograph with a message that said *You are my only reason for living.* After that, he had been unable to write again. He was embarrassed by their separation, and did not want to confess that even though she wasn't there, he was at peace, and feeling reasonably fortunate. Drunkenly, he wept like a child over all those things, and like a boy laid his head in the lap of the benevolent father he had never found in Cuenca when he was young. Old men allow themselves liberties they were not capable of when the world held them as a model of bravery and rectitude.

All the time Daniel was sobbing out his cares, Dr. Cuenca sat without a word, smoothing his son's hair with trembling, arthritic fingers, until sleep robbed Daniel of all his misery. It was December, two nights before Christmas. That was all Daniel could think of as he opened his eyes the next morning, his head still on his father's numb legs. He had no idea how long he had been there; he did not remember dreaming; his father's hand still lay on his head.

Dr. Cuenca died on December 23, 1912. Daniel's notification reached the Casa de la Estrella eleven days later. The fear Daniel had felt when he was sent off to boarding school, a fear he had conquered only after spending a night in the cemetery when he was thirteen, once again demoralized him. He was as alone and lost as he would ever be.

Josefa went to the hospital with the news, and Emilia was charged with telling Diego. For many years, his wife had resisted being the bearer of bad news. She didn't know the origin of that weakness, but knew she could not tell her husband about political reverses or personal losses without feeling guilty. As if she were the one responsible for the peace and long life of all humanity, as if she were the one dealing the blow to the troubled heart that was her husband's reaction to death.

Emilia took off her white smock, looked for Zavalza, and told him the news as if she were reading a verdict. He pressed his lips together, and touched her cheek. She closed her eyes and turned away.

NEARLY FOUR WEEKS LATER, without having been able to console either her parents or Milagros, Emilia arrived in San Antonio. She was carrying a tapestry valise, a case filled with bottles, a handbag with money from the whole family, the cello Dr. Cuenca had given her, and the certainty that the doctor had died to force her to come back to his son.

She leapt from the train to a platform swimming in the smell of biscuits and butter. So soon after the chaos that gripped her country, after passing through station after station that stank of gunpowder if not death, Emilia let herself indulge in that aroma as she anxiously sought Daniel. She spotted him in the distance and waited, without calling out, for him to find her. She wanted to engrave in her mind the picture of him looking for her in the crowd. She wanted to feel that she still could turn back. She wanted to take a last breath before accepting the fact that she was once again giving up her sanity. Then she raised one hand and waved as she called Daniel's name. As soon as he was near, she clung to the badgered animal who opened his arms to her.

They cried together all one afternoon and part of the night. For them, and for everyone else, for the dream the elder Cuenca had forged, for his lost world and his boundless world, for the murdered and the murderers, for the war that separated them and the peace they did not know where to find. Afterward, the call of their bodies revived them. They awoke in a perfect equilibrium of entwined arms and legs, and repeated that equation well into the day.

"I'm hopeless," said Emilia, as her fingers traced the bony trough that divided Daniel's chest.

THE NEXT FEW DAYS, they walked every morning along the river to where the city ended and fields of crops and fragrant grasses began. Emilia met Howard Gardner and became his accomplice and most faithful witness to his happiness and ambitions. She learned where to buy the best butter and freshest vegetables, she lost her fear of getting lost, and went to bed every night beneath a dark sky pinpointed by stars.

"For kissing," said Gardner, looking up as he told Daniel good-bye.

Emilia filled the small house near the river with plants and converted its two rooms into a haven graced with her boxes and possessions, where Daniel came to recognize even the aroma that reigned in the Casa de la Estrella. To come back there every afternoon was disorienting; to take off Emilia's clothes was to recapture everything, only to lose it as soon as he stepped outside again. All too soon, the consolation of having her with him turned into nostalgia for everything they'd left behind.

"You carry your world on your back," he told her one time when he came home from the newspaper.

"You, on the other hand, scatter pieces of yours everywhere," she replied, without looking up from the book in which she was absorbed.

Daniel bent down to kiss her, and took from her hands the treatise on anatomy she had set out to memorize.

EVERY AFTERNOON, Daniel came home from the newspaper accompanied by Howard and with news from Mexico burning his tongue. First, an uprising in Tlaxcala, then the eruption of a volcano in Colima, then the main port of the Yucatán destroyed by fire, then, one cold night, in a stuttering but precise telegram, the explosion, inside the army, of a conspiracy against Madero led by the most faithful adherents of the old dictatorship.

Like a gust of wind picking things up only to dash them to the ground, Daniel began recounting the details of the military insurrection. As he was telling them about prisoners freed by the dissidents, the bombardment of civilians, acts of panic and barbarism, he was throwing clothes into a suitcase, informing Emilia that they would be returning to Mexico the next morning.

"We can't stay here, content, doing nothing, while this is going on," he concluded. If he had fought with those opposing Madero the instigator, now he would fight against those who were betraying him for being a reformer.

Never changing expression, Emilia let Daniel talk on, curse, make plans and imagine battles, arrange with Howard how many weekly articles he would send, the places he would go looking for stories, the people he would interview, and the various newspapers where Howard would try to place his dispatches. Then, as matter-of-factly as Daniel had announced plans without asking her opinion, Emilia informed him that she was not crossing the border. She was still getting adjusted, she was haunted by the memory of her train trip through a country being torn apart, and she did not yet have the courage to retrace the journey. Besides, she claimed, what was the point of Daniel's going off to die in a war that no longer knew where it was headed or for whom it was fighting. She said her mother was right, that politics brings out the worst in men and that wars bring the worst men to power. She was sure that Daniel would go no matter what, but he should not count on dragging her back. He had promised to go with her to Chicago to meet Dr. Arnold Hogan, a famous pharmacist and physician with whom Diego Sauri had conducted a long, detailed, friendly correspondence.

"I'm not going to change my plans. I'm tried of being whipped about by the swings of your whims and about-faces of the Republic."

As a grinning Howard Gardner watched, Emilia was walking around with a coffee cup in one hand, exhibiting an aplomb that reminded Daniel of the little girl sitting in a tree swinging her legs, and talking a fluent, charming English that would have delighted his father and that was being used as a courtesy to their visitor. When she had had her say, Howard took the cup from her trembling left hand and kissed her on a cheek flushed with emotion.

Emilia poured Howard's coffee without breaking the silence, and he made himself comfortable in an armchair in the living room, settling in to observe the spectacle of their argument. Daniel, elbows on the table, head in hands, was half hidden from them. He closed his eyes, cursed in a low voice, and could think of nothing except how much he wanted to take Emilia with him. She destroyed him when she spoke to him as if he were a stupid little boy to whom she had to explain reality slowly and firmly enough so that he could understand. It destroyed him when a wave of indignation made the blood rise to her cheeks and focused her opinions, when she expounded with the authority of a historian and answered his fury with the condescension of a grande dame. Having lived so long among reflective adults had affected the way she thought, and it was impossible to argue with her because she was as unerringly perceptive as Josefa, as bold as Diego, and as stubborn as Milagros. He had very few arguments he could use to persuade her, none of them in public. He did not move or speak for a long time; the atmosphere grew so heavy that Howard drank a last swallow of coffee and said good-bye.

"Selfish!"

"Arrogant!"

"Heartless!"

"Martyr!"

What followed was a battle between desperate animals; they insulted and bit one another, threatened absence, oblivion, and eternal hatred.

"Drop dead," said Emilia, emerging from the wrestling and shoving they had descended to. Her forehead was scratched, her cheeks burning, the buttons torn from her blouse.

"Not without you," Daniel replied, stopping to look at her for the first time since their fight began. By his father, she was prettier than ever. "You're a savage," he said, bending down to lift his pants leg and look at where she had kicked him in the shins.

"Does it hurt?" asked Emilia, embarrassed.

"No," said Daniel, moving closer. Her breasts trembled beneath the open blouse. Daniel touched the hollow between them. The air lightened as their bodies joined in truce, making love as if they would not see a tomorrow, all anxieties forgotten. They recanted their oaths of hatred and signed a reconciliation. Nevertheless, neither of them retreated from the line they had drawn the night before, and although they swore tolerance, unbroken memory, and loyalty, they awoke without an agreement to exhibit in the light of day.

"You go looking for it so often that one day you'll find it," Emilia told Daniel.

"What?" he asked.

"Don't make me say it," she said, hugging him to frighten away the horror of death that hovered over their good-byes.

CHAPTER

20

DANIEL RETURNED to the Mexico he had envisioned the minute he heard of the military coup. Emilia, in turn, sold what little they had accumulated, boxed up all Dr. Cuenca's books, paid the last rent payment, and turned in the key to the house. Then she set off for Chicago to look for the university and a future that held no thought of war.

It was ten o'clock one dark morning when she arrived in a city in the grip of winter. It was snowing, and a cold wind was blowing from the lake. Emilia could not have imagined that cold could be so painful. As she struggled with the feat of walking on snow for the first time, she shouted her frustration at the gray sky descending upon her. Concentrating on everything except where she put her feet, she slipped on the ice. Laden with her luggage and her anger, she turned in a slow pirouette, trying not to fall, but she was carrying too many bundles and thinking too many thoughts to keep her balance. Unable to break her fall with her hands, she fell face first in the snow. She was soaked, freezing, but she believed she deserved what she got, for ignoring the evidence, for fleeing her destiny, for being so presumptuous. What was she doing? She had had the good fortune to be born in the warmth of a tropical country, and here she was flat in a puddle of dirty snow, out of patience, tired, and more lonely than she had known she could be. What was she looking for, when beneath the stars of the Casa de la Estrella was the warmest and most delightful haven in the world? All to be a doctor?

She wanted to cry but was stopped by the idea that her tears would freeze. She was seething over a multitude of indignities, but got to her feet. This was no place for disquisitions and nostalgia. In her purse was the address of a boardinghouse. She would get that far and not go out again until the icy wind died down.

Two months later it was still snowing. She had, however, learned to walk on the ice, and had enrolled as an auditor at Northwestern University and was working in the laboratory of Dr. Hogan, her father's friend, whom she had liked the moment they met. Hogan's interest in medicinal plants was equaled only by the Sauris', and he had welcomed Emilia into the beakers of his laboratory and the vacuum left by his wife's recent death with a warmth that was a blend of paternal affection and juvenile fervor. He saved her all the legal problems she would have encountered as a foreigner with only a tourist's passport had she looked for work elsewhere. He was a simple, wise man. When she was with him, Emilia felt conflicting emotions: on the one hand, she missed her father's enthusiasm and music more than ever, but in return she was infused as never before with his energy. In the mornings she went to the university, and in the afternoons helped Hogan in his lab near Hyde Park. She kept busy from dawn until long after the city sank into the early darkness of its long winter. Emilia's heart resembled the city landscape. Occasionally a ray of light shone through, the feeling that she was right, some irony to offset her homesickness and uncertainty, but most of the time her life was shadowed by the news arriving from Mexico. Each distant catastrophe tended to loom larger at night. She filled her days with sound; after dinner she entertained the woman who ran her boardinghouse, and the other guests, by playing her cello with the frenzy of a Hungarian violinist, but when the time came to be alone, to turn out the light in her bedroom, blackness spread through her body like a cancer. She missed her parents, Milagros, Zavalza, and if that wasn't enough, there was always the worst of her questions: was Daniel still alive?

She never got to sleep until early morning, and woke only a few hours later. She would leap out of bed even if it was Sunday, and begin some task or other. She studied with an intensity that amazed her professors. They did not know what to do about a student who had no documentation to verify her medical studies, but understood and talked about illnesses and symptoms as if she had already graduated. Dr. Hogan, who would have liked to soothe her wounds with honey and erase with a magic wand the sadness he could see in her eyes, invited her to make rounds at the teaching hospital with him and his last-year students. The way she had of moving, touching the patients, and, especially, reaching into her emotions to relate to their problems, fascinated him.

What most attracted Emilia to her new maestro was his theory that physical ills are connected with mental ones, his "crazy idea" that madness could be cured with medicines and longing forestalled with pills. Emilia knew, from her father and her own experience, that there were certain herbs that lifted depressions. Searching, always searching, with the help of Hogan and a constant stream of letters to Diego Sauri, Emilia began to experiment with preparations that would return a smile to the melancholy and lessen the pain of a disturbed mind.

Hogan had first begun to use folk medicine in hopeless cases when, after all avenues were exhausted, the patient still faced death. But gradually in less serious cases, too, some of which improved as if by witchcraft. In Emilia he discovered a flair for alleviating melancholia that was due not just to her preparations but also to the hours she spent listening to the afflicted. It didn't matter if their mumbling was incoherent, repetitious, or senseless, it didn't matter if they kept talking till midnight, Emilia never showed any impatience, and by listening and listening to the tangle of their desolate thoughts she was able to help find a loose end that would begin to unravel the knot. Hogan made her his assistant in all cases that dealt with mental or emotional problems. All the rest—the functions of the nerve cells, cardiac rhythms and their anomalies, which scientist was developing what antiseptic, why Dr.

Alexis Carrel had won the Nobel Prize, who had discovered how to detect diphtheria, and why it was advantageous for a doctor to read Shakespeare and Greek mythology—he taught her bit by bit as he discussed a hopeless case, a recent investigation, a doubt that seemed to have no solution. Sometimes, in the middle of a lesson the good Dr. Hogan was delivering with Saxon finality, Emilia would interrupt to recall one of her first maestro's maxims.

"Cuenca always said there are no hopeless cases, only doctors who can't find the answers."

Hogan was a tall, rosy, energetic, and infinitely tender man whom Emilia could turn purple with laughter. He regretted that he didn't know the Sauris, Milagros, the poet Rivadeneira, Zavalza, or, of course, Daniel Cuenca. In a brief time, he learned so much about them that it would have seemed perfectly logical to recognize them if he saw them on a street corner. Some of their customs were so attractive to him that he began to model his own Sunday afternoons after the ones Emilia described from her childhood. Hogan was a poet manqué, but the more he missed his wife, the more prolific he became. So he began every Sunday evening by reading one of his poems. Then Pauline Atkinson, an old friend of Hogan's, a great cook and descendant of Greek immigrants, would play the piano with her small precise hands, accompanying Emilia on the cello.

Dr. Hogan's passion was astronomy. He had a telescope installed in the upper story of his house and knew the names, colors, and movements of suns, comets, aerolites, and moons whose light had been extinguished centuries ago but still shone upon the sleep of mankind. So at night he would have his guests climb the stairs of a tower he had constructed on his patio and submit them to countless measurements and studies, all performed previously by someone in more scientific surroundings than his, but not with more fervor.

There was always a collection of visitors to enrich each Sunday with new obsessions, spectacles, and pastimes. At Hogan's Sundays, Emilia met everyone from a photographer famous not only for his skill but his storehouse of reverential knowledge about the beginnings of photography in the experiments of a sixteenth-century Italian, to Helen Shell, the niece of a well-known promoter and homeopath, a friend of Hogan's, a blond and bewitching student of philosophy recently liberated from the yoke that had been her life as a wealthy New Yorker educated not to make waves. The philosopher William James was one of her primary interests, another was falling in love twice weekly, always with a different man. She formed a friendship with Emilia that grew every Sunday as they told each other everything that had happened to them during the week. In the midst of a Belgian scientist's meticulous dissertation on the mysteries of the atom, in the midst of the sublime tones of a historian's musings on why the Chinese had not discovered Europe, in the midst of the humility of a mathematician who proposed that his science was not merely an instrument of exploration but a method of self-discipline as well, in the midst of an economist's monologue on the existence of paper money in the Orient some three centuries before Westerners printed their first bills in 1640, Emilia and Helen steered their way through minor incidents and plans that could not be delayed. Hogan, who would hear them whispering while some scholar documented his doubts or waxed eloquent on the numbers of discoverers who languished in anonymity, did not understand how Emilia could remember all of it and later talk about theories of time or marvel that the idea of including an index in a book occurred only in the eighteenth century, when it seemed she had not concentrated on a word that was said during the gathering.

When he asked how she managed to assimilate two conversations at once, Emilia answered that this facility was in the genes of the women of her family. And that some, like her Aunt Milagros, could grasp as many as four. Perhaps it had to do with the country they lived in. In Mexico, so many things were happening at the same time that if you didn't pay attention to more than one, you were always far behind events. The Revolution was an excellent example, because it quadrupled levels of events. After assassinating Madero, Victoriano Huerta—in Diego Sauri's opinion, the greatest traitor in the history of Mexico—assumed the presidency of the Republic and before the close of 1913 had eliminated Congress, silenced the press, jailed several legislators, and murdered the most prominent of them. With no public critics, he granted himself extraordinary powers and put off elections indefinitely. What had happened next, no one, however much they could watch and understand at the same time, could ever keep track of. The Zapatistas continued their fight in the south. In Sonora, Coahuila, and Chihuahua, everyone from a Maderista governor to Pancho Villa, an old renegade trained in the rough-and-ready wisdom of the sierra, had taken up arms. As Diego Sauri wrote in one of the long letters Emilia read and reread: "The country that buried Madero as a leader is resurrecting him as their symbol of hope." The forces of the counter-revolution had been strong enough to inflict the deathblow to the fragile Madero democracy but not strong enough to establish a national accord. Throughout the country, during a long, cruel year and a half, different forces rose up against the usurper Huerta, united in their hatred for him, though not in agreement on what must be done when the various warring groups and interests regained power. Which would happen only when the army left over from the Díaz regime Madero had not been able to crush was destroyed and Huerta was forced into exile like any defeated combattant—though with his freedom and his life, unlike the president he had unseated. The rebel armies entered Mexico City united in victory but divided in their causes and goals. Some represented the secular and enterprising north, enlightened and opportunistic, self-centered and ambitious; others rose up in defense of the Indian and colonial heritages, seeking a redistribution of lands and a justice that would compensate for a lifetime of poverty and misery. The hour of triumph, wrote the pharmacist, has also become the hour of rupture and confrontation.

With the past sealed away, Mexicans began to fight the future. And the war resumed. Daniel went back and forth, but his heart was with the Villistas and Zapatistas, however much his head told him that the ignorance and ferocity of those leaders could never govern a country as complicated as the one they had conquered with force. He felt an admiration for them that did not blind him to their ineptitude and excesses. At least that's what Emilia derived from repeated readings of the articles published in Howard Gardner's newspaper.

Letters from the Sauris arrived late or not at all; perhaps more than half the pages Josefa and Diego sent to their daughter reporting the most trivial details of everything happening before their eyes or in their imaginations during those years were still drowsing in the corner where wishes that once seemed impossible go to hide. Letters also came from Milagros, who although she constantly protested, asking what fool notion had caused her niece to go off like that, understood better than anyone the madness that prevented her from coming back. And then, like some scent of her childhood, Emilia began to receive letters from Sol, who had progressed from honeymoon to pregnancy, and then to another and another. Her missives conveyed a sense of boredom tinged with a fear she thought she hid, prudent and well mannered as always. The most faithful and precise letters were Zavalza's, and those that never came . . . Daniel's. Emilia became accustomed to living with the reproach of his silence, because from the beginning she had decided to mourn him the way we do those who die before we have paid our debt to them. Daniel, she told herself, could be two different people: one who rode the horn of the new moon with her, who soaked up all her dreams because no dream was better than reality when he was with her. The other was a traitor who mounted the horse of the Revolution to ride off and save the country, as if there could be a country anywhere except where they shared a bed.

"At first the world decayed, actually smelled bad, when he wasn't there. Today, some of his scent has faded, and I don't have to have it to breathe," Emilia confided one philosophical Sunday to her friend Helen Shell, eliciting a compassionate smile. As if despite her uncomplicated, good-natured, peaceful life, Helen envied the perfume of that passion she could not understand, not even in the light of the wisdom of her admired philosophers. The business of always thinking about the same man, of centering all your desire on him from the time you were a child, of missing him every day as much as the first, and going two years without sex with another man seemed outrageous, far more sinful and immoral than anything dreamed up in the filthy mind of the Protestant pastor whose sermons on sin she had grown up with.

With Helen Shell and her spirit of adventure, Emilia went to the theater when she felt the world closing in around her. With Helen she shared lectures, a passion for the latest novels, for avant-garde poems, for conversations into the early hours. With Helen she occasionally traveled to New York, where she was dazzled by the bridges and the craziness of a city that captured her gradually and for all time.

ONE MORNING just as Helen came to pick her up to go to the station to begin a trip to New York they had been planning for months, a telegram arrived from Mexico. Emilia was about to open it when Helen, who was strong on sticking to plan, begged her not to ruin everything by opening a telegram that would only upset her. Emilia hesitated, then heeded her friend's plea, sure that nothing good could be contained in an urgent message from a world at war. She did not dare look to see who had sent it; she knew the people it might have come from but did not want to know exactly which one. She was not, however, brave enough to leave it lying unopened on the table in her bedroom. She put it at the bottom of her purse and took it with her.

For several days she felt the need to dig down into her purse until she could feel it and confirm it was still there. And then one night she went with Helen to the ballroom of a luxurious hotel on the East Side where they were featuring the fox-trot, disposed to dance with the first person who asked her. At the university, Helen had met a man who was currently the dream of her evenings although, she said, she had not lost her head over him because his feet were too big. Nevertheless, the big night of the fox-trot, he passed the test of fire. Despite his clown feet, he fastened Helen in his arms and, face-to-face, whirled her around the floor with a panache that lighted a fire no other beau had been able to kindle.

Emilia watched them as they cut across the dimly lit, polished wooden dance floor, not envious, but wistful, as delighted as if she were Helen's older sister. Helen was actually three years older than she, but Emilia looked upon her with the indulgence of those who grow up before their time. Living among the dying, having at the center of one's memories the first rumblings of a war, and having already lost the love of her life, made her unquestionably less young than her friend.

It had been more than two years since the dawn she had said good-bye to Daniel. She knew through others, and through the dispatches Gardner regularly published, that Daniel had spent that time traveling through the country disguised as a woman, a gringo, a bandit, a priest—dressed like a northerner when passing through the north, and wearing white cotton peasants' pants when he lived in the south. She knew through Milagros that Daniel had come through Puebla six times with the hope she had returned, and that each of those six times he had left Puebla swearing he would never come back. That night, as Helen danced her fox-trot, Emilia struggled not to close her eyes, to watch her friend laughing, to hum the bouncy rhythm of the dance without so much as blinking, because she was afraid she would start thinking about the battles, persecutions, horror, and tenacity that filled Daniel's writing. But although the music made her feel mildly secure, it could not block out the words of Daniel's article of the previous week. "As things are, it no longer matters here which side is more courageous, or who is right. Any question of right was lost long ago, and the only cowards are those who fled elsewhere with their cause."

A hand before her eyes interrupted her dark thoughts; she rose to dance the fox-trot with the commitment of a soldier going into battle, losing herself in the dance, in the arms guiding her from one side of the floor to the other, in the mixture of Spanish and Scots her partner used to ask about her life, in her own smile as she listened to herself answer as if about another woman.

It was only when the music ended and they exchanged the ballroom for the skies of the last night of February that Emilia, still holding the arm of her high-spirited blond dance partner, felt her resolution not to open the envelope melting away. Anxiously, she looked through her purse and the minute she had the telegram in her hand stopped in the middle of the street to read it. It took only a moment to hear the voice of her Aunt Milagros, abrupt and unemotional: Daniel had died. They did not know where. The last town from which he had sent word was in the north of Mexico.

"What is it?" Helen asked.

The night air hinted of the coming months of spring, but Emilia could not imagine being there when they arrived. With her dance partner's arms still at her waist, she tried to speak, but ended up crying as if ordered to flood the world.

The next day she made inquiries about the quickest way to get home to Mexico. She did not want to go back to Chicago. She wrote Hogan a long letter of thanks and explanation and boarded a ship that would take her to a port near the Mexican border. Helen saw her off at the dock, stoic, joking, with not a word of how sad she was to be abandoned but with a quantity of gifts—among them a small satchel fitted with physician's instruments, two hats, and several concoctions that were in her view indispensable for traveling—that tripled the amount of luggage Emilia had brought to New York. Before she hugged her good-bye, she promised to send all of Emilia's belongings to her parents' house, and swore, on the photograph of her new sweetheart, she would come visit soon.

CHAPTER

21

EMILIA SAURI ENTERED MEXICO through a customs office that had not seen travelers in a very long time. As he was checking her passport and observing this woman dressed like an expensive foreign doll, the guard asked what she was looking for in a part of the world so remote from people like her.

"Would you believe my life?" Emilia replied, with no change in her aristocratic bearing.

"No," said the guard, stamping an entrance permit printed in the elaborate style of the Díaz dictatorship.

"Who runs things now?" Emilia asked.

"Whoever can," the guard said, and launched into a long, complicated description of the various military uprisings and the several, by his lights legal or illegal, governments of recent months. Emilia stood and listened to him speak the language that had not fallen on her ears for so long, and did not know what to do with the pleasure it evoked other than promise herself she would never again live more than a month anywhere else on the planet.

Before she had reached that border crossing, Emilia had stopped in San Antonio and learned from Gardner the name of the town from which Daniel had mailed his last article. Of course, it was almost two months since they had had any word of his whereabouts, but Gardner consoled her, reminding her that Daniel had disappeared before.

"He's a cat," Gardner had told Emilia when she showed him the telegram Milagros had sent telling her Daniel was dead and asking her to look for him.

"He was born with nine lives; he's lost one," he repeated as they began dinner. Then he drank nine whiskeys, neat. By the time dessert came he was crying more than Emilia.

"Try to remember I'm the widow here," said Emilia, with a smile like a rainbow breaking through the storm clouds of her tears.

She spent the night in the cluttered bachelor's room Howard had offered with the pride of someone offering a palace, and the next morning, after breakfast, the first she had wanted for many days, she set out for the border in search of Daniel's remaining eight lives. Her conversations with Howard had nourished her hopes to the point that during the journey she went so far as to reassure herself that her Aunt Milagros always exaggerated. But as soon as the guard handed back her passport and authorized her to go look for what she had lost, all her optimism deserted her. Where was she going with her silly hopes of finding Daniel? She was entering a country, not her living room, a country whose border with the United States was endless and whose expanse her eyes could never take in if she traveled across it the rest of her life. What had made her Aunt Milagros think Emilia could find Daniel "in the north of Mexico"? As if the north of Mexico would suddenly fit in the palm of her hand when she stepped across the border, as if the north of Mexico were a park, not that black, dry expanse she would wander across for days without finding anything.

IT WAS A TUESDAY when she came to a village that welcomed her with empty silence. As she had in all the others, she started walking around, expecting that the streets would be named after heroes, and there would be carefully laid dark stone sidewalks. The place had nothing to offer, however, but hot, dry air and squat houses Emilia did not know how to approach. She didn't know whom to ask what, what the devil she could do, in fact, but howl like a stray dog.

She saw herself reflected in the window of a store that sold nails and tools. Thin, hair uncombed, dark circles under her eyes, she was carrying four bundles and untold uncertainty, looking odd even to herself. She couldn't think of anything better to do than sit down and cry once again. It was from this village that Daniel had mailed his last dispatch to the newspaper in San Antonio, but that didn't mean he was there. Knowing how fast he moved, how restless he was, his dislike of being tied down, Emilia reasoned that if he had sent the article from there, it was probably as he passed through following who knows what rebel, what news story, what vanity, what glory, what change of power. She asked herself which of the bands Daniel might be with, and without a moment's hesitation answered her own question: with whoever was losing. And who would that be? Who was destined to lose the struggle that had been unleashed in her country? What did it matter, Emilia thought, drying her eyes with a handkerchief on which Josefa had embroidered her name with tiny, precise stitches. Why wasn't she like her mother? Why couldn't Daniel be as stable and generous as her father? Why had she had the singular bad luck to fall in love like this? When there were so many men. When there was Zavalza with his peace, even the pharmacologist Hogan with the adoration of an old man to whom everything was perfect? Why couldn't she escape the force that impelled her toward a man who might even be dead? Daniel: eyes like questions, hair falling over his brow, head swimming with ideas. Daniel, touching her where no other man had touched her, entering her as if she were his property, calling on her when he wanted her and going off when he was tired of seeing her. Daniel, who made the heart between her legs throb, begging her, cursing her. Daniel, who could be rotting somewhere on some remote mountainside. Daniel, who in two years had not written her a single line. If secretly she had thought about his death, why did she come running to look for him as soon as someone feared that he was a specter?

With her head between her knees, she wept under a desert sun that no one challenged at that hour, until she was too tired to think and instinct prodded her to seek the shade. In the late afternoon she got up again to walk through the half-empty town of squat buildings. She found no trace of Daniel in any street or voice, no scrap of the brown pants he had been wearing when he left, no billfold, no straw hat, no canteen left behind by chance; they existed only in her memory. It grew dark. So dark that Emilia felt the presence of a fear she had lost while wandering through the world with nothing but solitude to her name. She was starving, so hungry she could eat an ox the way they cook them in Puebla, slathered in some red sauce. She had never examined them too closely, thrown on the fire with the hide intact and blood shooting sparks like stars when a chunk was cut off. She stopped before a doorway where she smelled just that odor, the smell of meat sizzling over coals, and pushed open the door of a kind of tunnel that seemed be open to the public, although it had no sign and solicited no customers besides those already inside making so much noise. She looked for a table where she could collapse with her bundles, her sunken eyes, her fatigue, and then looked around to see if anyone would come ask what she wanted.

The place was filled with men drinking, but she was not bothered by what seemed to her an innocuous scene. When men gathered together they had to drink, because if they didn't drink they would have to talk sober, and men simply don't know how to talk unless it's about business. A tall, very fat woman with the most perfect features Emilia had ever seen emerged from the depths of the tunnel. Her voice was hoarse and her hands strong. She asked Emilia what she would like, as she would have asked an old friend. Then she brought what she had to offer and sat beside Emilia to watch her eat and ask her a string of questions. From where she was going and where she had come from to didn't she find the horse meat tough and why were her eyes swollen as eyes are swollen only from crying over some man's stupidity.

Emilia told her everything in her heart, from her passion for medicine to her bedeviled obsession for the man whose photo she carried in a locket beside pictures of her parents and her aunt.

"And is he worthy of all your tears? I don't see anything so special about him," said the woman after carefully examining the picture of the youth whose sepia face Emilia was stroking with her fingertip. She continued, not waiting for an answer, that she didn't know why she asked, that every woman carries her own stupidity in her bosom, and if this was hers, then it must be for some good reason—so good she had left the peace and soft life of the gringos to come looking for his corpse. Emilia was soothed as she listened to the woman's throaty, guileless voice, until the word *corpse* reawakened the apprehension that had consumed her since she received Milagros's telegram. Seeing her shiver, the beautiful fat woman got up from the bench where she had deposited her elephantine body and took Emilia in her arms, patting her as she would a baby. She offered to put Emilia up for the night and went back to the kitchen, saying that before she showed her the way she would bring her some hot water with cinnamon.

The kitchen lay beyond the farthest light at the end of the tunnel. From where Emilia sat, all she could see was that light and a wall; she imagined behind it a kitchen like her mother's: each clay pot set in a niche just its size, each baking dish hanging by a colored cord forming a perfect jigsaw puzzle on the wall and, right in the middle, a window looking onto a patio filled with jasmine like omens. Emilia was dreaming of Josefa's kitchen, her eyes fixed on the white wall that blocked her view of the kitchen of the *hostal,* when a man whose head was covered by a cloth came out into the light carrying a cup in his hand. He walked blindly, directed by taps of the *hostelera*'s cooking spoon. An apron covered the man's legs, he limped slightly, and he was skinny as a fish. Emilia's eyes were so heavy from crying, her heart so confused, that she could have been seeing a ghost, but instead, standing before her, whole and all of a piece, was Daniel Cuenca.

"Is this the light of your life?" asked the *hostelera,* whisking the cloth from the man's head.

Emilia stared at Daniel, up and down, as if she needed to fit together the pieces of his body in order to recognize him.

"What happened to your leg?" she asked, determined to control the trembling of her body.

"I tripped," he replied. "Are you cold?"

"I'm not sure," said Emilia, moving toward him to touch the many days' growth of beard on his cheeks. "Is everything there?"

"It's there," Daniel assured her.

"You didn't die?"

"Several times."

At a sign from the *hostelera,* all the men in the cantina rose to their feet and a teasing, humorous song rocked the room.

"And is that all you two have to say?" asked the fat woman.

"In public, yes," said Emilia.

With that, the *hostelera* put at their disposal the bed that had sheltered the scandalous love of her progenitors, a brassy Spanish woman and a Tarahumara Indian who was quite free of prejudice. Doña Baui del Perpetuo Socorro, which was the name she used to boast of her crossed bloodlines, would not accept the money Emilia placed in her apron as she would an Easter flower on an altar. She returned it, saying they would talk about money later, then spirited them both through the door. The next morning, she got up early to spread the news that a doctor was sleeping on the second floor of her house.

Daniel was using the village as his last center of operations: he came back there after forays through the sierra, visits to the oil fields, treks on trains that had no purpose other than to come and go and were taken by those who could take them. The region had once been prosperous, but as waves of uprisings swept across it over the last five years, no one was ever sure where the night's meal was coming from. Daniel paid for his bed and board by washing dishes and scrubbing floors, something, to his good fortune, someone still needed done. Because people had been doing without necessities with such dedication for so long that no one needed a baker, say, or a seamstress, much less a lawyer turned journalist. Nor were they hungry for good cooks, because to prepare the kind of food they could forage, all that was wanting was a fire and a little will. Laws were something that for the moment were kept in a drawer, waiting to be reintroduced in a far distant future, and lawyers, if they didn't know how to wash dishes or shoot a thirty-thirty, were completely useless. Of all the professions, the only one respected and needed was the medical profession. No matter the degree of training, much less the specialty, even an itinerant dentist was worth his weight in gold. So as it turned out, Emilia and Daniel, who could have stayed who knows how long closed up in that room, loving, asking forgiveness, wrapped up in themselves, were brought down from their cloud less than five hours after falling into each other's arms.

By seven A.M., more than fifteen people had lined up to see the doctor. Baui had classified them according to their ills, expecting Emilia to wake from the dream of love in which she was wasting time. But after a while, when she had not heard so much as a word from behind the door, the *hostelera* simply barged into her parents' former room and as if the intertwined couple on the bed were sitting talking at a table in her cantina, she asked them to get dressed as soon as they finished their dance, because Emilia was going to have to perform a different activity that morning. The Cyclops formed by an engrossed Emilia and Daniel did not even blink at Señora Baui's interruption: eyes closed, they continued to execute the task they had been engaged in nearly all night. The *hostelera* was not perturbed that they didn't answer, because she understood that they understood, and before leaving the room said she would give them ten minutes: three to repopulate the world they lived in, and seven to get washed and come downstairs.

By eight o'clock Emilia was already faced with a heterogeneous and volatile group whose ills ranged from simple stomach pain to the most horrendous injuries she had ever beheld: arms half torn off, hands missing fingers, gangrenous legs, ears torn loose, guts spilling from an abdomen. Under other circumstances, the spectacle of those she was being called on to treat would have made her weep with impotence, but buoyed as she was from the lovemaking, which can exorcize any sense of defeat, she started in, proposing to move from the impossible to the simple, seeking the solution for each pain placed in her hands. Daniel, with a humility new to Emilia, was from that moment prepared to be her helper, and as he trailed behind her, taking down the name and condition of each patient, he cursed himself for the weakness that had prevented him from being a doctor. He had always been aware that the mere sight of suffering immobilized him, and as he learned that such weakness was not supposed to be a male quality, he chose not to place himself in situations that revealed it. Which is why he had not wanted to study medicine, why there had been a chasm between him and his father that they bridged only at the end, why he fled from Emilia and her ease in confronting illness and pain without permanent damage to her spirit. Several times that morning, he wanted to run from the gruesome horrors Emilia addressed so naturally and sympathetically. He felt he might faint at every step, even though he tried to look as little as possible at the patient, instead concentrating on slowly writing his name, along with his age and his symptoms. Emilia had thought she would begin with the seriously injured and the children, but nearly all the patients were children and men wounded in the war. In that part of the world, a woman having a baby would never have considered taking the doctor's time. So she took them on all at once, in an undertaking Daniel assured her could only lead to chaos, but with the help of the *hostelera,* her *comandante*'s voice and organizational skills, progress became not only possible but nearly methodical as the morning went by.

Watching Emilia moving among the sick, Daniel realized that she was stronger than he, bolder than he, less egotistic than he, more necessary in the world than he with all his theories and all his battles. What did she have to fear from him if she had not blanched at the bullet-riddled body of a man who had survived the firing squad?

The day had been generous in misfortunes that had a name, and he, accustomed to walking among anonymous corpses, had felt true fear facing the named half-living whose corruption Emilia would have licked clean if that was what was necessary to cure them.

"And this is the war you're fighting to save us all?" Emilia asked Daniel that night after drinking half a glass of cane liquor and before tasting the plate of beans she was eating with him and the *hostelera.*

"All wars are like this," Daniel contended.

"That's what I told you," Emilia muttered.

"You think you're so perfect," he said, to precipitate the fight he'd felt building in him.

"She talks less and does more than some people," said the *hostelera,* throwing fuel on the fire.

After desires are satisfied, there is always a whole world to argue about. So Daniel and Emilia became embroiled in arguing and drinking that ended in the deepest melancholy Emilia had known. She was exhausted, and it did not take much liquor to inflame her tongue and turn two years' worth of resentment into hurtful, defensive retorts to the ironic tone Daniel used to describe her courage as disguised arrogance and her integrity as a pure lack of sensitivity. For an hour, Emilia teetered on the edge of the precipice, and then broke down and wept as she had longed to do since early morning. Two children whose only illness was caused by a lack of clean water had died in her arms, a soldier who had lost his arm beneath his general's horse, and a woman with the pus of an unknown disease oozing from between her legs. She had no medicines, she had no clean thread, and had only two needles for suturing. All her treatments had been made without an analgesic, and she had to send home to die at least six people who after ten days in a hospital like the one in Chicago would have been completely cured. Of course this war was obscene, no less so because all wars are. She had not wanted to face it, which was why she had fled to a different world when she saw it coming, but that night she knew with certainty that she could never get away from it now, even if she saw it only from afar, even if it was her role to repair its catastrophe and ruin whatever way she could.

"All wars are shit," said the huge Tarahumara-Valencian woman, who listened to their argument as one of many drunken quarrels whose flames she had fed.

"But there are heroes in all of them," Daniel replied, taking a long swallow of Señora Baui's *aguardiente.*

Emilia looked at him as if he had spoken a timeless truth, and wanted for herself the alcohol that shone on his lips, making him attractive and heroic as he had not been ten seconds before. She wanted that image to safeguard forever among those stored in her soul. She sucked the *aguardiente* from his lips, and led him to the bed of truce that called to them both.

CHAPTER 22

THEY HAD NOT SPENT more than three nights in the whitewashed adobe room they had rented from Señora Baui before Emilia Sauri had imposed a sense of home and hearth. On the broken-down bureau she set a photograph of Dr. Cuenca playing the flute, one of Josefa and Diego gazing into each other's eyes, and a picture of Milagros Veytia perched on the rim of a fountain. She transplanted two cactuses to pots and placed them with the photos, bought a china pitcher sold in the village plaza by a campesino who scavenged through abandoned haciendas, hung an embroidered shawl over the head of their bed, and transformed the room into a festive retreat where they forgot the hard, dismal life of the village.

As one could sleep in that dry climate with no shelter but a black sky studded with tiny mirrors, the *hostelera* converted her patio into a hospital. A hospital like so many that sprang up during those times, kept alive more by an abundance of patients and the humane efforts of a few dreamers than by their actual ability to maintain the breath of life left in the bodies of so many Mexicans. Baui's strength and Emilia's determination drove them to maintain their infirmary, dreaming like so many others that good things can result from pure will when there is no other source to draw upon.

Emilia started very early and worked into the night, but she came back to the room in the *hostal* combed and glowing as if she had just been bathing in the river. Watching her return one night, Daniel found her more beautiful than ever. Her cheeks were flushed from exhaustion, and some of the purple amapa blossoms that rained from a tree growing beside the well in the patio had caught in her hair. Daniel, nonetheless, gave her only half a glance, kissed her halfheartedly, and continued reading the yellowed newspaper that had reached the village two weeks before.

"We have no idea what's going on anywhere else. We might as well be prisoners," he complained.

Emilia did not answer. She knew those symptoms very well and feared them more than yellow fever, which was why she tried to confound common sense and not grant them any importance.

"Why are you so sour? Come here and I'll scratch your back," she said after a moment's silence.

Daniel folded the newspaper and lay down on the bed. Emilia's fingers followed the bones of his back.

"I'm not going to stop until I get that sick-dog look off your face," she said.

"It won't go away," Daniel replied, relaxing his body and his resistance.

Sometimes he was terrified at the thought of giving up his nomadic life, his certainty that there was no truer freedom than waking one morning in one bed and the next in a different one, of never eating at the same table long enough for the food to become familiar to the palate. He adored the Emilia who streaked through his life like a brilliant light that would blind him if it were permanent, and cherished the love he felt when she was in his arms, a devotion indestructible and intriguing as only new love can be, and nothing caused him greater panic than the idea that he would someday have his fill of that body, that it would no longer be desirable. When he was wandering alone through the world, when his bed was the earth beneath some tree, before he slept he would trace in the air the unforgettable arch of her eyebrows and tell himself that she was perfect, harmonious, beautifully drawn, like those lines. Then he desired her more than ever, and desire made him invulnerable and happy. He did not want to slake that thirst too often, he did not want the evening to come when because he had seen her too much her image could no longer stun his senses.

To protect herself from the danger she felt approaching, Emilia began to sleep in the patio with her patients, using the excuse of an emergency, or inventing one as the best way to blot out the day when Daniel would decide that things were not going well where they were, that life was becoming dull and that it would fall into the anathema of routine if something unforeseen, and therefore desirable, did not come along to rescue them.

AT THE END of April, a man came to the *hostal* who was fleeing Mexico City with his family, his belongings, and the latest news. He talked with Daniel from noon to early the next morning, feeding his anxieties. As they were eating, the man described the entrance of the campesino armies into the capital, the moment that Villa and Zapata watched the parade of their troops from the balcony of the Palacio Nacional, sat in the presidential chair to see how it felt, made long and confusing speeches in Xochimilco, agreed to continue fighting—one in the north and the other in the south—and then abandoned the political center of the nation, saying that all the sidewalks made them dizzy, that they were not interested in governing, that there were legal eagles for that and people they could leave to represent them, with the warning, of course, that hanging over their heads was a machete that would fall with deadly precision if they did not do well by the campesinos.

Such stories alarmed Daniel. To anyone with the least bit of experience, it was clear that leaving the capital and returning to the countryside was tantamount to yielding power that someone more ambitious and arbitrary would take for himself—and sooner rather than later.

Daniel went to look for a bottle of *aguardiente.* When he returned, Emilia kissed him and left for the hospital. Absorbed in his conversation, Daniel scarcely noticed her departure. The only thing he wanted to know was what the man had to tell. The war was continuing everywhere, the people of Mexico City were hungry and terrified, they lived at the mercy of the madness that every faction imposed when it took the city only to abandon it later. No one knew where all this was going to end; in fact, they were beginning to wonder if it would ever end.

With every drink, Daniel reiterated how important it was to install a power that would favor the weakest. He cursed the hour that the country had lost the generosity of the cause that inspired it to rise up in arms only to place its destiny in the hands of insatiable and bloodthirsty men. Emilia tried to put an end to the bottomless pit of that kind of talk when she came into the dining room that night, but Daniel was too wound up in drinking and talking to come to bed. Emilia left him there.

"I'm tired," she said, to avoid saying "You're insufferable."

It was very late when Daniel stumbled back to the room. Muttering incoherently about the useless horror of this battle or that, asking what had become of the old stupid ideals and what right the politicians had to toss on the garbage heap the purity of a cause for which all the best men had died. Furious with himself and, for good measure, with Emilia, he woke her to complain about the fate that had kept him so far away from the heart of matters. Because while all this tragedy was happening, they had been there gazing into each other's eyes, playing at marriage, curled up in a peace that was light-years away from what was going on.

All the next day Daniel went around kicking the walls, fuming over what he called his weakness, his lack of professionalism, his indolence, his . . . whatever word encompassed the simple but ineradicable fact that for too long Emilia had taken him in hand and made him forget everything in order to do her blessed will. As he stomped around in a blind rage, he howled laments and reproaches in which he blamed Emilia for having come to the village only a few hours before he was going to leave it, for preventing him from following his duty in the war, for making him forget journalism, which was after all the only thing he had left in life.

Only the morning before, Daniel had whispered ten times in her ear that nothing in the world made him as happy as she did, that he knew no better destiny than her body. Emilia was about to scream a few of the insults Milagros had coined during one of her inspired rages, when her mother's prudence whispered in her ear a more efficient way to calm Daniel without damage to her honor or her throat. She choked back the vitriol of her planned attack and went downstairs to advise Señora Baui that they would be leaving on the first train that passed through the village. Then she went back to the room where she had left Daniel talking to himself, and in five minutes' time had pulled the shawl from the headboard, put away the photos, folded the coverlet she had carried from New York, and filled a suitcase with two changes of clothing for each of them. As she did this, Daniel's blustering began to sputter until it was subsumed in one simple question: Where did she think she was going?

"To war," Emilia replied.

Daniel scrutinized this woman who stood before him, ready to travel, and asked her what she planned to do with her hospital. She hung her head for a second and then looked up, after biting her lip so hard she drew blood. It was in someone else's hands and she didn't want to hear another word about it. Daniel stared at her, not knowing how to deal with an attitude so different from the one he had expected to provoke with his tantrum. He had thought that after all his yelling, Emilia would let him go off alone to the war and chaos she so despised. Instead, her response was exactly the opposite of how she had reacted in San Antonio. He should have foreseen it, the woman was unpredictable, it was in her blood. There was a long silence as Daniel watched Emilia slowly disappear in the fading light.

"You're a bundle of surprises. Sometimes I detest you," he said finally, giving one last kick to the wall.

"My feelings exactly."

"Well, then, let's go to war," said Daniel.

A TRAIN PASSED THROUGH four days later. They heard the whistle in the distance just when they had given up hope of ever hearing it. All the air rushed from Señora Baui's massive lungs as she felt the terror of being left behind as an instant doctor. She ran upstairs to beg Emilia not to leave her with that responsibility, but all she got in return was a shower of kisses and a quick amplification of the thousand instructions Emilia had given as they worked together. As Daniel and Emilia were coming downstairs, Baui protested that no one became a doctor after only a month and a half as an observer, but as her babbling failed to move Emilia, she simply burst out crying. Never in the forty-seven years of her life in the desert had she cried. And the tears moistening her round cheeks surprised her so much that only because the train was leaving the station did she find the courage to acknowledge she had only herself to consult.

Emilia's right hand was clutching the metal bar at the steps of the car, so with her left, still holding her suitcase, she waved good-bye to the beautiful *gorda* who had given her so much and now was offering a lake of tears as a farewell gift.

"If you two have to die," Baui yelled after Emilia, "let it be without pain."

She was fast becoming a dot on the dusty horizon. Emilia licked the two salty drops that ran down her face from dark eyes focused on the friend now fading into the landscape. She turned to look for Daniel, who had already climbed to the roof of the car and from there was calling to her with the voice she remembered from many unexpected summonses. He had recovered the zest with which he looked upon life when it held danger, and offered Emilia a hand she did not try to, or would have been able to, reach. She left him to install himself among the troops whose affiliation was far from clear and looked for a place on the floor among the children, animals, and braziers of a group of *soldaderas* singing as if they had something to celebrate.

SHE KNEW from the first day: she would never forget that journey. One never forgets the experience of horror that becomes routine. And so much horror filled her eyes those days that for a long time afterward she was afraid to close them and find herself again at the whim of the war. Only Daniel could have led her into such a situation, and only following him could she swallow filth and pain as something she must accept. The train rolled past a long row of hanged men, their tongues lolling out, and she hugged Daniel to exorcize those distorted faces, the picture of a child trying to reach the boots of his father high overhead, the doubled-over body of a keening woman, the immutable trees, one after another, each with its dead man like a unique fruit in this landscape. They embraced each other, unable to close their eyes, the amazement of that first vision obliterating the right to miss those that followed. Several hours and a few kilometers later, they came upon a procession of ragged men fleeing from a second, men on horseback firing upon men too old to be of service, aged children, and women surprised behind burning houses from which a foul smoke poured, seeping into the bone and filling the imagination with atrocities. At times, the train stopped an entire day with orders to wait for a general to arrive and drop his load of purulent soldiers and take from their train a new haul of innocents eager to play with bullets. Emilia trembled, thinking that they might take Daniel, as they took the men of the *soldaderas.* She heard the women's voices fade, their singing change to tears of confusion, then begin again, like a moan: *What does it matter if I live, if it is man's fate to die, die, die. . . .*

Emilia didn't know which was worse, days plagued with images or nights of dark movement, ominous nights when they were crowded together, vague shapes between vague shapes, rocked by the rhythm of the rattling, dusty train they were traveling on. There was no attempt in any of the cars to set up rules for communal living; men and women used their space for whatever they wanted, whatever their bodies needed. Women lit fires to make tortillas, using the tattered velvet left on the few remaining seats; men urinated in corners or out windows, some slept half-naked, cursing their partners or taking them without thought for the opinion of the other travelers. At first Emilia had tried to maintain some of the gentility her parents had gone to such lengths to instill, but with time she learned to be guided, like the others, by bodily demands. Even to welcome the midnight black when she could lift her skirt and shelter Daniel beneath it, in a game of joined bodies that, faced with the certainty of death, reaffirmed life.

There was a feeling in the air that every morning could be the last, and that it was miraculous to live till the night and be able to make love in the flickering darkness of the train, or to lie in the middle of a field perfumed with tiny flowers when the steam engine had broken down and there were hours and hours of waiting that nothing except love could fill. Many times, while Daniel was scribbling his notes or talking with the soldiers, Emilia asked herself what she was doing just watching him, with no purpose in the world but to be at his service, with no possible task but to inspect a wound for which she had no cure at hand, day after day facing the reality that the practice of medicine is empty without the help of the pharmacy. To know that a woman could be cured with one of the compounds sitting on Diego Sauri's shelves and not be able to get it exhausted her to the point where she couldn't speak, laugh, eat, even react to the body Daniel offered as consolation. In her eyes, that train was carrying more sick people than well ones, more weak than sturdy, more people who needed a bed and tonic than needed a pistol and a general to follow off to the Revolution. She spent hours wondering what the vitamin deficiency might be that produced the white spots covering the faces of the children, what antiseptic could cure the venereal diseases that flowed from the men's penises to the depths of the *soldaderas'* vaginas.

All the length of the train traveled the news of the medical skills of the girl in the yellow car, talk of how she had remedies in her doctor's bag and gifted hands to sew up and bandage wounds, and from all the length of the train they came to consult her about complaints for which she could offer little more than the consolation of listening and making recommendations for the moment they would stop moving and could look for such and such an herb, such and such a powder.

One woman in her car had been lying on the floor with her knees drawn up to her chin for four days; Emilia had exhausted her painkillers the first morning and her words after the third day of watching the woman suffer. She cursed the time she had spent in Chicago, telling herself what poor training that was for practicing medicine among the poor, and with all her strength she prayed for some glimmering of knowledge that would let her extract a cure from nothing. But there was no answer other than what she had already exhausted, so she knelt beside the woman who was moaning quietly, as women learn to moan who know their destiny is not to displease, lending her company as the only treatment. She sat there feeling more ineffectual than ever, when a small, bent old woman came over to them, saying that she could help. Emilia looked at her, sure that she had reason to say that, and moved aside with all of what in the last few days she had come to consider her useless training to make room for the magic of the aged woman. Very formally, Emilia told her her name, and asked if she could stay to watch. The *curandera* nodded as someone might brush away a fly, and as she unwound her rebozo, revealed two strong, youthful hands that contrasted greatly with her tiny, seemingly weak and wizened body. With those hands, with nothing apparently in them, she began to rub the sick woman's head, slowly, as if looking for precise spots on which to place those gentle fingers. Then she massaged the back of the suffering woman's neck, her eyelids, the notch between the thumb and forefinger of her left hand, a specific point on the soles of her feet, which she kneaded longer than any other part of her body. Gradually, the woman stopped moaning and sank into the sleep she had not known in recent nights.

Kneeling before the old woman with obvious devotion, Emilia studied her as if she would will herself inside her.

"You know acupuncture?" she asked the *curandera,* who seemed to be returning from another world.

"My name is Teodora, I don't know what you call this I do," she answered, again wrapping her rebozo across her chest.

"Will you teach me?" Emilia begged.

"As much as you can learn," she replied.

They soon became a team. Emilia followed the old woman through the ramshackle train with the same fervor she had followed any of her other maestros, and there was no detail that escaped her, no question left unasked, no doubt that Teodora did not know how to calm.

"You have to feel it," she would say when Emilia introduced words the old woman didn't know or doubts that she believed had no answer except that mind could triumph over matter. There were times that Emilia despaired, because Teodora went too fast and assumed she knew things she didn't. At one of those times, the old woman asked Emilia caustically:

"Do I ask you how you go about stitching up holes? You watch and learn, that's all."

And she turned to suture a sick man's wound, something that until that moment had been the exclusive responsibility of the gentle señorita in the yellow car.

They passed the days happily, learning everything the other could teach. Emilia would always say that in this exchange, she gained the most. Teodora, nevertheless, treated her with the deference due those who know a lot about something you have always wanted to learn.

It is difficult to guess how much Teodora believed of everything she heard about the latest scientific discoveries, the possibility that human beings store their emotions in the brain and not the heart, the importance of antiseptics and clean water, the marvels of anesthesia and other modern developments, but neither did she feel that she had the best of their arrangement. She felt for Emilia a respect comparable to what Emilia felt for her after seeing her work the first time, and that was why she was teaching Emilia her treasured techniques, not disdaining Emilia's, but convinced she knew things Emilia needed to learn if she was to round out the madness of her calling. Little by little she trained Emilia in the art of drawing out bodily ills with the pure wisdom of her fingertips, and provided her with many lesser and greater grains of wisdom Maimonides would have been grateful to know.

When she discussed all this with Daniel, Emilia called her fortuitous meeting with Teodora her "course in itinerant medicine," and thanked him four times a night for having made her accompany him on such a fruitful journey. Daniel watched her grow thinner and more ragged with each day that passed, but also more fearless than the day before, standing up to misfortunes that had horrified her at the beginning of the trip. With a quiet respect and sober anguish he had learned not to externalize, he watched her every day as she tried to comb her filthy hair, wash her face, or occasionally smile as if the world were not falling apart, and understood that he would go on loving her forever, as he would never love another.

CHAPTER

23

THE STEAM ENGINE and the cars rattling along behind it like a gypsy caravan approached the outskirts of Mexico City just before dawn on a Wednesday early in June. The black night blew generous and warm on Emilia's face as she leaned out the window of the car to feel the dawn on her eyelids, the breeze ruffling her hair, the dew that was a foretaste of the high plateau. In the distance, sketched in the darkness, were the volcanoes, standing above the disaster moving across the land. Emilia's eyes followed their dim outlines. However great the disaster, if the volcanoes were there to observe it, there would be a remedy.

The odyssey of the train had been so troubled that its crew should have been celebrated as heroes. But all that awaited in the station was the noise of the train itself and a gradually lightening sky. Daniel, who sometimes could sleep like the dead, did not struggle awake until the train stopped rocking him with its clatter. He opened his eyes and saw Emilia near the window, face-to-face with Teodora, her hands locked behind the tiny woman's neck, whispering as if there were still things left they could tell each other.

After a few minutes, they hugged each other. Emilia kissed Teodora's cheeks and stepped back, crying with a naturalness that always evoked in Daniel the same blend of impatience and embarrassment. Emilia did not cry often, but when she did she wept as easily as one laughs, unmoved either by what anyone thought or concern for how long it might take to emerge from her anguish. That was how she had been taught to weep in her family, and had it not been for Daniel's criticism, it would never have occurred to her to think there was anything in that behavior deserving censure.

As he watched Emilia's farewell homage to the *curandera,* Daniel got up from the floor that served as his bed, ran his hands through his unruly hair, buttoned his jacket, and coughed to see whether Emilia would give him the time of day. The train had emptied, and all around them new passengers were crowding on. It was time to get off and find their way through the streets of the besieged, dangerous, and rowdy city the capital had become.

AT THE ENTRANCE to the station, they hailed an open cab pulled by two bony horses and asked the driver to take them to the *zócalo* in the heart of Mexico City. The man asked whether they were staying near the Palacio Nacional or if they just wanted to go have a look at it. If it was the latter, he suggested they not go anywhere near. So far that year, the Palacio had changed occupants several times; it had been in the hands of one band after another, following the tides of the advances and retreats of the armies fighting over the city. That morning, the rumor was that the Villistas and Zapatistas, fighting among themselves, had decided to seat a new president. The *zócalo* would be a hotbed of confusion. The whole city, in fact, was not the best place for a couple to visit for pleasure.

Emilia wanted to go directly to the house in the colonia Roma. She knew that a bedroom was always waiting for them at Milagros's home. Daniel took her aside and asked her not to listen to wild rumors collected by some cabdriver. They ended up by taking a turn around the deserted *zócalo.* One door of the cathedral was ajar and two women were going in to pray. A street vendor was blowing the steam whistle of the cart where he roasted sweet potatoes. A nursemaid passed by them, looking for some corpse or other to entertain the child of her employers.

Every morning there were bodies strewn around with no one to claim them but the wind, killed in the middle of the night without so much as a second thought. The driver recommended they not go out after dark, because, he said, the revolutionaries wandered around more freely and drunker than during the day.

Irritated by the man's chatter, Daniel asked him to drop them at the door of a nearby café. Emilia protested that she was too dirty to go in. They both needed baths.

"First comes internal peace, then cleanliness. What we need is something to eat," said Daniel, arguing that no one would give them a second look, the world now belonged to the poor and dirty; the country was governed by the likes of the campesino soldiers who had traveled with them on the train.

They got down from the cab after paying the driver a sum that seemed astronomical when they heard it in pesos and ridiculous when converted to dollars.

"For ten dollars, you can buy a killer," said the driver. "Be careful not to show you have that much," he recommended, a last offense to Daniel's ears.

They went into the café convinced that the driver was lying, and that a dollar could never be changed for that many Conventionist pesos. Emilia still had some of the money she had saved in the United States, where Dr. Hogan paid her a doctor's salary not only because he loved her so much, but also as part of the monthly income from the sale of medications they had concocted between them and with Diego Sauri's help by mail. Daniel had dollars left from what Gardner had sent him for past collaborations, but between them they did not think they had enough capital to allow them to throw money around for long. They were amazed that the bill for two fried eggs, breakfast bread, *café con leche,* and a cup of chocolate was so much higher than when they'd left three years before.

"You could have had a wedding banquet for that," said Emilia, wondering how many dollars they would have to spend for it.

In the meantime, Daniel had turned to talk with an emaciated woman who had a child wrapped in her rebozo. Talking in a whisper, she opened her fist to show him the finest diamond he had ever seen. She was offering to sell it for only six times the cost of their breakfast. Before Emilia—who was still scandalized that a plate of beans could cost two pesos—realized what was happening, Daniel gave the woman the money and took the ring.

While they were discussing whether anyone would open the door of the house in the colonia Roma, they stopped to take a good look at themselves. They were as filthy as a couple of hardened guerrillas and looked like what they were: two survivors longing for the paradise of soft beds and the twin tubs Emilia had enjoyed four years before, never dreaming that at some future date they would be one of the things she wanted most in the world. They rang the bell for half an hour before a frightened, shrill voice asked who was there. Emilia recognized it as Consuelo's, the caretaker she remembered from previous visits, and watched as the glory that door guarded opened to them.

She went in apologizing for their looking like vagabonds, but after a few sentences realized that Consuelo had lost her capacity for surprise. The house was as elegant and solemn as ever, but there was something in the upholstery of the furniture and the soft throbbing of the rugs that made it more welcoming, more like its changed custodian.

"If you knew what we've been through, you wouldn't waste your strength apologizing for the state you're in," said Consuelo. "After all, no matter how you look, you are a lady and deserve all the shelter these walls can offer you."

She later told them that for several months the house had been "borrowed" by one of Villa's generals, whose staff was quartered in the residence next door. The man, more foulmouthed than truly vulgar, desired a little privacy and installed himself there every night from November to a month ago, the date when General Villa had done everyone the favor of taking his war off somewhere else. Consuelo had waited on every whim of the man and the many women he slept with, not wanting them to claim the house because of anything she did. They had eaten everything in the pantry and drunk all the wines from the cellar, but not a book in the library, not a plate, not a glass had been lost.

After she told her story, sure that that was the worst the Revolution could do, she crossed herself and prayed for the soul of her nephew Elías, a boy of fourteen who had gone off behind the general.

"Have you been notified that he died?" Emilia asked.

"I've thought of him as dead from the day he left the house," Consuelo clarified.

"The boy must have had his reasons," said Daniel, with a voice like a bucket of cold water.

"His pigheaded idea that we're all equal," Consuelo replied. "Shall I warm your bath?"

Daniel decided he could put off any discussion about equality. At that moment, the possibility of a bath seemed an ideal as dear as any of the purest revolutionary aspirations.

NOTHING LIKE HOT WATER, thought Emilia, sinking into the clear water of the first tub. Daniel slipped in behind her and they set about ridding themselves of the filth of nearly a month. The tub was large enough for two sentimental people to move at will.

They soaped each other, embraced underwater, and played until their fingertips were wrinkled and two spots like hot coals lighted Emilia's face. Then, tired of soaking in their own dirt, they decided to move to the adjoining tub to rinse off.

"What a magnificent animal you are," Emilia, slow to leave the water, told Daniel when she saw him standing above her. Lazing there, she felt giddy from the glimpse of his testicles, and stroked his legs, kissed a bony knee, sat up to duck her head beneath the arch of his thighs. "You're the roof of my house," she told him playfully.

Daniel leaned down to kiss her and then pulled her from the water.

"You say such crazy things," he said, wrapping a towel around his waist and stepping out of the tub, acting as if he were looking for something.

Emilia began splashing in the clean water, waiting for Daniel to join her and stop wandering around the room.

"What are you looking for you can't find here?" she asked, placing her hand on the dark curls that guarded such rewards.

"I can't imagine," said Daniel, finally climbing into the smooth water where she was half-asleep. He wanted to span her waist with his hands, put his tongue in the navel that centered her flat belly. But first he sought her mouth and, inside, the imaginative tongue that always kept the promise of her eyes.

"It's been a long time since I've given you a stone," he said after they kissed.

Emilia felt a chill of gold scraping her teeth; her tongue felt its way into a circle of air and she closed her lips. Two tears like enigmas trickled down her scrubbed face. Daniel had left in her mouth the ring he had bought that morning.

"Don't cry, it wears me out when you cry," he said. "Do you want to marry me?"

THE NEXT DAY, ironed and perfumed, they went out into an indifferent city to look for a telegraph office, a store where they could buy some clothes, a restaurant where they could celebrate, and someone who had the time and will to marry them. The first thing they found was the telegraph office. Emilia sent the Sauris the longest telegram ever recorded in that office. Their second find was a luxurious restaurant that seemed not to have felt the demons of food shortages. There they reserved a table for three o'clock and continued their search for clothes and someone to marry them.

Nearly all the stores had closed their doors, but in the market they found a white *huipil* embroidered by the patient hands of a woman from Oaxaca.

"What a blessing to be free of enemies," said Emilia as they started walking with no destination in mind.

"Why do you say that?" Daniel asked.

"Just because."

Their route was determined by the whims of leisure. Suddenly, quite by accident, they found themselves at the gate of a cemetery.

"This is where Juárez is buried!" said Emilia, recognizing the Pantheon of San Fernando. She had visited it four years before with Milagros, looking for tombs of past heroes. She wanted to go in and look for it.

"You're not thinking of visiting a cemetery?" Daniel asked.

Emilia replied with a smile that was mirrored in her dark eyes. Daniel remembered how Milagros Veytia always said that Emilia was touched with a mysterious grace. The secret of her beauty perhaps lay in the fact that she was not perfect. She had a small space between her front teeth, a minute chicken pox scar that tempered the presumption of a goddess's nose, and a strange way of wrinkling her brow when a question seemed pointless.

As they went through the cemetery gate, Emilia walked ahead of Daniel, telling him that Miramón, Benito Juárez's enemy, had also been buried there until his wife Concha exhumed his body and took it somewhere else when she learned that Juárez was resting nearby. Daniel laughed at the story, and Emilia seized the opportunity to remind him how good it was not to have enemies or be wasting one's life in political squabbling. The one good thing you could do in life was forgive. And the only way not to be responsible for a landslide was never to be one of the grains of sand that formed it. Daniel laughed again and accused Emilia of being overly simplistic. Secure in her knowledge of the effort it had cost her to arrive at such simplicity, Emilia put her arm around Daniel's waist and walked on in silence.

Like all the rest of the city, the graveyard was untended and shabby. By noon, the benches were occupied by beggars and drunks. Emilia and Daniel walked past them and the ragged blooming hedges, happy to be happy and entertained by the idea of getting married.

A man older than age itself came up to ask them what day it was. They told him: hour, day, month, and year. Then, in exchange for such valuable information, they asked him to pronounce them man and wife.

"I can't," he said.

"Why not?" Emilia asked.

"Because I'm too hungry. I'm here waiting for my daughter to come back. She went off with the other women to raid a Spaniard's bakery."

"Marry us while you're waiting," Emilia pleaded.

"No," said the man. "I don't want to marry two people who are going to be separated."

"How do you know we're going to be separated?" Daniel wanted to know.

"Because I'm a prophet," he said, and went to take a seat on a bench. Emilia and Daniel followed, hypnotized.

"And according to your prophecies, who is going to come out on top in the Revolution?" asked Daniel, who since morning had been dying to ask anyone who came along what he knew or guessed about the political situation.

"The bad ones," said the old man.

"And which ones are bad?"

"That's where you'll have to be the prophet."

Emilia bent down toward the old man to assure him that they were not planning ever to be separated.

"That isn't something you can plan or not plan," said the seer. "You're going to be separated because right never follows a straight course. But if you love each other that much, I'll marry you. Stand over there."

He pointed to an ash tree a few feet from the bench. Then, with no authority except the look of an old man wise in matters of surviving, and with no formalities other than asking them their names, Don Refugio—for that was his name—pronounced them man and wife. Then he cut three leaves from the branches of the ash tree above their heads. He bit the tip of each of the leaves and handed them to Daniel and Emilia, asking them to bite them, too. He examined each leaf as if it were an important document, kept one, and handed the other two to the new bride and groom.

"This tree is nourished from the light of the dead. They're all the witnesses we need," he said. Then he asked them if in exchange for performing the ceremony they would buy him dinner.

CHAPTER

24

THE NAME of the restaurant was the Sylvain. It had an area open to the public that could afford to come there and a number of private rooms. Emilia and Daniel, with their unexpected guest, were seated at a small table near the window. Don Refugio ordered fish in green chili sauce, roast pork and beans, and a bottle of red wine, though Emilia doubted he could read the menu. Daniel was having a good time watching the people coming into the restaurant. While they were ordering their meal, the private rooms were filling up with generals with the look of politicians and politicians with the bearing of generals. They came in boisterously, shouting at each other across the room. Daniel watched them with the avidity of a man ripped too soon from the cocoon, and before five minutes had passed had spotted several friends with whom he had fought against Huerta in the north.

"Don't worry about us," Emilia told him, watching as he craned his neck, champing at the bit to rejoin the world of the adventures and passions he had left behind two months before. She smiled the smile of a princess granting permission for someone to go kill himself if that's what he wanted, and patted him on the back, suggesting he go talk to some of his old friends.

Don Refugio could have begun to congratulate himself on the veracity of his prophecy, but he thought it prudent to keep quiet and not stir up anything before the soup arrived. He took a hard roll from the breadbasket and criticized the service because the waiter had not brought butter at the time they placed their order: Then he began telling Emilia the story of his life, as if it had been only the two of them from the beginning. He had grown up on a hacienda belonging to General Santa Ana, where he had been taken under the wing of a Jesuit whose primary interests in life were mathematics, flowers, and the points of coincidence among religions the world considered in opposition. From him, he had learned to read and write, keep books, tend a garden, and confuse resurrection with reincarnation. When the Jesuit died, blind and out of favor with those who had never understood the need to reconcile extremes in mathematics, religion, or politics, Refugio was thirty-two. He found work in the house of a painter of religious murals and lived there until Porfirio Díaz took up arms, claiming to be a liberal and protector of the poor. After that, Refugio served two years in the army, long enough to learn, definitively, that the best thing one could do in life was live poor or rich, but always at a distance from the army. Poverty had not been eliminated with Díaz's triumph, and life was once again ruled by the denial of a better future for anybody who was a nobody. Refugio went back to working as a gardener, this time on a hacienda in Morelos. There he married a woman with crossed eyes and a noble soul, who died two weeks after giving birth to his daughter. It was shortly after that loss that he began privately to realize his prophetic powers. He knew that his daughter would die of typhus, and since then had run anytime he felt illness too near. They had traveled from city to city, working in a bell foundry in Querétaro, with a notary in Veracruz, with whores in Córdoba, with the inventor of a maguey harvester in Tlaxcala, with a Lebanese cloth merchant near Mérida, with a doctor who cured broken bones merely by touching them, and with miracle-working nuns who maintained a shrine. There at the nunnery, while trimming rosebushes in the atrium, he had met a nice-looking widow who had come from Zacatecas to solicit favors of the Virgin. Since what she wanted was a husband, and after three days had found none, she decided that Refugio had been sent by the mother of God and asked him to marry her. In order to accept her proposal, Refugio resolved to pay no further attention to his premonitions, because he was sure that all of them came to him through his first wife, who now was going to be so jealous that she would make him feel dangers he did not want to think about. At the age of fifty, he fell for the widow like a teenager, and under her tutelage learned to eat with a fork and dress like a *patrón,* to play chess, listen to Bellini, and go to sleep hoping the night would bring happy surprises. He had found himself obliged to abandon that marvel of a woman—who had done nothing but treasure him as she would a sultan's ruby from the day they first made love near the nunnery—because he dreamed that her children, who despised him and who from the day he arrived in Zacatecas had accused him of marrying their mother for her money, had decided to kill him. He fled from his destiny, and since then had wandered through the world, missing the widow's arms and hearing prophetic voices, his head filled with mezcal and visions of the future, his stomach with torment when the mezcal turned to him as the object of its curse. He lived with a granddaughter he called daughter, a girl of fifteen, sickly and pregnant but frisky and joyous as a young nanny goat.

Emilia, in turn, summarized her life, without slighting any important details. Beginning with her affection for a more than normally intelligent mother whom she remembered as a smile among the flowers of her gallery, and her devotion for a father who sang the way most people pray among the apothecary jars and antiquarian books of his pharmacy, and ending with her trip to Chicago and return following a man to whom she had lost her heart at the age of five and did not think she would ever be separated from. As she said that, she felt a slight tremor in her eyelids, but brushed it aside with an elegance Don Refugio did not miss, judging Emilia to be the best thing that had happened to him in many days—aside, of course, from the generous meal that put an end to his long fast.

"So you're a doctor," he said to help ease the embarrassment of her obvious emotion.

"Yes," said Emilia, for the first time acknowledging aloud that from the time she was a little girl she had been obsessed with that passion as well, one she never wanted to give up.

"Don't let it get you down, some things can't be helped," said the old man, his bony, trembling fingers patting Emilia's pale, graceful hand. "You don't know it, but you are many lives ahead of your man there," Refugio said, and spent the next half hour telling her how many reincarnations he thought the spirit lodged in her body had lived.

It was after six, and the roar of oaths and clinking glasses filled the air, when Daniel returned to the table, bursting with stories, each more fantastic than the last, recounting them for the next hour and a half. For Emilia, what they illustrated was that in all this quarrel among Villistas, Zapatistas, and Carrancistas, the one absolute was that the true losers were the liberals, those in the middle, people like her.

"It serves no purpose to bemoan the times you live in," said Refugio, who in order to gain strength to listen to the incomprehensible crimes, utter betrayals, and half-hopes Daniel was describing, had begun drinking anise and brandy.

"Refugio has a daughter who's not well," said Emilia, interrupting the excitement with which Daniel was reporting the twists and turns of the Revolution, as if they were anecdotes from some book of adventures.

"You're never interested in things that matter," Daniel replied. He kissed her indulgently and suggested she spend the rest of the evening visiting Refugio's daughter while he finished a conversation or two.

EMILIA AND DON REFUGIO went to his shack near the village of Mixcoac. There she met his granddaughter, frail and smiling, working hard to conceal the illness that had invaded her body with a violence whose symptoms she was trying to hide. In private, while Emilia examined her and asked her questions, the girl asked Emilia to keep her secret about the gravity of what was happening to her, to say that she was sick because she was hungry. After all, there was so much hunger and so many people looking like she did; who was going to imagine something worse?

"If you have to die," she told Emilia, "better to let it come as a surprise than to upset everybody beforehand."

There was no cure for her illness. Emilia knew that almost by looking at her. But rest and eating well would help her live longer than she would working until her body, like a beaten-down animal, dropped in its tracks. She asked the girl to let her help, not to work as hard, not to get up early to do the milking, or go with her husband to deliver milk in the city.

"Don't ask me to start dying today," the girl replied with inarguable self-possession.

Emilia promised to come back the next day, and allowed Don Refugio and his drunken sorrow to accompany her to the door of the house in the colonia Roma.

"My Eulalia is going to die, isn't she?" he asked on their way there, and then, without waiting for an answer, "It's hopeless. The bastards who brought so much hunger and fear are going to go away so that even bigger bastards will take their place. That's the prophecy I see from here on out: the others will win. And only because they're sure that's what they want, not because they're braver or cleverer than the ones who're here now."

Emilia hugged him without trying to answer and went inside. There was nothing she could say. She would have liked to fill the old man's silence with deceitful words to muddle his convictions, but she felt he deserved better than that. It was nearly eleven. She went upstairs, sure that Daniel would be home ahead of her, but Consuelo knew nothing of him; instead, she began babbling, intruding on Emilia's musings, complaining about how it was impossible to find anything in the market to prepare a decent dinner for them. All the grocery stores had closed, you never knew what currency was good, or for how long, and she wanted to use up the bills printed by the current government because if what everyone was saying was true, and the Carranza forces ended up winning, at the end of a year she would have *two* trunks filled with worthless paper money to cry over.

Emilia heard her as part of the increasing noise of the gathering storm whose only warning had been the passionate way Daniel was flirting with politics in the restaurant. She had always known that the war of their bodies was not enough to allow them to live in peace, that he didn't want to live in peace, and that however he strove to maintain peace in his mind, he would always need something more to satisfy his restless nature and idolatry of adventure. Perhaps that was also the stuff of which a political temperament was made, an inability to remain too long in a private world. She knew, however, that she was growing weary of battling a man whose commitment seemed to point toward denying the happiness of an ideal intimacy.

For a while Emilia paced back and forth in the sala, until her eye was drawn to the chair where years before she had waited up all night for this same Daniel, with his irrepressible laughter and magnetic body, to knock at the door. That one memory was enough to trigger the shudder of rage her pointless reflections always evoked. She did not want to indulge in them anymore. She said good night to Consuelo and put on a French silk nightgown Rivadeneira's English friend had kept in a wardrobe for the pleasure of his transitory lovers.

She climbed into bed, feeling the sheets slip smoothly over her body, a newlywed refusing to shed even one tear to lament Daniel's desertion on their wedding night.

Daniel came home before dawn. He tiptoed into the bedroom where Emilia was sleeping soundly as a statue. The darkness was streaked with light as he got into bed, still drunk from a mixture of news, conversation, and liquor. Emilia felt him slide toward her and woke up, opening wide, question-filled eyes that just as immediately closed. Her unconfined hair covered both pillows. Daniel lay upon the anarchical darkness of those curls, enveloping himself in their scent as if in a good omen, then, as she lay on her side, wrapped one arm around the sharply defined waist that divided Emilia's torso, and pressed his naked body against the only place he sensed awakened in her.

At nine the sun found them turned in the opposite direction, totally dissociated from any of the passions that at other moments tended to separate them. Captive in the body of the woman from whom stars exploded as she moaned his name as if blessing him, Daniel once again saw the world as flawed, a ridiculous place to roam. He drank Emilia like a potion that would soothe his restless spirit, then slept without a single desire to disturb his dreams. When he awoke, it was noon, and the place where Emilia had lain had been cool for hours.

He burst from the bedroom half-naked, yelling for her as if he had lost her in the midst of a battle. As soon as Consuelo saw him, she told him that Emilia had left two hours before to visit the Cruz Roja hospital. Daniel took that information as an insult, and cursed the moment Emilia had decided on medicine. Considering the state of the country, why hadn't she chosen to be a singer, or a general? Why a doctor? Why that profession she was practicing, without even having the degree, with the pride and confidence of some greater wisdom? That profession whose urgency made her inaccessible when he needed her as badly as another might need surgery? A profession knee-deep in shit, a profession that didn't allow you to forget horror, a profession that abandoned everything in order not to abandon a patient, a profession of madmen, of masochists, of narcissists. A profession for ugly men, for indecent women, for all those disenchanted with human weakness but longing to be heroic, but not a profession for the Emilia who had just left his side, because nothing, especially filth and pain, should claim the woman whose secret delights and treasures belonged to him alone, and always had.

He screamed a curse that made Consuelo cross herself, and took refuge in the bathtub with hopes of forgetting and finding relief for his sense of betrayal.

Daniel left the house fifteen minutes before Emilia returned looking for him, wanting to tell him about the conditions of poverty and abandonment in the hospital, to tell him that people were dying of typhus and that typhus indicated hunger, and that if he and his war didn't know how to correct such injustices, why had they ever started it? What bloody good had the Revolution *done?*

All Emilia found in answer to her questions was a brief note on the dining room table saying that Daniel would be at the Hotel Nacional after four o'clock. He had not even left her a kiss. She imagined he was furious. She scolded herself for having left him, then defended herself. She had done nothing wrong, she couldn't become a *soldadera,* she had her own things to do, her own destiny, and she was right to go after them. She ate a bowl of soup and damned herself once more, then went upstairs and started brushing her hair to see if that would help clear her mind. That rite, which she always associated with Josefa's counsel, made her miss her mother more than ever. What would she be doing at two o'clock on a Friday afternoon? Would she be sitting with Diego, eating and talking about their country and their daughter as two insoluble problems? It had been two years since she had seen them, but she carried them with her everywhere; they were in her actions, her rages, her weaknesses, in her hope. She saw them when she looked in the mirror, when she repeated the tired way her father rubbed his eyes, when she hummed the tune her mother whistled when she was looking for something she'd lost, in an exclamation of surprise, in holding back words of sorrow, in going on living. How much gray would Aunt Milagros's hair have now? Who would be the winner of the monthly chess tournament? How many new poems would Rivadeneira have written? Was it true what her father wrote her, that Antonio Zavalza came to see them every day? Would she have that to thank him for, too?

She admitted that she missed their world: her mother's soup, her father's music, their small arguments, Milagros's stories, Zavalza's arms, so good at frightening away the demons of her nostalgia. She had never dreamed the day would come that she would miss his arms only seven hours after sleeping with Daniel. She blushed suddenly. How fickle, to be missing Zavalza. As if the world weren't already full to overflowing with bizarre events. She put down the brush. Striking flirtatious poses before the mirror, she fastened her hair at the back of her neck and pinched color into her cheeks. Then, her head still swimming with thoughts of home, she went to look for Daniel, wondering whether he had the faintest idea of the size of the universe she had given up to follow him.

CHAPTER

25

Prepared to wait until Daniel appeared, Emilia Sauri made herself comfortable at a table, smiled tolerantly at the waiter who brought her coffee, and blocked out where she was by losing herself in her thoughts.

For Emilia, who had grown up in an atmosphere alive with conversations, the soliloquy had become a pleasant habit after traveling and living alone. As soon as she had a few minutes to spare, her head began to buzz with memories and ghosts that had never known each other in life but who met, even became friends, when she introduced them. She did not know at what moment that group of presences who came to her and talked among themselves had begun to manifest itself, but there were couples whose conversations and counsel she could not have lived without. One of the pairs was made up of Dr. Cuenca and Señorita Carmela, her grade-school teacher. Remembering those noble teachers always led to a discussion inside her head about Daniel's good and bad qualities. Dr. Cuenca, who in life had seldom defended his son against Emilia's criticism, in death created a monumental list of his praiseworthy attributes. In contrast, Señorita Carmela, who saw Emilia as the daughter her spinsterhood had prevented her from having, was the one who, anytime Emilia had time and willingness to listen, was charged with listing Daniel's defects.

It was beginning to rain when the argument between the contenders became so rancorous that Emilia did not want to listen anymore. That afternoon, in response to Señorita Carmela's accusations of egotism and coolness based on the way Daniel sometimes spoke with a steely voice that made him seem like the most hostile man in the world, even when he hadn't said anything hostile, Dr. Cuenca had set forth the virtuosity with which his son placed his hand upon the pubis of the sleeping Emilia and caressed her until her body was entirely awakened and the most extraordinary onomatopoetic sounds were exploding like lights from her throat.

Convinced that they both were right, Emilia tried to dismiss them by shaking her head, as if that were the only part of her organism that disturbed her. When she came back to the world around her, her legs were tightly crossed beneath her skirt and one hand was clenching the other to control the anger beginning to build because once again, and with the usual anxiety, she was awaiting the unpunctual arrival of the eccentric with whom she was traveling through life. At that moment, a stylish, slim man with dark eyes and black curls came into the dining room; he was pulling some kind of contrivance connecting five wheeled trunks. She watched him go over to talk with one of the waiters. She saw the waiter's face change with the stranger's words, and then saw the chef come out smiling as if it were fiesta time.

"The señor should proceed with his library to the storeroom off the patio," announced the boy assigned to show him the way and help with his luggage.

Emilia was wondering what mission a man like that might have in a kitchen, when she heard the waiters say that at last someone had come to the hotel who knew how to repair the refrigerator.

Slowly sipping her cold coffee, Emilia watched a parade pass by her en route to the kitchen, and then joined it.

Once there, everyone gathered around the new guest, who was facing the huge, empty refrigerator. He opened a suitcase that was small in comparison to the trunks, but large in comparison to a body that seemed made not to carry anything ever, and took out a screwdriver, some pliers, a monkey wrench, and an assortment of electrical cables. Then he opened two of the wheeled trunks, revealing four perfect bookcases. Time began to ripple over the general curiosity and the economy of motion with which the man plunged into the books, then delved like a physician into the guts of the refrigerator, which had not worked since 1913, the year the last expert in electrical appliances had left for Cuba. One hour and a number of consultations later, the refrigerator began to buzz like a wasp, and everyone who had known it in good health agreed that it had recovered its customary voice.

"How did you get to be an expert in refrigerators?" Emilia asked the gentleman of the trunks.

"I am an expert in books," he replied. "My name is Ignacio Cardenal. It's a pleasure to meet you," he said, bending over Emilia's hand.

"Emilia Sauri, at your service," said Emilia.

"My service? Be careful what you say."

"It's just a way of speaking, like saying 'pleased to meet you,'" explained Emilia, startled at the ways of such a strange man.

"I come from Spain," said Señor Cardenal, "and that's not what 'service' means there."

"Then I take it back."

"In that, you seem Spanish yourself."

"I'm a mixture," said Emilia.

"And a very nice mixture," Cardenal replied. "Are all the other girls like you?"

"We have a little of everything. Like an encyclopedia."

"You know about encyclopedias?"

"My father has one he adores but he gave it to me even though he's still alive. But I don't love it as much as you love yours. I leave mine at home when I'm traveling."

"Well, that's a bad choice. You see how useful they can be."

"Do they help you in everything?"

"Except selling them."

"You sell encyclopedias?"

"I make them, I bind them, I sell them."

"You take them for walks."

"I came to sell them, but was met with what's happened because of the Revolution. Now no one buys anything for idle days. And the minister who told me to come back isn't here anymore."

Cardenal, a Spaniard of educated speech and the demeanor of an intellectual, told Emilia that he had passed through Mexico four years before, and had taken orders for two dozen encyclopedias for libraries. He had returned with them, but no one was left who recognized him, and no one wanted his books. He was going to have to trade them for a few days at the hotel and a return ticket, that is, if someone was willing to make such a trade. If not, he would have to repair refrigerators until he got enough money together for his return.

Something about his manner of speech and the gleam in his unusually intelligent eyes made him as attractive and approachable as if he were a lifelong acquaintance. And he must have felt something of the same about Emilia. They sat down at a table and began talking as if they had all the time in the world. That was one good thing about the war: everything was as if suspended, waiting for something to happen that others would resolve at some distant moment. In the meanwhile, time was going nowhere, and people caught up in it did not have much reason to stir themselves. Waiting was the principal activity of those who weren't out fighting someone. And while waiting, there was nothing better than a good long conversation. Which was why Ignacio Cardenal, the deceived publisher, and Emilia Sauri, a doctor without a hospital, spent the rest of the evening chatting, as if they owed it to each other.

Beneath his unruly mop of curls, Cardenal had a noble mind. He was also an innocent at heart. He described his life to Emilia, and his loves in Spain. He had a very beautiful wife whom he remembered as the fieriest and best-looking woman in Bilbao, and three girls born in her likeness and blessed with the very eyes that had made him fall in love with their mother. He talked about his excessive love of books, and about the financial setbacks his family suffered because of that futile passion. Comparing herself to the destitute publisher, Emilia told her story: Daniel, medicine, her teachers, her travels, her destinationless destiny, her doubts. They left the restaurant and walked the streets around the hotel, as if assailants and calamities did not lie around every corner, as if the dusk were flooded with light, and the sparkles of rain left behind by the downpour weren't soaking their head and shoulders. The wounded, dark city seemed beautiful to them as they walked and talked, talked and walked. They would have walked all night, but a flicker of good sense, and a hunger for which they found no relief, brought them back to the hotel at about nine, with a sense that there was nothing to eat in the entire city except where the privileged gathered. By then they knew each other better than some who called themselves lifelong friends. They were comparing the size of their hands when Daniel came into the dining room, impetuous and smiling, as if it were four-fifteen.

"Who's this?" he asked Emilia, pointing to the Spaniard as if he were an intruder.

"This is the gentleman I've spent the evening talking with. And who are you?"

"A pleasure, señor," said Daniel, not looking at Cardenal, his hands on Emilia's shoulders.

"The pleasure is mine," said Ignacio, and, knowing perfectly well who Daniel was, and all his ancestors as well, "You must be the gentleman who kept this lady waiting all evening."

"I make no pretense of being a gentleman. And this 'lady' is my wife."

"She didn't tell me she was married," Ignacio said firmly.

"More than married," said Daniel, looking at Emilia.

"Worse than married," said Emilia, turning to face him. "Ignacio is my friend. I've told him everything, and he can't understand how anyone with a head as good as mine could get into something like this."

"Your friend? Since when have a man and a woman been able to be friends? And what does a head have to do with getting into 'something like this'?"

"I did not say *anyone's* head," Cardenal corrected. "I said someone with Emilia's wisdom and emotions."

"And what does he know about your emotions and wisdom?"

"Enough," said Emilia.

"Maybe you can tell me, then, what the hell you want from me?" shouted Daniel.

"That I can do," Emilia answered. "I want you to shut up."

Daniel snorted like a happy colt, pushed back the hair falling over his eyes, and ordered a brandy to celebrate Emilia's command. That morning, he said, when he woke up, who was the one who had already left? Who was the one who'd gone looking for trouble at the Cruz Roja, marched her shining clean ass into that hellhole swarming with communicable diseases?

"You're drunk," said Emilia, edgy and ready for a fight.

"We're all drunk. This whole mess is nothing but one long drunken brawl. People drunk with power. The smell of blood. Three A.M. altruism. In the best of cases, really drunk, from alcohol. We're all drunk, all the time. You, for example. Why do you have to go looking for death among the dying? What are you looking for when you put your hand in the mouths of people dying from the latest epidemic?"

"How do you know what I do?"

"Because I go away, but I don't leave you behind," Daniel answered. "I know everything about you. From that magnet between your legs to the stupid way you go around doing good works."

Emilia left her chair, went over to Daniel, ran her hand through his hair, and kissed his mouth, which tasted of a long evening's brandy.

Ignacio Cardenal, glued to his seat, was enjoying the spectacle. Since they had no reservations about showing their feelings, he saw no reason to hide his fascination. The way Emilia and Daniel had shifted so abruptly from quarreling to kissing amazed him.

"You deserve each other," he declared, laughing.

"You've got that right, fucker," said Daniel, abandoning lips he had sucked like caramels.

During the next week, the three of them went to a theater where a popular singer sang to stave off disaster, to an operetta where minor woes helped people cry out their major ones without shame, and to a circus, which in Emilia's mind was inextricably linked with the dark day in her youth when she learned Daniel was in jail.

The performance seemed absolutely unchanged: two clowns, the ever-present horseback rider, the animal trainer with his mangy lions, three disputatious dwarfs, a weary trapeze artist, and five showgirls of uncertain age. They applauded as if they had never seen any of it, as if the flimflam of the circus were the perfect image for the madness they were living in. When after several great swings, the trapeze artist hurled herself through space above the yawning void, Emilia whispered in Daniel's ear:

"Of all the risks I've run because of you, the only thing I have never risked is not having risked them."

It was not only they whose lives were up in the air, the entire city seemed suspended between two trapezes. Fighting in the outskirts could be heard as clearly as if it were in the city center. At night, people went looking for a wild time, like soldiers on leave. Every day was the last, every day something was lost and something happened to leave everyday customs, even the sun overhead, forever changed.

Daniel worked from early morning writing reports and articles for several foreign newspapers and spending time among revolutionaries of the two principal factions. Some he saw in their offices and in public meetings; he met with others surreptitiously, at night, in their homes, or the homes of those who took them in at great personal danger. He had known all of them when they fought together to unseat the president who assassinated Madero. He had not played a part in the discussions and quarrels that later divided them, and therefore believed that each group had some right on its side, refusing to give either claim to his conscience.

"You're chasing illusions," Cardenal told him with Spanish assertiveness. "You'll end up being branded a traitor by both sides."

"He's been chasing illusions as long as I've known him," said Emilia.

"Don't talk as if you lived in the real world," Daniel rebutted. "Every morning you dive into hell. Is there any illusion greater than that of fighting death every day, inch by inch?"

Emilia Sauri had offered her services to the Cruz Roja. They welcomed her as they would have water in a burning desert. They needed everything and everyone available. No one asked her for credentials, every day was a professional examination, and all that was required to pass it was the necessary courage. From eight in the morning to six at night, Emilia came and went, passing every test she could. There were too many patients and too few beds; a putrid smell filled the air, along with a sound of moaning that swelled into a sinister litany. But, Daniel said, that was the music that gave her strength. Her love for him wasn't enough.

When either of these subjects was raised at night, a chasm opened between them that they quickly closed. The rest of the time, their lives were blissful. At least that was what Emilia wrote her parents, and what she told herself when she had time to listen. Because time was not something she had to spare. As soon as she left the hospital, Daniel swept her off to the whirlpool of the city, eager to burst the confinement of the day and talk with as many interesting people as he could find. He made friends with doctors and politicians, ambassadors and singers, painters and bullfighters, all the amazing variety that city had to offer, although the only persons allowed into their private lives were Refugio with his premonitions and Cardenal with his emphasis on reason as the first and only method of analysis.

At the beginning of July, Carranza's army entered the city, after crushing the resistance of the Conventionists. Once again the capital changed government, money, and those who governed. More than ever, Daniel believed he could convince each side of the need to make peace with the other. He visited the general who commanded Carranza's troops, and talked and drank with him one night. Refugio was of the opinion that he was taking unnecessary risks by asking for compassion for defeated troops who weren't as yet defeated. Daniel laughed at Refugio's warning, but before a week had passed, had to apologize for doubting him. The Conventionists retook the city with a stroke of luck that surprised everyone except Refugio.

"Now's the time," he told Consuelo. "Go out and spend your paper money because they will never be back."

On August 2, the Constitutionists returned to stay. Then, to his horror, Cardenal found himself sharing Don Refugio's premonitions. That same night during the modest dinner Consuelo had been able to scratch together, he told Daniel:

"As soon as there's a clear winner, they're going to come after you. No one will believe that you're a true friend of both camps."

Daniel laughed at that premonition as well. But Emilia was shaken to the marrow of her bones. The hospital needed her more than ever;

the battles of the last month had left wounded whom she treated without asking which side they had fought for. Working among them, however, she had learned how deep the hatred and the fervor that moved both armies was, and she could imagine with no trouble at all what the strong would do with that hatred. There was no compassion on either side; the person who wasn't with you was against you, pure and simple. That was Daniel's situation, although he mocked it, laughing as if the cards were stacked in his favor and it was the wind that once again raked Emilia's world, leveling the house of cards she had managed to construct during her brief married life.

ONE RAINY SUNDAY MORNING, Salvador Cuenca came to town. He had been in Veracruz, the port where the Constitutionalist government, and its head, Venustiano Carranza, were temporarily located. Salvador had come as a part of a group of special envoys to work in the Ministry of Foreign Relations, and took time to have breakfast with Emilia and Daniel, who were ecstatic to see him after so many years. Salvador Cuenca had become very close to Carranza, and had his confidence and support. He was sure that the Conventionists would lose the part of the nation they still controlled, and that the sooner it happened the better. Daniel was so happy to see his brother, and so sure that they had always agreed about politics that, just as placidly as he had listened to Salvador, he began to tell him about the need to seek accords and not divide the Revolution, not to lose so many valuable men because of prejudices and hatred that only harmed the country and kept it from being governed with generosity and honor. Salvador listened, slowly drinking coffee he found insipid and sad. Then he explained to his brother that such advice had put him in danger, words spoken without malice but to people who listened with mistrust and suspicion. He had made enemies everywhere: among the generals he had talked with as well as the foreign envoys who read in the good faith of his articles praise for their enemies. He had created suspicion among the Villistas, who thought he was for Obregón, and among Carranza followers, who were sure he was loyal to Zapata. The only safe thing to do was to leave the country. He, Salvador, would arrange for his return when things calmed down, but in the months to come, it was best that he live somewhere else. There were too many uncontrollable murderers, too much unchanneled fury, for Daniel to stay and defy them with his writing and his speeches about civility and good governing.

"No one's in any mood to be sensible or thoughtful or good," said Salvador. "And with no offense to Emilia, I have to say that love is no friend to anyone talking with men who are at war." He explained that he had a proposition for Daniel, and that he hoped he would be wise enough to listen.

The next day, a group of foreign priests were traveling to Veracruz; they were being expelled from Mexico because of the current anticlerical sentiment. As these priests were more important than some of their fellows, and because Carranza did not want to pick a quarrel with the princes of the church, he had charged Salvador with getting them onto a train to Veracruz and, once there, onto the boat that would quietly take them back to Spain. Daniel could, and should, go with them, accompanied by Emilia, whom it would be easy to disguise as a nun until the boat was safely out of port.

The expectation of such an unusual adventure mitigated Daniel's reluctance to leave Mexico City just when, in his opinion, things were close to getting better compared to the bad times that had beset them in recent months. Always imaginative and an eager traveler, he began thinking of the dispatch he could write about the exodus. Furthermore, he could always return from Cuba in disguise and move around Mexico incognito; no one would know where to look for him.

He accepted Salvador's idea on the condition that he include Ignacio Cardenal in his clerical chain gang, rapidly summarizing his plight. Salvador was so happy with his brother's reaction that he accepted his provision and even promised he would try to sell the encyclopedias if the Spaniard wanted to leave them with him for a while. In short, by the time the slim, elegant, self-possessed Ignacio showed up, Daniel was already in a cassock, trying out his role for the next day, accepting that nothing better could happen to Emilia and him than to accompany the encyclopedia salesman at least part of the way back home. Ignacio was moved to tears at the prospect of returning to Spain and his wife, but after thanking Daniel for the opportunity asked him if Emilia had agreed to come with them. Surprised by the question,

Daniel turned from the mirror where he was contemplating the more comic aspects of his disguise. Emilia had not actually said she would go, although she had agreed that Daniel needed to leave as soon as possible. She had kissed Salvador when he agreed to include Cardenal among his soon-to-be exiles, but almost immediately got up from the table to rush to the hospital. Daniel was sure she would arrange everything to accompany them.

"You're that sure?" Ignacio asked. "Sometimes I wonder if you really know her."

"She would never betray me like that," Daniel replied, falling into a chair.

"Who's betraying whom, between the two of you?" Cardenal asked before he left to collect his belongings.

Daniel sat alone, doubt blooming like a crimson carnation in his chest. Emilia came home early. She found him in the bedroom pretending to be selecting books to take with him and acting as if he hadn't heard her drag herself upstairs. From the doorway, she watched his charade, then went to him, his body the amulet she needed to endure, and clung to him until the unpredictable light of the next morning.

CHAPTER

26

SHE PUT IT into words about dawn, when both already knew it had been said without words. She was not going with him. She did not even have the heart to dress and go with him to the station.

"Traitor," said Daniel from the door of the bedroom.

Still in her white nightgown, Emilia put her head beneath the pillows and burrowed into the bed covers. She heard Salvador's voice calling Daniel to hurry, and bit her fist to keep from begging him to stay.

One hour later, Daniel was on the platform of San Lázarao station, along with Ignacio Cardenal and twelve pale priests. Salvador was shepherding them, bringing up the rear. Raindrops drummed loudly on the roof tiles. Dressed in the black cassock and white collar he had tried on the day before, Daniel did not have to pretend in order to be the saddest and most solemn among the clerics. He was staring at the ground, his lips moving as if praying, when Emilia stepped into his path, kissed him on the lips, and pressed her body against Daniel's black robes. She was wet from the rain, and out of breath.

"I want to stay," Daniel said to Salvador.

"Don't ask for the impossible." Emilia's kiss shut off any words from Daniel. The train began to move. Emilia pushed Daniel toward the car where Cardenal was holding out his hand. A burst of icy wind intensified Emilia's trembling as she forced herself to smile until the clatter of the wheels faded into the rain.

SHE STAYED ON at the hospital for a few weeks. Waiting for those who were dying to die and for those who could be cured to reclaim the life in which every day they went looking for death. The city had regained a certain calm, but to Emilia it seemed a desolate place. She missed Daniel at every street corner, in every alley, in the middle of the indifferent traffic that ruled the Paseo de la Reforma, before the fallen-down door of a church, sitting at the table with her morning coffee, in the empty tub of the house that was closing in around her with its silence, awake at midnight, her mouth sore from chewing on her wedding diamond. She kept the ring in her mouth as a reminder of the guilt she could not shake. Had she betrayed him? Could the simple desire not to return to turmoil, to battles, to mornings with nothing useful to do, to renouncing the sane, productive world that was her vocation and her destiny, be called betrayal? She would wake up with those questions shining like miniature suns in the darkness, night after night distorting her normal sleep. Finally, she accepted that insomnia would rule her life and directed her energies to dreaming up tricks to prevent drowning in sadness when night stretched endlessly before her. She took up music again, practicing on a cello Refugio managed to borrow from a church, she read *The Thousand and One Nights,* kept long night vigils, and wrote letters as if they dictated themselves. She also kept a scrupulous diary, describing for Daniel her emotions and sorrows, her hopes and regrets. Someday life would be so generous that they both would have time to sit down and read what she had been doing during that dark period she despised every moment of but would not have traded for any other. Rather than follow him until she turned into a shadow, she had chosen to lose him. And having made that choice, she felt alone, wretched, proud, witless.

She again became the quintessential listener. She listened to everyone from the infectious patients to the women who looked after their wounded hoping fate would take pity on them. She listened to Refugio and his fears and to Eulalia herself, growing steadily more ill and more clever at disguising it. She listened with interest and without respite until she learned to see herself as one more needle in the needle-filled haystack where she had taken refuge.

One morning at the end of September, Refugio came looking for her. As if it were any ordinary morning, his granddaughter had milked the three drops of milk left in the two skeletal cows they shared the Mixcoac stable with. She had moved as if she were perfectly well, but since dawn Refugio had watched half her spirit cross over, and he was eaten with fear at being robbed of the one thing he had left in life.

Emilia followed him, and found Eulalia in the stable, pretending to be asleep beside the pail from the milking. There was nothing to be done but wait beside the placid Refugio for Eulalia's life to fade away in what she continued to pretend was her sleep. It was night when she opened her eyes; they seemed to be focused on something far away. Before her last words to her grandfather, she was able to tell Emilia:

"Don't cheat yourself. It isn't good to die before your time."

They bought her a white coffin and took her to the cemetery, crying as if hers was the only death among a multitude of deaths. Shortly afterward, trains began to carry civilian passengers again. Emilia decided to go back to Puebla. Claiming that she needed to see the other side of the volcanoes, and that her presence was not as urgently needed in the Cruz Roja, she told Consuelo good-bye and left with Refugio's agreement that he would follow as soon as he could. Then she boarded the train, eager to spend some time in the irresistible bosom of the world where she had grown up.

SHE HAD NOT TOLD ANYONE when she would arrive. Her experience with trains had taught her that it was impossible to predict. The trip, nonetheless, took less time than she had expected. Mesmerized by the still green and lush October landscape, she let time flow by without measure, not minding the jolting and discomfort of the car whose proud past had been brought down by war and harsh treatment. Once in the station, she walked down the deserted platform in the light of a late afternoon that brought back all her memories, propelling her toward the Casa de la Estrella like a sailboat pushed by the wind onto the waiting shore.

The pharmacy was still open when she leapt from the car she had hired and ran inside, calling out to her father. Diego Sauri was leaning on the counter before a stack of papers. His eyes opened wide, hypnotized by the image he saw approaching, and he spoke his daughter's name as if he needed to hear it to believe what he was seeing. Emilia felt the warmth of her father's voice like a hand upon her head. She hugged him across the counter, weeping and blessing him with such pure joy that Josefa, in her kitchen, heard jubilation ringing out like a pealing bell. She came running down the stairs—something she had not done since tumbling down the complete flight the year before. She found her husband and her daughter with their arms around each other, looking at each other as if they could not believe what they saw.

Knowing that if she let herself she would cry her eyes out, and that if she ran to Emilia she would be totally shattered, Josefa stopped in the doorway of the room behind the shop to catch her breath and wipe away two tears with her sleeve. Then she whistled as she had when her daughter was a little girl and she had gone to pick her up at the entrance to the school. When he heard his wife, Diego released Emilia and watched her move toward Josefa in a fog, like someone looking for a prayer.

Iconoclastic, beautiful, making more noise than in her prime, Milagros showed up that night with Rivadeneira, who, despite the war, had not lost a jot of his elegance. They all ate together, talking about everything and nothing, leaping from Mexico City to Chicago, from Daniel's exile to the war as an atrocity no one yet knew how to deal with. They had invested a good part of their lives in search of the spirited nation drowsing under the dictatorship; they had wanted a country of laws in which a general could not have his way. But nothing had come from the war against the dictatorship but another war, and the struggle against the excesses of one general had led to many generals and many excesses.

"The irony is that instead of democracy, we got chaos, and instead of justice, executioners," Diego Sauri said sadly.

"Daniel firmly believes that some good must come from so many deaths," said Emilia.

"As long as it's not to call more living to be killed," was the sentiment of Milagros, who suffered every failure as a personal wound.

They talked about Emilia's adventures as if they had happened to them, too, and about their own lives as if Emilia had been privy to every move they made. Emilia told them about Baui, the woman with the ferocious Indian-Spanish bloodlines who ruled the convulsed village in the north where they had improvised a hospital, and imitated her way of scolding Daniel for being in too big a hurry, her mocking tone as she said, "You're going to die when you die, no matter how hard you run." She went from back to back, illustrating the massage she had learned from the aged *curandera* on the train. She described Mexico City in the midst of catastrophe. She told them about Refugio, bone thin, amazed, his head filled with prophecies, marrying Daniel and her and then the same day predicting they would be separated. She told about Eulalia raiding a bakery because for more than three nights she had dreamed of an anise-flavored bun. Then she imitated the exaggerated, clerical solemnity Daniel had to affect in order to join the exiled priests, and how all his acting had gone for naught when she stepped in front of him and kissed him.

"The next day, my body hurt as if I'd taken a beating," she said, before indulging in the meringue, which she knew tasted like heaven. After she ate it, she started crying, for no reason beyond that.

It was nearly eleven when the bell at the front entrance rang and they heard footsteps crossing the patio and coming up the stairs. As the footsteps neared the sala, Emilia asked who would bother to ring if he had a key. And there in the dining room doorway, as handsome as she remembered, long legs, broad, judicious brow, eyes of peace, and hands of an earthly angel, stood Antonio Zavalza. A smile lighted Emilia's face that cleared away the tears, and she rose from the chair where she was bouncing up and down like a child. Never pausing to wonder what was expected of her, she threw her arms around Zavalza for being who he was, and covered his face with kisses, not wanting to know from where they came.

* * *

DOCILE, generous, the life opening before Emilia was less dramatic but more bold. Looking for formal approval of her training, she went to the university and asked to be examined. She went back to working with Zavalza in the hospital born in the time of calm and promise that had preceded her leave-taking. As if he had never been besieged by the disillusion and rage of losing her, Zavalza welcomed Emilia as naturally as one would yield to the enchantment of a moon crossing through the noontime sky.

Emilia seldom talked about her absence, shrugging it off as one of those things that are beyond our control. They worked as they had before, sharing the intimacy that came from dealing with the bodies of others when they did not dare deal with their own. They left the hospital late and began the day with the dawn, practicing their profession as if clinging to a life raft. Emilia diagnosed and treated, enjoying her work with a calm she had never known and with the self-confidence of a student who demonstrates things for her maestro she has not learned from him, but with the attitude of an apprentice.

With the modesty of those who know how much they know, Zavalza discussed new medical discoveries with Emilia and listened to her wishes, her curiosities, her failures. They spent late nights and Sundays imagining operations on the human heart like the one Alexis Carrel had successfully performed on a dog. They tried to isolate vitamin A in Diego's laboratory, because they knew it had been done by a chemist at Yale University, and tried to reproduce pills for depression according to a formula Emilia had brought from Chicago. They researched the curative qualities of herbs that, fermented by Teodora, had produced white mushrooms that Emilia had seen with her own eyes wipe out gonorrhea. As if all this were not enough excitement, the hospital and their practice were bringing in money. Not enough for Zavalza to recoup the wealth he had lost in the war, but enough to live well in those chaotic financial times. With her small but steady income, Emilia was able to help her parents, buy books, send rent money to Refugio, buy a new cello and, from time to time, even a new dress. In that way, with no formal bonds but the intimacy of their conversations and the passion with which they imagined the future, a year went by. They lived in their own houses but shared almost everything else.

Then, after the Christmas of 1916, when she received nothing from Daniel but a letter from Spain directed to all the family, Emilia lapsed into a period of silence she interrupted only to attend the ailing or discuss matters concerning the hospital with Zavalza. Nothing prevailed against that silence, not her parents, not Milagros, not the sweetness of Sol, whose lap had been the one haven for Emilia's tears as she wept over the painful void she sometimes felt at having lost Daniel.

"I envy how much you miss him," Zavalza told her one night.

"I don't miss him," said Emilia. "What hurts are my misgivings."

They had walked from the hospital, and it was cold. Zavalza did not want to come in for dinner. Emilia did not insist.

She slowly went up the stairs that led to the corridor of the ferns and slumped down between two large pots. There on the floor under the glass ceiling of the gallery palely lit by a myriad of stars, she sat a long time, brooding.

"Are you going to spend the night there?" asked Josefa, peering out from the sala.

"Part of it," Emilia said curtly.

"What a good idea. Before long there won't be anyone who loves you," said her mother, going to look for Diego.

Emilia heard them arguing and doing kitchen chores. Later she quietly responded to the "See you in the morning" they called out to her as they went off to the bed of their reconciliations.

IT WAS after midnight when Emilia Sauri knocked at the door of the house where Antonio Zavalza lived with his two dogs and the loneliness of his waiting. She had walked ten blocks in darkness occasionally pierced by a street lamp, and was freezing. She held out her arms as soon as Antonio appeared, seeking in his eyes the knowledge that she had come for him and not a substitute.

Everything in Zavalza's world was attuned to the simplicity of those who know what they want and do not long for lost paradises, only patches of light in which they can lose themselves. He was one of those persons who go through life convinced that happiness is something you find, not look for, that it always comes along, inevitably, and exactly when it is least expected. Emilia entered his house less as if she knew it than sure that she was known there. And everything, from the dogs to the darkness scented with the bouquet of its owner, welcomed her as if they had often seen her at midnight. Slowly they took off their clothes, slowly they probed the planes and longings of their bodies, aware of the conversation they must have but just then wanting only to touch each other, to celebrate their power over a kingdom whose blessings they did not tire of exploring.

Light on Emilia's eyelids alerted her that it was after seven. She opened her eyes because habit was stronger than exhaustion. The first thing she saw on her horizon was a tray with her breakfast and, after that, Zavalza's hands, reminding her of their many skills. She felt a flush on her cheeks and realized, seeing him there, like a force she had no desire to oppose, that she loved him as much as she did Daniel, and that she did not know how to handle that.

"Don't think about him too much," said Antonio, stroking her tangled hair.

Emilia's smile was a blend of light and doubts; she took the hands that smoothed her hair to guide them to other places.

It was ten o'clock when she walked into her own house with a spring in her step and the face of a naughty child. Gathered in the dining room, the Rivadeneiras and the Sauris heard her come in and looked at each other with the collusion the moment required. Among the four of them, they could prophesy as well as Refugio. They had eaten an early breakfast together to be sure they were in agreement that they did not have to worry about Emilia, who undoubtedly was at last asleep in Zavalza's arms. When they heard her come in, they looked at each other in silence and kept drinking their coffee. Emilia winged into that silence like a bird, and gave each of them a kiss. She sat down beside her father, poured herself coffee, took a deep breath, and said with a smile, "I'm a bigamist."

"Affection is something you can never use up," Milagros Veytia commented.

"Well, I'll find out," said Emilia, her feeling of well-being making it impossible to stop smiling.

"What a shameless pair!" burst out Josefa. "I've never seen such luck, not even in novels. A man like Rivadeneira never comes along. But two, two in the same family . . . If we wrote it, no one would believe it."

"They're not as saintly as you may think," said Milagros. "They've had their own affairs. Haven't they, Diego?"

"I don't know whether a man's strength could stretch that far," he replied.

"Well, I hope they have," was Josefa's wish. "That way I would feel less guilty."

"What do you have to feel guilty about?" asked Emilia.

"For putting up with you two," replied Josefa. "I wonder what god will protect you."

"Yours," said Milagros. "Yours will be enough."

CHAPTER 27

THE NEXT YEAR, 1917, according to all those who could still keep count, a new decree, vigorously enforced, demanded that federal taxes be paid in silver. Diego Sauri caught a raging cold brought on by bitter regret that the Revolution and its madness had gotten them a president who was no younger than he but looked less old, and, not because he was anti-Díaz, was imposing obligations different from those of the dictatorship. A congress of representatives chosen from the side that won the war approved a new constitution. Milagros and Rivadeneira survived the terrible fire that ravaged the Buenavista station as the train they were traveling on arrived there: a munitions car had exploded before their eyes, producing a terrifying display of lights and detonations that Milagros used as the pretext for running all sorts of risks, claiming that not even her real death would frighten her as much as she had been frightened there. Josefa once again fell down the stairs because she was hurrying. Rivadeneira could not stop dwelling on the puzzle that lodged in his gut when General Alvaro Obregón retired from Carranza's government to buy a ranch upon which to build an agricultural enterprise, he, a military man whose star had dazzled half the nation. Sol García gave birth to a baby girl three months after her husband's death, and Emilia learned, profoundly, that it is possible to reconcile serenity with the luxury of unrestrained passion.

She slept in Antonio Zavalza's house; with him she ate dinner at her parents' home, had breakfast on the way to the hospital, and supper wherever her stomach found her at midnight. Everything, even politics, which from afar seemed an attractive spectacle, raced through that year as angels flit through a room when a sudden silence falls. And Emilia kept a meticulous account of all of it, which was Zavalza's delight. Listening to her list the week's happenings as if they were far in the past and deserved to be recorded in the realm of memory pleased him so much that one afternoon, after dinner, he took her for a walk through the city to look for a present. Beneath the pale Saturday sun, they came to the narrow streets lined with the furniture shops that had sprung up during the Revolution for the purpose of selling the extravagant pieces brought in every day from sacked haciendas and houses the wealthy had abandoned intact rather than risk losing their lives defending them.

The rocking chair was hanging from a hook in the ceiling. It was one of those oak pieces with a carved back and spindles. On the headrest was the face of a smiling old man, nearly obliterated by his beard and mustaches. Zavalza asked them to take it down. He showed Emilia the face of the old man and asked her if she thought he would be a good listener. Emilia tried the seat, rocking energetically, and asked Zavalza if he was planning to go somewhere. He told her he would never leave of his own accord, but wanted to be sure that even if it worked out that way, she would always have a listener to help her pick up the thread of memories she wove so persistently and well, as one weaves a work of art.

"You can tell him everything," said Zavalza. "Even things you can't tell me."

Emilia called him jealous and got up to kiss him, to erase from his imagination everything his frown was communicating. They never spoke of Daniel but, knowing Emilia's inclination to remember as other women embroider, it was logical that Zavalza carried like a stone in his heart the certainty that, although two years had passed, she had forgotten none of Daniel's fascination or their adventures together.

They took the rocking chair home. At the door, Zavalza asked Emilia to sit in it so he could carry her over the threshold, chair and all. Emilia yielded to his wishes with an unaccustomed solemnity. She arranged the pleats of her skirt, lifted her feet from the ground, closed her eyes, and said she was ready. Zavalza saw her dark eyelashes flutter slightly and before he picked her up leaned down to hear what she was murmuring that sounded a little like a prayer. When she sensed his nearness, Emilia offered him a kiss like a blank check. The intoxication and audacity of one moment of heaven enveloped them. Then Zavalza picked up the chair and stepped into the house with that booty of sorrows and glory life had generously placed in his arms.

It had been a long day. Early in the morning a woman had given birth to triplets. Later a man arrived with his arm half chopped off by a friend's machete. And, to top it all off, at one in the afternoon Madame Moré was brought in screaming with an inflamed appendix, which they operated on without being sure she would survive. Madame Moré was a pleasant and affectionate old woman whose fame as a European whore had for forty years brought men from all parts of the nation to Puebla. With time, she had turned into a kind of exotic grandmother ready finally to broadcast that she derived the "European" part of her renown from a Zouave who had slept one night on the straw mat of a Zacapoaxtla woman, leaving behind the seed of a baby girl with green eyes and blond hair whose birth shamed the entire village. Horrified to have produced such a freak, the baby's mother had traveled to the city to leave her in the care of someone who had the misfortune of skin as light as hers. The only place where there were white-skinned people and she would not be thrown out at eleven o'clock in the morning was the honorable brothel near the railroad station. There, sound asleep in the middle of a room of soundly sleeping white women, she left the baby with the tranquillity of knowing that among them no one would find her coloring or her features strange. From the first afternoon she came to their office, Emilia and Antonio had adopted the woman that baby became without blinking an eye at the malodorous reputation that accompanied her. They loved her endless store of proverbs and intimate details about the many men who had found refuge in the thick Zacapoaxtla thatch that covered her snow white Breton mound of Venus.

It was midnight when Emilia was awakened by the chill of her body pressed against Zavalza's nakedness. All those thoughts were racing through her head as, drowsy and shivering, she pulled up over them the eiderdown she thought of as the perfect symbol of the protection this man provided to everything around him. She snuggled up against his back and between his dreams heard him say those words that permeate the night with meaning and that stay forever in the ears of those who hear them. This, she thought, must be what her parents always called happiness.

By March 1919, the hospital had twenty beds and seven additional doctors. Sol García, because of reverses the Revolution had wrought upon her family's and her husband's wealth, had become the hospital's administrator, the most perfectionist and rational in the world. Zavalza said he could not have found a miracle like her with a magnifying glass, not even in Germany, and when she heard that, Emilia was as proud as if Sol's blood circulated in her own veins. Had they been interested to know, they would have learned the low opinion some people had for women of their class who worked. Neither of them, however, had time to spare for opinions, and so took pleasure in their jobs, their hearts at peace.

That spring, Emilia and Zavalza accepted Dr. Hogan's invitation to give a paper on intestinal parasites at the Geneva College of Medicine in New York. It was a subject that until then no one knew more about than Mexican physicians. Even in that period of epidemics and killing, Sol had given them the statistic that of every ten illnesses, four had something to do with stomach problems.

Emilia had a particular fondness for Geneva College, because in 1847, when no North American university would admit women to medical school, the alumni of that college, when asked by the dean whether they would accept a woman among them, wrote back a unanimous "yes," thinking the question was a joke. Elizabeth Blackwell, which was the name of the young lady in question, armed with that document, set up such a commotion that she convinced her future colleagues that there was no reason to back down from what they had decided in jest. Then, although the authorities had predicted grave incidents brought on by the presence of a woman in their classrooms, a mutual appreciation gradually developed between the male students and their female colleague. So much so that when one of the professors asked Miss Blackwell to absent herself during anatomical discussions of the male reproductive organs, her classmates seconded her refusal to leave the room. After the two years then required to complete the courses for the degree, Elizabeth was graduated with the highest grades of her group.

Dr. Blackwell had been Hogan's teacher, and he felt for her story and her life a profound appreciation that he instilled whole in Emilia's awareness. As if she had been there, Emilia knew the tribulations of Elizabeth's residency in London, where she was allowed into the classes and the hospitals but was rejected by many of the women she tried to attend. No less difficult was her time in France, where in her eagerness to learn she agreed to work in the school of midwifery, the only place she was allowed to practice obstetrics.

Dr. Hogan and the intrepid Helen Shell traveled to New York to meet Emilia and Zavalza. They had fallen in love as if one were not thirty-five years older than the other—or perhaps for that very reason. Helen was still the impulsive woman who had captivated Emilia five years before, and touched by the magic of the young philosopher, Hogan looked like the photographs taken when his wife was still alive to light his youth.

When they returned to Mexico, Emilia devoted every night of the following month to rocking in her rocking chair. She had the theory that everything she wanted to remember when she was an old woman should be stored there, as if in an envelope from which she could pull enigmas and dreams when life dwindled down to a handful of impulses and blurry forms. No one would ever be able to expel her from that paradise woven of memories.

Zavalza saw her rocking both when she wanted to confess some error and when she had dreams and afflictions to tell. He had learned to understand everything about her, and he knew, perhaps as well as she herself, what obsessions, what alarms roused her, what abysses of nostalgia she was passing through on some silent afternoons, how much sugar she put in her morning coffee, how she had come to like salt, how she slept curled up on her right side, and what paths he must follow to touch her dreams.

He was grateful to Emilia for the happiness of knowing he was loved, and for the daily pleasure of watching her pursue some new revelation. She did not know how to give up, she never used the word *incurable,* she did not believe in God but, rather, in something more like a Divine Providence. When one treatment failed to work, she tried another. She had taught Zavalza that no one fell ill of the same disease in the same way, and that therefore no one had to be cured of the same disease by using the same treatment. She could diagnose someone's illness merely from the color of his skin or the opacity of his eyes, simply by noting the tone of his voice or the way he moved his feet. Zavalza thought of her as a peripatetic laboratory. He never heard her ask questions as essential as the simple and direct, "Where does it hurt?" And when no one dared pinpoint the origin of an illness or when others found a disease unknown and perilous, she would come out with three conclusive statements, and most of the time she was right. Thanks to her conciliatory instincts, the hospital sometimes seemed more like a council of madmen than a scientific center, but deep down, Zavalza agreed with her eclectic search for answers.

When the entire country was laid low by an epidemic of Spanish influenza, besides their own team of licensed physicians, Emilia called in an equal number of unlicensed healers whose presence gave the hospital the reputation of being a place where everything was possible. Living together there, enriching each other with an indiscriminate exchange of knowledge, were three celebrated homeopathic doctors, two Indian authorities who called themselves traditional practitioners, and a midwife more skilled in the critical art of birthing babies than the most famous New York gynecologist. In addition, at Hogan's prompting, each semester the hospital had a visiting physician eager to pursue innovative treatments.

As if drawn by an echo, tiny Teodora appeared one noontime in the Sauris' pharmacy. When Emilia and Zavalza came to the Casa de la Estrella around four in the afternoon, dead with hunger, they found Josefa lying on the floor with Teodora on her back, pressing the places that had hurt ever since her fall. Zavalza had heard Emilia talk about the aged woman and her artist's hands, and so was not taken aback when he heard his wife speak to Teodora with the untarnished devotion of a student, and was happy, and not at all surprised, that she had come.

And then to top everything off, assuring that the hospital would more than ever resemble a three-ring circus, one blazing sunset Refugio appeared with his collection of enigmas under his arm. When she saw him walking into her office, escorted by Diego Sauri, Emilia felt memory's butterflies fluttering in her stomach, and as she embraced him wondered what had become of the husband he had predicted would not last. It had been almost four years since she had seen Daniel, and although she was living a peaceful life, and her heart was in better hands than ever before, Emilia knew as well as she knew her own eyes—something she did not spend every minute thinking about—that her body conserved an ineradicable devotion for the other man in her life. She did not dwell on that admission, she kept it as everyone keeps secrets beneath a smiling facade. At times, however, she had allowed herself to nurture that admission, and although she had never asked a single question as Milagros summarized Daniel's letters when Zavalza was not around, she knew all she needed to know about him. That he was alive and well, that he continued to write for a number of newspapers, and that he still loved her, despite the fury of his hatred the first year following the separation he summarily referred to as her "arbitrary desertion."

Milagros had the gift of accidentally leaving Daniel's letters in the drawer of Emilia's dressing table in the Casa de la Estrella that still held her mending. Every two or three months, Emilia took them from there, always returning them at siesta time, well read, the day after finding them. He was writing long letters again. They began with a brief "Dear Aunt," and from there on out used the plural: "How are all of you?" "Would you like . . ." "I'm sending you . . ." "I miss you all so much . . ." There was never a word about coming back, little about politics, a lot about other countries, nothing about other women. Sometimes he was able to make Emilia feel guilty without mentioning her name, and sometimes the letters sent her running to her rocking chair to invoke the magic of other times. Later, time, curiosity, or the love at hand would descend over her like a filter between real life and the fantasy of remembering the man of so many personal wars.

Refugio brought to the hospital the responsibility of being the official conversationalist. At first, only Emilia had confidence in the healing powers of his tongue, but experience taught almost everyone there to consider him an unparalleled practical tool. Refugio was as effective with women who had just brought life into the world as patients who were leaving it, with injured children as men reluctant to tell anything more about themselves than their name, and as he had more time than ever to listen, he was a splendid compiler of the phases each patient passed through.

Over the course of the years, Emilia had developed a particular preference for cases related to the brain and spinal column, those two misanthropes that, enclosed in their cases of bone, control everything we do, with no explanation but an occasional glimmer we usually do not know how to interpret. She ended up with all the cases having to do with abrupt changes in state of mind, disturbances in memory or language, paralysis, convulsions, blurred vision, lack of coordination—any uncommon behavior. She took on the task of classifying the symptoms and signs that originate in what was still being called the central nervous system, something only slightly more arcane than it would be eighty years later. Refugio helped her by listening and by patiently observing each of the sensations, images, impulses, and oddities patients exhibited when she could not be there.

The eventful year of 1920 saw the uprising of generals who did not agree with the restorative calm of the Carranza government, led by Alvaro Obregón, the military guiding star Josefa had always recognized in her favorite agriculturist. Emilia passed that year fascinated by the desolate interior landscape of a woman with sudden periods of depression, the strange dreams of a man agitated for no visible cause, the snatches of angelic music a girl always heard before falling into convulsions that her confessor considered to be satanic possession, difficulties in the speech of a boy who was extremly intelligent in his writing, an otherwise reasonable man's mulish insistence that his wife was an umbrella, the clear recollection of the past and absolute obliteration of the present that confused the lives of some elderly patients, and the warm purple light that bathed the world of an adolescent boy minutes before a swoon from which he recovered five minutes later as exhausted as if he had scaled a mountain. Nothing dominated Emilia's professional life more than the distress, pleasure, and fascination contained in the mysterious relationship between what everyone thinks, feels, imagines, and what is lodged in the body under the denomination "brain." Because of that passion, Emilia decided to travel to the United States for a seminar Dr. Hogan invited her to attend in that gentle but slightly bullying way in which teachers continue to address their best students. Zavalza could not go with her because the trip was so long the hospital could not function if both of them were away for that period of time. So Emilia turned to the company of Milagros, who was always ready for a trip—at her age, she said, travel was the only sensible way to take risks and feel she had just fallen in love.

Zavalza saw them off on a ship sailing from Veracruz to Galveston and New York in October, the day after the Chamber of Deputies had declared Alvaro Obregón constitutional president of the Republic. Emilia glimpsed the beaten-dog expression Antonio tried to conceal, staring straight ahead as if focusing on something he had lost in infinity. He was a generous and sensitive man who would have borne any pain before contesting Emilia's right to the trip, but despite his effort not to show his uneasiness, he could not summon the logic to reassure himself that he was not losing her forever, that separations make the heart grow fonder, that at one time he had been able to live without her, that he would not expire no matter how close he felt he was to dying.

"If you want, I won't go," Emilia said, with sympathy but also more than a dash of mischief.

Zavalza smiled, grateful for the way she winked as she moved from his arms. He told her to think about him every minute and left the ship that was announcing its departure with a raucous blast of its whistle.

"That sounds full of promises," said Milagros after the second or third deafening roar. Then she lifted an arthritic arm to match the fervor of her niece's athletic waving in honor and benediction of Antonio Zavalza, left quivering behind on the dock.

CHAPTER

28

JOSEFA VEYTIA had always said it was not necessary to pursue destiny, because nothing was less foreseeable yet so surprising in its innate predictability than fate. Knowing the way her parents had met, Emilia had always thought of Josefa's sayings about chance and its eventualities as nothing more than an account of her personal experience, which, as everyone knows, is never the same for any two people. Even so, when she walked into the hotel in New York and experienced the thrill of seeing Daniel there, like a mirage in the desert, all Josefa's words collected in a knot beneath her ribs like a whirlwind of illogic with which she could only agree.

Daniel was sitting in the lobby of the hotel, chatting with a man so blond he was nearly albino and a man so black his skin verged on blue. Emilia's first reaction was to accuse Milagros, who was walking behind her, talking to the bellhop. She was the only person who could be guilty of arranging such a rendezvous. But so great was the surprise on a face incapable of feigning emotion, that Milagros's reaction exonerated her.

Emilia knew how deeply Daniel engaged himself in conversation, and as her only wish was to gain time to set her emotions in order, she hurried straight to the desk clerk, a bleary-eyed man used to dealing with people whose haste and lack of cordiality no longer surprised him. Not even curious as to why this woman was so pale and behaving as if she were being chased by an elephant, he gave her five words and the key to a room on the seventh floor of that brightly lit palace. Emilia slipped into the elevator, where Milagros was waiting, her conversation with the bellhop seemingly unending, and disappeared from view.

As soon as the door to their room closed, Emilia threw herself down on the bed, cursing the curiosity that had lured her from the hollow of the world where she was so happy, as well as the evil moment she had accepted the poet Rivadeneira's offer to pay for her stay in a hotel that he himself had reserved. In the meantime, she was getting a headache she did not know whether to attribute to a disturbance in her brain or her heart. She suddenly felt a great sympathy for all the trapped people of the world.

After hours of listening in the dark to Milagros's quiet but wide-awake breathing, Emilia managed to sink into lethargy and dream that she was sleeping with Antonio Zavalza. Daniel came into their room covered with medals and woke her to give them to her as if she were a little girl who desperately wanted them. He was naked, and soon climbed into bed with them. Later he left the room noiselessly, but left his shoes at the foot of the bed. Emilia watched as the shoes flew through the air to land in the middle of her chest, where they pressed upon it as if they were made of lead. Unable to free herself of that weight, she remembered in the dream of her dream a sign painted on the back of a rickety cart the two of them had ridden on one afternoon to the village of San Angel, looking for someplace less saturated with war than the Mexico City of those days: *Pick up your tiny little feet; you're walking on my heart.*

They were awakened by knocking at the door. She got out of bed still recalling the perfume of her laughter against the sky above the village market, and went to the door. There, touching a gloved hand to his hat, looking exactly like the memory that had invaded her night, stood Daniel, speaking her name like an echo she had not wanted to hear.

"Don't you know the air changes color when you pass by? Are you coming with me or shall I take off my clothes here in the doorway?" he asked, loosening the knot of his necktie and taking off his jacket.

Emilia went with him, realizing it would have taken much less of a challenge to get her to follow him. She went in her nightgown, her hair loose, her feet bare, creeping down the hotel corridor trembling like an inexperienced thief to steal from life another bit of that man whose fate she had sworn never to follow again, and also sure as never before that all her oaths had been bogus.

They went into a room barely illuminated by the pale glow of a lamp. With the index finger of her left hand, Emilia traced the bones in Daniel's naked back.

"Every time I run into you, you look like a starving dog," she said, and leaned down to touch the tip of her tongue to the salt and splendor of his skin.

They spent two days locked in that room, until there was nothing beween them but air and the silence of two people who had cursed and blessed one another without truce or surfeit. When finally they emerged to eat with Milagros Veytia at one of the seafood restaurants near the docks, she found them luminous and infuriating, as they had been as children. Daniel speared a lock of Emilia's hair with his fork, put it in his mouth to suck on it, and sparked in Emilia the smile of a roused animal to whom medicine and its pitfalls seemed to have no importance at all.

"I'm not going to the seminar," she decided.

"That's the luck of men who are spellbinders," Milagros commented as she tried to pry open a clam.

"And the curse of the women in their lives," Emilia replied.

DURING THE WEEKS that followed, Emilia and Daniel walked through the city as if it were a fair: the circulation of the automobiles a merry-go-round, going up in the buildings, riding a Ferris wheel. They dipped into theaters as they would into grab bags, they watched ships arriving from other worlds like invitations, they ate exotic dishes until the tang of remote seas wafted from their ears.

One evening when night fell early, the first notice that winter was upon them, Rivadeneira arrived on a Spanish ship. It had been nearly a month since Milagros and Emilia left Veracruz and a week since the end of the seminar, where Emilia stopped by only to ask for the silence of her friend Dr. Hogan, and to receive in exchange a scolding and the gift of his complicity.

"You'll miss a variety of discoveries," Hogan told her.

"But I'm gaining another," Emilia replied with an angelic smile.

"Are you making yourself some promise?" asked Hogan, dazzled by the light in her face.

"It *is* a promise."

"Of what?"

"Of the present," said Emilia, kissing him good-bye.

Three nights later, Daniel pulled out the last stop on his charm during a dinner at which Hogan was prepared to be distant and inhospitable. He succeeded until the end of the soup course, but from then until dessert could only surrender to the intelligence and charm of that man whose pact with adventure he had considered reprehensible. Hogan repeated his invitation to Emilia to spend some time in his home in Chicago, which she and Zavalza had not been able to visit during their stay in the United States. Daniel was excited about the offer and promised that very soon Emilia and he would come to enliven one of Hogan's Sundays, and perhaps stay a week in that city. He sealed his promise with an impetuous farewell embrace that captivated Hogan entirely.

AS SOON as they were alone, aimlessly strolling through the streets of a contemplative November, Emilia Sauri wanted to know where Daniel had gained the impression that she could go to Chicago with him.

"Because I can go," he replied, with the assurance that he spoke the truth.

"Daniel, what am I going to do with you?" Emilia said, directing the question more to herself than to him, with the thought of her profession and the man with whom she shared it a sudden, deep wound Daniel not only could not heal, but had not even noticed.

"Marry me," Daniel said, leaning down to nibble her earlobe.

Emilia shook her head to avoid his teasing.

"I already married you," she said.

"But you're deceiving me with that doctor," Daniel admonished her.

"You don't understand anything."

"What I do understand is enough."

"You're the one who goes away."

"My body leaves. My head is always with you," said Daniel in a tone Emilia did not recognize.

"And what good is that to me? How does that help me live? What difficulty does it get me through? What children does it give me?"

Daniel had no defense but to awaken her desire, so they hurried to the hotel room, where the only rule was the reason of their bodies.

The next day they went back out into the fair to celebrate the joy of having each other, of wandering through that tumultuous, hospitable city always ready to offer refuge to unpardonable passions. Daniel was working for a newspaper and was living in a small apartment on which Emilia made no effort to impose order. They moved in there to sleep and make love while the world was working. They put off their disagreements. Both feared the distasteful territory of reproaches and explanations. Each for a different reason, but each with the same reluctance to delve too deeply into anything other than their current irresistible caprices. They were together, with no future beyond the night before them. Life was fine, generous, irrevocable, and filled with promises.

They went to Chicago. They spent not one but two weeks in Hogan's home, turning Sundays into festivals and nights into parties. They walked and drank with Hogan and Helen as if the four of them were prepared to die, as long as they did not lose one moment of the joy they were living.

"This man is more your type," Helen told Emilia one night when they were exchanging confidences, which had begun with Helen's praising the way her friend's skin and eyes glowed when Daniel was near.

"Not when I want peace," Emilia replied.

"Why do you want peace, if you have happiness?"

"That's what I think now, but life is not always *now,*" Emilia answered, recalling her life with Antonio as one remembers a lost paradise.

THEY RETURNED to New York to spend Christmas with Milagros and Rivadeneira, whose role as go-betweens had caused them to stay a little longer in a city they had begun to fear after two weeks. Emilia found them noticeably older, in the way children seem to grow immoderately when we haven't seen them for a while. She was afraid something had happened to her parents. She hadn't written more than a brief note to anyone in Puebla. Nor had she drummed up an excuse to explain her delay in returning. She summed up her days by sending hugs and saying she was well and happy. Identical letters for recipients as varied as Zavalza, Sol, Josefa and Diego. Nevertheless, she had felt an occasional gust of remorse that was frightening in the certainty that eventually it would turn into pain. But no amount of reason, no guilt, no memory was allowed to intrude on the present.

One afternoon two days after a magnificent and cheerful Christmas dinner, Daniel informed Emilia that they needed to leave immediately for a place where he was going to interview visiting Mexicans, one of whom was a representative of Obregón's government. He was ecstatic, making plans and remembering friends, ready once again to plunge blindly into the clandestine world of intrigue and disputes. As they were drinking their rum with sugar and lime, Emilia listened in silence, knowing it was pointless to try to divert him, concentrating on his voice like someone putting together a jigsaw puzzle, knowing the finished picture requires infinite time and patience. They sat there drinking one rum after another until very late at night; Daniel grew tired of hearing himself without hearing her, and began to interrupt his imaginings to kiss her between thoughts, communicating to her in bits and pieces the euphoria that had claimed him.

The next morning, the pull of a banished impulse broke into the opulence of Emilia's slumber and burst the bubble of the spell. She awakened in the grip of a fear she recognized of old: she knew she was incapable of forgiving another desertion. She remembered how Daniel's eyes glittered when he talked of getting back into politics. It was time to go back to Mexico. She needed to flee from Daniel while the flame was leaping, otherwise, before she knew it, he would disappear into the fire of an adventure more public than the war of their bodies.

She could barely make out his features in the darkness, gazing at him with the sadness of someone renouncing a kingdom. She did not kiss him, not wanting to wake him, wanting to believe that because she hadn't said good-bye some part of her was left behind. "What I am taking away is my body, my head is always with you," she wrote in large letters on a concert program. She left the note on the pillow beside him, in the place that had held her dreams.

Some time later, still drowsy, Daniel reached out to touch her. When he didn't find her beside him in the bed, he called to her in the sleepy voice she liked to hear as she was drinking her coffee and reading the newspaper by the window. When there was no answer, he opened his eyes, saw the note, cursed, and with her absence like a bottomless chasm ran to look for her at Milagros's hotel, where he found Milagros still half-asleep.

"What does the woman want?" he asked his aunt, puffing like a dazed and wounded bull.

"She wants it all," Milagros answered, for the first time unable to offer consolation.

EMILIA RETURNED to Mexico invigorated. She did not say why she had been gone so long. No one wanted to know. Zavalza least of all.

"Do you want a baby?" he asked her the night they reclaimed their love.

"I was with Daniel," she replied.

"I know," said Zavalza. And nothing more.

CHAPTER 29

ANTONIO ZAVALZA always knew. That knowledge was from the beginning the thread of the fabric of his relationship with Emilia Sauri. He was a rare man among men, a man to be cherished above all others because he was capable, unlike any other, of understanding the magnificence of a woman who—uncontrollably and uninterruptedly—had the power to love two men at the same time.

The long Revolution was ended. Diego Sauri celebrated it with the caution of a man who no longer waits for the world to change before trying to live in peace. Josefa convinced him that was the way, not with words but the way birds sing after the storm.

"Let's go see your ocean," she said one night.

Two days later they set off. From then on, Josefa's vision of paradise was colored with the blue of the Caribbean.

"We should stay here until we die," she said, moved by her incorrigible romanticism.

"I would miss the air of the volcanoes," Diego replied.

They had three grandchildren, and lived to see them grow up under their daughter's indefatigable wing.

Persistent as rain, Milagros took them to the pyramids,

to the sea, to cemeteries, to the kingdom of the stars and the unforeseen. Sundays they had dinner overlooking the silvery water of a dam, in the stone cabin Rivadeneira had built for playing chess and keeping a sailboat.

NO ONE EVER KNEW how many times Daniel returned. The house Milagros left at his disposal on the Plazuela de las Pajaritas was the undisclosed inn where he and Emilia found periods of truce in their unending war. They met there sometimes for an evening, sometimes at mid-morning; there their torment, their frustrations, their accords, their memories became clear.

Once, pawns of chance, they met in San Fernando cemetery. Another time, pregnant and smiling, bright as a bird, Emilia looked him up.

"You're like one of those Russian dolls," he said. "If someone opened you up, would they find another Emilia inside, and another, and another?"

How many Emilias went through life as if wanting to devour it? Daniel was sure that no one knew them all. Some, he preferred not to imagine.

"Is this baby mine?" he asked.

"All the children are Dr. Zavalza's."

How many Emilias? The Emilia who woke every morning in the same bed beside a man more understanding than he? The one who plunged into the terrors of a hospital as easily as drinking a glass of milk? The one who concentrated on studies of the brain and its enigmatic responses? The Emilia who lighted the daily lives of so many?

"Is Octavio my son?"

"I already told you. The children are Zavalza's."

"But Octavio likes music."

"All three like music."

And all the Emilias were Emilias who stole his. The Emilia afire only for him, the Emilia who never tired of exploring the elusive universe of her heart.

"Marry me."

"I already married you."

"But you're deceiving me with that doctor."

"You don't understand anything."

"I understand you're deceiving me with the doctor."

How many Emilias? Zavalza's Emilia, her children's, the Emilia who slept with his stone beneath her pillow, the one in the tree, the one on the train, Emilia the doctor, the pharmacist, the traveler . . . his Emilia. How many? A thousand and none. A thousand and his.

IN 1963 the key to Milagros's house was still the same. Daniel had gone back to wearing it around his neck. The sun was setting upon the hospitable and unpredictable volcanoes when Emilia came into the room with her desires intact, despite the years that weighed upon them. Daniel had opened the balcony doors and was looking out on the street.

"Is the girl who brought you to the door my granddaughter?"

"You know the answer to that. All the children and all the grandchildren are Dr. Zavalza's," Emilia answered.

"The way that one pushed the hair back from her face was like me."

"When did you get here?" Emilia asked him, kissing him as she had when their lips were smooth and unwrinkled. The eternal throbbing beat below her breastbone.

"I never leave," said Daniel, stroking her head with its scent of mysteries.

ABOUT THE AUTHOR

Ángeles Mastretta was born in Puebla, Mexico. She is the author of the novel *Tear This Heart Out*, which has been translated into twelve languages. She lives in Mexico City with her husband and two children.

ABOUT THE TRANSLATOR

Margaret Sayers Peden is professor emerita of Spanish at the University of Missouri, Columbia. Among recent translations are works by Isabel Allende, Laura Esquivel, Pablo Neruda, and Sor Juana Inés de la Cruz.